Ian Townsend is a journalist with the
Australian Broadcasting Corporation. He
lives in Queensland with his wife, Kirsten,
and their daughters, Charlotte, Josephine
and Gabrielle. *Affection* is his first novel.

affection

Ian Townsend

HARPER **PERENNIAL**

Harper Perennial
An imprint of HarperCollins*Publishers*, Australia

First published in Australia in 2005
This edition published in 2007
by HarperCollins*Publishers* Pty Limited
ABN 36 009 913 517
A member of the HarperCollins*Publishers* (Australia) Pty Limited Group
www.harpercollins.com.au

HarperCollins*Publishers*
25 Ryde Road, Pymble, Sydney NSW 2073, Australia
31·View Road, Glenfield, Auckland 10, New Zealand
77–85 Fulham Palace Road, London W6 8JB, United Kingdom
2 Bloor Street East, 20th floor, Toronto, Ontario M4W 1A8, Canada
10 East 53rd Street, New York, NY 10022, USA

National Library of Australia Cataloguing-in-Publication data:

Townsend, Ian.
  Affection.
  ISBN 13: 978 0 7322 8627 9.
  ISBN 10: 0 7322 8627 1.
  I. Title.
A823.4

PS Material prepared by Denise O'Dea
Cover and internal design by Natalie Winter, HarperCollins Design Studio
Cover photograph from 'Townsville 1888', reproduced by HarperCollins
  with permission from the North Queensland Photograph Collection,
  James Cook University
Author photograph by John Bean
Typeset in Baskerville BE Regular 11/15.5pt by Helen Beard, ECJ Aust Pty Ltd
Printed and bound in Australia by Griffin Press on 50gsm Bulky News

6 5 4 3 2 1   07 08 09 10

For my lovely wife, Kirsty

Acknowledgments

This book was researched and written with the help of an Arts Queensland grant and a fellowship at Varuna, the Writers' House.

A number of people gave me encouragement, suggestions, and information including editor Judith Lukin-Amundsen, Peter Bishop from Varuna, and Stephanie Smith, Rod Morrison, Linda Funnell and Vanessa Radnidge from HarperCollins.

I'm especially grateful to Dr John Thearle for his enthusiasm for Dr A. J. Turner.

As part of the research for this book, I read and enjoyed Dr Thearle's University of Queensland thesis, 'Dr Alfred Jefferis Turner: His Contribution to Medicine in Queensland', as well as Christina Louise Amiet's James Cook University thesis, 'The Second Angel: Plague in North Queensland 1900–1922', and the numerous books on Queensland's political history by Professor Ross Fitzgerald.

I'd like to thank the staff of the James Cook University Library in Townsville and the John Oxley Library in Brisbane, as well as Di MacGregor in Townsville for her advice, friendship, and newspaper archives.

Thanks also to Dr Humphry Cramond from the Australian Medical Association in Queensland, Mrs Dorothy Row, Vic Jackson from St Andrew's Presbyterian Church in Townsville, Geoff Thompson from the Queensland Museum, Artie Rentoul from the museum at Dunwich, and Peter Ludlow.

And thanks to Heather Townsend, for never doubting that I could write this book.

Affection \af*fect"tion\, n: 1. Kind feeling; love; tender attachment. 2. Disease; a morbid or abnormal state of body or mind; malady.

moreton bay

1921

I'D BEEN SEARCHING THE faces of passengers as they chattered past fearing twenty years might have changed him, and then there he was in front of me conjured from a flurry of parasols and hats and peering up at me like I was some damned specimen he'd misplaced. Of course, I'd have recognised him even if he wasn't wearing the topee and waving a butterfly net in my face.

'Your eyes are worse, Row.'

'There has never been anything wrong with my eyes, Dr Turner.'

A woman pressing a large feathered hat to her head gave us a queer look as she hurried past with two bawling children.

I said, 'Welcome to my asylum.'

As the ferry grumbled away, I was looking at a man who'd in fact changed little in two decades, although he must have been now, what, seventy?

'For Heaven's sake.'

Well, sixty then. Nearly.

He smiled and tucked his pith helmet under an arm and I thought for a moment he was going to salute, but he simply patted down his hair, which was thinner. His beard was grey and trimmed to a neat Bolshy goatee. Thick, round, wire-rimmed spectacles magnified many fine lines around his eyes.

He'd accepted my invitation, he said, because he rarely had an excuse nowadays to escape town. The pleasure of seeing me was a sort of bonus.

His little joke.

We walked up the road from the wharf, slowing to let holiday makers hurry ahead to their buggies and motorcars, or clamber on to the flat bed of Dalton's lorry that would take them to the ocean side of the island.

'And where is this asylum of yours, Row?'

'Just ahead a short way.'

The vehicles clattered away and we were left with the wind and sand.

Formalities first, I supposed.

'Hilda?' I asked. 'Is she well?'

'Yes. Maria?'

'Yes. Yes.' Perhaps I should have told my wife Turner was coming, but she'd already made her plans. 'In town. Shopping.'

'Oh?' he said.

He asked about Allan, Marjorie and Eileen, but as I answered he gazed off into the hazy hills, as if he didn't really care or already knew. I tried to think if he had any family, and we fell into silence.

'*Nesolycaena alboserica*,' he said, eventually.

I chewed at an icing of salt on my bottom lip.

'I've been meaning to add it to a tray of Lycaenidae,' and he looked at me. 'That's a butterfly.'

'So I gathered.'

'Found only here. On this island. Apparently.'

'Really.'

Turner was slapping the net against his leg and looking around with a restless, boyish energy. I remembered that about him now.

In front of us were scrubby hills, and hard clouds shot over the top like cannon shells. We walked up the road through the village towards the asylum, a few cottages on our right, the fishing co-op on our left, some thin shrubs here, a pine there, mostly sand with some ragged islands of grass. There'd not be an insect left alive if I had my way.

'I don't remember mentioning any butterflies when I called,' I said.

'No?' He twirled his net as if preparing for tennis. 'Do you remember the Blue Tigers, Row?'

A sudden image dragged up after twenty years made me breathless.

'No,' was all I could say, and kept walking into the wind.

He looked over at me. 'Are you writing your memoirs?'

'I'm not writing my memoirs, Dr Turner. The last thing I want to do is dredge up the past.'

'But that's what we have in common. That's why I'm here, is it not?' he said, twirling his net. 'The past?'

I'd begun to regret inviting him.

Turner stopped to poke his net into an exhausted low cottonwood to see what he could flush out.

'Why didn't you keep in touch?' he said. 'You know I named a moth after you?' He pronounced it 'moff'.

'Really.'

'*Eupterote rowii.*' He gave up on the bush and we kept walking. 'How long have you been here?'

'Ages. Before the War. And then back here afterwards.'

We were approaching a long yellow hut. 'Your namesake is a very small moff, even for small moffs. Not just that but he hides on the bark of the ghost gum. Dashed hard to see. Has this remarkable colouration, a bit like blue cheese.' He looked up at me. 'You're very pale for someone who's been living on an island for all these years.'

'I caught some gas in Ypres.'

'Really.'

'I've been busy.'

'You should have kept in touch, Row.'

Then he gently tapped me on the shoulder with his net. Silly, I know, but it moved me and I had to turn away.

We walked in silence for a while.

'So,' he said. 'Why am I here?'

I cleared my throat.

'Pardon?' he said.

'Plague.'

His stride faltered a little, I was pleased to see.

'Well then.'

'That's the short of it.'

'You'd better tell me the long of it. It seems I have plenty of time.'

The long of it.

Well, Ronald Merriment had sent a telegram ordering me to the hospital to see a patient. I sent a telegram back suggesting a nurse could accompany the patient on the barge. I assumed it was leprosy, you see. My only speciality, as far as the Health Department's concerned.

But no, a telegram came back insisting I go, a matter of medical urgency, and no further explanation. This had happened once or twice before, so I went.

And there he was. I couldn't have been more surprised, as you can imagine. I took a smear and did a microscopic examination there and then. There was no doubt about plague, but they must have already known that. The symptoms were quite obvious. The hospital telephoned the ministry and Ronald sent a motorcar.

Turner was nodding as I told him this, and I stopped walking.

'You might ask why,' I said.

'Why what?'

'Why me?'

'You mean, why you and not me?' he said.

I nodded.

'I'm retired.' He smiled. 'I suppose they wanted the next best bacteriologist in Queensland.'

I walked off and Turner caught up.

So. Picture me standing outside the office of the Under-Secretary of Health. I'd had time to wash, of course, but I had no change of clothes. It was all very rushed. I noticed a spot of blood on my shoe, so I asked the young woman there if anything else about me seemed odd.

'No,' she said.

'Nothing in my hair?'

She shook her head. 'No.'

I leaned closer. She shook her head again, more slowly. I straightened my jacket and the woman knocked and opened the door in one movement.

I was surprised to see someone else behind the table. My first thought was that the room's usual occupant, Under-Secretary Ronald Merriment, finally had his promotion to Tax and they'd given his job to someone older and in poorer health.

The man didn't stand, but said, 'Dr Row? Come in. I don't think we've met. I'm William McCormack.'

I shouldn't have been surprised, I suppose, but I usually came to Brisbane only for budget meetings and dealt only with Ronald at that table. Home Secretaries didn't have their hands in departmental pockets, but they often had them around departmental throats, as it were.

He waved me over and pointed to the creaky red leather chair. The room was lit by large vertical windows opaque from grime on the outside, and it wasn't until I sat that I noticed Ronald standing in a dark corner. Under the circumstances, no one shook hands.

'So I take it you've seen the poor chap?' said the Home Secretary.

'Yes.'

'Sorry to send you straight to the front, but we needed an opinion fast. How bad is it?'

'Well, he died. He was dead when I arrived.'

'Yes.' He leaned back and blew out a long stream of pipe smoke towards the ceiling. 'I take it that's not a good sign.'

'No.'

'And the hospital's coping? Can cope? In your opinion?'

I'd been at the hospital only for the two hours it took to watch the autopsy and look for bacteria.

'They isolated the patient,' I said. 'They seem to have done the right things.'

'The superintendent seems to think the hospital's going to go broke over this.'

Ah, I thought. 'He did ask me to ask about more money,' I said, picturing the harried little man. I hadn't taken much notice. 'I suppose it depends on how many more cases there are. Isolation is expensive. A whole ward had to be cleared for one man.'

The Home Secretary leaned forward as far as his belly would allow. 'It's only this one case so far.'

'But it is plague. There are bound to be more. In my opinion.'

The Home Secretary slapped the table suddenly. 'Bound to be more. Did you hear that, Ron?'

'Yes,' I heard Ronald say from the gloom. 'That's Dr Row's opinion.' It obviously wasn't Ronald's.

'What is your opinion on isolation hospitals?' said the Home Secretary.

'It would be wise. To build one,' I said, carefully, feeling like a rabbit with one foot already in the trap. 'Or find one. As soon as possible.'

He leaned back and puffed for a while, staring at a point above my head.

'What about Peel Island?' As if he'd just thought of it. 'That's under your jurisdiction already, I understand.'

I should have seen this coming. I didn't have a pipe to light, so I took off my glasses and rubbed at the lenses.

'To be frank, Mr McCormack, I wouldn't even put my lunatics there, let alone anyone who needed urgent medical attention. A large amount of money would have to be spent. The lepers moved.'

Through the smoke, I saw him wince. 'I thought Peel Island was closed.'

It was no longer a quarantine station, yes.

'Well for pity's sake. Lepers?'

That seemed to be a cue for Ronald Merriment to step into the square of light from the window.

He stood there like a newspaper advertisement for Gentlemen's Tweed Suits, looking a little sad in a way many younger men affected nowadays. In Ronald's case I put it down to *pes planus* and I knew this because Ronald had told me – and, I assumed, the world and his wife – that flat feet had let him down and he had to stay behind for the War, which no one believed, but I suspected was true.

It felt suddenly stuffy in the room and I wished I were back home.

Pipe smoke curled like a vine through a shaft of light and Ronald seemed quite unhappy standing there, leaning backwards slightly in his comfortable loafers and avoiding my eye.

He said, quite sarcastically I thought, that in such matters as Peel Island and Dunwich, I was the Home Secretary's best advisor, and the Home Secretary had asked about lepers.

'Yes,' I said. 'Peel Island is a lazaret. There are fifteen of them.'

'Why?' said the Home Secretary, pressing forward, the table moving slightly.

'Lin?' said Ronald. He was looking at me, his head at an angle, as if one of us had nodded off.

I was blowed if I knew where these sensations came from, but there you go. I had a ringing in my ears and my head felt squeezed as if a shell had exploded nearby.

I said, 'Could you open a window?'

'Jammed. Would you like some water?'

'Thank you.'

The Home Secretary and Ronald exchanged glances and McCormack himself reached for the jug on the table, poured a glass and pushed it towards me.

'Well,' he said, suddenly jovial. 'Lepers. Fancy that,' sitting back, looking to me and then to Ronald. 'I didn't know we still had lepers, Ron.'

Ronald completed the ridiculous triangle by telling me, 'Mr McCormack has a large portfolio, Lin. I'm sure you understand.'

He turned to stare out the window again, and the Home Secretary faced me. I finished the water and wondered why the Under-Secretary ('please call me Ronald') had left it to me to mention the lepers.

In fact, I wondered why I was there in the first place.

I took a deep breath and explained that, yes, in years long past the old Peel Island quarantine station had been used for cases of fever: cholera, typhoid, smallpox, and the like, any ship's company who arrived in suspect health. He either died, or recovered and moved on. Modern medicine had put the quarantine station out of business. After it closed some lepers were sent there, never recovered and so never left. It was convenient, I supposed, to have them on an island. They took care of themselves, there was an administrator, and there'd been no reason to move them. I visited Peel nowadays to treat them for pneumonia or childbirth and, apart from the obvious, they were generally in good health.

'Ha! Lepers!' said the Home Secretary. He picked a piece of tobacco from his tongue and placed it carefully on the table. 'And they can't be removed?'

'Yes, but we'd have to put them somewhere.' I didn't say, of course, that they'd be moved over my dead body.

'Do they have to be moved?' He looked at Ronald.

'I believe this is a good example of the difficulties inherent in this suggestion by the Premier that we need to find a site for a plague hospital now,' said Ronald to the window. 'As Dr Row suggests, it will cost money and a great deal of inconvenience. In the case of Peel Island, for example, if the island is something we must consider, then in this case we'd have to allow that we'd be exposing the current residents to plague, and I think Lin would also point out that we'd be exposing the plague patients to leprosy.'

It was all absurd, of course. They both turned towards me, and I was forced to play along, determined to protect the island.

'The trouble also is that it's a long way to send someone who's very ill,' I said. 'If someone is ill enough to present with plague symptoms, he might not survive. And you'd need medical resources. At the moment it's just me and I have to row out there as it is.'

The Home Secretary stared at me for quite some time, but I'm a good starer. 'I think Dr Row has some good points. Can we get them in the report to the Premier? Ronald?'

'Of course. Lin?'

'I suppose so.'

'Good-oh,' said the Home Secretary.

There were a few moments' silence.

'Why was I asked to see the patient?' I said.

'What?'

'Why me?'

The Home Secretary raised his eyebrows. I heard Ronald say, 'We understood you had some experience in these matters.'

'Recommended,' said McCormack, nodding, but clearly unsure himself. 'Best man for the job. Undoubtedly.'

'What job?' I said.

'Head of the Epidemic Board of course.' The Home Secretary studied me, probably thinking I was mad. I'd seen that look before, on occasions when people asked what I did and I mentioned the asylum. I never mentioned the lepers on such occasions, of course.

'We just want you to keep an eye on this. Ronald thinks it's an isolated case, man infected in Sydney or some such place, but the Premier wants options. You're the options man. The Premier will be happy with your appointment, your experience, and such. Congratulations.'

'You don't mind moving into town for a while? Until it blows over,' said Ronald. 'Be a bit of a change for you.'

After a beat, he added, 'I don't have to tell you, do I, Lin, to keep this hush-hush.'

I pulled out a handkerchief and wiped my forehead. 'But people must be wondering.'

'About what?'

'About quarantining the port. Activating the plague regulations. Informing the Commonwealth of the outbreak.'

They exchanged glances again and the Home Secretary re-lit his pipe, slowly, building up a cloud.

'No, no. We're not at that stage yet. Just one case. Hardly call it an outbreak. Ron?'

'I agree.' They both looked at me.

'But the public will at least be told to watch for symptoms,' I said.

'It would be dangerous to alarm people unnecessarily, don't you think? We don't want a panic. If someone has a headache they'll think it's plague and we'll have them beating on the doors of every damn hospital in the city.'

I didn't know what to say.

'Well, good. That's settled then. We need to keep a lid on this. Report back to me only. We'll meet next week.'

'That's all. Thank you, Dr Row,' said Ronald, and I found myself back in the hallway with three hours before my ferry.

I'd wandered down to the foyer in a daze and hesitated at the heavy glass and bronze revolving doors that opened to the city of Brisbane.

It was past noon and the Ann Street trams were filling with office workers going home for Saturday lunch. A motorcar flashed by in a blue cloud and across the street were the brightly modern display windows of a new department store.

Two women arm in arm went out through the doors, letting in the sickly odour of burnt gasoline. Not even the smell of blood brings back so vividly that *je ne sais quoi* of Belgium, of ambulances steaming in the mud. I looked for a seat.

The Board of Medical Health is a brick nest of bureaucrats and I found a hard bench in its colonial foyer. I picked up a magazine from a pile in front of me, pretending I had some business there, and closed my eyes for a minute, breathing deeply. The feeling passed. I could hear across the hallway that the young men were finishing typing, scraping chairs and clearing their desks for the weekend.

It fell quiet after a short time and I opened my eyes and found I had a *Medical Gazette* in my hand, and so I thumbed it while I took my breather, realising I needed something to eat, wondering what else I should do with my time in the city, not really reading.

When I felt better, I looked up to find that the clerks had already vanished. I stood, and with the magazine still in hand walked across the hall. I poked my head inside, ready to beg a light if asked, but the typing pool was deserted.

I walked in and looked around. The desks were in neat rows, swivel chairs and overflowing ashtrays. I spotted a telephone near the door and ambled over to it, examining it as if I had a particular interest in the damned thing. I looked over my shoulder before taking the earpiece off its cradle, and in a world of electric humming a voice asked to whom I wished to be connected. I asked if there was a number listed for an A. J. Turner, doctor.

There was. But there was no answer at his surgery.

Well.

Would I like to be connected to his home?

He has a number at home?

It's listed; he's a doctor, said the woman.

Well, so was I, but I asked politely to be connected.

I waited and heard a woman's voice, a long way away, saying she'd take the call.

Mrs Turner? I said. Was Dr Turner there?

Dr A. Jefferis Turner couldn't come to the telephone, she said, but who was I and what was it that I wanted?

When I told her she seemed unsurprised, though I couldn't have expected her to remember me. She said she'd ask the doctor and I imagined him bent over one of his trays in a parlour patiently listening to Hilda relay my questions. After a pause, and some repeating, she told me Dr A. Jefferis Turner was not free today, but would be free tomorrow.

I said I was in town only for a few hours, but not to worry, I would … I heard some discussion in the distance. She said Dr Turner would meet me tomorrow at my residence.

'But I live in Moreton Bay,' I said.

Yes.

So I gave instructions, the ferry time, she passed them on, and I heard her voice fade until there was just the crackle of the wire, and after a minute the operator asked me if I'd like to be reconnected. I told her I'd hang up, and placed the earpiece back in its cradle feeling vaguely foolish.

And here we were.

There were now low, grey clouds flying over Moreton Bay and the whole damned Asylum for Inebriates felt as bleak as it could manage as we walked across the compound from Block F back to Block B, where by chance Turner found someone he seemed to know sitting on the verandah with a rug over his knee.

The sight of this frail old man might have saddened Turner, but he didn't show it. Anyway, the old man was one of my happy ones and a very good bluff, saying 'There you are,' but there was little substance after the introduction. The old man, a former doctor himself, hid his own confusion well. He posed a few testing questions about the care of his horses, but his humour trickled away when he learned we had failed to bring a bottle for which he'd apparently asked.

Turner spent a good half an hour by his side, managing to get him talking about some ancient and amusing treatment for dengue, and I was happy to see the old man on relatively firm ground.

Then, having satisfied himself that his old friend was in good hands – mine – Turner accepted an invitation to coffee in my office.

'Coffee,' he said. 'How vewy appwopwiate.'

My office and surgery was a free-standing building distinguished from the others by having its own garden, Maria's handiwork. The red and yellow cannas tried hard to be cheerful.

We left our hats and his net by the door.

Inside it was just a little less grey. I showed him around, but there was not much to see. A humble surgery, a dispensary, and then my office. Along one full wall of the office was a bookcase. Amongst the reports and books of previous medical superintendents, the medical books and temperance texts, were some novels, which Turner was now surveying. For some reason he went straight to *Great Expectations* and took it down. He must have seen the silver flask hidden behind it, but he replaced the book and kept browsing without a word.

I felt compelled to explain that I sometimes took Dickens down when the weather closed in during winter and read it by a fire, just for atmosphere, this was that sort of place; ' … *for the night-wind has a dismal trick of wandering round and round a building of that sort, and moaning as it goes; and of trying, with its unseen hand, the windows and the doors; and seeking out some crevices by which to enter.*' That sort of thing.

He seemed amused.

On such occasions I'd take the flask and risk a nip, I said, a little cheer-me-up.

He nodded.

As it happened, just as we took our seats by the window, the sun came out and spoilt the splendidly grey scene. Just offshore was Peel Island, the lazaret and the old quarantine station. It occurred to me that I should invite the Home Secretary to inspect it, but I suppose he never had any serious intentions for it. On a day like today it was a bleaker version of Dunwich, if that was possible.

I made coffee and we watched the traffic out on Moreton Bay, more barges than steamships and even fewer sails nowadays. It was mid-May and the bay was simmering under the south-easterly trade.

I told him that it must have been this time of year when he, Dr Alfred Jefferis Turner, then the Government's agent, crossed these waters heading northward on what he would later dismiss as our 'little adventure'.

'You know, you're right, Row. I can just see myself out there now, about where that steamship is, looking back to Brisbane and thinking, hooray! Off hunting again.'

The way he said 'hooway' made me smile. And I remembered 'hunting' was a Turnerism for any project from netting butterflies to performing autopsies. Or, in the case to which he referred, chasing the plague.

'I'm sure you can manage them,' said Turner. 'We managed up North.'

I looked at him, searching his face for irony. He just blinked.

'It was a catastrophe,' I said.

'Your hindsight's worse than your eyesight.'

'You're saying I'm wrong?'

'Catastrophe's a strong word. The *War* was a catastrophe. Tell me it was worse than that.'

I went to get more coffee and placed the cups carefully on the rickety table by the window.

'It just so happens that lately I've had the opportunity to visit Townsville,' Turner said.

'My God. Why?'

'Hesperiidae.'

Of course.

'There were gaps in my collection of skippers,' he said.

I told Turner I'd be happy to put the whole Northern experience in one big gap, cover it in quicklime, and stamp it down with the heel of my boot.

'Have you had any medical treatment since the War?'

'I know what you're getting at.'

'For the gas I meant. But no matter.'

He wanted me to ask about his trip, I suppose. 'It's a funny thing,' I said, 'but quite by coincidence a man who said he worked for the Howard Smith Company was here a few years back. Said he was a steamer captain. I asked what ship he'd captained, wondering if it was one I'd been on, and he mentioned the *Leura*. I don't believe he was a captain at all, of course, probably some engineer or steward. But he said he remembered very well the Government doctor on board in 1900 when the plague was prowling up and down the coast. He described you.'

'Oh yes?' Turner looked out through the big panelled windows. 'I remember that trip very well. You know, Row, I have an unrequited love for the sea. I love the sea; it despises me. Always puts on a show when I'm about in boats. Had the most awful trip back from Home after the War. I believe I'll take the train to the next war. Much more civilised.'

Afterwards, I walked him back to the ferry.

We crossed the compound to the shore, where small hard waves were slapping the rock wall. As we waited Turner spied a gnarled tree in the cemetery and cut to it.

Casuarina equisetifolia. It was his curse on me that I knew its name. I hated the she-oaks; they picked up a breath of wind and moaned about it. In a gale they sounded like the pits of hell. I'd been meaning to have this one felled for firewood.

'Cemeteries are marvellous spots for moffs,' he said, circling the tree. I cleaned my glasses. He wanted me to ask, but I wasn't going to be tricked into any more lectures about blasted insects so I said nothing, walking over to the grave.

Even on a dull day it shone with flowers. I crouched beside it. A few had turned brown and I tossed them away.

I heard Turner walk up behind me.

'You think I've been here too long, don't you,' I said.

'It's not for me to say.' But of course he couldn't resist saying, 'There are moments in our lives when we're given the chance to stay or move on. Sometimes we let those moments pass. It's not easy, either way.'

We shook hands at the jetty as it started to rain.

'Why don't you and Maria come to Highgate Hill one evening? You'll be in the city for a while and there'll be no excuse. Hilda would be delighted to meet you.'

'I haven't decided if I'll accept the job yet,' I said.

'No?'

'It was your recommendation, wasn't it?'

There were small drops on his glasses and he took them off to wipe them.

'Perhaps it was. The Premier did ask me a few days ago if I knew anyone who was as stubborn as me and who knew as much as I did about epidemic disease.'

'And you said no, of course.'

'Very good, Row.'

'And you mentioned my name nevertheless.'

'I couldn't think of anyone else. He didn't mention the job he had in mind, by the way. A remarkable coincidence, don't you think?'

I tried to work up some anger, but he was smiling now and I supposed I should be flattered.

'Whatever you decide, come into town. I'll show you your moff,' and he saluted this time with his net, turned and hurried up the gangway.

The rain trickled down inside my collar and I shivered. As the ferry kicked up a stink and pulled away, I saw Turner continue forward. He was soon separated from the other passengers. The ferry swung in a circle before lurching towards the far shore and as it turned I saw the doctor standing near the bow, a hand on the railing, looking like a small Captain Ahab off to catch his big fish with a butterfly net.

And I had the image again of Dr Alfred Jefferis Turner twenty years younger leaving this bay, the trade wind behind him, the palm of God gently coaxing the steamship *Leura* like a migrating Blue Tiger, a giant Nymphalidae, past Cape Townshend northwards up the Queensland coast for His purposes, inexorable and perhaps fatal for fragile Lepidopterae.

townsville

autumn, 1900

Drunkenness is a very great evil unquestionably, and it is very common in the North. Men, and even women, go recklessly on, drinking whatever comes in their way, and consequently suffer untold misery. How much happier and better off they would be if they kept sober and drank only West End Beer.

Advertisement, *The Northern Miner*

IT HAD BEEN A NORTHERN summer that had driven even the fish to despair. The mackerel had washed up dead in vast runs along the Strand and the old Chinamen were out on the beach every morning reading the fish calligraphy before loading them into carts for burial in market gardens at Kissing Point.

The smell of fermented sugar and spilled molasses, the tang of explosives and sweet dead things from Ross Creek hung about east Flinders-street in dark swarms.

I leaned my bicycle against a hitching rail. A couple of horses were letting themselves be eaten by flies outside the offices of the shipping companies as I waited for someone to come along and open up.

Punctuality, Humphry had pointed out, was a vice in the North and I'd have to change my ways. But I hadn't yet kicked the habit of my thirty-six years so I spent my time worrying a loose rock on the road. A few birds were snapping up the insects that hung over horse pats in the street and a dog explored rubbish in an open drain. I picked up the rock and threw it, but the dog simply ambled over to sniff.

It was well past nine when a man came along and opened the door of the Adelaide Steamship Company office. I followed him in and sat on the wooden bench just inside, already worn out by the day.

A number of other clerks arrived and started moving between machines and tables with papers. A telegraph chattered every so often, someone was using a typewriter and had trouble finding the keys, and there was the sound of a rubber stamp. No one spoke, and they ignored me as the temperature climbed.

When the manager finally came over and asked if he could help, I introduced myself. Dr Linford Row, the municipal medical officer. I was waiting for a colleague who'd telephoned him the day before. We were due to go aboard the *Cintra* and examine a patient, I said. The suspected case of plague?

The beat of the office stopped; even the telegraph was silent.

The manager chewed an arm of his spectacles and looked about the room, 'And where is Doctor Humphry?'

He was to meet me here. At nine.

'It's almost ten,' said the manager.

Perhaps I could collect the list of passengers and the medical report wired from Mackay so we could leave as soon as Dr Humphry arrived?

He chewed for a while and then told me that the Townsville municipality had no authority over the port and he would prefer to wait for the district medical officer before handing over any sensitive company information.

I had no idea if that was true, so I sat down. The office went about its business, the slow percussion of machines composing a sort of languid marching tune.

It was stupefyingly hot and I began to feel drowsy.

Truth be told, some part of me welcomed the plague. It had crept out of China and had touched the Pacific islands and was now steaming up the coast from Sydney. It would give me something to do.

Plague! I could have yelled, though even panic appeared to be too much of an effort here. I watched the clerks and waited for Humphry.

The shipping office was tucked away safely in the centre of town, but out on Cleveland Bay the SS *Cintra* rested fitfully, its fifty-two passengers and dozen crew probably anxious, perhaps frightened, and no doubt scared the whisky would run out.

Those aboard the *Cintra* had already had an adventure of sorts. One of the crew had fallen sick out of Rockhampton and when the ship arrived in Mackay, the medical officer there had diagnosed plague.

The news was taken calmly. It had been expected, after all, following the Sydney outbreak. The Mackay passengers had been promptly quarantined in the local gaol and the rest sent on to Townsville. The Queensland Government had asked for confirmation before considering pratique. And that was Humphry's job.

In fact, the whole colony was waiting for news on the plague and the African War, while I waited for Dr Ernest Humphry.

So when the door swung open and Humphry stepped inside, I didn't get up.

He looked around and seemed surprised to see me sitting there.

His suit was crumpled and his moustache wild. I pointed to the clock behind the counter.

'Good Lord,' he said, and he sat down heavily beside me and winced. He took a silver flask from inside his jacket and offered it to me. I pushed it back and he took a nip.

As casually as I could, I went to the counter. I caught the manager's attention again and he came over, chewing his glasses, determined to outdo me in nonchalance.

'Doctor Humphry would like to see the passenger list and medical report,' I said. 'When you're ready.'

He tapped the lenses against his teeth, *click click*, and looked at Humphry, who had his eyes closed, and then at me before fetching the report as well as two sheets of paper with the list of names in blue carbon-copy ink.

I sat back down next to Humphry and put them in front of his face. He waved them away.

'Just tell me.'

I began paraphrasing the medical report. 'The steward's name is Storm.'

'His *name* is Storm?'

'That's what it says.'

'I suppose that's appropriate.'

'Sickened on April the twentieth. Syphilis in the secondary stage and an illness that might be the first stages of plague. Some swelling of the glands in the groin, lethargy, brain fever.'

'Brain fever,' snorted Humphry. 'That's a medical report?'

'Isn't that enough?'

'I don't know.' He sighed. 'Who's on board then?'

I ran a finger down the passenger list. 'A few Townsville-ites.' Some names looked familiar; most were probably from Charters Towers. 'Here are three ministers of religion.' I recognised a name. 'Methodist.'

'What a comfort they must be.'

And then two names jumped out at me. If they weren't one after the other on the list I might not have noticed.

'Oh damn.'

'Eh?'

'It appears we have the Honourable Members for Charters Towers aboard.'

'That's not amusing.'

I jabbed him with my elbow and held the list under his nose. Humphry snatched it from my hand and held it at arm's length.

'Dear God,' he said. 'How many plagues can one ship bear?'

'Maybe it's not plague.'

'Maybe. I've never seen a case before. Have you, Lin?'

'No. But it could be cut and dried. Buboes, high fever, lethargy, blood poisoning.'

'Ah, happy days.' But Humphry was suddenly more animated. He slapped me on the knee and stood. 'Well hurry up, we haven't got all day,' and marched out of the office.

I stepped out into a world of aching light. Humphry's horse drooped in the sun, too miserable to fight the flies.

'You drive,' said Humphry, putting on his hat. I collected my bicycle and put it carefully in the back of the buggy, the front wheel and handlebars hanging off the tray like a corpse. I gave it a shake and it seemed secure enough.

'You should get yourself a bicycle,' I said.

'Ha!' said Humphry as I climbed up beside him and took the reins. 'Why should I push pedals around when I can ride a buggy without expending any energy? I'll wait for a combustion engine.'

He proffered his flask again. 'Hair of the dog?'

'Not the dog that bit me.'

'How long have you been in this town?'

'Six months.'

We'd had this conversation many times before. We set off for the wharves.

The Customs launch SS *Teal* slid from the tidal grasp of Ross Creek and flopped across Cleveland Bay chased by gulls. Our destination was moored at the Fairway Buoy and I could see a few becalmed clippers anchored well away from it, sitting on a sea so brittle it might crack under their weight.

The sun was high and I pulled the brim of my hat further down, gathering the world to within a few feet. My boots needed a polish, the wooden deck had been scrubbed grey, Humphry's silver flask appeared under my nose again and I pushed it away again. It was a short trip and, frankly, I was a little anxious now.

A rope ladder dropped as we came alongside and Humphry was on it and clambering up immediately. I followed, looking up past his swaying arse to the faces looking down, who perhaps were hoping we'd fall. But then we were on deck and a man greeted us with a hand like a rope and said he was Captain Thompson.

Humphry introduced us and flapped a copy of the Health Act under the captain's nose.

'We've been waiting all morning,' said Thompson, brushing it aside. He gestured with his chin to the crowd, which was dressed for town and watching us. A few women stood stoically under sunshades. They were all gathered behind two men in shirt-sleeves chomping cigars and cutting such a presence they had to be Dawson and Dunsford.

'Some of these gentlemen have business to attend to,' said Thompson.

'I hope they haven't been out too long in this heat. It's not healthy.'

'Well, what kept you?' said Thompson.

'Business. Anyway, they must be keen to get the medical examination out of the way. The sooner the better, eh? Let's not dawdle,' and Humphry asked the captain to have all hands on deck, except for the sick steward of course.

'Is it necessary? We went through this at Mackay.'

'It's the law,' said Humphry and we stood back as the captain reluctantly got the stewards to round up all the passengers and crew.

When it appeared they were all there, Humphry addressed them, asking them if they would be so kind as to line up, as best they could, so he and his colleague could ask them a few questions and conduct a medical examination. They did as they were told and weren't happy about it.

They all looked tired, some looked a little frightened and I felt sorry for them, but Humphry was jovial and in no mood for mercy. He had them form a queue around the smoking saloon and we sat with our backs to it on two deck chairs, in the shade. We opened our bags and began.

We asked each to open his mouth and say 'ah', took his temperature and asked if he had any aches or pains. The first dozen were polite in answering questions, but they were otherwise quiet and I had a sense of brooding resentment.

Then it was the turn of the two cigar men. They were a pair in their dress and manners; they both wore bowlers and smoked cigars. I had the shorter one first.

'Name?' I asked.

'Andrew Dunsford,' he said. 'Member of Parliament.' He made it sound like a threat.

I asked Mr Dunsford to remove his cigar so I could take his temperature and I thought for a minute he was going to refuse. I had no idea what to do if he did. But after a few savage chomps he took it from his mouth and tossed it over the side and I heard it sizzle when it hit the water. I replaced the cigar with the thermometer before Dunsford said anything.

Next to me I heard Humphry say, 'Please open your mouth and say "ah", Mr Dawson.'

Dawson hesitated just long enough for Humphry to say, 'Come now, that's surely not difficult for a politician.'

Dawson took a long pull on his cigar and threw it after his colleague's. He exhaled slowly and then opened his mouth for Humphry.

'Have you experienced any pain in the joints, headaches, sleeplessness or fondness for any kanakas in the past two days?' asked Humphry.

'Is that your bedside manner, Dr Humphry, or the whisky?' Dawson had drawn himself up. His moustache cast a shadow.

Humphry didn't seem to care. 'I'll take that as a yes and have you quarantined then, shall I?'

There were a few titters from the queue. Dunsford was looking daggers at me so I let him go. He pulled a new cigar from his pocket, lit it, and walked off through a cloud.

Dawson was telling Humphry, 'You and your apprentice forget who you're speaking to.'

'No, I don't.' Humphry pretended to be aggrieved. 'You're most definitely Anderson Dawson, one of a pair of Honourable Members for Charters Towers. Or at least you're a fair impression of him. And this is Dr Row and he's not an apprentice. He's the Townsville municipal medical officer and he deserves your respect. He has as much authority as I to carry out whatever is necessary to protect this town from plagues and rats. Isn't that right, Dr Row?' Humphry looked over to me and winked, before turning back to Dawson. 'Dr Row is from Brisbane and a champion pugilist so I wouldn't upset him if I were you.'

Dawson was staring at me now. 'Does McCreedy approve of this interrogation, this abuse of ratepayers?'

'I'm actually here on behalf of the Townsville Joint Epidemic Board,' I said.

Dawson considered this and turned back to Humphry. 'You seem to think this is amusing.'

'No, I don't, but you seem to be in your usual robust health, Mr Dawson. Congratulations. Next.'

Humphry had to look around Dawson to call the next passenger and the MP turned slowly and walked off to join Dunsford and the captain.

'They're plotting something,' Humphry said to me. 'I hope you've been practising on that punching bag lately.'

I wiped the sweat from my forehead and dipped the thermometer in alcohol for the next person.

After the parade, the captain took us below to see the sick steward, Storm, whose cabin was near the stern. Captain Thompson opened the door and stood by it. Storm lay on his bunk with a blanket about him looking wary and feverish.

'After you, Dr Row,' said Humphry.

There was a strong smell of sweat and onions. I looked over my shoulder before entering and saw that Dawson had followed us and was now standing behind Humphry in the hallway. Behind him smoke and passengers were filling the narrow corridor.

The cabin was small, hot, dank and airless and I couldn't stand straight without knocking my head on something. One wall, which I assumed was the hull of the ship, had a large suppurating brown sore. A single lamp hung from the ceiling and spread a sickly yellow light.

I wondered how the man had stayed alive in there for the three or four days he'd been laid up. His eyes had withdrawn into two black pits, but his face turned towards me as I stepped into the cabin. I reached for the blanket.

'Not here,' I heard Humphry behind me say. 'Captain? Can we move this man to a larger cabin?'

'There are no larger cabins that aren't occupied.'

'What about Mr Dawson's suite?' said Humphry. 'He's for the working man. I'm sure he wouldn't mind.'

Captain Thompson hesitated and looked back down the corridor, perhaps wondering if Dawson had heard. He asked, 'How long is this going to take? Can't you tell what's the matter with him here?'

Humphry poked his head further inside the cabin. 'I don't know about this gentleman, but I'd suffocate if I had to spend a minute in here.'

'Yes. All right. I'll make the smoking saloon available then.'

'Thank you,' said Humphry, stepping backwards into the captain and then vanishing down the corridor. I heard him say 'Make way, damn you,' and some other men swearing. The captain shot me a sour look and followed him.

I was suddenly alone in the cabin with Storm. The poor man was gasping as he tried to raise his head to see what the commotion was about.

'Can you walk?' I said.

He nodded and made a weak effort to rise, but couldn't get himself up on an elbow. I grabbed him under the arm and pain flashed across his face. I let him fall back.

'Here,' said a voice behind me.

I turned and saw a man in the white linen uniform of a steward. His face was an assortment of odd angles, as were his teeth.

'Captain said you'd need a hand.' He held up a large and calloused hand, but didn't move from the doorway.

'Grab an arm and we'll see if we can get him up,' I said, pulling at Storm's elbow again. The man groaned.

'Should we be, well, touching him?'

I gave Storm his elbow back again.

'You won't catch it,' I said. 'Not like this.'

The steward looked back down the corridor, no doubt wanting to be somewhere else.

'If it's plague, it's spread by fleas,' I said.

He stared at me. I must have been a sight myself with the perspiration streaming down my face and my shirt soaked through, staggering as the steamship rocked.

'That's a new one. I've heard rats, I've heard Chinamen and now it's fleas. Here's Mr Storm sick and he's none of those, far as I can tell.' He nodded to himself and stood firmly at the door.

'Well, if Mr Storm has it, it's from a flea that bit a rat.'

The steward just stared. The stench, the lack of air, and the motion was making me queasy.

'The ship was fumigated at Rockhampton? Mr Storm went ashore? Well, Rockhampton has the plague and he might have caught it from a flea. Do you see? No fleas on this ship because it's been fumigated. Unless a flea bites him and then you, you're safe. No fleas; no worries.'

I was about to gag and wasn't going to confuse matters with a few qualifications. I had to get out of the cabin. I turned and grasped Storm's elbow, heaving him to a sitting position and feeling the heat like a coal fire in the man. And then a white shirt sleeve reached across and seized the other shoulder and we had Storm up on shaky knees. He buckled, but between us we steered him to the door.

'Captain orders him up on deck,' said the steward. 'But I hope for both our sakes you're right, doc.'

We manoeuvred Storm into the corridor and I gulped the fresher air. Storm sagged drunkenly between us, moaning, and the steward said over the sticky back of his bowed head, 'My name's Gard. Walter.'

I told him who I was.

'You really a boxer?'

'No.'

'You are a doctor, right?'

'Yes,' I gasped.

'Need a drink,' Storm mumbled.

'Don't we all, mate,' Gard told him.

The sick steward's bare feet made a feeble pretence of climbing in mid-air as we frog-marched him up the steps and onto the blessed open deck. I stumbled into the fresh air as if it was a lake and I was dying of thirst, and we lowered Storm to his knees. He groaned long and loud with his eyes shut tight against the glare. Passengers backed away in terror at the sight of us dripping, groaning and gasping.

'Down here,' said Gard, collecting Storm up again. His toes scraped along behind us, leaving a wet trail into the smoking saloon where Humphry had ordered all portholes closed. He'd set up a card table for his medical bag and had spread a tablecloth on the floor for his patient. We let Storm down and the man shuddered. Gard stood back and wiped his hands on his trousers, and I looked about for somewhere to wash.

Outside, the crowd had regathered and there was more smoke wafting into the saloon than out, which must have been a first.

Humphry, the captain, Gard, Storm and I were inside. Dawson appeared at the doorway.

'Clear the room and close the door, please,' Humphry told Gard. Gard went towards the door, but Dawson took two steps forward. He stood there with an unlit cigar in his mouth, his hair sharply parted as if by some newfangled machine.

'And what is your particular interest, Mr Dawson? Medical? Philosophical?' said Humphry.

The captain swore under his breath.

'I'm representing the passengers,' said Dawson.

'Political then. Is this your new constituency? Was there a vote taken?' Humphry seemed somehow fortified and I wondered if he'd been sneaking more nips.

'The passengers have a right to know everything is being done and done correctly to ensure they get off this tub as soon as possible.'

'Mr Dawson, this is a private medical examination and there is a chance a very dangerous, probably lethal and highly contagious disease is aboard this ship,' said Humphry, raising his voice so everyone heard.

Dawson took the cigar from his mouth and pointed it at Humphry. 'That's rubbish and we both know it.'

'Be quiet!' Thompson's shout made me jump; even Storm opened his eyes and tried to sit up.

'This is my ship. I'm in charge here. You're both forgetting that,' the captain said, mopping his face.

'Right you are,' said Humphry. 'Let's get on with it.'

Dawson rolled the unlit cigar in his mouth, and then turned and closed the door himself. He walked across the room and stood over the sick steward, facing Humphry.

I wondered if Dawson was armed. I knew Humphry sometimes carried a pistol for crocodiles, if he ventured to the Burdekin or to the shanties along Ross River.

Humphry opened his medical bag on the card table and Dawson brought out a tin of matches and made to strike one.

'No smoking, Mr Dawson, if you please,' said Humphry. Dawson looked at the captain who shook his head, and Dawson put the matches away, but kept the cigar in his mouth.

We all stood over Storm's prostrate body, Gard a little further away. Humphry took a thermometer from his bag and gave it to Captain Thompson.

'You can make yourself useful if you like, Captain, and take the patient's temperature. I'll have to wash my hands.'

Humphry held up his hands and wiggled his fingers and Gard pointed to a door that led to the galley. The captain knelt beside Storm mumbling about where to put the blasted device. Dawson was standing, his cigar bobbing violently, offering no help, staring now at me, so I followed Humphry and found him washing his face over an enamel basin.

'Damn those politicians. If I was a vindictive man I'd wish Dawson a good dose of buboes.' He found a cloth and wiped his beard. 'But I'm not, so here's to his good health.' He fished out his flask and took a mouthful. 'And may he avoid the painful death he deserves.'

We found some more water and washed our hands with soap.

I said, 'Mr Dawson could be a dangerous enemy.'

'He's all bluster.'

'Still. Might be best not to annoy him.'

'He's taken a shine to you.'

'He thinks I'm on your side.'

'You are, aren't you?'

'Absolutely not.'

'You know,' said Humphry, 'I'm starting to hope now that it is plague. Might curb everyone's insolence,' and as we dried our hands he started whistling. I suspected then that he'd already made up his mind.

'The other steward says Storm has had typhoid,' I said.

'Yes. So the captain tells me.'

'What do you think?'

'I think I need some air,' he said, and then contradicted that by saying, 'I wonder if the bar on this bucket is open yet.'

We had both read the medical papers that were being posted around the colonies since the first case of plague reached Sydney in January. A Dr William Fox had produced one of the first happy pamphlets: 'The Bubonic Plague or Black Death: the Pestilence that Walketh in Darkness'.

The problem I noticed was that several other tropical fevers, including typhoid and particularly dengue, had similar symptoms. And as Humphry pointed out, some other symptoms of plague – slurring of speech and vertigo – could well describe half of Townsville on a Saturday night.

We went back into the saloon. The captain was standing over Storm. Humphry asked him to remove the thermometer.

'Well?'

Thompson held it and turned his head to one side. 'He has no temperature.'

Humphry took it. 'You've put the wrong damned end in.'

Dawson let out a short explosive laugh.

Humphry ignored him and put the thermometer back in Storm's mouth, and then undid the man's shirt. He peeled away the sticky grey cloth from Storm's chest and put his fingers under the armpit. He grunted, and then pulled the man's trousers down. I could see a bruise at the groin.

'Hand me a syringe, please, Dr Row.'

I found the large needle and syringe in the bag and passed them to Humphry. Storm was in a feverish daze when Humphry took the thermometer from his mouth.

'One hundred and four, Mr Thompson.'

Humphry asked the steward Gard to hold Storm by the shoulders while I held him by the feet, and he took up the frightening needle. The captain turned away and Dawson's cigar stopped moving as Humphry, with some effort, punctured the swelling and drew some viscous pink liquid. Storm stiffened and groaned, but took it well.

Humphry started putting the equipment back in his bag.

'Well?' said Dawson.

Humphry ignored him.

'What do you think?' said the captain.

'We'll tell you what we think tomorrow,' said Humphry.

'Tomorrow?' said the captain, but it was Dawson who stepped over Storm's body. He took the cigar from his mouth and jabbed it at Humphry's chest.

'Make a decision now.'

'You're putting us in a difficult position, Mr Dawson,' said Humphry. 'Dr Row has to inform the Townsville Joint Epidemic Board and I have to seek instructions from the Home Secretary.'

'Nonsense.'

'But you're right, it is within our power to make a decision now, I suppose, if you're so keen to have it.'

Humphry paused and Dawson glared at him.

'What do you think, Dr Row? From your observations.'

All eyes turned to me. I swallowed hard. 'I think we should speak with the Epidemic Board,' I said.

'But what do you intend to tell the board? From what you've seen of Mr Storm's symptoms.'

Storm was lying on the deck shivering and moaning quietly.

'From what I've seen, Mr Storm appears to have the symptoms of bubonic plague.'

'I agree,' said Humphry. 'Pending the results of our test and the advice from the board and the Home Secretary, this ship and its crew and passengers without exception are to be quarantined for twenty-one days. You'll all have to go to the quarantine station at West Point.'

The captain gaped. Dawson dropped his voice ominously and said, 'You fool.'

'Well, that's our decision. Anyway, you have your wish. You'll be off this ship tonight. Captain? You do understand? The *Cintra* is denied pratique. You have to proceed immediately to Magnetic Island.'

There was a shocked silence. Dawson popped the cigar back into his mouth.

Humphry said, 'I suggest you make your passengers as comfortable as possible, and hoist a yellow flag.'

Dawson put his hand inside his jacket and I was about to shout a warning when he produced his tin of matches.

'Is there anything you want to add, Dr Row?' said Humphry.

'Fumigation,' I said, as Dawson struck a match and lit his cigar. 'The ship and its cargo and luggage will have to be brought back here to be fumigated with sulphur.'

'We'll arrange that once the passengers disembark at West Point. Who's in charge there?'

'Dr Routh,' I said.

'That's right, Routh. I'll have him make the necessary arrangements for your arrival at West Point. I think that's everything.'

Thompson and Dawson both started speaking at once, but Humphry said, 'Right then,' and pushed past Dawson.

'You're being unreasonable,' said the captain, following him. 'We'll wait until tomorrow and the decision of the board.'

'No. I don't think so. Mr Dawson was right. A decision had to be made immediately. This is too serious a disease to be taking chances.'

Gard was first to the door and opened it to let Humphry and me out. Several men were leaning against the railing.

Dunsford stepped forward in Humphry's way.

'You'll have to ask Mr Dawson,' said Humphry, pushing past him. I followed with the captain close behind.

'What'll I do with Storm?' shouted Gard.

'Get the man back to his cabin and make sure no one goes near him,' said the captain, and strode off in a dark fury towards the wheelhouse.

Dawson remained inside the smoking room, his exit blocked unintentionally by Gard at the door and the crush of men who milled around wanting to know what was going on. Dawson bellowed at the steward to get the hell out of the way.

I had to squeeze past the passengers who'd crammed the narrow deck between the saloon and the sea, ignoring questions about when they could leave the ship, they had family waiting, businesses to attend to. The sight of Townsville so close had made them optimistic, but Humphry hadn't stopped to explain and I followed his lead.

The boat suddenly shuddered beneath me. I grabbed the railing and looked back. The captain was at the wheel and the stacks coughed a cloud of black smoke. The ship shuddered again and moved sideways.

Humphry called to me, 'We'd best go now. I think the captain's keen to get to West Point.'

'He's going now?'

The ship heaved again, as if trying to make matters worse, and everyone stepped to port in a sort of bow-legged jig. We headed for the rope ladder with Humphry muttering 'Bloody fool'.

Beneath the ladder there was confusion on the *Teal*, which had kept its engines going and now was riding the wake of the larger ship as it ran up to the buoy.

'The man's gone mad,' shouted Humphry. Men with hooks were leaning over the front of the steamship to snare the ropes and cast her free.

Humphry was halfway down the rope ladder and I'd just stepped over the side when he yelled up past me, 'Regulations, Mr Dawson. It's your Parliament's law after all.'

Dawson's face was near me. He hissed, 'Do something.'

'There's nothing I can do about it,' I said.

He grabbed my arm. 'But you can. Humphry's a funk. Tell this Epidemic Board of yours that it's a remittent bout of typhoid. Because I assure you, that is what it is.'

I could feel the engines thumping and the boat in motion. I shook my arm loose. 'I'm sorry.'

'You're making a grave mistake,' he said, as I found another rung and stepped down the swinging rope ladder.

'I must get off this ship,' I heard Dawson say. 'Your boss will hear of this.'

I climbed down backwards, and when I looked up again others had appeared beside him. Dawson's face was stone, but the others looked fearful. I thought it was for themselves. But then I looked down and realised that I was the one in peril.

The wake and the rocking of the ship was uneven and below me I saw Humphry throw his bag, which was caught by a crew member, and then he suddenly launched himself out towards the moving deck of the *Teal*. He was caught smoothly by two crewmen before he could stumble over the other side.

I looked up at the crowd and imagined my own public death.

'Tell the captain to stop the ship,' I yelled, but no one moved. I continued down.

I reached the point from where Humphry had jumped. I threw my bag and it was fumbled and dropped into the launch. The *Teal*'s crew were yelling for me to be steady and wait for the crest of the wake, and one of the passengers above me yelled the opposite. All this time the ship was moving crabwise and the *Teal* banging into the side, and I imagined my body being scraped along the ship's hull like jam.

I waited, and when the crew beckoned I jumped.

A woman screamed at that point and I wondered if God would seize this eternal moment to Act.

Then hands grabbed me and three of us fell to the rolling deck.

By the time we got to our feet, the launch had pulled away from the steamship and Humphry had his flask out. He handed it to me and I drank. I looked back at the *Cintra*. A crowd had gathered around Dawson. I was glad I couldn't hear. A few people watched us depart, but nobody waved.

chapter two

> *So far the plague ... is a very small affair. It isn't a patch on the daily, hourly typhoid as a means of slaughtering the public, and so far it has proved about as safe as football, and much safer than it was a few weeks ago to have doubts concerning the absolute justice of the war in South Africa.*
>
> *The Bulletin*, 21 March 1900

THE REVEREND KERR HAD found a rhythm so I left him to it and closed my eyes, just for a moment. His baritone voice washed over me and out the door where it was consumed by the heat haze, devoured by a dust devil.

I started awake, blinking, and had the impression that Maria had been watching me. She was now staring ahead a little too intently, holding her small chin high. A droplet of perspiration ran past her ear and she dabbed at it with the floral handkerchief she held in her hand. She swallowed, once, but didn't give her game away.

Allan sat between us and kicked at the pew in front.

Eileen and Marjorie were quiet and out of sight beyond their mother.

The heat radiated from the wall at my back and I forced myself to sit straight. An infant cried with little conviction.

'And Moses was very wroth ...' droned the Reverend Kerr. I knew this passage. The Lord had been angry with some of his chosen people and this was what came of it – as Allan's mother often told him, the wages of sin being death to the Levites and a stubbed toe for a tardy boy.

I closed my eyes, ran a finger under my collar, and felt the wages of my own sins also being paid out on a troublesome tooth.

In the South, this time of the year would be called autumn, but in the North autumn didn't properly describe a season that couldn't make up its mind if it was still supposed to be stewing people, as it had since I'd arrived, or whether it was merely as hot as the place the Lord had sent the sons of Levi.

'...and the earth opened her mouth and swallowed them up ...'

A well-chosen passage; since Humphry and I had sent the sinners aboard the *Cintra* to Hell the week before, ministers of all denominations in Townsville were scouring the Bible for something apt. The obvious choice was Revelations. I admired the Reverend Kerr's choice of Numbers, a much better story of sin and punishment and a valuable lesson in Acts of God.

Everyone was looking for biblical references these days. Plague plus war equalled a well-thumbed Bible. And a crowded church. The iron roof of St Andrew's not so much kept the sun off the congregation as roasted those tardy enough to attend the late service. Maria was normally the early service sort. I took after my father, God rest his soul.

I opened my eyes a crack. Maria was staring determinedly ahead and the windows let in a white haze so I closed them again.

A man must make his own choices and the North had been a choice of sorts. I might have chosen the Queensland Mounted Contingent. I'd probably been foolish to point out to my wife that some married men had enlisted, and I had to agree I wasn't the type to wave the flag and whoop it up, but no matter. There is duty, but of course I am a doctor and a married man, and for my family's well-being the choice was made and Townsville chosen. Make no mistake, Maria had a hand in the decision.

'...and the Lord spake ...'

Townsville was abnormally warm for this time of the year, the Reverend Kerr had assured her, as if the weather was betraying him by giving her the wrong impression of the place.

The roof stretched in the heat.

And somewhere to my right, on the other side of Melton Hill, across the dusty streets that ran down to the Strand, through creaking iron-sheeted cottages and over a bay as thick and warm as blood, Mr Dawson was no doubt scheming revenge.

Incarcerating the *Cintra* passengers had enhanced my reputation. Humphry and I were now regarded with the sort of wary respect given to people who were mad and dangerous.

'...they that died in the plague were fourteen thousand and seven hundred, besides them that died about the matter of Korah. And Aaron returned unto Moses unto the door of the tabernacle of the congregation: and the plague was stayed.'

The Reverend Kerr paused, allowing the congregation to shift its weight and cough. When we settled into a new stupor he went on to urge us to 'recognise the plague in our own hearts'.

How fortunate to be a pastor in a time of pestilence.

We shared the pew with Mrs Duffy, who handed out the Bibles. Usually, we were the only back-pew sitters. Mrs Duffy came to both the early and late services and undoubtedly made no judgments of her own.

But across the aisle today was a young woman with red hair and a white frock. Few in the congregation looked, but a couple of men stole glances in her direction, at which I could sense Mrs Duffy bristling.

The young woman seemed better at dozing than I, and beside her was a child of perhaps two or three kicking her legs listlessly.

'There are other plagues in the community that we suffer without complaint,' said Reverend Kerr, his sonorous voice filling the church to its hot iron roof. 'There are plagues of Saturday night shopping, Sunday labour, gambling, the drink evil.'

Someone coughed and I snapped my head up.

Townsville had seemed a good choice. Its winters were warm. It would do the children good. Men were making fortunes in gold and sugar. The North was prosperous and exotic.

But I'd been disappointed to find the streets unpaved, the water foul and a frontier disregard for sobriety and manners. There were some grand buildings along Flinders-street, but the housing was generally poor, thin-skinned and prone to invasions of rats, insects, reptiles and amphibians. Not that Maria complained. She said, when we first arrived, that she supposed she should be thankful I was not being shot at. Humphry had told her that wasn't out of the question.

'...but the worst plague of all, the plague of sin, which is a lack of love and loyalty to God, and which, like leprosy, is subtle, incurable by human means, and fatal.'

I yawned behind my hand and stretched my back by leaning forward. I could see around Mrs Duffy and noticed the young woman was praying, or asleep, with her head on her arms leaning against the back of the pew in front of her.

A sudden cough racked her and she lifted her head.

Those seated in front drew away. The Reverend Kerr continued to talk about the Great Physician.

She coughed like a horse. In profile I saw the top of her neck white and slender above a tight collar, and a pretty face, if a little gaunt.

The child kicked the air beside her and seemed deaf to her mother's fit. The coughing ceased after an agonising while, she laid her head back into the material on her forearms.

I wondered if the pair had escaped from the consumptive ward. I hadn't seen her at church before, but then perhaps she'd been there and I hadn't noticed. I'd just blown in and the jury was still out, I'd heard, on my long-term ability to commit to the North. Doctors, unlike priests and public servants, rarely travelled far from their comforts and were viewed with suspicion when they did.

Perhaps the girl and her child had just arrived from some hard outback station between Townsville and the gold fields. It may be that they'd escaped the brute of a station manager by walking to the railway line and hailing a train. Such things happened. But they were too pale to have been out west.

The woman looked beaten by some ailment. Young, perhaps eighteen, maybe twenty-one. Possibly ... well, possibly younger, possibly older. My heart went out to her child though.

I decided to speak with the mother. Parents often passed serious ailments on to their children.

The Reverend announced the 'Old Hundredth' and we all stood, but for that pair, who seemed not to have noticed.

We waited near the door. A breeze brushed my neck. Just a tickle.

I could see the trees on Castle Hill swaying and Mrs Duffy took Maria's Bible and told her it was the south-easterly trade arriving late, but at least arriving, which was more than could be said for the mail, blaming me no doubt for the delay.

Allan squeezed through the forest of legs and escaped outside, but Maria held the girls back. Eileen was tall, almost a young woman herself, holding her hat in front of her and refusing her mother's hand. Marjorie clung to her mother's dress. Maria fanned herself with a free hand.

The Reverend Kerr stood just inside the porch, holding the congregation in purgatory, releasing us one at a time after interrogation.

'Feels like Salvation, Mrs Row?'

My women put their hats on and carried their skirts quickly down the cement steps. The Reverend grabbed my hand and didn't let go.

'An Act of God, do you think?'

'Just the grace of God, I'm sure,' I said.

'I meant the case of plague.'

'Oh. I believe the steward is recovering,' I said. 'An act of natural disease perhaps this time.'

'Well, a warning no doubt. I fear God's been warning us for some time.' He looked off into the distance, perhaps for a sign, and there was the gurgle from a crow. 'Modern times. We rush headlong like a locomotive. Into a new century. A new country. I wonder sometimes. Pride, you know, is a sin. Too fast progress, but it could be an Old Foe that overtakes us.' He looked at me earnestly. '*And behold a pale horse: and his name that sat on him was Death, and Hell followed with him.* Interesting don't you think that God chooses this moment, this year, to visit us again with pestilence and war.'

He let go of my hand, but grabbed my forearm and leaned forward. 'I want you to know, Doctor, that I do think there is a lot going for modern medicine. I do, unlike some, and I know you do your best. But our first consultation, if you will, has to be with our Heavenly Father. The Great Physician. You did like the sermon? If you have faith, the plague will not touch you. Tell me, was he an Irishman?'

'Who?'

'The man struck down.'

'I don't think so.'

Kerr nodded and kept hold of my arm. 'You look tired.'

'Work.'

Someone behind me cleared his throat. Maria was near the front gate speaking with a group of women who were dressed all in black. She glanced back.

'A family is a blessing,' he said. 'You're a lucky man.'

I said, 'Mr Philp's sending up another doctor from Brisbane. He'll be here by the end of the week.'

'Ah.'

'He's a doctor who makes a study of germs.'

'Germs.' He held the word in his mouth for a moment. 'Let's not discount God's hand in this though, and the healing power of Prayer. Perhaps this Brisbane physician is Presbyterian? What's his name?'

'Turner.'

'Turner. Turner.' He seemed to be tasting the name. 'Dr Turner. Hmm.'

'Jefferis Turner.'

'The entomologist?'

'Bacteriologist.'

'Dr *A. Jefferis* Turner. My word.' He let go of my arm and stared up into the bell tower.

'You know him?' I said.

'I do. I know *of* him. Moths, you know.'

I'd met Turner. Briefly. He had a reputation as an expert on a number of things. I thought the Reverend had the wrong man, but I wasn't going to argue with him.

Kerr was saying, 'My interest too. Well, butterflies. A small group we have up here. Lepidopterists. How interesting. Acts of God can giveth as well as taketh away, you know, Dr Row. They're called *blessings*. Remember that.'

Some in the crowd behind me had started to complain and several fellows no longer able to wait pushed past. Kerr ignored them and said to himself, 'Well, well. Turner is coming.'

The Reverend gave my arm a final pump, and I escaped.

I stood under the lone fig tree that shaded a corner of the churchyard next to the road. It rustled in the breeze and was gloriously cooler. I kept an eye on the rest of the congregation as they were delivered from the church. They milled near the bottom of the steps, splitting into groups, stiff-necked women in threes now wearing huge feathered hats, men in boxers and three-piece suits lighting pipes, children running around on the gravel. For all the talk of 'one people, one destiny', North Queensland was still firmly anchored in the Empire.

Maria had rounded up Allan, who was now sullenly kicking at the gravel. Eileen glanced my way, quickly, from under her hat. Marjorie was still clinging to her mother, whose ear had been taken by Mrs Kerr, the Reverend's wife and president of the Women's Guild. Allan saw his chance and slunk away again.

I was happy to have a few moments' peace, and decided that, if I saw her, I'd approach the young woman in the diaphanous dress to ask about the health of her child.

A hand came down on my shoulder.

'I startled you, Dr Row. So sorry.'

'You're right,' I said, trying to keep composed. The Mayor had somehow outflanked me. Behind His Worship, the Mayoress sat primly in their buggy.

'She's in a hurry to be off,' he said, as if I was delaying him.

I'd had the McCreedys pegged as early service types. I'd never seen them in church before.

The Mayor's lacquered moustache was as dark and shiny as a liquorice strap. He pulled a gold watch from his fob pocket. 'Your watch keeps good time, I take it? Yes, of course it does.' He put his back without looking at it.

'Now, a quiet word.' No one was in ear-shot, but he leaned forward. 'About the plague issue. Man to man. You follow me?'

McCreedy started making a speech, in the sort of tone he used in council chambers, his eyes drifting over my shoulder into the distance as he sought his words and found a rhythm.

'... and the Home Secretary, no less, instructed our own Government health officer not to go about bothering the shipping companies over fumigation, even if the damned ship in question came from Sydney or Brisbane. I must say I support Dr Humphry on this one and insofar as the council can make such demands, I'll be insisting every ship from any infected port be fumigated for a good twelve hours before being unloaded ...' and so forth.

My mind had a dangerous habit of drifting in council meetings. Maria was now looking my way. She still had the girls but Allan was nowhere to be seen and had probably made a dash for home. His mother pointed in that direction and I nodded and she marched off with the girls, leaving me to McCreedy.

'...leading the way in fumigation. Now Brisbane wants to adopt our tight restrictions and what earthly good will that do them now, for Heaven's sake? They've already got the damned disease ...'

I heard someone coughing. A cough in itself could mean anything. How many ailments were a product of phlegm or the lack of it? Asthma, consumption, any number of relapsing fevers. I started ticking them off.

'...you follow me?'

'Yes, yes.'

'I knew we were of one mind on this, Dr Row.'

I wondered what I'd agreed to.

'A necessary evil, if you like. We have our differences Mr Dawson and I, but on this we agree. White workers need as many jobs as we can find for them these days. Kanakas are suited to the plantations, I agree with Mr Philp on that one. Australia for Australians, but who'll cut the cane, eh? Mr Dawson, of course, wants them packed off or bleached or something, well, I ask you where would we be? White men can't work in the sugarcane fields, but by Jove the railways need as many white workers as they can get. Can't just knock a spike in anywhere, you follow me? And you have to build train lines; the modern businessman can't run a show without them. The North especially needs the railways now. One day soon, Row, you and I could catch a train from the station in town here and travel all the way to Brisbane. What do you think of that?'

I supposed, unlike a steamer, I could just pull a cord and get off.

I said it would be pleasant.

'Pleasant? It'd be a bloody triumph of the modern age. Now Dawson, I grant you, is as red as he is white, if you follow me, but you've got to respect the man, a former Premier, even though that was a debacle. Anyway, he's due to appear at the railway hearings here later in the week. What are the chances of him being released in time for that?'

Released in time for …? I nearly choked. 'You want me to release Mr Dawson from quarantine?'

'That's what I said.' McCreedy was watching me closely now, having apparently come to the point.

'I can't do that.'

'What, even for a few hours? Why on earth not? We both know he's not infected. No germ would dare. Ha.' McCreedy put a heavy hand on my shoulder. 'Mr Philp will win this one, Row, if Mr Dawson doesn't show, and if that happens it'll be a blow to the North and to progress, let alone good sense.'

It occurred to me that Dawson and McCreedy had reached some agreement about some railway line. The only railway project I could think of was the proposal by Charters Towers businessmen to build a spur line to link up with Bowen, so they could bypass Townsville.

But he was the Townsville Mayor and this couldn't be what he meant.

'I can't cut quarantine short for anyone,' I said. 'I'm not even sure it's Dr Humphry's decision now.'

'Well, put it to Humphry, will you? Mr Dawson must front this hearing,' said McCreedy, 'or the project's scuttled. You follow me?'

I said I'd see what was possible.

'Good, good. You know Mr Dawson and Dr Routh are saying the man has typhoid?'

I nodded.

'And he's recovering.'

'Yes.'

'If there's some disagreement about Dr Humphry's diagnosis, could not the Epidemic Board reconsider the quarantine period? I believe the passengers have another, what, week to serve?'

'Fifteen days,' I said.

'Well, there you are, in those harsh conditions. Away from their families. It may be we are putting them at risk of infection from some other diseases, you follow me? A quarantine station by definition is not a healthy place. You'd have to agree.'

I supposed I had to.

'Good, good. And what about this other Government doctor they're sending up. He's an expert in the damned disease, isn't he? Maybe he could do something. In the interests of Queensland's development.'

'Maybe,' I said.

'Don't know how many Government doctors we need, maybe one for each rat, eh? You know this fellow?'

'Dr Turner? I've met him.'

'Right. Well, whatever he needs, keep him sweet, but I won't stand for any meddling, you follow me? Neither will the rest of the town. See if he can get Mr Dawson off the island.' He slapped my shoulder and leaned forward. 'If you can do this for me, Row, you won't be sorry.'

The Mayor looked around at his wife, who was fidgeting with her parasol. '"The wrath of the Lord" indeed,' he said, nodding towards the Reverend Kerr who was mingling with the last of the congregation. Buggies were raising dust along the road.

'Anyway,' McCreedy was saying, 'one case does not an epidemic make. Would you be able to tell, Row, the difference between plague and any number of tropical fevers that touch this city in any given year?'

'I hope so.'

'Right. Northern stock are tough and it's the Chinaman and kanaka who'll cop it. They're the ones we need to damn well quarantine.'

Most of the buggies had gone. I saw the back of Reverend Kerr.

'...Brisbane medico,' McCreedy went on, 'an expert in these matters I read about, whatshisname? Lukin or something. Lucas. You follow me?'

The Mayor took his watch out again. 'Blast.' He tapped his head, 'One mind, doctor,' and crushed my hand.

The stragglers of the congregation were climbing into their carriages and I saw that the Reverend and Mrs Kerr had found an invitation to lunch and were already on their way to German Gardens.

And then I was alone. Behind St Andrew's, dry scrub and boulders climbed the side of Castle Hill. The only sounds came from crows and insects, the wind in the trees, and the fading rattle of McCreedy's buggy.

The church door was open. I looked around and stepped out of the shade and over the gravel.

The church was an oven when I poked my head inside. Perhaps the young mother had fainted.

The pew where she had been sitting was empty, but I leaned over it to make sure she wasn't lying full stretch. Coughing politely I walked slowly down the aisle, looking up and down the pews.

'Anyone here?' Apart from the Almighty.

The church grew darker and the iron roof creaked as a cloud passed over. Ahead was the communion table, pulpit, and the dark opening of the doorway leading to the vestry.

An empty church is an eerie place. You can never shake the feeling you're being watched, which is, I suppose, the point. If you're alone, though, you're the centre of attention.

Even my socks were damp with perspiration.

Something moved near the vestry.

'Who's there?' My voice was pitched a little high.

I walked slowly over, tilting my head, trying to get a clear vision of what lay in the gloom. A figure in black stood by the wall.

'I'm a doctor.'

Not necessarily the most reassuring thing to say in these parts. I stepped closer.

He didn't move. I stood at the vestry entrance. A sudden shaft of sun lit a column of rising dust and I was looking at the Reverend Kerr's black robe hanging from a hook.

I straightened, ridiculous and apparently alone. And yet I had heard something. To my left was the door, behind which a homeless thin woman and a child could hide. I stepped into the vestry and touched the knob. A dark shape rushed me.

'Christ!'

I leapt back. The rat darted between my legs and went for the far wall, hitting the skirting board and running along until it reach the hem of the robe. It stopped there, thinking it was hidden, but I could still see its greasy tail and I took two strides towards it, lifted my foot and brought it down.

The robe slid from the hook to spill over my boot, under which the rat squirmed. I leaned my weight to it until it stopped moving.

I took a deep breath and pulled my leg away. It had all happened so fast. I pushed the cloth aside with the toe of a boot. The rat kicked feebly in death, blood blossoming from its nose onto the floor. A great deal of blood. I saw black blood on the cloth.

I stood there feeling shaky, expecting footsteps, someone fleeing, or someone arriving to investigate the desecration. But it was quiet.

I gathered up the black robe and then used it to pick up the body. I started to wipe the bloody floor.

Damnation.

I carried the corpse in its bloody shroud to the front door and, holding it out at arm's length, let the dead rat fall to the dirt. Blood, dust and rat hair were smeared over the cloth. I gave it a shake, and then debated whether to take it with me and burn it.

But I simply went back to the vestry and hung the thing up again, walking out of the church as quickly and casually as I could manage.

I reached the fig tree before turning around. If the young woman and her child were still in the church they could stew. I cursed myself for trying to help. I could see the small broken body of the rat in the dust near the steps. A crow swooped down and jumped towards it. I turned.

I felt a little ill as I walked away, my boots raising puffs of dust that the wind blew ahead, down a road empty at noon on a Sunday.

chapter three

The flaunting flag of progress
Is in the West unfurled,
The mighty bush with iron rails
Is tethered to the world.

'The Roaring Days', Henry Lawson

THE WHEELS OF HEAVY wagons had maimed the road to the wharves, but the Carbine negotiated the lesions with a certain panache, I felt. I passed two men walking their bicycles and I even managed to raise my hat.

The thing about the Carbine bicycle, the thing that made it suitable for the North, was that it was built completely of English parts, as I said, but had been assembled in South Australia to be raced between towns. It was painted red and had pneumatic tyres, the pillion modified to take my medical bag, but I couldn't say the streets of Townsville were ideal for the sport. It was mostly flat going, but rough, and everyone had a dog.

I picked a path between the grooves, flicking the bicycle deftly around muddy holes and hard clay spines, but eventually the road was in such bad shape I had to get off and walk it the last hundred yards.

The passenger wharf was closer to the mouth of Ross Creek than the Government wharf, but even here against the sea breeze were the oily odours of industry. A steam shovel was working out into the bay to extend the harbour so that bigger coastal traders could actually tie up. At the moment lighters were used to take cattle, gold, and sugar out to the ships, and it wasn't unusual to see steer swimming in the bay.

The water was now flecked with whitecaps and I could see a few ships at anchor.

The plague news up and down the coast hadn't done much to slow the steamer traffic and the port was busy despite the burden on ships to be fumigated. I doubted many captains actually took the trouble. The regulations probably meant more backhanders for port officers.

That was the talk, anyway.

The northern railway lines terminated here, all the cattle, gold and men channelled through this point. A spur line ran on to the wharf, and there was a train parked beside the steamship.

The gunwale of the SS *Leura* was still slick with sea spray. Despite McCreedy's vision of long-distance train travel, the steamship was the only civilised way to get to Brisbane.

I searched the crowd for Humphry.

Passengers lined the deck ready to disembark and there was a fair number of people to welcome them.

Women in white skirts and muslins paraded beneath red sunshades and men in flannel suits stood around in small groups.

I saw the back of Humphry's black boxer several yards in front of me. I knew it was Humphry because it was at an unlikely angle, pushed far back on his head in the manner of a bushranger I'd seen in a photograph, who wore it that way only because he was propped up against a wall, dead. I think Humphry enjoyed looking mad and dangerous.

He was standing with the dignitaries who'd come to the wharf to welcome the Government's new health officer. As I was unsure of my own status in that crowd, I stood behind them while the ship tied up.

I knew their figures well enough now to recognise them from behind under their charcoal suits, hats and billows of smoke. Counting myself, there were five here to welcome Dr Alfred Jefferis Turner.

His Worship the Mayor stood beside Thankful Willmett. Alderman Willmett was the chairman of the Townsville Joint Epidemic Board and appeared to be a level head in a town largely run by lunatics.

Beside Willmett, taller and thinner, was Dr William Bacot, the chief surgeon of the Townsville General Hospital. Bacot was older than I, but not by much, and he was perpetually angry.

Beside Bacot was Humphry.

Three doctors and two aldermen.

I guessed that the aldermen outweighed us, even though we outnumbered them.

McCreedy was facing the ship and he said loudly that it was a shame there were no Members of Parliament to receive the Government's agent today, Townsville's own Mr Philp being caught up with matters of state in Brisbane and the MPs for Charters Towers incarcerated at West Point on Magnetic Island.

McCreedy leaned forward and turned to Humphry at the end of the line. 'But I suppose that's not your fault.'

'Clearly not,' said Humphry.

'I've heard you've been going about startling people with unsubstantiated claims, Dr Humphry. Some people have come to me asking if the town is overrun with the Black Death.'

'Black Death?' Humphry snorted. 'I wouldn't say anything of the sort.'

McCreedy was about to say something more, but Willmett whispered in his ear and he turned his attention back to the ship.

There was some excited shouting as people on the wharf recognised passengers, but our group in black, like pallbearers waiting for the coffin, remained in dignified silence as the gangway rolled out before us.

The Wesley Military Band struck up the Doxology. Humphry's elbow rose as he took a nip from his hipflask.

The first passenger appeared at the top of the *Leura*'s gangway. He looked around and seemed to take a deep breath before starting down. As he came closer I saw spectacles, a white linen tropical suit and a white pith helmet. There was no movement from the party as he came towards us, but then Dr Bacot took a coughing fit and Humphry pounded him once, hard, on the back.

The man was carrying a medical bag and tottered down the gangway towards us.

I'd been nervous about the reception the doctor would get in Townsville and seeing Jefferis Turner again, his stature, I was certain now that he would be quickly crushed.

Except for the white suit he was exactly as I remembered: small and dapper. His slight build hardly tipped the scales in the doctors' favour.

As Mayor McCreedy had said, they were a tough breed in the North. They were quick to note any weakness in Southerners. The man seemed unsteady as he negotiated the moving gangway and McCreedy appeared to swell as the Government doctor approached.

He was the centre of everyone's attention now; even the other passengers watched as he stepped off the gangway as if off a Brisbane tram.

Humphry in front of me went to step forward, but the Mayor in one long stride beat him, reaching out a practised hand.

'Doctor Turner? A. E. McCreedy. I'm the Mayor. Good of you to come.'

I caught the 'fank you'. I saw McCreedy's face now and it was beaming, and Bacot was staring with his mouth open. My God, I thought, Turner was lightweight, English middle class, bookish, with a speech impediment; the antithesis of the northern male.

The Mayor eclipsed the doctor as he stepped forward, causing the rest of the party to move forward and surround him. For a moment I fancied they'd eaten him.

I heard McCreedy introduce the others. I could just see the top of Turner's oddly large head.

'And where is Dr Row?' I heard him say.

'Who?' said McCreedy.

Humphry looked around, saw me, and stepped aside.

'Here I am,' I said.

I took the hand that Turner extended between Bacot and Humphry. 'I never expected such a crowd.' *Cwowd.*

Bacot, I swear, sniggered.

Turner smiled at me as if we were old friends. In his eyes I saw a confidence no doubt naïve and dangerously misplaced.

I said I was glad to see him again. I wished I'd meant it.

Alderman Willmett, as chairman of the Epidemic Board and a gentleman, asked Turner if his trip was comfortable and Turner told him it was, but for the last leg from Rockhampton, which was 'wuff, vewy wuff, but jolly good fun'.

I stood back and Turner vanished again among the black suits. The other passengers were now coming down the gangway and the Mayor was gesturing at the locomotive, one of the train's carriages having been especially organised for the dignitaries. I heard Turner from within the scrum assure him he shouldn't have *bovvered*, but the Mayor wouldn't hear of anything but the best for a respected medico and escorted the doctor to the carriage.

Humphry fell back beside me as we moved off.

'We've been sold a pup.'

'Why do you say that?' I said.

'*Weally*?' mocked Humphry. 'Come on. You didn't tell me he was a jockey.'

I saw Turner walking between McCreedy and Bacot. 'He's no jockey.' I supposed he didn't look like the man who could fight our battles. 'He's the Brisbane featherweight boxing champion. Took my title.'

'Ha!' said Humphry. The train whistle blew. 'Wonder if they have beer and sandwiches.'

We stopped by the carriage.

'I brought my Carbine.'

'You know, Lin, when you say that, I look around for your gun or your horse.'

'It's only a mile back to town. Seems silly to take a train.'

'Nothing's too silly for the Government's bacteriologist, apparently.'

I left them and walked back to my bicycle with mixed feelings about Turner's arrival.

I'd just put my foot on the pedal when I heard a shout. Our chairman Willmett was waving me over. I wheeled my bicycle back to the train.

'Dr Turner was wondering where you'd got to,' he said as I came nearer. Turner's head without the helmet appeared from a window.

'I have my bicycle,' I said.

'Bwing it on board and wide back with us,' said Turner.

I could see Humphry through a window waving a sandwich. I reluctantly wheeled the bicycle over to the wooden foot step. There was no platform at the wharf, so with the help of a fellow who was apparently the conductor I lifted the bicycle aboard, Willmett climbed behind me, and the train moved off.

The solid figure of the Mayor sat opposite Turner, making the little doctor appear even smaller on his seat. Willmett squeezed next to the Mayor. McCreedy began asking Turner if he'd been north before. Turner said he was sorry to say he hadn't but he'd been jolly well looking forward to it. He was watching the townscape unfold through the carriage window.

It seemed extravagant to have the short trip catered, but the council had put silver platters of beef sandwiches on board and Humphry passed one to me. Turner had two, and the conductor came with tea.

'Do you have coffee?' said Turner. The man went away.

McCreedy and Willmett kept exchanging glances, having difficulty comparing the man they had in front of them with the one they'd been told to expect.

Willmett had a go at the weather. 'Heat's gone now, so that's a good thing.'

'I'm afraid that won't help you at all,' said Turner. He was looking out the window at the tents and iron shanties beside the spur that linked the wharves to the town.

'Won't it?'

'The plague bacillus isn't bothered one way or the other about the weather,' said Turner. Some grubby-faced children appeared and ran beside the train. I saw undergarments hanging on a wire strung over a dusty yard, a drunk leaning against the rusty side of a tin shack.

'Of course, you know,' said Turner, not taking his eyes off the scene now, 'it's the rats we have to watch. They'll start wandering around in search of food in cooler weather.'

There were piles of rubbish beside the track, and some of them were smouldering. I caught a glimpse of children playing cricket in a dusty lane with kerosene-tin wickets.

'I wouldn't take too much comfort in the weather,' said Turner again. All the carriage windows were closed, and Turner stood to open his. He had trouble getting it to budge.

'Don't do that,' said McCreedy, putting out his hand, but the window suddenly shot up with a bang and Turner put his head outside. A fetid smoke from burning rubbish and cooking fires filled the carriage. I saw a dog carcass in a drain.

McCreedy leaned forward and put a hand on the window. 'With the drought and everything, men have been arriving in town in droves. You know the type.'

Turner shut the window and sat down again. 'Disease loves poverty.'

'Eh?' said the Mayor. 'Is that so? Well, what we need are projects, you follow me? Get these coves working. Railway lines, that sort of thing. It's the patriotic thing to do. And, as you say, disease prevention.'

Willmett was frowning and I suspected the Mayor didn't have complete support for all of his private projects.

'This is fun,' said Humphry in the uncomfortable silence. 'We should do this more often.'

The train rumbled over the Ross Creek railway bridge and as we were approaching the station Turner leaned into the aisle and asked Humphry and me about the *Cintra* passengers.

'Still quarantined,' said Humphry.

'And the man who is sick?' said Turner.

'Oh, he's recovered,' McCreedy cut in, 'fully recovered.'

'Splendid.'

'Yes, we think it may not have been plague after all,' said the Mayor, shooting a savage glance at Humphry.

'Really?' said Turner. Weally? 'Why do you think that?'

'Well, because the man's recovered. Dr Routh's our man on the island and he thinks it was just a bout of typhoid.'

'Rot,' said Humphry.

McCreedy glared. 'Well, it *was* Dr Humphry who diagnosed plague in the first place so I suppose he has every right to defend his position.'

'I'm not taking a *position*,' said Humphry. 'The man has plague. It's a fact, not a matter of opinion.'

Turner looked to McCreedy, who rolled his eyes.

Turner said, 'I can only go on the advice of the district medical officer over this, but I'll keep an open mind. Until I see all the facts for myself.'

'Of course,' said McCreedy. 'Only right, I'm not saying otherwise. Just saying what the West Point medical superintendent reports.'

'West Point?'

'That's the quarantine station they're at. Magnetic Island.'

'An island? And how far is that?'

'About six miles,' said Humphry. 'Across the bay.'

'And is this the preferred place for a plague hospital?' said Turner.

Dr Bacot leaned forward from his seat behind McCreedy and Willmett. 'It hasn't come to that yet. We won't be needing a plague hospital.' He nodded to himself and sat back, folding his arms.

'Well,' said Turner, 'I can't imagine an island's the best place to put people who are sick.'

The Mayor grinned and leaned forward. 'My thoughts exactly. Exactly.' He slapped Turner on the knee and sat back, nodding. 'Completely inappropriate.

That's what I told the Premier. You just can't incarcerate people on an island willy-nilly. Thank you, Dr Turner.'

The train rolled slowly into the station and shuddered.

'Well,' said Turner. 'The most important thing now I think is for me to examine the patient as soon as possible.'

Humphry stood and said, 'Whenever you're ready.'

'This afternoon,' said Turner.

'Not sure I can arrange the launch by then.'

'Tomorrow morning.'

'Difficult.'

'I see. How do you get to the island in an emergency?'

'There's never been an emergency.'

Turner stared at Humphry for a while. 'I'm sure someone can arrange transport.'

'All right,' said Humphry. 'I'll see what I can do.'

'Tomorrow morning,' said Turner, firmly.

Humphry nodded.

'Jolly good,' said Turner, and he stood. We all filed out of the carriage on to the platform.

As I collected my bicycle, Humphry whispered to me, 'You know what they call him in Brisbane, don't you?' Actually, I did. 'Gentle Annie. I thought it might have been a joke, like calling a big man Tiny.'

Humphry then started whistling the tune 'Gentle Annie'. He stopped.

'McCreedy thinks he'll have this fop of an English doctor around his finger soon. I'm not so sure.'

I didn't say anything.

Outside in the full sun, small eddies of dust and paper played across the drive at the railway station's entrance. McCreedy was bustling Turner into his own buggy, almost grabbing the doctor by the arm. Dr Bacot and Alderman Willmett found a hansom cab and were negotiating who should get in first. I left Humphry standing at the bottom of the station steps and walked my bicycle around the traffic.

It was Turner who called out. 'Where are you off to now, Dr Row?'

'Back to my office.'

'Good. I'll meet you there. There are matters I'd like to discuss.'

'But we have a lunch organised for you now,' said McCreedy.

'Even better. A good chance for Dr Row, Dr Humphry and me to brief each other,' said Turner.

I saw behind him the cab roll by, the faces of Willmett and Bacot looking out at us.

McCreedy said, 'I believe Dr Humphry might have other matters to attend to.'

'My lunch date cancelled.'

'Oh, all right then.'

I followed the dust from McCreedy's buggy. It was only a short distance down the main street to the Town Hall. Humphry, who found himself without a lift, said he'd walk. His tuneful whistling faded behind me.

* * *

I waited in my office for Humphry and we went together to the Mayor's chambers, where McCreedy had invited his peers and the aldermen to a reception for Turner. Humphry and I, uninvited, stood at the door. Men were standing around in small stiff groups.

'Let's go,' said Humphry, and he started to turn away, but I saw Turner, who waved.

'There are beer bottles on that table,' I said, and Humphry followed me in.

The mayoral suite was panelled with cedar. Red velvet drapes were drawn over what would have been large windows opening on to a balcony overlooking the street. McCreedy always kept them drawn against the heat and dust, so even in the day the room had to be lit by gaslight. The furniture was dark and heavy, as were the unsmiling portraits of four previous mayors. McCreedy's own face hung behind the mayoral desk so that when he conducted interviews, the effect was like being interrogated by large twin uncles.

Men stood around with drinks and it would have been all very civilised if a dog fight hadn't then started up in the street below.

'I hope to Christ we missed the speeches,' said Humphry.

Turner seemed even smaller in the large room of large men. I saw McCreedy offer him a whisky and Turner shake his head, and with that I knew he'd failed the last test of northerly manhood. Bacot was hunched with some aldermen near the table of food, looking furious and hungry.

Turner might as well be bleeding in a pool of sharks.

Willmett came up with a tray of tropical fruit and Turner took a banana.

Humphry had veered towards the table of bottles. Willmett offered me some fruit and I thanked him but shook my head, and he wandered off.

'It's good to see you again,' said Turner.

'Yes.'

'Under better circumstances this time.'

I nodded. They could hardly have been worse.

'Your wife?'

I nodded again but said nothing.

He looked around the room. 'You and Dr Humphry have created a bit of a kerfuffle.'

'Have we?'

'Incarcerating two Members of Parliament. One of them a former Premier, no less. And three ministers of religion. You've made quite a few people uneasy.'

'Well, the man had plague,' I said.

'Quite.'

Humphry came over with two glasses of beer.

'I was just telling Dr Row that you've both done an excellent job so far,' said Turner, shaking his head at the glass Humphry offered.

'The Board of Health even mentioned it to me in a letter,' he continued, patting his breast pockets. 'I have it here somewhere.'

'Really?'

'It's what we'd hope from our medical officers along the Queensland coast. Unfortunately, not all of them are as thorough.'

'That's true,' said Humphry.

'Ships are going to and from ports without check now. Local councils are thumbing their noses at Brisbane. Well, that's hardly news, I suppose. Anyway, it will be a disaster.' Turner finished his banana and looked for a place to put the skin. I held out my hand. 'Thank you. Of course, as you know Townsville is especially vulnerable, being in the tropics, with its port and … how many people live here?'

'Seventeen thousand,' said Humphry. 'Not counting blacks, of course. About twenty thousand in the gold fields.'

'That many? Anyway, it appears you've made Townsville a shining example of disease prevention. So. Well done.' He reached out and shook our hands again.

I felt the suspicious gaze of men from all corners of the room. I saw McCreedy look away.

'There are still a few problems,' I said.

'That's why I'm here.'

Many of the aldermen were openly smirking. I had the impression they'd made up their minds about this little man and had already dismissed him. He was a southern intruder who had no business in the North anyway. When they came up to shake his hand, there was a patronising politeness. Enjoying the weather? Not too hot? Best avoid the Commercial Hotel.

Between these introductions, I told Turner about the problems we had arranging quarantine. Supplies had been slow in coming. There'd been a backlash from some doctors and many local authorities.

I then told him about the Mayor's request to free Dawson for the Bowen railway hearings.

'Did he? Preposterous,' blurted Humphry.

'Keep your voice down.'

'What did you tell him?' said Turner.

'I said I'd put it to you. He's the Mayor.'

'It's simple. Anyone who tries to break quarantine will be arrested,' said Humphry. 'You can tell the fool that,' and he shot a tight smile at the Mayor who was looking at us.

'Keep it down,' I told Humphry. 'The man's just asking.'

'Just asking! Do you know *why* he's just asking?'

I had to admit I didn't.

'Sleepers,' said Humphry. 'Railway sleepers. From McCreedy's sawmills. I suppose he wants the contract for the Bowen line.'

I was wary of Humphry, the natural cynic.

'Nothing to do with northern development. It's business,' Humphry was saying, looking pleased with himself as the implications occurred to him. 'So Dawson wasn't just whinging. When's that hearing?'

'Late next week. Several days before quarantine ends.'

'Well, well. It seems incarcerating Dawson's really put the wind up them. I'm beginning to think this plague *is* the Almighty's punishment on the wicked.'

Turner said, 'Whatever the reason, if there's one thing we can't do it's compromise the regulations. Once we start making exceptions, laws become useless and civilisation is in peril.'

'Right. I'll get us something to eat,' said Humphry, happy with his theory.

Would the Mayor of Townsville really jeopardise the city for personal gain? McCreedy prided himself on 'doing the right thing'. I wasn't sure.

Humphry returned with sandwiches, took one and pulled apart the two slices of bread to inspect the meat.

'I'm tired of sandwiches,' he said then. 'Can't we do anything else with this stuff?'

'Bread and corned beef? I think it's rather good,' said Turner.

'You'll be sick of it soon enough.'

The lunch dissolved, Turner thanked the Mayor for his hospitality and Humphry took him to his new office.

'It won't be easy,' I said. 'Dealing with the council.'

'I'll manage. How are you managing?'

'The Mayor's stubborn.'

He seemed to be examining my face. 'I meant your family.'

I said, 'The summer was very hot. My wife is tired. I'm hoping the winter will suit her better.'

* * *

Turner had been given a bare room that still smelled of ink and dust. It was across the hallway and down from my own.

McCreedy had been generous to Turner. Large glass doors opened out onto a balcony over Flinders-street. The office was spacious. Someone had wasted no time in looting it.

'I'll find you some furniture,' I said.

'How far away are your rooms, Dr Humphry?' said Turner.

Humphry went over to the glass doors.

'Down the street,' he said, pointing. 'The post office is next door here. You're only a block from your hotel. You can just see the top of the Bellevue. The Prince of Wales is in front, around the corner there.'

Turner undid the latch of the door. It opened with a kick on to the small balcony.

'And a gas lamp, right outside,' Turner said. 'How wonderful.'

He gazed up at Castle Hill, and when he turned around I noticed the man looked delighted. He clapped his hands like a child and Humphry caught my eye.

'Well,' said Turner, 'there's a lot to do. Tell me everything.'

The plague scare has many advantages over the war-fever. Kipling hasn't made any great songs about it. It doesn't move any great crowd of idiots to sing patriotic songs every five and a half minutes. It leads to cleanliness.

The Bulletin, 31 March 1900

THE WIND HAD SPRUNG TO TWENTY-FIVE knots overnight and now overtook the launch, pushing the smoke in front of us so that if anyone had taken a daguerreotype at that time it might look like this: a small grey boat appearing to go backwards through a grey sea. That illusion and the sensation of the engine made me queasy. I studied the horizon, looking beyond the activity on board, the crew tending the ropes, Humphry his flask.

Turner was standing on the bench seat with his back to me, his head over the side and eagerly facing forward, and if he had a tail it'd be hitting me in the ear.

He'd insisted on an early start and, in spite of Humphry, had managed to arrange things so that when I arrived at the Government wharf in the dark, the SS *Teal* was already belching loudly.

'A telegraph to the Board of Health,' Turner explained. 'And one back to the port office.'

More surprising was the appearance from the shadows of Humphry's buggy.

'Just don't say a word to me until sun-up.'

The dawn touched the whitecaps turning them pink, and they chased each other over the sea like galahs. The *Teal* rolled heavily and for the first time since I'd come north, I shivered. Behind me, Castle Hill sat on Townsville, a granite paperweight lit pink by the rising sun. Ahead was the deep blue strip of Magnetic Island.

I'd never been there. I didn't even feel a morbid attraction to the place. All quarantine stations were alike on their glum islands. West Point would be more desolate than most because the regulation quarters, stores and sheds were carried away or wrecked by a cyclone in '96.

The island heaved above the waves before us, a natural gaol where people who arrived by a ship carrying some fever or other were left for a quarantine period to sicken, recover or die.

During the previous two weeks, Humphry had come to my office to tell me stories that I didn't want to hear. He'd sit on the other side of my desk and say things such as 'They're sending a petition to the Home Secretary.'

I'd been making a list of hygienic household practices: the importance of light, fresh air, sealing food scraps, poisoning rats, and the like. Humphry had a knack of interrupting when I was busy.

'Every one of them signed it,' Humphry continued. He rustled a sheet of paper loudly.

I gave up. 'What's that?'

'The petition. Look here. They've spelt your name wrong.'

I looked. Humphry held up three ink-smudged sheets of paper pinned together and jabbed a finger at it. I squinted from my side of the desk.

'They sent you a copy?'

'Hell no,' he said. 'This is the original. I promised I'd take it to the post office.'

I put my pen in its stand and sat back.

'They asked *you* to take a petition that demands your dismissal and just, what, pop it in the mail?'

'Your dismissal too. But no, of course they didn't ask me. It was the bloke who runs the supply lighter who begged me to post it for him, with the other mail.'

Humphry had then just come back from giving the *Cintra* passengers another check-up.

'Saved him the trip from the wharf,' he said. 'And he did give me a lift over and back, so it was the least I could do.'

I leaned across and snatched the petition from his hands and began to read it through.

'You're breaking the law, interfering with the mail,' I said. 'You know that?'

'Not at all. I'm still on my way to the post office.'

'You're going to post it?'

'I haven't decided. I might. Might even sign it myself.'

I sighed. Even the Methodist ministers had signed it. I handed it back to him.

I heard no more about it after that, but it added to my growing anxiety about the island. I was in a difficult position and Humphry wasn't helping. He liked to poke sticks into wasps' nests and didn't seem to care if other people got stung.

It was hard to avoid him. Given the nature of our jobs, Humphry the Queensland Government doctor and I the municipal one, our paths crossed when it came to the public health of Townsville, so it seemed sensible to work together.

That's what Humphry said.

The difficulties we would face in trying to protect Townsville from the plague had by then begun to appear in an acute form at West Point and we should have learned our lessons there.

The first problem was Dr Routh, the quarantine station's medical officer.

He'd been thrown from his buggy at Hermit Park three weeks earlier, cracking his head and three ribs. Quarantine station duties were normally a doddle, but then *The Lady Norman* arrived from the Solomon Islands with a load of kanakas infected with measles. The *Cintra* arrived soon after. Routh had to move out there, to his horror, where the white passengers imagined they would be ravished, murdered and eaten in their sleep. Although they were well provisioned with newspapers and tobacco, the *Cintra* passengers never ceased complaining.

There wasn't a murmur from the kanakas.

The only person relieved of company on West Point was the sick steward, Storm. Soon after his arrival, he had his own tent ringed by barbed wire to form a regulation compound twenty yards square with yellow quarantine flags sprouting from each corner.

'See,' Humphry told me, after his first visit, before Routh was dispatched. 'Anyone who wants the North to separate from the rest of the colony only has to get plague and we could peg it out tomorrow.'

There was some confusion about the laws under which the *Cintra* passengers now lived. The quarantine station was provisioned and run under the Health Act, but convention also allowed Captain Thompson to maintain the law of the sea, and it was convenient, because of the lack of any other authority on the island, for him to divide them into steerage and saloon, and organise quoits and religious classes.

Dawson and Dunsford had apparently wanted some decision-making collective, but Captain Thompson, to his credit, said he'd consider that mutiny.

The kanakas had moved into the most habitable buildings by the time the *Cintra* arrived, of course, so the white passengers were given tents and removed themselves as far away as they could which, said

Humphry, the kanakas must have considered a blessing.

Dawson particularly resented his incarceration and sent telegrams daily, via the supply lighter, protesting to the Premier that conditions were terrible, there was no plague, and demanding to be freed to appear before the railway hearing. Mr Philp never replied, and somehow Humphry knew all about that as well.

So we arrived at West Point after dawn. The wind on this side of the island curled around and beat the sea into short meringue peaks. A broken wharf struck out uncertainly from the beach and with the crew all the time worried about hitting a reef, we tied up at an unlikely-looking pylon halfway along.

I couldn't see much beyond the beach, apart from some drifting smoke.

Because there had been no way of contacting the station, no one knew we were coming, but two men, who must have seen the boat approaching, appeared on the bank above the beach.

'I hope the natives are friendly this time,' said Humphry as we picked our way across the shambles.

The wharf groaned and shuddered where it leaned against the *Teal* and the *Teal* against it, like a pair of drunks. I was in the lead, followed by Humphry and Turner, jumping over gaps of churning grey-green water. To anyone on shore it might have looked comical: grown men playing hopscotch.

When I reached the end I saw that one man had gone and the other had come down to meet us. He stood at the end of the jetty with his hands clasped behind his back.

'Mr Gard, isn't it?' I said.

'Yes sir, Dr Row.' But he didn't look happy to see me. He didn't look happy at all.

Turner was still picking his way. We each carried black medical bags.

'Three doctors,' said Gard. 'One doctor's enough bad news, isn't it? Not sure what they'll make of three.'

'They don't have to make anything of it,' said Humphry, pushing past him and taking a steep path up the bank.

I followed, reaching the top and seeing Humphry trudge on along two wagon tracks that wound through the dry, low scrub. I looked back. We'd left the crew smoking and the launch looked particularly ugly beside the broken wharf. The mainland was a line of blue and brown.

I cleaned the salt from my spectacles as I waited for Turner.

Gard beside me said, 'What's the chance of going ashore today then?'

'Quarantine ends in a week's time. I doubt that'll change.'

Gard shook his head. 'They're not going to be happy with that news, you know.'

Turner arrived at the top of the bank.

'My word,' he said, looking about before following Humphry.

I started to follow Turner, but Gard suddenly grabbed my arm.

'You know,' he said, 'they're getting more fidgety each day. Some people have been stirring them up.'

'Dawson?'

'And others. And seeing how Storm's better . . .'

'That's what we're here to find out.'

'Well, I'm just saying they won't be pleased to see you. Or him.' He nodded at Humphry's back. 'It's been three or four weeks since some of these people left Brisbane or wherever, you see what I'm saying? Could be trouble.'

'What sort of trouble?'

He shrugged. 'Just saying be careful.'

'Thanks for the warning.' I started walking.

'Me, I'm busting to get off this island too. You a married man, Dr Row?'

I ignored him.

'You know what I mean?'

I caught up with Humphry.

The wooden buildings we passed might have been the bones of some giant saurian, picked over and scattered. The area was flat for maybe a hundred acres and then rose suddenly into dense bush. There was a racket of birds, but also a sort of peaceful charm to the place.

Gard began chattering aimlessly, pointing things out. The grass, he said, was kept trim by goats. They shot a few goats for meat, but they were too fast to catch for milking. Over there were two mighty stands of bamboo beneath the hill. That's where kanakas buried their dead. On the other side of the clearing was the white man's graveyard.

'Years since it's been used.'

Charming, as I said. A building slumped exhausted on the ground beside its stumps and looked as if it had been long abandoned by flesh. The roofs of the huts were a patchwork of badly fixed, dull and rusted iron sheeting.

A couple of black faces looked out from holes where the windows had been.

'Ain't them who'll be causing you any trouble. Whatever Mr Dawson says, they're all too lazy to butcher us in our sleep. Wouldn't like to get too close to any of them but. There's your disease carriers.'

Old large paperbarks had been left standing through the site and a few other smaller trees and shrubs grew here and there, thickest on the sea side.

Humphry nodded towards Turner who'd wandered off the track.

'Man could be mad,' he said.

Turner started plucking at some leaves, and as if to prove Humphry's point he came towards us with his hand out, two green leaves on his palm. He poked them with his finger and one moved. He turned it over.

'It has legs,' I said.

'A leaf with legs,' said Humphry. 'My word.'

'Look how well camouflaged this caterpillar is. This is the leaf from the same tree. Almost identical. Dashed hard to see.'

'What is it?' I said.

'Don't recognise the species. A moth or butterfly, but I've never seen anything quite like this one.' He pulled from his bag an empty bottle with a cork and popped the caterpillar and leaf inside.

'In case she gets hungry,' he said.

Quite.

We walked on.

The trees opened out and there was a building ahead. As we came closer I saw it was better kept than the others.

'That's the surgeon's cottage,' Gard told me. 'Dr Routh sleeps in there. Seems he has visitors though.'

Three men were standing casually about the front as though they'd posed themselves there a minute earlier. One of them was standing in a flower bed and leaning against the stairs. The other man might have been the one who'd left Gard at the beach.

'I didn't know doctors got up so early,' said the tall man as we approached. Dawson wore braces over a woollen undershirt. He hadn't had the chance to shave or wash, but he'd acknowledged a sort of formality by wearing his hat and fiddling with an unlit cigar.

Humphry ignored them, marched up the stairs on to a porch, and banged the flat of his hand against the wall. 'Wakey wakey.'

'The doctor might not be in,' said Dawson. His friends tittered.

Humphry just sighed at the coarse unpainted boards under his hand and then banged them hard three times.

'Dr Routh?'

'I'm coming, I'm coming. Who's that?' came Routh's voice from the belly of the cottage. Humphry kicked the bottom of the door, it banged open and he vanished inside.

Dawson turned his glare to Turner and me. I'd just put my foot on the bottom step to follow Humphry when Turner said, 'You're Mr Anderson Dawson.'

Turner walked over and introduced himself, extending a hand. Dawson stopped chewing his cigar when Turner said 'Jeffewis'. I wondered if the doctor had the short man's inclination for picking fights.

'Have we met?' said Dawson.

'Brisbane. British Medical Association. Amalgamation dinner?' Dawson shrugged and Turner said, 'January?'

'I don't recall.'

'You probably had more important things on your mind.'

Dawson finally accepted Turner's hand. 'What are you doing here?'

'The Government's given me the job of making sure northern and central Queensland don't catch plague,' said Turner.

'Who sent you?'

'Mr Foxton.'

'And you've come here to look at Storm?'

'Yes.'

'All the way from Brisbane?' Dawson looked confused, as if Turner had appeared on the scene out of context, which I suppose he had. 'You're English.'

'Quite.'

'Turner. Name does ring a bell.'

'Parasitic anaemia.'

'You've been hounding the Government.'

'I wouldn't say hounding. I've brought a condition that's affecting scores of children to its attention. It requires a scientific approach –'

'Science,' interrupted Dawson, taking the cigar from his teeth. 'Science needs evidence, proof. Am I right?'

'You are.'

'That's good. That's very good.' He glared at me then.

Humphry appeared at the cottage door with Dr Routh at his heels. Routh's big moustache dragged the eyes down his face.

'This is Dr Turner,' said Humphry to Routh.

'Yes, of course, how are you?' but he clearly didn't know who Turner was.

Humphry told Turner, 'And this is Dr Routh, the medical superintendent.'

They shook hands and Routh winced.

'Are you all right?' said Turner.

'Had a fall. I'll be right. Well, what's all this then?'

Turner explained who he was and what he wanted to do, and Routh seemed actually to brighten at the prospect of professional support.

'Good. Good. You're very welcome. Let's get you some breakfast.'

'Do you have coffee?' said Turner.

'Coffee? No.'

I think Routh was about to invite us inside, but Dawson said, 'Follow me,' and he popped the cigar into his mouth, turned and left. Dunsford and the other man followed.

'Oh all right, if you like,' and Routh followed. 'Coffee. Now there's something.'

I caught a glimpse of tents. Wood smoke from breakfast fires hung about the trees. Dawson stopped at a campfire where a large kettle hung from a tripod over the coals. A man stood as we approached and used a stiff length of wire to pick the kettle up and put it on the ground. He took several careful hand measures of tea and threw them in before sitting down again.

On a log were about a dozen tin mugs. I heard Turner say, 'I didn't realise the conditions were this primitive.'

'Conditions have improved,' Dawson said. 'You'll have to take it black.' He poured the tea and handed a mug to Turner.

'Don't we have enough doctors today?' said Dunsford, looking from Turner to Humphry to me with our black medical bags.

Dawson said, 'I can tell you, you won't find plague here.'

Turner blew on his steaming cup. 'I very much hope that's true, Mr Dawson.'

Dawson had taken the heavy kettle and poured tea into several other mugs on the log. I picked one up. Humphry stayed back, but Dawson collected two and took them to Humphry. He put one under Humphry's nose and I thought Humphry might knock it away, but without taking his eyes from the politician's, he reached into his jacket, produced his flask and poured a good nip into both mugs. He took the one Dawson offered. Dawson took his, walking back to the fire without saying a word.

'And how are you going to help us?' Dawson said to Turner.

'By making sure you don't actually have plague when you leave this place.'

Dawson snorted. 'There's still a week of quarantine left. There are women here without their children, husbands without wives, children without fathers . . .'

'Politicians without soapboxes,' offered Humphry.

'Doctors without manners. One thing that would improve conditions markedly is if you could leave Dr Humphry with us so we can string him up.'

Humphry sipped his tea.

Dawson took a couple of steps and pointed his unlit cigar at Humphry.

'It's this cur's misdiagnosis and the compliance of his, his lapdog here,' he waved it at me, 'that's put us all unnecessarily and at great inconvenience on this blasted desert island.'

He picked up a twig from the fire and lit his cigar.

Turner said, 'However much you feel you've been treated unfairly, Mr Dawson, Dr Humphry and Dr Row have been following the law.'

'Pah,' said Dawson.

Turner turned to Routh. 'Perhaps we should see the sick steward now?'

'Certainly. He's right here.'

There was a moment's confusion. 'Here?'

And the man who was tending the fire when we arrived stood to attention. It took a few seconds to understand what had happened. I think we'd overlooked him because we were expecting to see a man pale, ill and supine in a tent. But here he was, looking a little uncomfortable in front of so many gawping doctors.

'Dr Humphry,' said Turner. 'Is this the man you treated on the ship?'

Humphry looked the man up and down. 'I believe it is, yes.'

'How long has he been out of the quarantine tent?'

'Just yesterday,' said Routh.

'Well, dash it, who gave permission to release him?'

'Permission? He left the tent of his own accord.'

Storm raised his hand, a little embarrassed acknowledgment. He looked weak but otherwise healthy.

Dawson was standing back and had folded his arms. Turner spun around and Dawson shrugged.

'Nothing to do with me.' He took the cigar from his mouth. 'I just found him chopping wood for the nurses. Can't say I'm surprised the man's better.' And he stared at Humphry. 'Seeing it was just a re-bout of *typhoid.*'

'And how would you be able to tell typhoid from tremens?' said Humphry.

'I don't have to. It's the opinion of Dr Routh. He says it's typhoid.'

We turned to Routh. 'Well, I've said that before.'

'Dr Turner,' said Dawson, 'what do you think of this evidence?'

'It's evidence of the man being well and apparently recovering from whatever had afflicted him. What that was is still to be determined.'

Dawson went over to Storm and slung an arm around his shoulders.

'If it was plague, Mr Storm here would be dead, wouldn't he?' Storm kicked at the sandy dirt. 'And we'd all be sick by now.' He left Storm to his embarrassment and walked over to Turner. 'This is a farce.'

Turner spoke softly. 'I have to examine the patient and complete some tests.'

Dawson nodded. 'Well, do that. I'll be interested to hear what you find,' and he walked back to the fire.

Turner asked Routh to lead the way to the plague tent where he could examine Storm. Storm seemed terrified by the suggestion. 'But I'm feeling orright.'

'I just want to make sure you don't get sick again,' said Turner.

So Humphry and I followed Routh and Turner to the tent where Storm had apparently spent the past two weeks, less a few days. Dawson and the others stayed at their fire.

When we were out of sight, Gard appeared at my side and leaned very close. I could smell smoke and sweat.

'Storm just said he felt better and got up,' he whispered. 'Said he'd chop some firewood, and we said, no, you're in the plague tent, mate. You can't leave. We was talking to him over the fence, and he said, well bring me the wood and I'll chop it in here.'

Gard pointed to the tent we were approaching, its wire fence, and a chopping block inside with wood chips all around.

'And we did bring him the wood, but then Mr Dawson saw him and asked him if he felt better and would he like some breakfast. He said bloody oath and just stepped over the wire and off he went.' Gard was rubbing the palms of his hands against his forehead.

'Are you all right?' I said.

'I hafta get home, doctor. Hafta get back. I gotta see my wife.'

The tent was set apart — a new military-style tent, square, peaked and white like a fancy iced cake. We stepped over the wire and entered through the flap.

It was bare but for a stretcher, a chair and a small table. It appeared clean enough, and the stretcher had a fresh starched white sheet. The nurses obviously kept it ready should Storm decide to return.

'Where are the nurses?' said Turner.

'I sent one back. Didn't need her,' said Routh. 'I use the other one at the dispensary. Matter of fact she's making breakfast.'

Turner sat Storm on the stretcher and made his observations. There was a yellow bruise at the groin. It remained fixed and firm when pressed, but there was no visible swelling. The sight of the needle proved to Storm that he hadn't been wrong about doctors, but we held him and Turner got his serum.

'Well,' said Turner, holding the syringe of dark blood to the light, 'we'll see what lovelies are in here.'

But most of Storm's symptoms had vanished. What remained was lethargy, a backache and sulkiness. Turner gave Storm a wide glass jar.

'What for?'

Turner said would he mind using the lavatory. He tapped the glass.

'What?'

'Have you been to the lavatory this morning?' said Turner.

The man's eyes darted to each of us. 'Whatcha want that for?'

Routh handed Storm a bedpan, pointed to soap and a basin of water, and gave him instructions. We left the tent to stand outside where Gard was smoking one of Humphry's cigarettes.

'Should we keep him here until quarantine's over?' I said.

'If it was plague, he's past infecting anyone,' said Turner.

'Wasn't plague, you know,' said Routh. 'Wasting your time.'

'Let me be the judge of that,' snapped Turner. Routh reddened and, mumbling about breakfast, excused himself. We watched him walk back through the campsite. The call of black magpies echoed around the hills.

Humphry struck a match and lit a cigarette. 'Anyway, what do you think?'

'Oh, I don't doubt your original diagnosis, if that's what you mean,' said Turner. 'The swelling's gone, but I'll make a bacteriological study.'

'But it is plague?'

'I can't say that Storm still has plague until I've seen plague bacilli. It doesn't mean he didn't have plague before, though.'

Gard smoked anxiously, glancing furtively at each of us and looking away quickly. We contemplated the pastoral scene around us, while Storm could be heard trying his best to fulfil Turner's request.

'Anyway,' said Humphry, 'What's wrong with typhoid? Perfectly good disease. Why does typhoid get a good wrap, but everyone runs screaming from plague?'

'You know, you're right. We've become familiar with typhoid and we treat it with contempt,' said Turner. 'Plague on the other hand produces a superstitious terror.'

'Not in Townsville.'

'It's not in Townsville yet. And it's easier to deny it than deal with it. In Sydney, it's another story.'

'Surely to God we don't want that,' I said.

'What we do need is some sort of balance. I think there's something to be said for having a healthy fear of disease.'

Storm let out a curse from the privy. Gard came over and asked Humphry for another cigarette.

Humphry lowered his voice as Gard walked away and said, 'It's a pity in some ways then that Mr Storm recovered.'

Humphry was right, but even then would they have believed that it was plague?

'We have to convince people that plague is near, that it's a real threat,' said Turner, 'and to reinstate fear proportionally, not by causing them to panic, but to make people take the proper precautions.'

'God help us all,' said Humphry.

Storm came over to us with his jar and held it out to Turner.

But Turner had Storm place the jar on the ground, slosh germicide over it and make sure it was well sealed. Then he wrapped it in a cloth and handed it to me to carry. We made our way back to Routh's office, skirting the tents.

Gard was back in my ear like a sticky fly.

'You said before I could only catch this plague through fleas and not to worry, but then here we are all in quarantine.'

'In case someone else has the germ. You can have a germ and not get sick for a few days; perhaps longer.'

'Well, why are we stuck here for three bloomin' weeks?'

'It's the law.'

'Damned stupid law, you ask me.' He smoked in quick puffs. 'We're not going home, are we.'

'Not today.'

He turned and strode away through the trees.

About twenty of the passengers, mostly sullen men, had gathered outside Routh's cottage. Word had spread quickly that we were there, and I suppose they were hoping for reprieve. I felt sorry for them. None spoke to us as we walked by, but I could feel their frustration. Dawson wasn't amongst them.

Inside, Routh and his nurse had organised breakfast. We washed. The station doctor appeared to be sulking and wouldn't look at Turner. I'd lost my appetite somewhere between tea with Dawson and collecting the steward's stool, which now stood wrapped and tied near our bags by the door.

'It's not such a bad place for a holiday,' said Humphry, holding up a thick slice of salted bacon on the end of a fork. 'I don't know what they're all complaining about.'

'That's what I keep telling them,' said Routh, gloomily.

There was a single knock and we turned. Dawson filled the doorway.

'This is cosy.' He'd found his jacket and his cigar was lit and in place.

'I'd ask you to join us,' said Humphry, 'but we've just done a faecal examination.' He popped some bacon into his mouth. 'Come to think of it, why don't you join us?'

Dawson ignored him and pulled a chair over to sit next to Turner.

'There are a number of people outside who'd like to know when they can get off this blasted island.'

'I know,' said Turner.

'Well?'

'Another week, Mr Dawson. I'm sorry. The quarantine period can't be broken.'

'So, as a man of science, can you say that the steward has plague?' Dawson was trying his best to intimidate.

'Had plague,' said Turner. 'He certainly appears to be recovered and his illness is consistent with *Pestis minor*.'

'Minor? Well, then. I have a meeting on Thursday; it's an issue of the utmost importance to my constituents.'

'Give me two bob,' said Humphry, 'and I'll put it on that nag of yours, if you like.'

'The railway hearing,' said Dawson, ignoring him, 'is about the future. The future, Dr Turner. A new

Australian nation. This line will employ hundreds of white men. Thousands will benefit from it. You don't want to be responsible for scuttling that, surely.'

'The future of the colony and its railway lines isn't my responsibility. I'm not a politician, I'm a doctor. We all have to work within the law and twenty-one days' quarantine has to be endured. I'm sure you can get the hearing rescheduled.'

'Rescheduled!' Dawson suddenly banged his hand on the table and the glowing end of his cigar rolled across the surface throwing sparks and leaving a trail of ash. It was such a violent punctuation that even Humphry stopped eating and stared at the politician.

'Don't you understand? The Tories won't let it be rescheduled. This is what they want, for me to miss this hearing. That's what I fear this is all about. This is some blasted conspiracy, isn't it? Isn't it? I'm beginning to think it must be.'

Turner said, quietly, 'I assure you it's not. It's the law. There's nothing I can do. Do you expect me to break the law?'

'The law! It all smells like one of Foxton's plots to me. I know their tricks. The law!' Dawson stood, pushing his chair back. 'You agree this is no place to hold people in quarantine and you say the steward is no longer sick and not a danger and yet you insist we stay. This is more than just incompetence.'

Turner stood and assured him it was in fact a very serious matter and it was being handled in the correct way, but Dawson turned and stormed out of the office.

'Perhaps,' said Routh, looking sad beneath his watery eyes and walrus moustache, 'you'd better leave.'

We could hear Dawson outside telling the mob that they'd be here for another week. There was a general hubbub about this and I could hear a woman crying. Someone yelled that the doctors then should stay as well and this was greeted with applause.

Routh looked out the door and said, 'I'm not sure I can guarantee your safety. Maybe you'd better stay here after all, until they quieten down.'

'They may try to blockade the office,' said Humphry, 'if they get it into their heads. I think we should go now before Dawson puts it to a vote.'

Turner agreed. He gave me the jar and took my bag up with his and we moved out on to the verandah. We were greeted with booing.

Humphry cleared his throat and looked as if he might be about to address the crowd, but it was Turner who grabbed his arm and said, 'Don't,' and pulled him down the steps. Two men stood in front of us with their arms folded and seemed determined not to budge. I looked back over my shoulder to see Dawson chomping his damaged cigar on the verandah. He smiled tightly and the circle closed around us. Humphry and I both took a step back and I looked over the heads of the crowd. I couldn't see Turner, but I saw the captain.

'Mr Thompson?' I said. The crowd cheered. He pushed forward to the front of the crush, looking worried.

'Let us through,' I said.

'It's nothing I can help with.'

'But you'll be held responsible.'

'Where's Turner?' said Humphry. 'If we come to any harm there'll be hell to pay.' A few people laughed.

'All three of us are employed by the Government,' Humphry continued. 'Does that make this treason, I wonder?'

Thompson turned and said, 'Let them through,' but it appeared he'd lost control over the crowd. He looked up angrily to Dawson, who shrugged. Turner was suddenly pushed into my side. He said quietly to me, 'Where's that jar?'

'Here.' I had the cloth bundle in both hands.

'Why don't you hold it up in front of you so everyone can get a good look at it.'

I managed to unwrap the jar as the jostling continued. And that was how we made our way through the crowd.

Humphry shouted, 'We have to get this shit back for scientific examination. Get out of the way.'

Humphry was in front and Turner behind. Someone yelped as Humphry stood on his foot, but those closest could see the jar's contents.

'Plague or typhoid, Dr Row? What do you think is in this jar? I hope to God we don't spill any,' and we kept moving forward.

A few people insisted on jostling us with their shoulders and so I took the added precaution of unscrewing the jar's lid. Humphry needed to say no more after that.

The crowd thinned out behind us, but a hard core of men continued to shadow us through the grounds.

Captain Thompson strode after them and said, 'Gentlemen, please. Let them go.'

We went Indian file and I still held the jar up like a talisman.

'Could you put the lid on that blasted thing now? I'm going to be sick,' said Humphry.

Some men had got ahead of us along the track and may have had it in their minds to somehow stop us when we got to the wharf. We finally got to the bank above the beach and I saw the *Teal* still belching smoke, rubbing against the stricken wharf.

Humphry and Turner went down the embankment in an undignified rush and I followed. My heel hit some soft dirt and skidded from under me, and I landed on my backside. Mercifully, the lid was secure and I kept a grip on the jar.

A hand reached down towards me.

'You right there, Dr Row?' Gard was standing over me.

'Yes, yes.' As I sat there, half a dozen men surrounded me.

Gard took my elbow and pulled me to my feet and walked me through the group of passengers. There seemed to be no logic in what they were doing, which made it even more disturbing.

Gard whispered, 'Could you take a letter to my wife?'

'Your wife?' Men pressed around and eyed me hungrily. I felt a rising panic.

'Yes. Just give her this.'

I felt an envelope thrust into a pocket. Humphry had been well ahead of me and was coming back now that he saw I was surrounded.

'Is there a problem, Dr Row?' Humphry yelled.

'Why don't you send a telegram,' I told Gard. Telegrams were free. They just had to be sent ashore with the mail.

'This is personal. A letter from a husband to a wife. You understand?'

'Dr Row?' shouted Humphry, marching towards us. Did he really have a pistol in his hand?

'Where do I find her?' I said to Gard.

'I dunno.'

'What?'

'I helped you. You help me. You'll find her.'

I heard Humphry up ahead bellow, 'Excuse me,' and Gard stepped back and his place was taken by a grinning man with a big white beard and bad teeth. I felt a hand grab me and I tried to knock it away, but then they all stood back and I was suddenly with Humphry, stumbling over the uneven planks of the pier.

Behind me the mob watched. Perhaps they thought they'd achieved some sort of victory in our flight. There was some scoffing, public-bar laughter.

Humphry's pistol had vanished.

* * *

Turner was already at the *Teal* and the crew was casting off. It bucked as I stepped aboard, and I stumbled on to my knees like a drunk, raising a few more distant laughs. The jar rolled from my hands but didn't break. I managed to pick it up.

'All right, Row?'

I stood and it was hard going but I managed to construct a smile.

Just as we pulled into the passage the wind caught my hat and I lunged instinctively to pluck it back. The jar fell to the deck and shattered. I gave a little skip backwards and looked dismally from my shoes to Turner.

'No matter,' he said, and he might have considered rescuing the damned mess as it streamed towards the stern, but for a quick-thinking crew member who threw a bucket of water at it. And another.

I turned to the receding jetty and saw my boater ride a foaming crest before it flipped over and vanished.

chapter five

Dead rats in the east,
Dead rats in the west,
As if they were tigers,
Indeed are the people afraid.

Shih Tao-Nan

THE WIND WAS BREAKING the tips off the waves and throwing them into the air. A wad of foam slapped me in the face and I peeled away a damp butterfly.

I stared at it for a while, wondering where it had come from, and then noticed another flopping on the deck, and another. One flashed past as we raced into the wind and I saw that the bay was full of them.

Thousands of butterflies were being swept by the wind that was now hitting us hard from the east, as the launch corkscrewed through the bay.

The butterfly stuck to the palm of my hand was lampblack splashed with Reckitt's Blue.

'*Danaus hamatus*,' said Turner. 'A Blue Tiger.'

He gently teased its front legs and it climbed on to his finger, raising its wings in the air to dry.

'Was that fear in the right proportion?' I was still shaken.

'That was just a good old-fashioned riot, Row. Born of fear, but orchestrated for political effect. All show and strictly for Mr Dawson's benefit.'

'I'm sorry about the faeces,' I said.

'We have the serum. That may tell us something.'

A gust knocked the butterfly sideways on Turner's finger and it steadied itself.

'What are they doing all the way out here?'

'Migrating. Must say I've never seen anything like this before.' Turner looked around the bay. 'The tigers must have come from over there.' He pointed into the wind to a thin strip of navy blue land that kept disappearing behind waves.

'Cape Cleveland,' I said. This appeared to be a mass suicide.

Turner stared out to the sometimes visible cape. I watched his face in profile, his extraordinarily high brow, the spray on his beard. When the violent rocking of the boat let him, he used a finger from his free hand to wipe his glasses.

'You haven't told me much about your Maria. Is she better for her move north?'

Somehow I was surprised always when he remembered her name. 'Yes.'

He waited for me to elaborate, and then said, 'Your boy?'

'Allan.'

'He's …?'

'Eight.'

'How is he?'

'Runs around like a savage.'

'And two girls if I remember. Well?'

I nodded.

Turner took his glasses off and wiped a sleeve over his eyes. 'And you?'

I spread my arms. See for yourself. It wasn't much of an answer. What was I supposed to say?

Turner held his hand up. The butterfly faced the wind and spread its wings, and a sudden gust blew it backwards over the deck and into the sea.

The deck was now littered with small flapping blue and black bodies. Turner bent down, stumbled as a wave slapped the hull, then picked up another, although this one appeared to be dead already.

'I've seen this species in Brisbane.' He turned it over in his hand. 'Never a riot like this, though.'

'Seems to be a day for riots,' I said. The boat lurched again and threw us both into the railing, and I grabbed Turner's jacket so he wouldn't spill overboard.

'Thank you, Row.' We sat on the wet bench.

'You know,' he said, 'we can't have plague patients making this journey. We need to find a site on the mainland for an isolation hospital.'

'That means new buildings, though.'

'Tents should be adequate. If there's an outbreak, it won't be permanent. Finding the right site will be the thing.'

I had to stand again and find the horizon. The motion was making me queasy.

'The wind is actually helping them make their trip,' Turner was saying, picking up another live butterfly and holding it high. 'They use it. The strongest survive. The survivors breed.'

'The others are food for fish,' I said.

'Well. No effort is really in vain then.' His butterfly was snatched away.

'Do you really believe that?'

'What I mean is, nothing is wasted in nature.'

'Didn't seem to be any good reason for losing my hat.'

'Maybe someone who has a greater need for your hat will find it.'

'I don't have another.' I looked out to sea. 'I suppose this isn't the weather for hats.'

'Perhaps Mr Darwin's theories apply to hats as well. Survival of the best fit.'

Turner fetched his medical bag from beneath the bench and produced a jar similar to the one that had contained Storm's stool. He opened it and put a few wet butterflies inside.

'For a closer look later,' he said.

It felt as though we were moving fast, but the land was getting no closer. Turner pointed to the long stretch of coast, a small headland rising north of the city.

'What's that area?'

'Cape Pallarenda,' I said.

'That's where these butterflies will end up. We should pop out and investigate.'

Absolutely not. 'No one lives there. It's sand. And behind it is swamp.'

'Splendid,' said Turner. 'We must ride out there. Do you have a buggy?'

'No.'

'Perhaps we could borrow one. What about Dr Humphry's?'

Humphry, at the wheelhouse, must have heard his name. He turned around.

'Can we borrow your buggy?' shouted Turner against the wind.

Humphry raised his flask.

Splendid.

The waves became sharper and less predictable, and we didn't speak again until we pulled into the harbour.

Humphry had commandeered a shed at the wharves for fumigation. We had to traipse into it, remove our clothes and wash while Humphry burned sulphur. Each item was to be fumigated in turn and anything that couldn't be fumigated had to be burned. It was a miserable exercise and we emerged smelling like rotten eggs.

When I was putting on my jacket I felt the envelope. I took it out, remembering the circle of hostile faces, wondering what the message might be. I turned it over.

It was sealed and on it was written 'Mrs Walter Gard' in the careful hand of the barely literate. There was no address.

It was another burden I didn't really want. I put it back in my pocket.

Humphry dropped Turner and me back at the Town Hall and drove off through the afternoon shoppers in Flinders-street.

I had the beginnings of a toothache. It had come and gone for weeks and I knew I should get it seen to, but a toothache was something to be put off until the pain overwhelmed the terror of getting it pulled. Anyway, a good dentist was one with experience and the best were in Brisbane, not in the colony's back blocks.

For the moment I simply wanted to go to my office, close the door and put my head on my desk for a few minutes. Turner, though, had his serum to study.

I found myself in his room, where someone had delivered a remarkable amount of luggage. A number of trunks were in the middle of the floor. In our absence, someone had returned or replaced his missing table, a hard swivel chair and had hung a picture of The Royal Couple on the wall.

'These days,' said Turner, patting one of his steamer trunks, 'you never know where your luggage will end up.'

Peking? Bombay? Cape Town? I stood over them and noticed labels for Liverpool, Sydney, Brisbane.

Disappointing.

Turner took off his coat and put it on a hook behind the door.

'My laboratory equipment is in there,' he said, and asked if there were any more tables to be had so he could spread it out. 'But not as wide as that one. Longer if possible.'

I said I'd see what I could find and went off to raid the storeroom. I found three smaller office tables, so I collared a junior clerk and we brought them up the stairs, each delivery finding Turner surrounded by more cloth-wrapped and boxed instruments.

He wanted the tables placed along the wall so they formed one long workbench.

I took out my watch. It was four in the afternoon.

Turner began unwrapping his treasures and placing them on the tables. Glass beakers, a tripod, a lamp, three more kerosene lamps. Bottles of spirits. I looked at the labels.

'You didn't have to bring all of this.' I picked up a bottle of ether.

'I thought it best to bring everything I needed.'

'You can get almost anything you need up here. Anything I can't find in Townsville will almost certainly be in Charters Towers.'

He opened a large square box of polished wood held shut by clips and two leather straps for good measure. Precious scalpels gleamed in red velvet.

There were several autoclaves, the most modern design of two-piece pressure sterilisers in their steel cylinders. There was a box of surgical gloves and masks and an ether mask. Another wooden box contained slide trays.

The room now smelled exotically of steamer hold and machine oil, brass polish, dust and ether.

From one solid box Turner produced a brass microscope. This new sort was rare. I hadn't seen its type before.

'I've been afraid travelling with this would loosen the lenses.' He placed it carefully on a table and looked through the eyepiece, satisfied.

'Hasn't happened yet.'

Inside one box was a paper bag. He offered it. I opened the twisted top. Inside was a bright mass of boiled lollies. I prised an aniseed humbug from the conglomerate and he chose a butter ball and popped it in his mouth. We sucked noisily.

'What about that one?'

One trunk remained unopened.

'That one can wait,' he said, pushing it against a wall.

The other empty trunks were dispatched to the storeroom as Turner set about arranging his exquisite microscope.

I leaned close to read the label. *Bausch and Lomb Optical Company.*

'German,' I said.

'American. The lenses aren't as good as the Germans, but it's easier to use. Three nose pieces and a double mirror.'

He sloshed alcohol from a bottle on to a cloth and wiped the desk tops, and he handed me a cloth and we did the same with his equipment, piece by piece. He lit a kerosene lamp and positioned his microscope in front of it. He fetched the glass slides and held one up. It had tiny handwriting along the bottom and I couldn't make it out.

'Take a look at this, Row, and tell me what you see.'

He placed the slide on the round stage and adjusted the screw at the top of the limb and, when he was ready, stood back and let me look. I made a slight adjustment. There were some fuzzy grey objects that were cells, but the objects I was looking for would be much smaller.

I stood back and rubbed my eye and put it to the eyepiece again.

'Can you see?'

'I think so.'

'What do you see?'

'Some oval cells.'

'Bacteria.'

'They look like safety pins.'

'*Pasteurella pestis.* Dead of course, but in good enough shape to use for identification.'

I kept looking. This was plague? Turner said, 'Remember the face of your enemy.'

And here, I realised, looking into this other world, was the power of a machine to reveal the powerhouse of nature. I could see the enemy and I could imagine some other machine with which I could reach out and squash it. A shiver ran down my spine. Science would conquer all sickness one day. It was surely just a matter of time before the causes of all diseases could be put on to a glass slide and annihilated one by one. A world free of illness and suffering. It seemed possible.

'Now, we go hunting,' said Turner.

He took the cloth from his leather bag and withdrew the bloody syringe. He then found two clean slides and prepared them with a drop of fluid smeared on the glass plate.

He put it under the microscope and began his hunt.

There were some muffled sounds of traffic, voices down the hallway, the tick of a clock. The room was hot, but I no longer felt drowsy. Turner pulled away from the eyepiece occasionally to blink and pull faces, but otherwise his only movement was a delicate touch of the screw.

After an interminable time he sighed and said, 'You look.'

He let me sit on his chair and I rubbed my eye and put it to the lens. What I saw was soup. There were a few intact cells, but the rest were like beans and carrots floating in a grey liquid. I adjusted the screw and found it difficult to focus on anything that I could readily identify.

'It's pus,' I said.

'Apart from a few blood cells, yes.'

'Did you see any bacteria?'

'Nothing.'

'Shame.' I pulled my eye away.

'Good news for Mr Storm.'

'I mean it's a shame we have no proof.'

'Yes, I know what you meant. But we have pus from a bubo, we have Humphry's diagnosis and your observations of the sick steward, we have a steward aboard a steamer that visited an infected port, we have an epidemic of plague in Queensland.' He looked at me. 'What do you think?'

'He had plague.'

'In this case we must assume the disease is close, and if it's not here yet it soon will be.'

We washed our hands in alcohol and then with soap and water from one of Turner's metal bowls. We sat and he shared his lollies.

'What should we do now?' I said.

The council building had emptied. Turner's lamp now provided more light than the window. A lolly clattered against his teeth.

'Wash and pray.'

Maria had reminded me that back in Moreton Bay the frangipani tree would be losing its leaves.

Here in Townsville the frangipani at the front verandah still had its flowers, although they'd been dropping *plop plop* through the night. The cannas growing in the old bath buried in the front yard were a bright showy red. Seasons here lost their logic.

The wind had also dropped and the heat had crept back during the night. The air was thick and warm as I sat alone in the kitchen.

I worked a thumbnail into the surface of the table, a rough piece made from local pine, scoured by carbolic acid and still smelling of onions. Our furniture hadn't caught up with us. It was still at Dunwich.

This, though, was a solid house with wide verandahs and a garden of dripping tropical shrubs. It sat above the town, catching a breeze and rubbing shoulders with other grand homes.

It had a view of the harbour. A wealthy trader could enjoy the sight of his ship returning from the South Sea Islands under white sails with a black cargo.

It was the home one George Busby had built. George had lost two of his three blackbirding luggers in the cyclone in '96. It had ruined him and he shot himself, just there, outside the kitchen window.

Burns Philp and Co. was kind enough to buy the remaining lugger, and Mrs Busby had moved to Brisbane, but rented out the house. Mr Philp himself still owned a house down the street, so we were in good company, even if that company chose to be somewhere else.

The stove spat a glowing splinter and I watched it smoke on the floor. I heard someone coming and I stooped to flick it back through the grate.

Allan was in his night clothes. There was a ritual we'd fallen into. I'd be up first and make tea. Allan would come in and we'd sit and drink our tea. It was the best time of my day.

I sat.

From the sideboard he fetched the chipped porcelain cup with horses on it.

'You came in late. I heard you.'

'I was working,' I said. The milk hadn't come yet. I watched Allan put four teaspoons of sugar into his tea.

'Is it true,' he said, 'that they were going to hang you on Magnetic Island?'

'Who told you that?'

'Dr Humphry. He had to save you from being hanged.' He blew into his cup and sipped. 'I'm glad you didn't hang.'

'Thank you, Allan.'

Humphry was a friend of Mrs Busby and it was he who had arranged for us to rent the house. It apparently gave him the right to pop around unannounced and scare the children.

'Dr Humphry gives me bull's-eyes,' he said. 'You never give me bull's-eyes.'

'I hate bull's-eyes.'

'You like liquorice, don't you. A lot.'

I nodded.

'I don't mind liquorice,' he said, conversationally. It had grown light outside.

'The Reverend Kerr says the plague is coming to kill all the sinners in Townsville,' said Allan.

'Don't worry about the plague.'

'What's a Levite?'

Marjorie toddled into the kitchen. I picked her up and put her on my lap. She nestled back with a thumb in her mouth and we sat there for a while, the three of us.

As I said, it was the best time of the day, but also the worst. It reminded me of what I had and what was lost.

I washed and dressed. My jacket on the peg hadn't yet been cleaned. It still smelled of sulphur. I went through the pockets and found the envelope.

'Damnation.'

I'd been trying to forget the humiliating retreat from West Point. And why on earth didn't the woman's own husband know where she was? It seemed absurd now, but I supposed I owed Gard the delivery of a letter. I'd go to the post office and ask for an address.

What did a husband say to a wife when he was in quarantine? I looked at the seal, just to make sure nothing could fall out. I gave it a shake. There was a thick wad of paper in there. I held it up to the window, but couldn't see its outline, let alone the contents. I put it in my bag, and then found another jacket and slipped out of the house.

My office was smaller than Turner's and the view from my window was south. If I cared to open my curtains I could look out over Flinders-lane to Ross Creek and South Townsville, and the distant hazy mountains.

Flinders-lane was lined with shacks and its main businesses, I'd been told, were run by Chinamen:

gambling, grog, and prostitution. I didn't take much interest, although Humphry insisted on describing the more colourful details.

The Mayor's chambers had two views and he chose neither, so perhaps I shouldn't read too much into the aspect he had chosen for me. McCreedy always kept his drapes closed and instead had hung an immense landscape near his door. It was an English pastoral scene in a frame that was riddled with worm tracks.

On my first day he had made a point of showing it to me. It was of a field of wheat, a water mill in the background. Two noble shire horses harvesting the grain. He asked me what I thought.

'Picturesque?'

'Yes! A masterpiece.'

I looked for a signature and couldn't find one. It was from Home, he said; a previous mayor had brought it out with him and given it to the council, but some fool had shoved it in the storeroom. McCreedy then ran a finger along the base of the frame and rubbed the dust with his thumb as if it were rich English loam.

Now I left my own pastoral scene hidden behind the curtains and went to my filing cabinet.

Turner had asked me to go through my records to see if any undiagnosed cases of plague might have appeared; anything suspicious worth investigating. Pernicious fevers with swellings at the neck, armpit or groin, I supposed.

Every Tuesday a list of deaths registered at each receiving hospital in Townsville and Charters Towers fell on to my desk. It was my job to include these as part of my fortnightly report to council. If there was a spate of fatal diseases or accidents, I'd know and council could act – the essence of public health, modern medicine in practice, and my job. I'd made many recommendations and each had been duly tabled and ignored.

In most cases, northern fevers came and went mysteriously, and were out of my control anyway.

Now I pulled out the death lists for the previous six months.

I regularly swapped lists with the medical officer in Charters Towers, a man I'd never actually met, but we both had this in common: a scientific knowledge of what killed people in the North. At least, it was as close as one could get. One of the problems was that there was no consistency of diagnosis. Doctors and hospitals often had their own descriptions of diseases, and in the North medical practice hadn't caught up with medical science.

Medicine was advancing daily in the rest of the world, but many of my colleagues weren't aware of the discoveries or, if they were, they simply didn't trust them. Even Pasteur's germ theory was still widely treated with cynicism. What in the blazes would the French know? The result was that medicine in the North was mired in practices and prejudices at least a hundred years old.

And this in the age of the telegraph and the steamer. I ask you.

My finger slipped down death's ledger, written in my own hand. *Morphine poisoning,* I read. *Gunshot wound to the chest.* Well, those at least were straightforward.

Not all causes could be properly described, even by autopsy, of course. Hospital superintendents often looked at the corpse and took a stab at it: apoplexy, debility, phthisis, born dead. The list was naturally long and sad.

Children still died in droves.

I closed my eyes and saw Lillian's grave, and had to open them again. I forced myself back to the list.

For adults the greatest plagues, as such, were mining, industrial and firearm accidents. The Charters Towers Hospital dealt with most of the mining accidents, but some appeared in Townsville, brought to town by people suspicious of their own doctors.

Brought in dead was common, with crush wounds, gangrene, fractured skulls.

Gunshot wound to the abdomen.

My finger slid down the pages searching for patterns.

Gunshot wound of mouth. Carbolic acid poisoning. Rat poisoning.

If there was a bright side to this, it was what was not included in the reports. In my short time, there'd been no outbreaks of smallpox or typhus. Measles and tuberculosis seemed to be a problem mainly of blacks and kanakas, and they didn't normally appear on my list because few dead or living blacks turned up at a hospital. The gunshot rates were steady. There were no strikes, riots or rebellions, and if Dawson remained in custody it might stay that way.

My little joke.

I made notes of patterns, of other doctors' diagnoses, and put these in my reports.

Then I went back to the filing cabinet and took out a separate folder, a single page, a separate list, one that didn't appear in my reports.

This was a private study, if you like.

Each month, under *Acts of God*, I'd noted possible cases.

A woman had been struck by lightning, for example. A man died from a fall down a mine shaft. I included him because I'd learned he'd been running from a snake. It didn't necessarily qualify as an Act of God, but the circumstances warranted a closer look.

I was working on a medical definition.

I'd mentioned it to Humphry, who agreed that it might be just as important to know when God was as cross as two sticks as it was to know where pernicious fevers were burning.

The Reverend Kerr tried to find a Presbyterian definition, but the best he could come up with was Jonah, where the Lord sent a great wind to break up his ship when Jonah was fleeing to Tarshish. The Bible itself, of course, was full of them.

Maria told me not to speak of it to her again.

I was looking for the inevitable death: the fist of a God determined to kill – and man could do nothing to avoid it. Being bitten by a snake and then falling down a mine shaft was the sort of thing.

One may have caused the other, but Death was persistent. If there'd been another factor, if the man had survived the fall and the snakebite and had been eaten by scorpions, then you'd have to say his number was up.

An Act of God.

By their nature, Acts of God might be difficult to spot. For instance, someone crushed by a Castle Hill boulder might make the list, but it would depend on the circumstances. Was the boulder pushed, or subject to human intervention of any sort? Had there been a storm?

If there was a cluster of Acts, it might be possible to do something about them, to predict them, to avoid them.

I supposed I was boiling down my definition to this: was there anything man could have done to prevent the event, or did the event in any way serve nature?

The answer needed to be emphatically 'no' in both cases. If God had a hand in evolution, he would show His hand occasionally in an observable, if as yet unfathomable, way.

I put the list aside.

Finally, I noted that there had been a rise in malaria cases over summer, some dengue, but nothing was worth another look and I put the files away with relief.

Turner's office had now settled on its own pungent character, a mixture of alcohol, ether, coffee and sugar.

The door was open and I was about to knock anyway when I noticed McCreedy sitting across from Turner, his back to me, tapping the table with a forefinger. Turner sat straight and still, the light was at his back, and I couldn't quite see the expression on his face. I stayed at the door.

'You follow me? You can't treat them like blackfellows.' I gathered McCreedy was talking about West Point. 'Now, I'm not saying to ignore the regulations, but a little mercy wouldn't do any harm, neither to the city nor to your new position here. You said yourself that those people shouldn't be there.'

'I said it was the wrong place for a quarantine station under the present circumstances. But we have no choice at the moment. Are you suggesting we break the law?'

'Even under law there can be extenuating circumstance.'

'Not in this case.'

McCreedy tried to poke his finger through the table. 'Some humanity. That's all I'm asking.'

Turner held up his hands. 'I'm agreeing with you, except on the point of law. The fact is, the passengers will be released on Tuesday and no earlier. But I take your point. I think we both agree that in future no one should be sent to West Point.'

'That's right.' McCreedy sat back, happy with a concession. 'Damned right.'

'We need another site closer to the city. For medical services and supplies.'

'Yes, but that doesn't solve the current problem, does it now.'

'There is no problem if you don't make one.'

'Look. This railway hearing, for instance. Can't you make an exception of Mr Dawson? This is damned important. Damned important. To a lot of people.'

'Sawmill owners?'

McCreedy fiddled with something in front of him and struck a match. A plume of smoke rose to the ceiling.

'Mill owners employ many men,' the Mayor said. 'They support families.'

'Why don't you ask Mr Philp for a delay in the hearing?'

'The last damn thing he wants. This has played well into his hands.'

'Well, there's nothing I can do.'

'Right then. I suppose that's it.'

'Unless you have any suggestion for a site for a plague hospital.'

He tapped the ash on to the floor. 'Is it really going to be necessary?'

'A precaution. We need a flat piece of land, good drainage for tents, preferably sandy, good access by a single track, fresh water. Out of town. Near the sea if possible.'

'The only place that fits that description is Three Mile Creek.'

'Ah,' said Turner at last, 'there's Dr Row. Are you familiar with Three Mile Creek?'

'Cape Pallarenda,' I said, 'north,' walking in as if I'd just arrived.

'Good. We might pop up there, with the Mayor's permission, and stake out a site for the plague hospital.'

McCreedy got up. 'Blast the plague,' he said, as he fumed past me. 'And blast all blasted doctors.'

However wide Flinders-street might be and however modern and solid the buildings, they still couldn't disguise the town's precarious position. Castle Hill had ruined any attempt to impose order. Try to build a straight road and it invariably hit granite and took a kink. Build a church and it was dwarfed by the unmoveable pagan monolith towering over it.

Every day it reminded the residents, if they ever needed it, that this was a frontier teetering between civilisation and savagery. The rock was bald and unbalanced and sent the occasional boulder crashing down in the middle of the night. It defied civilisation. It was an Act of God waiting to happen.

I was on Turner's balcony.

'Have you ever climbed it?' he said.

'What for?'

'Imagine the view.'

'Imagine the climb.'

Below us, some shopkeepers had already opened up, or were about to, and were chatting and smoking in the street. A dray piled high with lumber was making lazy progress without the whip.

'We've been invited to afternoon tea,' I said.

I pulled out one of the invitations that had arrived on my desk the day before, the handwriting smooth and formal.

Turner opened it. *The esteemed Dr A.J. Turner.* It signed off, *Your humble servant in God, The Reverend Richard Kerr.*

The Reverend Kerr seemed to think Turner was some sort of visiting aristocrat, and even went as far as to consider Townsville 'unworthy' of the presence of such an Eminent Scientist.

My invitation had been less the gush and more the trickle, but the essence was that we'd both been invited to afternoon tea at the Manse on Saturday, today, to meet the members of the local Natural History Society. I was invited by association, it seemed.

I had already planned not to go.

'Are you interested in insects, Row?'

'Only in ways to exterminate them.'

He pretended to look disappointed. 'I thought you wanted to go hunting for your Blue Tiger.'

'That was your suggestion.'

'You need the education.' He went to the part of his office he now called his laboratory, where a small stove boiled water.

'What about that boy of yours. Why don't you bring him along?'

'Allan? To the Manse? For a lecture on insects?'

'What does a boy do in this town?'

I frankly had no idea. I tried to picture Allan doing something and couldn't manage it. What did the boy do? He must go to school. Did he play cricket? Did he have friends? I really didn't know.

'Let's collect the boy on the way,' said Turner. 'He might find it fun.' He held up a bottle of Symington's Essence Coffee.

'You can buy that, too, at Wiltshire's store,' I said, and he poured some into two cups and filled them with water.

'Try this.'

I sniffed and sipped. It was terrible.

'Well,' he said, 'I suppose you know where the Manse is?'

I started to protest.

'I won't be able to find the place on my own,' he said. 'Do you have something else to do?'

'I need a tooth pulled.'

'I can do that.'

I said I'd rather have an expert do it and would go to the barber.

'You'll have more fun with me. I wonder what sort of afternoon tea the Reverend Kerr provides.'

'Corned beef on stale bread,' I said. 'No coffee. You'll be sorry.'

chapter six

There is but one gospel and I preach unto you,
When the plague comes like the spectre that
haunts the sombre yew
And its bony feet are on the street and tread
them night and day
Wash and pray!
But more especially wash this earthly tenement
of clay —
Wash and pray!

The Bulletin, 14 April 1900

THE FIRST THING I NOTICED was the picture.

Actually, there were two pictures, both in gold frames. One was a painting of Christ at Calvary, and the other a blue and gold tapestry.

'Please,' said the Reverend Kerr behind me, and Allan and I stepped through the doorway. Turner was inspecting the tapestry.

'What do you think?' said Kerr.

It was only when we joined him that I saw the details of the tapestry. Punctuated by a myriad gold beetles and blue butterflies were sewn the words, *Among whom ye shine as lights in the world.* But when I peered closely at the endless, finely stitched insects I realised there was no stitching.

'They're real,' said Allan, solving the puzzle.

The little creatures were pinned to the canvas.

I looked again at Christ crucified. It appeared to be a genuine print, free from insects, the dying Christ beseeching Heaven, looking away from the gaudy scene to His left.

'My word,' said Turner.

'God's word,' said the Reverend Kerr. 'Philippians 2:15. Eight hundred and thirty-five golden scarab beetles. *Anoplognathus parvulus.*'

'Must have taken for ever to catch all of them,' said Allan.

'I had some of the parish children catch them for me. The butterflies were the most difficult. Caught those myself.'

Turner put his nose to the glass. '*Papilio ulysses.*'

Kerr nodded.

'Beautiful.'

'Won a prize at the Exhibition.'

'I'm not surprised.'

The Reverend Kerr beamed.

'Please,' he said, and gestured towards the dining table where afternoon tea was laid out. There were scones on a tray, with a bowl of cream and another of jam, and a jug of milk. A few flies hovered around the jam and the Reverend attacked them with a tea towel.

'So glad you could join us. Rarely do we get a visitor of your stature.' He was talking to Turner, of course. Allan stared at the table with his mouth open.

'Mrs Kerr's scones,' said the Reverend, ruffling the boy's hair. 'She's at the Women's Guild.' He held up a finger. 'I'll just fetch the tea,' and vanished through the door.

We waited. Allan fidgeted. The room was cool. A weak light came through two large sash windows that opened to a wide verandah. The windowsill was at floor level and they were open for air. Allan poked his head outside. I told him to come back and be still. I was sorry we'd brought him, for his sake.

Kerr returned carrying a large teapot. He told Turner, 'I read your "Notes on Australian Lepidoptera". Most concise and informative,' and I knew that it would be a long afternoon.

Apparently Kerr had arranged for a friend of Turner's, Fred Dodd, to come.

'Splendid,' said Turner.

Unfortunately, he was still up the coast, on a hunting expedition.

'Never mind.'

'Crocodiles?' said Allan.

'No,' said Kerr, chuckling. 'Nothing so mundane. New species.'

Turner explained that Dodd now supported his family by collecting insects.

'He gets money for beetles?' said Allan.

'Yes, but mainly butterflies and moths,' said Kerr. 'He has orders from all over the world.'

'How much?' Allan sat on the edge of his seat. Was he genuinely interested or just being polite?

'I really don't know.'

Allan wanted to know what sort of insects people paid money for and whether he'd get any money if he found some.

'You have to be very observant,' said Turner. 'And patient. And they have fragile wings. You mustn't damage them.'

Allan strung together more words than I'd heard him speak for months. He quizzed Turner on who would buy insects.

The Reverend Kerr, sitting beside me, said, 'Any Acts of God this week, Dr Row?'

'None that I'm aware of.'

'Well, that's good news.'

Allan excused himself.

'Full of beans,' said Kerr.

When the boy hadn't returned after five minutes I went looking for him, leaving Turner and Kerr in a deep discussion about the local ants.

There was a breeze in the hallway. I could see the front gate, the dusty street on my right. I turned left. The open rear door framed hot distant hills.

I passed a small room, stopped and took a few steps

back. I had the uneasy impression that things were crawling over the walls. It was dark in the room, but something was moving.

'Ghosts.'

Kerr reached past me and pushed the door open further. There wasn't much light, but I saw a figure.

'Allan? What the devil?'

'I was just looking,' and something clattered on the floor.

Kerr pushed past me and I saw a match struck. The room filled with light from a lamp. Allan was by the bookshelf, looking as if he'd been caught with something he shouldn't have. At his feet was a rifle.

'I was only looking.'

'Looking?' I was staring at the gun. 'What in the blazes?'

'I saw things.' He was on the verge of tears, watching my face.

Kerr bent and picked up the rifle. 'It's my fault. Shouldn't have left it lying around.'

He put the gun back on a shelf, and then changed his mind and put it on the highest shelf he could reach. Allan looked at me fearfully and then looked up at the wall.

'Come here now,' I said. 'Come out of there.' I felt alarmed and angry in turn.

'Ghost moths,' said Kerr. 'Startling, aren't they.'

I only noticed then what it was that had made me stop. On the wall was a large case of luminous moths.

In fact, on every wall as I turned around were insects in framed arrangements. I imagined the rustling of dry wings.

Allan had moved towards me, but stopped out of reach, looking around the walls and giving me wary glances.

'Are they all dead?' he said.

'Of course,' said Kerr.

'Allan,' I hissed. 'What were you doing?'

'*Aenetus*,' I heard Kerr say. 'They're called ghosts, but I think of them as angels.'

Their wings were chalky white, pastel blues, yellows, some even green.

'Creatures of the darkness, Dr Row, and yet they almost glow, don't they. Shine as lights.'

Despite the colours, there was still the sense that this was a room full of dead things. I took a step towards Allan, grabbed him by the arm and led him back into the front room.

'You really shouldn't blame the boy,' said Kerr.

'He was where he shouldn't have been,' I said. 'And he had a rifle.'

'I only stopped because I saw the moths,' Allan pleaded. 'I saw the rifle and I picked it up. I just wanted to see what it felt like.'

'There,' said Kerr to me, as if it was a perfectly good explanation.

'What if it had gone off?' I said.

'Oh no,' said Kerr. 'I never keep it loaded. I don't even have any bullets. It's just for show. When I'm out collecting.'

He appeared to be serious.

Turner said, 'No harm done then,' which annoyed me even more, but it seemed I was outnumbered.

We sat. I fumed, but my anger was evaporating. Allan appeared contrite, at least.

I forced myself to construct a scone with cream and jam. Allan reached out, but drew his hand back under my glare.

'I was just telling the Reverend Kerr about your interest in the Blue Tigers,' said Turner. 'The Reverend says he's sure we'll find some at Three Mile Creek.'

'What a coincidence,' I said.

'What's a coincidence?' said Kerr.

Turner said, 'We have some business there as well. It might be a good site for an isolation hospital.'

'Ah. The plague you mean. Is it that serious?'

Kerr and Turner talked about the need to slaughter rats, and I whispered to Allan, 'Don't you ever pick up a gun again.'

He shook his head, eyes wide. I was rarely angry.

Kerr was saying, 'Found a rat dead outside the church a few weeks ago.'

'Really?' Weally? 'What did it look like,' said Turner.

'Looked as if it had been trampled by a horse. That was the day I found blood on my gown. Such a shock though. I can't think who would do such a thing. But I take comfort in the Bible: *And when I see the blood, I will pass over you, and the plague shall not be upon you to destroy you.*

'Exodus,' said Allan, full of surprises today.

'Can't seem to get the blood out either.'

Allan scouted a tree in the front yard as we were leaving and Kerr dashed back into the Manse and emerged with a cigar box.

'A Hercules moth,' he said, presenting it to the boy.

'You shouldn't,' I said.

'Nonsense. The boy seems to be interested.' And Allan did peer into the box with a sort of reverence.

'What do you say, Allan?' I said.

'Thanks.'

'Not at all.'

'Biggest moth in the world,' said Turner.

'Did you shoot it?' I heard Allan say. Turner proceeding to describe some interesting aspect of the creature.

I took the Reverend by the arm and led him further up the path.

'I'm terribly sorry,' I said.

'No harm done.'

'He's been at a loose end lately.'

'Boys,' Kerr said, shaking his head.

'In church a couple of weeks ago,' I said, 'there was a woman and her child sitting up the back. She had a bad cough.'

'Terrible time of the year for coughs. I could shut my

eyes and tell you what month of the year it was, just by the coughing in church.'

'But this particular woman was right up the back. With a girl about three. I'm worried about her health.'

Kerr put a finger under his chin and stared off into the hazy distance. 'Girl with a child? I may have seen her once or twice, but her name?' He shook his head. 'Flits in and flits out, barely a word.'

Perhaps she'd be in church on Sunday?

'Perhaps,' said the Reverend.

Turner and I dropped Allan home. He was silent on the trip. Other fathers would have whipped the boy.

When we returned to Turner's office, there was a gift waiting.

'My my,' said Turner, opening the shoebox outside his door.

I looked over his shoulder. A rat was lying on its side slightly bent, so big it filled the box, its tail curling back over its body. Its fur was wet.

'Must be a joke,' I said.

'A joke? I hope not. No, I think this is just what this doctor ordered.'

He opened the door and lit his stove, explaining that he'd asked a health inspector to bring him any rat he found dead of natural causes.

'Didn't take him long,' said Turner.

'I'm not surprised.' There were plenty of rats around, if one cared to look. I preferred not to.

When the water had boiled, Turner spread out a clean cloth and began sterilising a scalpel, shears and a syringe.

He laid the rat on a metal tray under a lamp.

'Nothing out of the ordinary, Row?'

'I'm not familiar with what's ordinary in rats.'

Turner flipped the thing on to its back and forced the legs apart.

'Hold them back,' he told me, and I grabbed the small limbs and held them as he took a scalpel and cut down from the chest to the anus.

'Male,' he said.

'I can see that.'

'Please don't interrupt,' he said.

Some bloody fluid oozed, but the animal had been dead for some time and was already stiff. Turner pulled the skin back from the stomach exposing a swirl of entrails.

He picked up the small shears and delicately snipped, once, at the rib cage, exposing the white ends of tiny bone.

The animal was spread apart.

With the tip of the shears Turner swiftly separated the organs, displaying them around the body so we could examine them closer.

'See here, Row?'

I bent forward, smelling the wet fur, a distinctive rodent smell.

'Intestine. Look at the colour.'

I shrugged. 'Green.'

'It's actually milky. The green is what's inside.'

'Heart,' he said. The thing was bright red.

We went through the organs one by one and then Turner made incisions along the underside of the legs.

He stood back and sighed.

'Plague?' I said.

'I doubt it.' He fished out the lungs and cut them open. They were grey and watery.

'Well,' he said, turning away and picking up the syringe. 'I'd say death by drowning. What do you think, Row?'

'Is that natural causes?'

'Our inspector seems to think so.'

I thought about it too. Did man, nature or God kill this rat?

'Why the sample, if it drowned?' I said.

'Just to make sure.'

I carried the rat in its shoebox out to the Town Hall's back yard. Walls of rusty corrugated iron were hard up against the back fence and there was an awful smell of the creek. A fitting place for a rat crematorium. I threw the box into the council furnace, doused it with kerosene, set it alight and hurried back inside.

That evening we sat on the balcony of Turner's office. A man with a ladder made his way down the street lighting the gas lamps one by one with a sleepy efficiency. The act softened Townsville's hard edges.

It had always been a happy ritual for me as a boy in Brisbane to see the lamplighter come down the street, the day's heat evaporating, being called home and dinner not far off.

The wind had died and the air was drier and cooler than it had been for months, and so it was pleasant to watch the gas lights come on. Castle Hill vanished into the purple evening.

Soon the street lamps were the only ones by which we could see each other. Insects were already forming halos.

The hotel on the corner was becoming rowdy. Townsville was a place of limited distractions and a shortage of women, and most men worked and drank the harder for it.

Turner was outlining the things we should do the next week, but my mind drifted along its own current until it caught up against the girl in church.

'Why don't you go home?' he said.

I didn't know. I said nothing.

He stood and disappeared inside, and then re-appeared dragging some cleverly folded contraption, something that turned into a hinged box on legs, perhaps a portable meat safe. Turner lit a carbide lamp and its white light filled the length of the balcony. He put it carefully in the box and rolled a sheet of calico down over the front.

The light challenged the street lamps and black things came out of the night.

'It's easier to hunt, Row, if you get your quarry to come to you.'

Something large passed in front of my face and I flapped a hand to brush it away.

'Be still,' said Turner. I saw he had a small net in one hand. I looked to where I thought he was looking. 'See it?'

'No.'

'Here it comes.'

A big dark shape flitted from the dark and startled me again. It beat its wings near the calico and retreated and then came back, a moth the size of a small bird. It made swift attacks and then rested on the cloth, its dark wings casting a frightening shadow into the street. Slap. Turner suddenly had it under the net and it struggled violently. With one hand he found his killing jar and lifted the lid, then grabbed the net and moth all together and held it over the top as if cooking it. The moth stopped moving. Gas from the jar.

'Got him,' he said, removing the moth and holding it up to the light on the palm of his hand. 'Isn't he a beauty?'

The creature was like a japanned chest spattered with white and yellow paint.

'Dead?' I said.

'"I went to heaven",' he said, turning it over, '"Twas a small town."'

I yawned and shook my head. He put his great moth on the table and turned his attention to some smaller insects swarming over his trap.

'Allan's a bright boy,' he said.

'Yes.'

'Enjoying the North? Your family?'

I pushed my seat back and made to move. I shouldn't have stayed so long.

'It's hotter than I thought it would be.'

Slap.

'It's difficult to know how things will turn out.'

I watched as Turner put another fluttering animal over his jar of death, and then tipped it on to the table where it lay still.

'I was very sorry about Lillian, you know.'

My heart stopped. The crowd was louder. Turner was holding up a pair of tweezers.

'*Micro-Lepidoptera*. These small moths, Row, are exquisite. The smaller they are, the more intricate the patterns and the more subtle the colours. See?'

He brought the tweezers to my face.

Lillian, my daughter, had been nearly three.

She'd been running a fever all night and had a sore throat the next morning.

'Shall we take her into the hospital, Linford?'

'For a sore throat?'

I waited. That night I saw her tonsils swollen, the left one covered with a white membrane.

I bundled her up and took her across the bay then. The small Dunwich launch had struggled against the tide and the darkness.

* * *

Turner was holding something beneath my nose. I raised my spectacles to see it, a moth flecked with grey.

'Difficult not to damage them,' he was saying. 'This is probably a species new to science.'

He gassed it and put it at the end of a row of little dead bodies. A cheer rose from a hotel down the street.

'I suppose a lot can happen to us all in a year. Here we are, for instance. Who'd have thought it a year ago?'

He slapped his net over another insect and dispatched it in one smooth movement, the fragile little body exposed on the table.

'Steamships,' Turner was saying. 'I suppose it's not such a coincidence really. Steamships are spreading plague and doctors. One causes the other, and here we are. Nine hundred miles from Brisbane.'

'Fate,' I managed to say.

'Fate? I don't think so.'

The air was a rich soup of insects, beer fumes, and the sound of men getting drunk.

There was a plop in the dark beyond the lamp and a large green frog suddenly jumped into the light, looking up at the carbide lamp and the meals flying around it. The frog lunged and then immediately seemed to have trouble trying to swallow whatever insect it had caught. It closed its eyes and gulped.

'He's eating your specimens,' I said.

'There's enough for everyone.'

Turner leaned forward and appeared to be looking at something on my face. I brushed my cheek.

'What do you mean, "fate"?' he said.

I felt exhausted. 'Serendipity. I suppose.'

He nodded to himself.

'Maria is well?' He'd asked me all this before.

'It's been difficult.'

Turner picked up a magnifying glass and studied his new collection. He showed me his small drying box, how he pinned them out, and a collection of tobacco tins in which he mailed his specimens, packed with cotton and sealed tight, to the museum in Brisbane.

Another giant moth thumped against the sheet and the frog lunged at something just beyond the light. There was laughter from the street. We sat quietly for awhile, the three of us, watching the crowd of insects around the sheet, waiting for something to suggest itself and be swallowed.

chapter seven

Congratulations on your heroic defence of Mafeking and the dear old Flag. Invite you to visit Townsville at your earliest convenience.

Telegram to Col. Baden-Powell from the
Mayor, 19 May 1900

MARIA WAS A STRANGER to me.

I knew she was watching, though.

I sometimes tried to catch her eye but was never quick enough. After a while, it became normal, this circling.

I was at the table. She was at the stove, stabbing the grate with a poker.

A coal fell to the floor and she flicked it expertly back with her fingers.

'*Maudit!*' Ladies never swore, and if they did it was never in English.

I watched her when she had her back to me. Sometimes lately, staring at the bow of an apron, I could imagine that I didn't know her at all. Once, a few days before, I couldn't remember her name. I'd had to think back to when we first met. I'd been studying in

Ireland, and had admired her riding. She taught French, she said. I thought she was frightfully aristocratic. Miss Maria Mahood.

Australians could ride, but it turned out most were a linguistic disappointment, and Mrs Linford Row had made a habit of voicing it, I suppose. It had been amusing at first.

Maria put breakfast in front of me.

I stared at the sausages and eggs. The toothache had returned and I wasn't hungry.

'Allan says you've been angry.' Her voice was quiet, flat, uninflected.

I pricked the sausage and it spat at me. 'Did he tell you why?'

She picked up a tea towel and stood over the tub, looking out the window. I watched her now in the light. 'Perhaps if someone took the time to teach him how to shoot.'

I put down my fork. This was almost a conversation. 'Are you suggesting I teach him how to shoot?'

She suddenly screamed, '*As-tu perdu la tête?*' and rushed from the kitchen, throwing the towel to the floor as she ran.

Damn it! 'It's not me who's out of his mind,' I shouted back. I stood and followed her out the front door.

Maria was on the road, swearing at the man driving the nightsoil cart.

'My children walk here, *debile*!' pointing at the road.

The man had stopped and was looking over his shoulder from my wife to the place on the road she pointed at. He then turned to me, shrugged, and drove off.

'*Va chez le diable!*' and lifting her skirts Maria turned and stormed past me.

I found my jacket and decided to get the devil away myself.

A breeze had sprung up and brought with it the smells of other breakfasts. A dog which had come out through a gate pattered happily beside me until I reached the top of Denham-street. The dog stopped at a telegraph pole and was left behind as I gave the Carbine its head, and in a moment of furious exhilaration I passed the nightsoil cart and executed a smooth sweep into Sturt-street.

I'd had one victory in council. The municipality had agreed to employ a team of workers to sweep Flinders-street daily. Sturt-street, though, which ran parallel to it, was still covered with the drying scabs of horse pats.

I dodged as many as I could, but couldn't avoid the smell of rotting scraps from rubbish piled in back yards. Here in the ditch were paper bags and green beer bottles, and there a dead dog, black with flies. And another dead dog. If a shopkeeper didn't move a carcass, it could stay there for days. Some of the more exceptional carcasses became landmarks by which people would be directed to some shop or other. They were particularly useful to strangers because few of the streets were signed.

The boarding house faced two streets and had wide iron-laced verandahs along each frontage. It would have been a handsome building if it hadn't been painted green. Also in white lettering on a green board at the front was: *Glendinning Townsville Boarding House.*

I leaned my bicycle against the picket fence. The gate was open, the door wide for a breeze, the hallway empty, but I could hear creaks and the groan of water pipes.

I walked up the path and through the open door. On the hallway wall were some drab prints of Ireland. The front room had been set for breakfast. I followed the sounds of cooking to the kitchen, and knocked on the green doorframe.

A stout woman with grey hair appeared, holding a towel.

'Take a seat,' she said, and disappeared.

I stepped through the doorway.

'Blimey,' she said, from the stove. 'I'll be with you in a tick. Take a seat.'

I started to say something, but then decided to wait until she'd finished, and went back into the dining room, listening to the scrape of a frypan, more sizzling sausages.

A man shuffled into the room and looked at me with red eyes, nodded and took a seat at a corner table. He produced a bottle of beer from the folds of his coat and put it on the table, stared at the bottle for a moment, then opened it deftly with a flick of the wrist and perhaps a coin he had in his hand.

'You one of mine?' The woman I assumed was Mrs Glendinning was at the door. She looked me up and down. 'You're not, are you. If you're after a room we're full up.'

'I'm looking for someone,' I said.

'You won't find him here.'

'If I told you who –'

'Whoever it is, he's not here,' she said, and went over to her other guest, grabbed the beer bottle and strode with it back into the kitchen. The man at the table simply stared at the place where the bottle had been. The landlord taketh away. I followed Mrs Glendinning into the kitchen.

It seemed unlikely Walter Gard's wife would still be here, or Gard would have known, surely. The Post Master had simply looked the name up in his directory.

'I've a message to deliver, that's all,' I told Mrs Glendinning.

'Is that right?' and she poured the beer on to a pile of greasy plates in the sink.

I looked around at the kitchen's turmoil. The floor looked as though it had been washed a few days earlier. The stove was clean, but a grey scum and beer foam lapped the plates in the sink. A rooster crowed loudly near the back door, which was open for the flies. A dog was sniffing at a large bucket of scraps and slunk away with a chop bone.

'I'm not a constable,' I said.

She looked me up and down, suspicious now I'd mentioned the police.

'You got no business in here then.'

She stood in front of me, her hands twisting a filthy dishcloth into a rope, and I thought she was about to shoo me out like a child.

'Mrs Gard?' I said. 'Is she still here?'

'I already told you she's not.' She flicked the cloth, 'Sorry,' and turned away.

'Mrs Glendinning, I'm the municipal health officer.'

Without turning she said, 'Ah bloomin',' and threw the dishcloth on the floor, standing by the sink with her back to me. 'You can't close me down.'

I looked around the kitchen and thought I probably could.

'I keep the place clean,' she said, gesturing at the cracked floor. 'You take a look. I do what I gotta. Oh bloomin'...' She turned and her chin was wobbling.

'I'm just here to deliver a message to a Mrs Gard.'

She didn't seem to believe me. 'I can't ... I don't ...'

She picked up the dishcloth and wiped her hands on it.

'If you tell me she's not here and I learn later that she is here,' I said, 'I'll be back with a sanitation inspector.'

She threw the cloth down again.

'Number eight,' she gestured behind me with her

chin. 'Up the stairs. She won't take kindly to someone visiting this early.'

She followed me out of the kitchen. The man who'd lost his breakfast drink had his head in his hands. I set my foot on the yellow stair runner.

'Hope you are who you say you are,' she said, but added, 'Left at the top. Second door on yer right.'

I put my hand on the banister. A cockroach scuttled between my feet, hit the bottom board and then ran into the hall. Mrs Glendinning tried to tread on it and then followed it down the hallway stamping a foot. 'Git. Go on, git yer little bugger. Bloomin' ... '

I climbed the stairs.

Outside number eight I paused, trying not to breathe too hard, turning an ear towards the nicotine-stained door. The hallway smelled of tobacco and stale beer.

Someone was coughing, and I knocked. Silence. I knocked again and there was a muffled voice.

'Mrs Gard?' I said.

'Who is it?' A woman's voice.

'My name is Dr Row. Are you Mrs Gard?'

'Why?' The voice caught and there was a cough and then breathlessly, 'Who's this?' louder, and I imagined both of us now pressing our heads together, a door's thickness apart.

'I have a message. From your husband.'

A long pause. 'My husband?'

'You are Mrs Gard?'

Another long pause. 'Is he here?'

'He sent a message.'

A cough. Then a child's voice and the woman saying, 'Shoosh,' and then, 'What's the message?'

'It's in a letter.'

'Slip it under the door.'

I stood back and looked at the thin gap beneath the door and took the letter from my pocket.

'I can't,' I lied.

There was a curse and then the shuffle of feet, and eventually the scrape of a bolt being drawn and the door opened a few inches. Part of a face appeared, a pale blue eye, pale powdery skin, light red hair over a smooth white forehead.

She held out a thin hand. And then she opened her mouth and coughed.

I stood there, stunned, and watched her, the red hair tied back, her thin white neck, as her body shuddered.

'Bad cough.'

She nodded.

She eventually raised her head, wiping her hand across her mouth, her eyes watering.

'Mummy,' from behind her.

'I said shoosh.'

I tried to catch a glimpse of the little girl.

'I've seen you before,' I said.

Her eyes narrowed suddenly and she went to close the door again.

'Wait. The letter.' I held it out and she tried to snatch it, but I pulled it out of her reach.

'I don't know you,' she said.

'Church. We go to the same church.'

She seemed to relax a little, and looked me up and down. 'How'd you know where I was?' she said.

'I found your address at the post office.'

'Does *he* know I'm here?'

I shook my head. 'He just gave me the letter.'

'Where is he then?'

'At the quarantine station.'

She screwed up her forehead. 'Sick?'

'No. No.' Hadn't she heard? She grabbed at the letter again and this time I wasn't quick enough. I thought she'd close the door in my face, but she kept it open and held the letter up. Her pale red lips formed the words of her own name. Her skin was slightly freckled and dusty dry.

Then she slammed the door. Somewhere down the hallway, a man was shouting for someone to damned well shut up.

I stood there wondering if I should go, but I thumped the door again with the palm of my hand. It opened a fraction.

'What?'

I didn't know what. I could smell her scent.

'I'm a doctor.'

'So?'

'I could examine you both.'

Her eyes narrowed again. 'I have my bag,' I added quickly, holding it up.

'What for?'

'Your cough. You sound ill. There's medicine I could get for you.'

I had to press myself against the wedge of the door and lean close to speak with her. She kept hold of the knob, looking me up and down.

'You don't look like no doctor.'

I could see past her a narrow slice of room, a glimpse of her life, an impression of cobwebbed ceiling, bottles on a dresser, clothes on the floor, a doll. I couldn't see the child.

Mrs Gard wore a dress so thin that the light from behind her seeped through, outlining a sliver of her body, her hip, the sketch of a breast pressed against the cotton.

'I'm a doctor. With the council.'

'I'm all right.' She drew an arm across her nose and looked down at the letter again. 'Don't tell him I'm here.'

'He's your husband,' I said.

She looked into my eyes and for a moment it seemed as if I was looking into the face of a drowning woman.

Then she shut the door.

'Maybe I'll see you in church?' I called out, but there was no reply. Down the hallway someone started laughing.

* * *

I was still shaken when I walked through the door to Turner's office.

'Roll up your sleeve,' he said.

'What?'

'Come.'

He picked up a huge hypodermic syringe from an enamel kidney dish on his table and squirted a little yellow fluid into the air.

'Haffkine's serum.'

'I've already had one.'

'This one's better. New batch just arrived. Twenty-six doses. Sleeve.'

He came around the table and plunged a hot steel ball into my arm.

'Jesus Christ!'

'No need to blaspheme, Row. And don't tell me that hurt.'

'It bloody did.'

'Nonsense.'

He put some blotting paper on the blossom of blood and I held it there, flexing my arm, trying to get the ball rolling. He went back to his laboratory to clean up, and appeared more excited than usual.

'Why the rush?' I said.

'Just had a look at another rat,' he said, and he pointed to the microscope. 'Take a look.'

I knew what I'd see, of course. Nevertheless, when I took my eye away I felt a little out of breath.

'*Pasteurella pestis*?' I said.

'No question. Not many, but enough.' I thought he was about to applaud, but he wrung his hands together and said, 'Coffee?'

He went through his coffee ritual.

'As I say, only twenty-six doses. It's nowhere near enough, of course. All medical staff, health officials and contacts? No. I'm hoping to get some dried serum, but we don't have enough for an outbreak.'

'I can give you your shot now if you like,' I said.

'Very kind, but I've done it myself.'

I inspected the wound and the bleeding had already stopped, but I pressed the paper to it again and rolled the sleeve down carefully.

'No need to be alarmed, Row. That's just a booster. More vaccine's on its way from India,' Turner was saying. 'In all the Australian colonies there are only five hundred doses left. We're lucky to get twenty-six, I suppose. Now,' he checked his watch, 'let's go for a stroll.'

Turner was whistling a tune. It may have been 'Annie Laurie', but I couldn't be sure. He may have been tone deaf. We stopped to watch a sea-eagle.

'"A fing of beauty is a joy for ever",' he said.

I asked him if I should have my family vaccinated.

'Do you have rats?'

'No.'

'I wouldn't worry just yet. We need all the doses we have at the moment just for medical staff.'

The raptor made lazy circles as it followed Ross Creek west. Another joined it.

'It's quite a beautiful spot. From up here,' he said. 'Don't you think?'

He waved his hand over the town. The tableau in front of us was more grey than green, the coastal plain stretching south into swamps and saltpans, a slate-grey sea, grey scrub rising to blue-grey mountains, and in the west smoke and dust to the horizon.

'It's not jolly old England though,' I said.

'No. Did I tell you – I was actually born in China.'

He started prattling on. His father was a missionary, and the family lived in Canton until his parents fell ill with some Oriental disease and they all moved back to London. Public school, University College Medical School, and then to Australia, for his health. He took a deep breath and slapped his thin chest.

'And you believe you've come to the right place?' I said.

'Of course. What about you, Row?'

'I'm a native, I'm afraid.'

'I meant here. Why Townsville?'

'You know why I'm here.' I didn't want to answer any more of Turner's damned questions. 'Maria's health.'

'She's ill?'

'You know what I mean.' I snapped, I suppose, but Turner of all people should understand.

We walked in silence for a while. I gathered we were heading for the hospital. It was on the other side of the ridge that ran from Castle Hill towards the mouth of the creek. It was a good site for a hospital, away from the stench of the creek and its beard of swamps and bogs, the coastal waterholes, and the stagnant drains that criss-crossed the settlement. The sick convalesced on its screened verandahs with their backs to the town and had a splendid view of the sea if they could enjoy it.

We were too heavily dressed for the outing. Turner took off his pith helmet to wipe his brow and the wind caught his hair and blew it across his head. Everything he did seemed to be done with a boyish enthusiasm, a clumsy disregard for how it made him appear, a sort of guilelessness that I supposed would become either annoying or endearing.

'What you gain from risking an adventure more often than not compensates for what you've left behind,' he said. 'In fact, the soul usually makes a profit on the deal. In my experience.'

'You think I did the right thing? Coming north.'

'Don't you?'

'I'm not sure what I'm doing here,' I heard myself say, before I could shut my mouth.

'Well,' said Turner, 'it's probably a question we should all ask ourselves from time to time.'

The chief surgeon, Dr William Bacot, was pacing the hospital corridor. He had his hands in his pockets and his head bowed as he marched towards us, but just before we collided he turned on his heel and went the other way.

I cleared my throat and he looked back over his shoulder, annoyance passing quickly, replaced by a tight, thin smile.

Bacot looked older than I, but younger than Turner. He must have been in his late thirties and had a long face and the professional man's moustache: the carefully tended variety in the shape of bicycle handlebars, worn by the men he thought of as his peers. He also had a reputation for having a short fuse and I tried to avoid him.

'Blasted suicides, you know. Should be a law. Well, I suppose there is, but who's ever charged, eh?'

He led us down a long corridor, explaining how he was treating his second attempted self-poisoning for the week. Rough on Rats. Hadn't we noticed?

No, I said. I read the list of registered deaths and hadn't seen that many poisonings.

'Ah, that's because they usually have to find something else to finish the job. A gun, a rope.'

'I have noticed a few gunshots.'

'Rough on Rats,' spat Bacot. 'There you go.'

A trolley hummed past on rubber wheels.

I said, 'So, there could be an epidemic of poisonings and they wouldn't show up on my weekly lists.'

'There certainly is an epidemic.' He stopped and looked at us. 'What are you doing here?'

'I wanted to discuss preparations for the plague,' said Turner.

'Plague,' he snorted and we followed him into a large room at the end of the corridor. 'I suppose you'll want coffee.'

Turner smiled.

The window in Bacot's office was open. A draught that ran the length of the building was expelled here, so that the window appeared to be trying to swallow the curtains. I could see Kissing Point and West Point, the sea in between, salted with whitecaps.

I envied Bacot. He'd been given a small garrison up here and managed to fortify it so that, although he was hounded occasionally by Humphry, he was left for most of the time to run his own show. He had a staff of doctors and the most coveted collection of single women in the town. He was living in a detached house nearby, but there were never any of those sorts of rumours about him.

Bacot called a nurse to bring coffee and slumped into his chair with the window at his back.

'I'm busy,' he said. He tipped his head back and shut his eyes, waving a hand around his office. It was cluttered with papers; some had blown on to the floor and were making a scratching sound. To be fair, he'd probably been working all night. He never slept, I heard.

'What we really wanted was your opinion,' said Turner. 'About the plague hospital.'

He snapped his head forward again. 'Not here, you don't.'

'No. It needs to be further out of town.'

Bacot leaned back again and looked at us both with suspicion.

Turner continued, 'We're considering Three Mile Creek instead of the quarantine station for an isolation hospital.'

Bacot spun in his chair and looked up the coast. He spun back to Turner.

'A rough drive.'

'Better than the six miles by launch to West Point,' I said.

Bacot stared at me, probably wondering what I was doing there. He'd refused a position on the Epidemic Board, and may not have known or even cared that I'd taken it up.

'Yes. Tents, I assume,' he said.

'That's right,' said Turner.

The surgeon shrugged. 'All right. What's it to do with me?'

'It would have a lot to do with you,' said Turner. 'I presume, if it comes to the worst, some plague patients would first arrive at this hospital and after being diagnosed would need to be transferred to Three Mile Creek. We have to make sure that is done as quickly and efficiently as possible to spare the patients further discomfort and to protect them, and the staff and the other patients here, of course.'

'I won't be treating plague patients here.'

'You might have no choice. We won't know who has plague until they're diagnosed. It's reasonable to assume some sick people may turn up at this hospital.'

Bacot made an exasperated sound and shook his head, looking at us as if we were idiots. 'It won't come to that.'

'I hope you're right,' said Turner. 'If it does come to that, Dr Row here, Dr Humphry and myself are to be responsible for making the official diagnoses. We'll have the power to compel infected people to go to the plague hospital –'

'And that will make you all very popular,' he snorted.

'. . . and to use force if necessary.'

Turner stood then and opened his medical bag, taking out a syringe and a small corked bottle.

'Arm or thigh?'

Bacot stared and gave a short laugh. 'What?'

'Haffkine's serum. We have to inoculate everyone who'll be dealing with plague patients.'

'Not me.'

'Especially you,' and Turner produced a copy of the plague regulations, putting it on the table and pointing to the paragraph on the protection of staff.

'I'm not having you give me that jab,' said Bacot, watching Turner draw the fluid up into the syringe.

'Would you rather Dr Row?'

'God, no.'

'I had a rat brought to me this morning,' said Turner. 'It had plague.'

Bacot drummed his fingers on the desk, staring from the syringe to me.

'Nonsense,' he said.

'Are you frightened of a little injection?'

The nurse arrived just then with coffee in china cups and looked startled by Turner's needle. It was quiet for a moment except for the rustling papers and the flapping curtains.

'Oh, all right.' Bacot took off his jacket and rolled up the sleeve of his left arm and Turner, with more care than he'd used on me, pushed the needle under the skin.

Bacot was determined not to wince. 'Damned waste of time,' he muttered, as Turner put a wad of cotton on the wound and removed the needle.

'Hold it there.' Turner packed the syringe away, and Bacot sat.

'What if people don't want to go to this ... this isolation hospital at Three Mile Creek?'

'I hope by then everyone will be clear as to why it's necessary,' Turner said, picking up his coffee.

'I'm not clear.'

'About what?'

'As to why it's necessary.'

'To stop the spread of infection.'

'It wouldn't work.'

'It's the law.'

Bacot spun his chair around again to look out the window, still grasping his arm. 'I heard about the commotion at West Point.'

'We'll be asking for police assistance. But I believe all reasonable people will understand.'

Bacot turned back to Turner and gave another short snorting laugh.

'Glad I'm not in either of your shoes,' and he examined the cotton and rolled his sleeve back down.

Turner stood. 'Thanks for the coffee.'

We shook hands and turned to leave. Turner reached the doorway and turned around. 'One more thing.'

Bacot had just brought his cup to his lips.

'I'd like you to be in charge of the plague hospital.'

There was a long pause before Bacot said, 'I'm sorry, what authority did you say you had here?'

'I'm the government medical officer for north and central Queensland. The Queensland Government's given me the authority to make these arrangements. I'm not ordering you to take this on, but you're the only man with the administrative experience to run a hospital. In fact, the Central Board of Health's already approved your appointment.'

'You're joking.' Bacot put his cup down with a clatter, spilling quite a bit, a brown stain spreading.

'No.'

Bacot smiled uncertainly. 'Impossible.'

'Why?'

'I have a real hospital to run.'

'You're the best man for the job.' Turner turned to me. 'Dr Row?'

'No question.'

Bacot came around his desk looking ferocious.

Before he could say anything, Turner held up his hand and said, 'There's more money. You'll have to use some of the hospital staff, but I have two hundred pounds for wages, supplies and equipment.'

Bacot was breathing heavily and stopped quite close to Turner's face. 'Two hundred pounds?'

'From the Central Board of Health. The money's been approved. It can be wired to you immediately. We're pushing this through quickly, because of the emergency. You'll buy the supplies you need yourself. Brisbane is taking this very seriously. All you have to do is set up the hospital. You can have someone else there to run it day to day. If you like.'

Bacot said nothing so Turner continued. 'I expect it'll be a matter of keeping an eye on things. As I said, the government doctors – that is Dr Row here, Dr Humphry and myself – will be taking full responsibility.'

Bacot rubbed his forehead hard. 'So I can put a superintendent in there?'

'You have a budget. It just needs to be organised. As you say, it might not come to human cases.'

'It won't, you know.' He turned around and went back to his chair, and Turner and I departed.

I waited until we'd left the hospital grounds. 'Was that an ambush?'

'That's a colourful expression. Completely inappropriate.'

'You'd appointed him before you saw him.'

'It's his own fault if he didn't see this coming. The facts are laid out. I'm sure he'll be happy to do his duty.'

'I'm not completely sure that he'll see it your way.'

'What?'

I held up my hands. 'You might have handled him better. The man's highly strung. Those facts are laid out, too, if you'd cared to ask. It could have gone badly, that's all.'

'Really?' said Turner. He looked at me with genuine surprise.

I told Humphry later about the incident. His admiration for Turner seemed to be growing. I also told him Bacot's theory of a poison epidemic. I had to re-examine my lists.

'It sounds about as far from an Act of God as you can get,' said Humphry.

Exactly. Poison would mitigate *against* an Act of God. I could never be sure that someone hadn't taken poison and then, their reason impaired, gone out into a thunderstorm or fallen down a well.

'Or got hit by a buggy,' said Humphry.

Every suspected Act of God would need an autopsy.

The town was whistling and clanging as we descended into it, the bells at the fire station ringing non-stop.

'What's going on?' Turner's pace quickened.

We were a block away from the main street when a small dog tore out of a lane in front of us, eyes white and ears flat, its tail sprung beneath the body. A lean kangaroo dog followed and caught up with it easily in the middle of the road and they both went tumbling in the dust. The smaller beast cowered, dropping what it had in its mouth. The large dog went to snatch it, but the small one changed its mind and took hold of an ear. There was a distressing howl, a blur of teeth and dust. A man appeared with a whip and the big dog loped off. The other one reclaimed its soggy grey prize and fled, the rat's tail swinging from its jaw.

Turner wanted to find more rats and I left him at the Town Hall. I did need to see a dentist.

I'd put it off too long, dreading it. But when I arrived at the shop the barber who, I'd been told, 'pulled teeth painlessly' had closed for the day to celebrate the great British victory in South Africa, and the damned tooth had stopped aching anyway. I wandered back to my office, relieved.

I must have left my door open. The curtains were still drawn and I was fumbling for the coat hook when a shape came out of the gloom.

I took a quick step back, 'Get away,' and I flapped my arms in front of my face.

'Steady on,' said Humphry, striking a match and lighting a cigarette. 'Is that the way to treat a colleague?'

'What on earth do you think you're doing?' I was gasping.

'I was looking for you. Anyway, I don't have time to hang around while you dawdle in to work.'

'I had business.' I put my coat on the hook and straightened it while I recovered.

'Who did you think I was anyway?' said Humphry.

'I've had bats in here before.'

'Well, you keep it like a damned cave.' Humphry came closer and lowered his voice. 'I have good news and I have bad news.'

'Well?'

'It's awaiting us in Turner's office now.'

chapter eight

The northern stirp beneath the southern skies –
I build a Nation for an Empire's need,
Suffer a little, and my land shall rise,
Queen over lands indeed!
    Rudyard Kipling, from 'The Seven Seas'
            (Song of the Cities), 1896

'TYPHOID?' SAID TURNER.

Humphry rolled his eyes.

'My opinion,' said Routh.

'Well, keep it to yourself,' mumbled Humphry.

I'd followed him through the door, and he stood at the back of the room, leaning against the laboratory tables.

'My opinion, Dr Humphry,' Routh turned to him, 'and it was confirmed yesterday.'

Turner was sitting behind his desk polishing his spectacles. It was stuffy in his office as we held another meeting of what Humphry had dubbed The Bubonic Society.

Turner was saying, 'I don't understand. Confirmed? Who confirmed it?'

'The damned steward did himself, of course,' said Routh, 'when he died.'

'He died?' I was genuinely shocked. We'd taken samples. The man seemed to be recovering. It had been typhoid and we could have diagnosed it if I hadn't thrown away the stool.

It was my fault.

'Don't suppose you could open the doors to the balcony, Dr Row?' said Turner.

I walked over unsteadily and unlatched them. The hot stale air inside was as greedy to escape as the ballyhoo outside was to enter. I went back and sat heavily in the chair next to Routh.

Turner was saying, 'I know he's dead, Dr Routh. What makes you think typhoid killed him?'

'I know typhoid when I see it, Dr Turner.' Routh shifted in the chair.

Turner put his elbows on the table. 'Well, you could have at least informed us when he got sick?'

'For God's sake, it's an island. There's no telegraph. No supply lighter since Friday. How in the blazes was I supposed to contact you? Smoke signals?'

Humphry laughed and Turner looked exasperated.

Routh blustered on. 'I was there, I'm the doctor in charge and I did what I could. It was brought to my attention that he was sick on Friday, and in the space of two days he died. I couldn't very well leave him and there was no boat until this morning anyway. So here I am.'

'Yes, I do see. I am sorry.' Turner patted down his hair. 'And Mr Storm? How's he?'

'Storm? He's –'

'Hang on,' I said. 'Who died?'

'The steward,' said Turner. 'Walter Gard.'

'Gard?' I fumbled for the edge of the table. 'He wasn't sick.'

'Well, he's dead now,' said Humphry. 'Something must have been bothering him.'

I stood. And then paced the floor, trying to grasp what had happened.

Turner had asked Routh again about Storm.

'Fully recovered. Which proves my point, that it's been typhoid all along. Look, Gard must have caught it from Storm. They're both stewards, you know how those sort live aboard steamers, and I'm told he helped Dr Row here carry Storm when he was sick. Probably didn't wash properly.'

My stomach lurched at the suggestion, probably true I realised then, that I might have had a hand in Gard's death.

Turner said, 'So tell me exactly what happened.'

Gard had died at five minutes to noon the day before. Sunday. The business sounded particularly harrowing.

Routh told us he'd had to administer opium because of the terrible ache of which Gard complained. The man was weak and tremulous and his tongue white and furry. His nose bled freely at times and his stools were distinctly typhoidal in character.

'When you say typhoidal, do you mean bloodied?' interrupted Turner.

'I mean typhoidal. The blood was dark and old at first and towards the end bright and fresh. There was some sloughing of the gut.'

'Did you bring a sample?'

Routh nearly choked. 'Of course not,' looking around at Humphry and me as if Turner might have said something crazy, but Humphry was engrossed in the instruments and I continued pacing, wondering if I could have had anything to do with Gard's infection.

Routh continued. The morning Gard had died, yesterday, he'd passed a quart of blood through the bowel and gone quite cold. His pulse weakened and he never rallied.

Poor Mrs Gard, I was thinking. He must have been dying when I was at her door telling her he wasn't sick. I saw her face. My God. Her child.

'What did you do with the body?' said Turner, but we all knew there was only one thing that could be done.

'Buried the poor bugger immediately.'

Routh, Captain Thompson, Dawson and Dunsford had apparently decided to keep the sudden death to themselves and a few of the other men. They were worried the women might become hysterical.

'We decided Gard must be buried quietly and without delay.'

'Even though you say the man died of typhoid and not plague?' said Turner.

'Now you're cross-examining me as if I was some criminal. You'd have done the same. No ice. No *ice*! The body would start to putrefy within a day,' said Routh. 'The tent was full of flies as it was. And it was typhoid.'

Routh then apparently had the problem of giving the man a Christian burial. Although there were three ministers of religion, all refused to conduct the service because Gard was a Catholic.

'Well then, it's his own fault. Damned cheek to be a Papist on an island full of Protestants,' mumbled Humphry from his corner.

I was thinking that Mrs Gard was Presbyterian. She was in my church. Gard was Catholic? I was astonished. Such mixed marriages were rare, but maybe not so much in the North, where men weren't spoiled for choice.

Routh was saying that eventually one of the passengers, John Cook, who was also Catholic, volunteered to read the burial service, and Gard was interred in the cemetery while the clergy occupied the women with a Bible reading.

'I suppose it's too much to ask if he was buried according to the plague regulations?' said Turner.

'No. I said it was typhoid, not –'

'It was septicaemic plague, you fool.' Humphry didn't turn around. 'That's the truth, though you don't want to hear it.'

'Yes, all right!' Turner snapped.

Routh appeared to be trembling.

'I'm actually glad you didn't anyway,' said Turner. 'Bury him in lime, I mean.'

Routh blinked several times before he understood what Turner meant. 'You can't dig him up now.'

'Wouldn't have to if you obtained some serum as you were required to do in such a case.'

'But as I said ...'

'And we'll have to keep the *Cintra* passengers on the island. At least until I finish the post-mortem examination.'

'Well,' said Routh, 'I'm afraid that really *is* impossible.'

'Why?'

'Why? Why? The quarantine period is over. They're all off today. Surely you realise that they're on their way back to the mainland.'

'Dash it,' said Turner, jumping to his feet. 'Humphry?'

Humphry had turned in surprise. We'd all thought the quarantine ended on Tuesday, the next day.

'It's a day early. Hang on.' Humphry walked over to the table, counting his fingers. 'Yes. Twenty-one days. Tomorrow.' He stared at Routh, who squirmed in his seat and looked to Turner.

'Twenty-one days, from the first day, is today,' said Routh. 'That was clear.'

'But they didn't arrive there until the evening of ...'

said Humphry, adding up on his hand. 'Anyway, you're still a day short.'

'Not if you count that first night at the Fairway Buoy,' said Routh, a little uncertain now. 'That was, strictly speaking, part of the quarantine period.'

'No, it wasn't. Who said that?'

'It was agreed.' Routh's jowls shook.

'I didn't agree. Lin?'

I shook my head, hardly able to speak.

'Well ...'

Turner held up his hands. 'All right. Let's see if we can stop them. When do they leave?'

'Six-thirty,' said Routh. 'This morning's lighter. Some of them. Sent the launch back for the rest.' He took out his watch. 'They'd all be ashore by now.' We looked at him in disbelief and his face was livid. 'Well, I told you.'

There was a moment's silence and Routh tried to excuse himself, but Turner asked him to please stay where he was.

'How dare you!' Routh suddenly screamed. 'You've no right! *No right!*' He got up too quickly, and his chair fell with a bang that made us all jump. He was shaking and pointed a finger at Turner. 'I'll not be bullied by you. *You*! Who ... who gave you the right? I'm the medical officer in charge of the quarantine station. In *charge!* I'll not be treated like this. *Not* –' and half choking he turned and collected his coat from the door, fumbled for his hat and was gone.

* * *

'I say.' Turner had taken off his spectacles again and was examining them.

'Man's hysterical,' said Humphry, picking up Routh's chair and taking a seat. 'Mad as a meat axe. Best he takes himself off and has a lie down.'

Turner wrapped the spectacles back around his ears. 'What to do now?'

'You're not going to be able to stop them from coming ashore,' said Humphry.

'I think we should try, don't you? We can get the police to help. We have the power under the Act to compel quarantine.'

'We might need their co-operation,' I said, still feeling winded by the revelation. 'Later. I mean, if the passengers get sick. We'd need them to come to us to report it, wouldn't we? Not enough police anyway to round them all up.'

'Yes. I suppose you're right. Now they're ashore, who knows where they'll go.'

'The Adelaide Steamship office will have their addresses,' I said.

Turner nodded. 'Well. All right. Let's say it's too late now. The next thing we have to do is find out what killed Gard.'

'It wasn't typhoid,' said Humphry.

'Yes, but we still have no proof, thanks to Dr Routh, so we need to confirm it.'

We were all quiet. I supposed each of us was thinking about the business of digging up a man.

I still found it hard to visualise the fellow I'd spoken to only days before now lying in his coffin. I remembered his anxiety the last time I saw him, and wondered if that was a symptom. He hadn't complained of any pain. He just wanted to get off the island, like the others.

'I wonder if his wife's been notified,' I said.

'That's not our job, thankfully,' said Turner. 'That's a matter for the police. It's important we maintain a professional perspective, especially if it is plague.'

But I was still thinking of Mrs Gard, who'd already seemed unwell. And what of the daughter? The letter. Did the man have any inkling he was ill when he gave it to me? What the letter contained now seemed far more poignant. And the disease must have at least been hiding in his blood when he put that envelope in my pocket.

'We'll need the magistrate's permission to exhume the body,' Humphry was saying. 'Once a man's planted, it takes a lot of paperwork to dig him up again.'

'And we must do it soon. The organisms won't last long in the cadaver,' said Turner.

'Trouble might be the magistrate,' said Humphry. 'He might not allow it if it's just to settle a medical disagreement. If that was the case, we'd be spending more time digging people up than putting them in the ground. I mean, he might get to know that Routh thinks it's typhoid, and if Dawson gets wind of any exhumation, the bastard will try to stop it out of spite. I know him.'

I realised then that Dawson was off the island and probably plotting revenge.

'This is far more serious than just a medical disagreement,' said Turner.

'Exactly, so let me handle it,' said Humphry. 'We'll also need a grave-digging party.'

Turner sighed. 'I do think it's time we brought in the police.'

Humphry and I were alone in the hallway outside Turner's office.

'What was the good news?' I said.

'Eh?'

'You said earlier there was bad news and good news. I hope the death of Gard was the bad news.'

'Right. Well, we're vindicated, aren't we? Our decision to put them into quarantine –'

'Your decision.'

'Well, anyway, don't you see? Dawson's going to have to eat his words. He slandered us. I'm going to make sure he gets his comeuppance.'

'If it's plague.'

He slapped me on the shoulder. 'I'll put a guinea, no, two guineas, on it being plague.'

'I'm not going to bet on that.' I wasn't sure if I wanted Humphry to be right or not. 'Maybe Mr Dawson will take the bet.'

Humphrey clapped his hands together. 'Now that's a thought!' he said. I watched him go, a stalwart of the

English Church, and I tried to fathom his contrary ambitions.

Just a few weeks before it had been as flat as a stove top. Now the sea was boiling again. Foam flew from the crests of short waves and a cold spray stung my eyes. The trade wind had returned overnight and at dawn was blowing steadily. I blinked back towards the pink rock of Townsville and thought that at least we were making good progress. Turner was a stoic on a bench. The two constables were coughing and cursing over the railing.

I went to join Humphry and the captain in the wheelhouse. They were singing 'The Last Rose of Summer', Humphry punctuating the heavy ship rolls with a deep loud baritone and offering his flask around. I started to wave it away and then changed my mind and took a sip. It warmed me, but I felt no better for what we were about to do.

We anchored at the quarantine station's crumbling wharf again and made our way ashore, leaving the crew behind. Constables Clark and O'Donnell collapsed against their shovels when we reached the sand, the colour returning slowly to their faces. Turner was already fidgeting. He'd brought his net with him this time. The constables looked, but didn't dare ask, probably imagined it had something to do with the body.

It had taken the rest of the previous day to get the order to open the grave and persuade Sergeant Moylan to release two of his men and have them inoculated. All of the *Cintra* passengers were scattered. Even the kanakas had gone. Every soul had deserted West Point with due haste.

'I've missed the old place!' said Humphry. 'The times we had here, eh?'

We were in the lee of the island, the sun was warm, and none of us was keen to move.

'Right,' said Turner, setting off up the bank.

The constables picked up their shovels and we followed Turner, who was swinging his net. I carried his bag and my own unshakeable sense of foreboding.

Gard's grave was easy to find, a pile of fresh orange clay brought up from beneath the sand and a nailed cross that wouldn't last the year. There were no flowers. Perhaps Mrs Gard would come to maintain it. I pictured her daughter in black, a veil, kneeling beside the grave, perhaps planting a flower.

'Friend o' yours?' said Humphry, coming up behind me and putting a hand on my shoulder. 'That's right. Shipmates. I remember. Dearly beloved, for what we are about to do may the Lord make us truly thankful amen.'

'Go easy on the grog,' I whispered, glancing at Turner who was speaking to the two constables.

Humphry handed me the flask again and said 'Speshull occashun,' winking, and I wondered if he was putting it on. I pushed it away and Humphry went over and offered the bottle to Turner, who looked offended, and then to the two constables, who took a mouthful each and spluttered.

'Let's do it,' said Humphry and the constables reluctantly hefted the long-handled shovels, sinking the blades deep into the earth.

I stood there between Humphry, who was humming, and Turner, who was slapping his net against his leg and looking about the tree tops. Each time a blade entered the ground it whispered like a membrane being ripped. The constables found a rhythm, making their way down into the earth.

The last time I had stood beside a grave I was burying my daughter.

The thought pierced my heart and I had to turn away from the unbearable image to look back through the trees towards the camp. I shouldn't have come.

'Give it a rest,' said Turner, eventually.

The constables weren't grave-diggers, and probably not used to any form of exercise. I heard them throw down their shovels, panting.

'Any water?' said one.

I volunteered to find some. Each of the buildings had corrugated rainwater tanks, and I searched for a bottle. Turner appeared at my side.

'Is there something wrong with Dr Humphry?' he said.

I looked back over my shoulder. 'He might be off colour.'

'We shouldn't have let him come.'

'No.'

I'd never seen Humphry rolling drunk, and I wondered if we might have problems getting him back to the boat.

I found a tank with a tap and there was a beer bottle in the dust under one of the huts. I raked it out, washed it as clean as I could, filled it and walked back towards the cemetery.

Halfway back and Turner called me over to a log. He pointed at the surface and something moved. I put my nose closer and saw the indistinct shape of a moth, flecked grey, the same colour exactly as the wood.

Turner put his net gently over it and it didn't struggle.

'Does it realise its fate, I wonder?' I said. The grey thing just lay there in the bottom.

'I think it did everything it could. Being clever will only get you so far.' He folded the thing into his net and carried it back to the grave.

The constables quickly emptied the water bottle. Humphry had chosen to sit against the grave of the victim of some previous horror and had apparently fallen asleep. *Here lies* – Humphry's carcass obscured the name.

The flask was still in his hand. Turner walked over, picked it up, and stood it behind a nearby headstone. The constables resumed digging.

* * *

A spade thumped the coffin. There was some nervous laughter and then the hollow scrape of the lid. The earth smelled ripe, as if it had just rained.

'Give us a hand,' said a voice, and I had to turn around and face the open pit.

One of the constables climbed out and uncurled two ropes, the other put his hand down the side and tried to lift the coffin so they could get the ropes under. It was a bit of a puzzle in the narrow hole, but they finally managed it. With the four of us taking an end of rope each we hauled the box out, staggering over the grass until the coffin was clear.

Then we all stood back and stared at the thing.

Gard had been in the ground now for two days. I glanced at Turner, who must have been thinking the same thing.

'The glands of the groin and armpit. If that's impossible, one of the organs might still have integrity.'

I nodded. *Integrity.* What we all prayed for.

The constables picked up their shovels and went to prise the lid off.

'Wait,' said Turner. 'Wait till I say.'

They stepped back and waited.

As he sorted through his bag, Turner asked me to get Humphry's flask. I took a swig of Dutch courage on the way back. Turner had opened his bag, setting beside it a clean cloth and an enormous syringe with a long needle.

'Oh Jesus,' said one of the constables. 'What's that for?'

Turner took four other clean handkerchiefs from the bag and handed them around, taking Humphry's flask and wetting each with whisky.

We tied these over our noses and mouths.

Turner nodded to the constables and they began removing the lid.

Its nails screamed a little as the wood released its grip. I lifted my mask and went to take another drink, but Turner took the flask from my hand.

'The idea's to sterilise the body,' he said, 'not the brain,' and he sloshed the liquid over his hands. 'Now, when the lid comes off I'm going to try to get some samples. It shouldn't take long, but I want you to help me find any buboes.'

'Is it safe?'

'That depends on what we do with it. But if you mean could the plague still be alive, I don't really know.' The two constables had been given the prophylactic, but Turner warned, 'Try not to touch the corpse if you can.'

They both laughed, a brief girlish giggle.

The lid came up and the constables flipped it over with the shovels, and then both turned quickly and walked away swearing. Turner lunged forward and I followed. There was a whiff of something vile creeping through the whisky fumes.

I'd never seen a corpse look so devilish. The mouth was open and snarling. The gums had drawn away from the teeth. The tongue was black.

The body had swollen to fill the coffin, a fat snarling maniac in a narrow bath. The features were so distorted I was almost certain we had the wrong man, but then I saw the nose, the crooked teeth. One eye still had its penny, but the other had fallen off. Turner bent over the corpse.

'Blast Routh. He could have saved you this indignity,' he told the corpse. He called to the constables, 'We'll have to get him out.'

'How?' The body was still tight in the box and I couldn't see a way of loosening it without upending the coffin and banging on the bottom as if it was a bucket of slops.

Turner ordered the constables back over to pry loose one of the coffin's sides. It didn't yield easily. After a few minutes with their shovels, the nails popped, an arm flung out and a sigh escaped Gard's mouth. The constables were too shocked to speak.

'Gas,' said Turner.

I supposed they'd seen death before, but the grave held its own horrors.

One of them said something about having enough of being a witness and the other sat down heavily with his head between his legs.

Turner was crouching beside the body and moved the arm further back out of the way. It looked as if they might have been mates, the way the arm was crooked, suspended stiffly as if about to embrace the little man. He cut away the undershirt and then started on the trousers.

He produced a scalpel and searched the blotched, stretched skin. The whole thigh had swollen.

Turner pressed the skin and when he took his hand away the indentations remained.

'This is going to be difficult.'

He palpated the thigh, but couldn't find anything, which was hardly surprising.

'I'm going to have to pierce the skin to let some of the gases out,' he said.

'Well, if you don't need us then we might …' and the two constables started edging further away.

'Stay,' said Turner, not looking up. 'I might need some help.'

'Ah bloody hell, don't say that.'

Turner pushed the scalpel into the thigh and I took a step back. There was a hiss like a gas lamp and then the handkerchief couldn't disguise the smell. I heard one of the constables cry out and I shut my eyes.

'That's better,' said Turner. 'Now.' He probed the thigh again. 'Here's that gland. My word.' He took the scalpel and made a circular incision around the now visible swelling at the groin. 'Where's that jar?'

Turner plopped the bubo inside.

'One more,' he said. Working fast, he found the gland beneath the armpit.

Plop. I sealed the jar as tightly as I could.

Turner was drenched in sweat as he stood and poured the last of the whisky over the jar, and then wrapped it in a clean heavy cloth bag and packed away his equipment.

'Didn't you bring any alcohol from the laboratory?' I said.

'Yes, but no point in wasting it.'

The constables were now at the far end of the small cemetery, staring back at the scene. The coffin had been pulled apart, the arm and leg spilling from the open side, and it was obvious it wouldn't fit back in even if we did have a hammer. Turner called them over. They shuffled back.

'We'll just have to push it back in like it is,' said Turner. 'The poor chap won't care.'

And so the constables made a desperate final lunge towards the coffin and pushed it back over the grass towards the hole. It slid easily, but in their hurry they pushed it straight in, one end hitting the bottom of the grave with a thud. The coffin stood upright.

'Oh Jesus Christ and all the saints, what'dya do that for ya idiot?' said Clark.

'You're the idiot. I stopped pushin' back there,' said O'Donnell.

'Just tip it forward,' I suggested, and Clark put his foot to the top and pushed. Gard's body fell stiffly face first out of the box and into his grave, letting out a sound as if he'd been punched in the stomach. The box remained standing at one end.

'Oh Christ,' Clark said and danced away again holding his arms over his head. His mate just stood there gaping, mesmerised by the scene.

Humphry then rose stiffly from his own grave and staggered over. He looked down at Gard's body. 'Good job.'

He noticed I still had hold of the empty whisky flask and he snatched it away and shook it. 'You lot've been going at it a bit, haven't you?'

Turner ignored him and continued packing his bag. Humphry went to the foot of the grave, put his shoe on the exposed end of the upright coffin, and said, 'You finished here?'

I nodded, and he kicked. The coffin toppled in and the sound roused O'Donnell from his coma. With a sudden, manic energy the constable began shovelling dirt back into the grave.

'Where's that lazy mate of yours?' said Humphry looking around.

I crouched next to Turner. 'What do you think?'

He snapped his bag shut. 'I think we should reserve our judgment until we see what little nasties have been eating Mr Gard.'

The wind made for a miserable trip back, the SS *Teal* at full throttle because the captain knew our business and, I supposed was anxious to be rid of us. Humphry slept the entire trip, or pretended to, opening his eyes only to transfer himself from the launch to the police wagon.

The wagon dropped Turner and me at the Town Hall, and no sooner had our feet hit the ground than O'Donnell flicked the reins and was off, pulling so hard the vehicle lurched dangerously in a half-circle, spraying gravel. It disappeared at a gallop, the constables anxious to get to the Shamrock with the pound Turner had slipped them. Humphry had said he'd make sure they didn't waste it, and Turner and I were left outside the Town Hall in the twilight with the dust settling on our shoes.

There was still a small crowd of late shoppers in the street and being set down by the police was enough to get tongues wagging.

A few watched us closely, men dressed in black suits, handkerchiefs poking from the top pockets, starched collars and ties, civilisation out of context, I thought. They probably all knew who we were, but they couldn't have guessed where we'd been or what Turner had in his bag. Still, I started to worry and hurried us inside just the same.

In his office, Turner set up his kerosene stove and started organising his autoclave. I wiped the microscope with a rag dipped in alcohol. Turner was fastidious and it took a good half-hour to have everything ready.

He removed the gland, already looking brown and dry, from the jar. He placed it on the metal tray and took a scalpel to it, smearing fluid and tissue on a slide and placed that under the lens. He twiddled a screw, adjusting the lamp, and stood back.

'There you are, Row. Tell me what you see.'

I bent down and put my eye to the piece. 'I'm not sure ...' I adjusted the screw.

'You're too close again. Take your eye back a bit.'

Then the squat oval rods were suddenly in focus.

'Well?' he said.

'*Pasteurella pestis*,' I said, but my voice was croaky. There was a cold significance, of course, in seeing the devil in a man rather than a rat. The hairs stood on the back of my neck.

Turner took a look.

'Quite a few. They're alive. The grave isn't as cold as they say.'

He was excited and my next thought was that it was good news for Humphry: he'd been vindicated. But, of course, something sinister was happening. We were heading into a new world and this capering disease was coming with us. We could even see it, but it acted with indifference, as if nothing had changed since the Middle Ages.

It was already dark outside. Steam from the autoclave and boiling beakers filled the room.

'Now. We have to sketch what we see.' Turner had placed a pencil and paper beside the microscope and started drawing. It looked like something a child would do.

Afterwards, we cleaned everything carefully and scrubbed ourselves raw with phenol. There was so much alcohol and steam in the room I felt light-headed. The rag, the syringe, the soupy remains of the steward, all went to the incinerator out the back. Then we sent for the Mayor.

McCreedy was in no mood for small talk. He was dressed in a blue suit, his collar stiff, but his necktie loose. He'd just come from dinner. I realised I hadn't had a bite since breakfast.

'Just the facts, gentlemen,' he said, sitting noisily opposite Turner.

Turner explained the exhumation of Gard, the examination of fluids taken from the body, the identification of the plague bacterium. He showed an astonished and pale McCreedy the sketch he'd made.

'There's no doubt,' said Turner.

The Mayor looked for a long time, bringing his face closer and then further away from the drawing as if it were an optical illusion. He was probably a little drunk.

'Mr Dawson says it was typhoid. He was adamant. Told me that Dr Routh confirmed typhoid,' the Mayor said, and I suddenly knew with whom McCreedy had shared dinner.

'We found no typhoid bacterium in the sample we took from Gard's body,' said Turner. 'Just plague.'

McCreedy opened his mouth to say something and then closed it. He looked at the sketch again and frowned.

'Could there have been some mistake? If Storm had plague, as you say, he got better.'

Turner said, 'I can tell you that typhoid did not kill Mr Gard. We would have found the bacterium. So something else killed him and we found plague bacillus in his organs, in great quantities.'

'All right, all right,' McCreedy said. 'What now?'

Turner stroked his beard. 'I'd have liked to have traced all the contacts. Impossible, apparently.'

'We have the tightest plague controls in the colony,' said McCreedy, ignoring what Turner was saying and looking over at me. 'The fact that the damn thing's not in the town is testimony to that, isn't that right, Dr Row?'

I still felt uncomfortable that Dawson and McCreedy had been having dinner.

'I mean, we've done our best to protect the town and it seems to be working. This is just proof of that,' said McCreedy. 'You follow me?'

Turner was gazing out into the dark and appeared to be thinking aloud.

'This may be two separate cases. I can't say where Gard contracted the plague bacillus: it may have been directly from the other steward, but more likely on the ship. A virulent bacillus, considering how rapidly the disease took hold in the end. Septicaemic certainly.'

'So?' said McCreedy. 'The man was in quarantine.'

'So, it's an example of how cases can pop up anywhere at any time, seemingly unrelated. It's just a matter of time, I'm afraid, before there's a case right here.' Turner pointed into the night.

'Well,' said McCreedy, slapping both hands down on both thighs and standing, 'I'm not sure what else I can do.'

'We can all do more to *prepare*.'

McCreedy spoke as if he were in chambers. 'I've just said, we *are* prepared. No town is better prepared. Dr Row has seen to it. We've swept Flinders-street from end to end. Fifteen hundred horses a day going up and down the main street, you follow me? A man can cross it now without having to scrape his shoes clean on the other side. We've flushed drains and sloshed so much carbolic acid around I don't think there's a germ alive. So many ships have been fumigated one actually caught alight.'

'I was in Chinatown yesterday ...' said Turner.

'Didn't know we had a Chinatown,' said McCreedy, with a chuckle, looking at me for some reason and winking.

'Flinders-lane, I think it's called,' said Turner.

McCreedy's face swiftly changed and flashed annoyance. 'What the devil were you doing there?'

'I've not seen conditions like that since I visited Shanghai.'

Turner could not have chosen a worse comparison. McCreedy stiffened.

'Should plague take hold in this town, and today I believe that is more likely than it seemed yesterday, it will be conditions like those in that squalid street which will give it a home.'

McCreedy mustered his height and weight. 'I told you what we've done. I'll not be told how to run my town.'

'Plague is at the door, Alderman McCreedy. You might think the main street is clean. I don't — not enough to stop the disease. And despite what you say, in my time here I've seen a great deal of rubbish piled up, not just in Flinders-lane but everywhere behind the main street. Drains choked by rubbish. Dogs fighting over rats. Just yesterday there were children sliding down Denham-street on the slime left behind by the nightsoil cart. I counted nine horse carcasses on the town common alone. It's all perfect cover for rats and disease. I've looked at Dr Row's correspondence book. There are many things he has suggested which you have not done.'

McCreedy gave Turner a vicious look and strode to the door, before turning. 'I'll not be lectured —'

'And I'm going to urge the Home Secretary to declare Townsville an infected port.'

McCreedy took a step back towards Turner. 'What the devil are you talking about?'

'It's enough to have one confirmed plague death. I plan to send a telegram tomorrow.'

'You'll bring this town to a standstill.'

'Plague is directly associated with the sorts of unsanitary conditions I've seen here. Filth and overcrowding. If you don't move to clean the town up now, there will be no trade,' said Turner. 'And if it gets a foothold, nobody will want to build railway lines up here. To Bowen or Charters Towers or anywhere else. Do you follow me?'

I could have throttled Turner myself. McCreedy stood at the door with his mouth hanging open. He looked at me, and I looked at Turner.

'Perhaps, Dr Turner, if the council had some time?' I said, wondering how in the hell this mild man could turn so caustic.

'Time's run out,' Turner said.

'Another day?' I said. I was trying to be conciliatory, on behalf of the council more than McCreedy.

Before Turner could reply the Mayor shook his head and said, 'I'll not be bullied or blackmailed,' a hoarse whisper. He gave me a furious look and left.

Turner went back to his table. I closed the door. If anything he looked pleased with himself, but he apparently didn't like the look on my face.

'Calm down,' he said.

'Calm down? My God, are you crazy? That was the Mayor. He's trying to help.'

'No, he's not.' Turner looked at me as if I was the crazy one. 'Not at all. He's acting as if it's a political scrap rather than a mortal danger. We have no time for tact.'

I threw up my hands and left Turner with his bacteria. Of course, Humphry would have applauded him, but Humphry enjoyed pointless acts of bravado himself.

I thought about finding Humphry as I had promised, to tell him what he said he already knew, that Gard had the plague. But I was tired and angry.

Out in the street I felt my cheeks still burning. A couple of drunks were singing their way down east Flinders-street and bats were diving through the darker edges of a galaxy of insects around the lamplight. One creature making a meal of another.

I walked my bicycle around the spinning circle of moths and started up Denham-street. In the dark beyond the lamplight I could hear the drunks laughing. Shapes flickered around my head and my unreasonable instincts told me that there was, indeed, danger in the dark.

chapter nine

Liphyra brassolis: The moth butterfly

... He climbed the tree and started chopping at a branch with a small axe. Oecophylla smaragdina had made a nest by sewing the leaves together with the silk of their own young, which they held and used like darning needles. The nest was in turmoil when it came down, the ants swarming at us, rising on their hind legs and spitting. Seizing a pair of scissors and mindless of the ants biting his arms, he cut open the nest, showing me something the size and colour of a halfpenny. This turned out to be the armoured and flattened larvae of our Liphyra brassolis *which lives inside the ants' nest and, unlike any other caterpillar I know, eats the ant grubs, its head safe from what must be daily attack underneath its burnished copper back. I remembered Dr Turner saying 'Heads or tails?' and made as if to flip the thing, which then was still a mystery, a good puzzle for Mr Darwin, and an eloquent example of God's hand in nature if ever one was needed ...*

Observations of My Father (unpublished),
Dr Allan Row (1948)

THE FAT BLUE GRUB of Gard's canvas bag rested against my legs.

Boots at the bottom, clothing, letters and postcards tied with a bootlace, a pipe, tobacco, buttons, razor and strop. I knew this without opening it. Every man's life could be boiled down to these mundane things.

But I owed the man something, I felt. He had helped me carry Storm; he tried to warn me. He put his trust in me and perhaps I'd let him down. I felt a certain amount of responsibility for his death. There you go.

The man who spoke over Gard's grave had, it seemed, delivered his personal effects to the police station, and Sergeant Moylan had duly locked them in the cell they used for such things. They had been fumigated with the rest of the *Cintra* luggage.

A dead man's kit is a heavy burden. It might have sat immoveable for days or weeks or years with all the other abandoned possessions the police collect, until someone claimed it or it was dragged out and burned.

Moylan had been surprised when I mentioned that Gard had a wife in town, surprised I knew where she lived, but he'd offered me the bag, probably relieved to be rid of it.

'Are you sure you want to do this?' he had said then, as he dragged it from under the bunk.

'Yes.'

'You knew her?'

'No. I delivered a message. From her husband.'

'Poor woman.'

I nodded.

'It's a terrible thing.'

Moylan was sitting on the bunk with a suitcase on each side and scratching his mutton chops.

'Would you mind asking the poor soul if she'd like a visit from Father Walsh?'

I had said I would ask, of course, not wishing to cloud the issue by telling him what I knew: that she wasn't Catholic, that she might be ill, that she had a child, that I might have broken quarantine by delivering the letter, that I might have been partly responsible for her husband's death.

I had picked up the bag and tested its weight. It wasn't much to show for a life.

I'd managed to balance it across the handlebars of the Carbine, *corpus delicti*, to Glendinning's Boarding House. The place was quiet. I met no one on the stairs.

And so, resting the bag against my leg, I knocked on number eight.

'Mrs Gard?'

There was no answer and no movement. I knocked again.

'Mrs Gard. It's Dr Row. Please open the door.'

But it was quiet and I sensed only space within. The canvas bag slumped slowly to the floor in despair and I kicked it away with childish anger. And then, feeling bad, I bent to pick it up and found myself face to face with the door knob.

I put my hand on it, it turned and I pushed. The door opened. When I let go, it swung fully in of its own accord, revealing a slice of dingy room.

'Mrs Gard?'

But she wasn't there. I dragged the bag through and toed the door closed behind me before I'd fully considered my actions.

I set the bag against the end of the iron bed. There was clothing on the floor. One door of a wardrobe was open and some dresses hung limply. The room was hot and heavy with her scent, but I resisted opening the window for air.

I felt like a thief and wondered if I was now adding to the woman's woes by violating her life.

On a washstand was a jug and cracked basin, a washer still wet. Red hairs clung to a comb. I picked it up and put it down. On the dresser were some creams, a bottle of Eno's Fruit Salt, no jewellery.

There was a pencil in my pocket and I was looking about for paper when I realised how stupid I was being. I shouldn't be in the room, no matter the urgency of the news. But what to do?

Should I leave the bag or take it with me and try again later?

If I left it and Mrs Gard came back and saw her husband's things, what would she think? That wouldn't do.

If I could find some innocent piece of paper I could slip a note under the door.

I was reaching for the knob, suddenly anxious to leave, when there was a light knocking. I froze, mortified, the knob turned and the door opened towards me. I thought of jumping into the cupboard; ridiculous. There was no time.

Mrs Glendinning saw the bag against the end of the bed and put a hand to her breasts.

'So sorry ...' I began, and at the sight of me she recoiled, her eyes wide.

She mouthed the words, 'Jesus Mary and Joseph,' but nothing came out and if she hadn't reached out then and clutched at the doorframe she'd have fallen back into the hallway.

I led her to the edge of the bed and closed the door again. She was gulping and I hoped I hadn't killed her, too.

After a minute or so the colour came back to her face.

'I've brought her husband's things,' I said, trying to sound official, pointing at the bag. 'The door was open.'

'Wasn't,' she said, gasping and wiping a tea towel over her face, 'when I come in.'

'I came to drop off her husband's things,' I said again.

She took a deep breath. 'Her husband's *things*?'

'He's dead.'

She looked at me as if I might have killed him. 'Oh dear.'

'Do you know where she is?'

She shook her head.

I looked at the clothes in disarray on the floor. 'When was the last time you spoke to her?'

'She keeps to herself and minds *her* own business. Haven't seen her since day before yesterday,' she said. 'Her rent's due.' She shook her head. 'Dead. Oh my gawd.'

I tried to help her up, but she brushed away my hand. She stood and straightened her dress and her hair.

'It's not proper for a man to be alone in a room with a married woman,' she said. Was she talking about herself or my visit to Mrs Gard?

'I told you, I'm a doctor.' It seemed she didn't believe me. 'Why did you open the door?' I asked.

'Thought I heard a noise; thought she and her little one might have come back.' But I suspected she was snooping.

'Back from where?'

She stood and backed out of the room, her hands at her cheeks. 'Oh gawd.'

I picked up the bag and followed her.

Downstairs, in the hallway, she turned to me and said, 'Well, what did he die of then?'

I took a little pleasure in saying, 'Plague.'

She stopped and fanned her breast. 'Oh my gawd,' she said. 'And that's his things?' She pointed at the bag.

'It's been fumigated.'

'I don't want that here.'

I had no intention of leaving it with the woman.

'When you see Mrs Gard, could you tell her to see me?' I said. 'Or I can come and see her. My office is at the Town Hall.'

I lugged the bag down the front steps to my bicycle. Mrs Glendinning followed.

'What's your interest in them then?' she said. 'Her and her husband. Were you his doctor?'

'Yes.' In a way.

'So you'd know all about them then.'

'I didn't know him that well.'

She smiled, having caught me out.

'You have no idea where she is?' I said. She shook her head, determined not to tell me anything more.

I looked at my watch. 'I'm late.'

'Well that ain't my fault.'

Balancing the bag as best I could on the front, I threw my leg over the saddle.

'Hoy.' Mrs Glendinning stood by the front gate, snapping the green tea towel at flies. 'If you're looking for trouble, you won't find it here.'

But she was wrong.

Did digging up a man and taking his possessions make me a grave-robber? I felt like a villain. Sulphur had seeped from the fumigated bag and my clothing smelled of rotten eggs.

Back at the Town Hall it was still too early for most employees to be at work so I managed to get the bag into my office without attracting questions.

I stood over it, wondering what in the blazes to do with it now. It had to be concealed, of course. It already invited questions I couldn't answer, like why I didn't just throw the damned thing away. I told myself I was holding it for Mrs Gard and her daughter. I should have taken it back to the police station, I supposed, but I was still worried that the woman had phthisis and might easily pass it on to her little girl. And I didn't want Moylan asking me any more questions.

There was only one place for it. I had a corner cupboard of the public-service type, large and strong and stacked deep with old reports and stationery and useless things requisitioned mistakenly by the gross.

It had hanging space and I managed, with some rearranging, to stuff the bag inside and close the door. I walked away and heard the door open, Poe-like, with a long moan. The bag slowly tumbled out. I put it back and this time locked the damned thing in.

I sat down to finish a report to council on what we'd found in the West Point grave, but then my tooth started throbbing.

A dog charged us and disappeared into our dust.

'What's the rush?' I said.

'No rush.'

We were still within the city limits. 'The police will have us.'

'Nonsense,' said Turner.

He had the whip in hand, but just the sight of it seemed to have been enough to encourage Humphry's horse to gallop. Allan sat between us with a hand on his hat and a wide grin.

Three children cheered as we flew past the last house.

Once out of the town, heading north, Turner let the horse find its own pace.

'Beautiful,' said Turner, looking around the countryside. 'I never realised.'

The hard road had turned to packed sand, which cushioned the wheels and gave us a comfortable ride through a forest of creamy paperbark trees, past a lagoon of flowers and waterbirds. The sea sparkled through the trees on our right.

I'd never been out to the common, but I could see why people took the trouble.

'Are you all right?' Turner was looking closely at me.

'Tooth,' I said.

'You really should get that seen to.'

We seemed to float over the sandy ridges above the sea. 'I can see why it's popular for picnics out here.' I was starting to enjoy the expedition, despite myself.

'You mean you didn't bring a picnic?' said Turner.

'It didn't seem appropriate when you first mentioned popping out to look at the plague hospital site.'

Allan had said nothing, but his grin couldn't have been broader.

We arrived in a flourish, braking abruptly at the edge of a small clearing. The hot hush of the bush wrapped around us with a swirl of dust.

'Here it is,' said Turner. Here it was indeed. There was a surveyor's peg with a yellow ribbon in the middle of a low flat hillock. Coarse brown grass crackled under our feet. Just ahead were dark green swamp trees marking the course of a creek.

'When do we start hunting?' said Allan.

In the back of the buggy was Turner's butterfly net and a large sugar bag on the end of a pole.

'Business first, then some fun.'

Turner and I paced the site, imagining the tents, while Allan explored the perimeter.

'It's a hike,' Turner said. 'But there's not much we can do about that.'

Initially there'd be three tents: a ward, a surgery and staff quarters, as well as a privy. Then there'd be the well, waste pit, incinerator, all surrounded by a barbed-wire fence.

And then a cemetery.

Clouds of small insects fled from our feet and I could see Turner's eyes flick over them. I pinched at the grass seeds burrowing through my socks. Allan was off at the far end of the site, poking around a dead tree.

We found the spot we were looking for in the north-western corner, below where the tents would be, flat and out of sight. Turner dug his heel into the ground.

'Seems porous enough.'

Behind, the land dropped away into a paperbark swamp.

'Do you think the water climbs this high when it floods?' he said.

I said I didn't think so. The gloom I'd lost briefly on the trip seemed to have caught me up.

'Wait there,' and Turner went to the buggy and fetched his butterfly net and the sack on the end of a pole.

'What on earth's that for?' I said, pointing to the sack.

'It's a surprise.'

I called Allan over, Turner handed him the pole, and we headed off down into the thicker scrub.

The ground was muddier and carpeted with branches and leaves. It was even quieter down here, a hidden glade, full of biting things, no doubt.

'This insect's dead,' said Allan, picking something from the tree bark.

'It's the skin of a cicada. It sheds its skin as it gets bigger and leaves it behind,' said Turner. 'Possibly *Cyclochila australasiae*.'

Allan appeared to be repeating the words under his breath. He pocketed the thing.

Turner showed us a cluster of brightly coloured beetles. He poked a finger at the metallic mass so it moved as one.

'*Tectocoris diophthalmus*. See here, this one has eggs,' and he put his finger near a beetle and pushed it back, revealing a tight cluster of tiny lavender eggs. 'What do you make of that?' he said.

'A clucky hen,' said Allan.

'Maternal concern. Rare in insects. A quality that eludes even some human beings.'

It was airless in the hollow and things kept brushing my cheek.

A butterfly flickered past and off into the tree tops. Turner's net twitched in his hand. There was another, closer, and the net snaked out from his body and swallowed the insect. He and Allan examined it carefully.

'A Blue Tiger, Row.'

Fancy that.

There were more, I noticed, and Allan wandered further until he was out of sight.

'Dad!'

I took a few hasty steps and my foot – boot, socks and all – plunged into mud.

'For the love of God.'

'Around here.' Allan's voice echoed through the trees. I hobbled over, annoyed.

And then I saw the butterflies. They were hanging in their thousands from the bush like glossy black fruit.

Turner was already there. '*Here* are your Tigers, Row.'

Allan took a step closer with his bag and they took flight, most of them, creating a black cloud around the bush. Turner then walked over and stepped into the vortex.

Where the man ended and the swarm began became blurred. He held his arms out and the butterflies settled on them like a black cloak and he turned slowly and faced me, a strange bird. The insects had also perched beneath the brim of his pith helmet, obscuring his face, and the effect was like a mourning veil and a little grotesque. And then he flapped his arms and they rose in a cloud and began circling again, and he stepped away.

Allan clapped, Turner bowed, and I tried to dislodge the mud from my shoe.

'The survivors of your little pretties blown across the bay,' Turner said. 'Aren't you glad you found out where they went to?'

'Are you going to catch some?' said Allan.

'They're not actually my cup of tea,' said Turner.

I told Allan, 'Dr Turner's cup of tea is coffee.'

'Very droll, Row.'

I left Allan with Turner and returned to the clearing. Then I climbed the bank. Halfway up I stopped and looked around, savouring the quiet. Tree trunks rose around me like the columns of a Greek temple.

My eye was drawn to a stick. It appeared to be moving. A sinuous shape. I couldn't see the beginning or the end of the snake, but its body threaded through the litter on the slope. I turned and strode uphill. It was impossible to run. I didn't dare look back. The bush became a thick tangle and swallowed me. I pushed, it grabbed, and then with a snap it let go and I stumbled into the clearing. I backed away, panting, checking myself for spiders.

The waterbag was cool and I drank from a tin mug, sitting on the buggy's footplate. I'd removed my shoes and socks and cleaned them as best I could, scraping the mud with a stick and plucking at grass seeds. The insects hummed. A sea breeze blew at my back. It wasn't such a bad place to be laid up, I thought.

I walked down to the sea, mindful now of snakes. The entire sweep of bay was in front of me. I traced the horizon from West Point to the tall ships and steamers at anchor in the middle of the bay, and then to the dark line of the harbour and the whitewashed houses at the foot of Castle Hill. The tide was out and I walked down on to the firm sand, filling my lungs with clean sea air.

There were worse places to die.

I found Turner up a tree.

He'd taken his jacket off and was lying along a branch like a stick insect, waving a bread knife in front of him and expressing his efforts with small grunts.

'Hold the dashed thing still now, Allan. Almost there.'

Allan gazed up at the little man with his mouth open in serious concentration, steadying the open bag beneath Turner. Ants were swarming all over the Government doctor, biting his bare arms and face.

'Uh. Uh. Hold it, boy. Up. Up. That's it. Unh. Unh.'

Allan tightened his grip on the pole and the bag seemed to sway all the more.

'Here we go.' The small branch fell away and into the bag, remarkably. Allan lowered it to the ground.

'Get that cord around the end, Allan.' Turner dropped the knife and slapped the ants from his face, before pushing himself backwards along the branch. Within seconds he was on the ground and madly brushing his arms, head, and clothes.

Allan had removed the bag from the end of the pole and cut the twine that held it to a wire hoop, tying the open end with cord so the nest and the raging horde were sealed inside. He seemed to know what to do. Amazing. He was picking ants from his arms when Turner came over and slapped him on the shoulder.

'Good show,' he said. 'I don't think we damaged it at all.'

Turner's face was a rash of bites and one of the Lilliputians clung to an eyebrow. He looked delighted.

'Something Dodd had mentioned,' he said. 'A little surprise sometimes inside these nests. I've been keen to take a look.'

I noticed then that there were several butchered nests nearby, and ferocious ants everywhere.

Allan was holding out his hand. In the palm was something that looked like a coin or a flat nut, brown and round.

'What is it?' I said.

'I have no idea,' said Turner. 'The larvae of some moth, perhaps. Won't know until it hatches.'

It just lay there. 'Is it dead?' I said.

Allan turned it over and pointed to where he said its little legs were.

'It lives inside the ants' nest, Dad.'

Turner said, 'The ants might actually protect it from other predators. Remarkable.'

Allan put it back into a paper bag.

Turner said, 'We'll try to hatch one, and then we'll see what sort of creature it is.'

'We're going to put it in this nest,' said Allan, pointing at the bag, 'and keep it in a cage in the back yard.'

I said, 'Not in our back yard.'

Turner and Allan looked up at me, their faces scratched and bitten.

'Those things bite,' I said.

They glanced at each other.

'Just don't tell your mother.'

We pulled up outside my house and Allan furtively vanished around the back with the bag of ants. Turner had suggested making a cage of an old meat safe under the mango tree. It was somewhere even Maria avoided. The mesh on the meat safe would let the ants out, but trap anything that might hatch. The thought of it made me shudder.

Back at the Town Hall, the corridor was full of chatter and pipe smoke.

I escaped into my office and shut the door, wishing I could take a bath, knowing I should see the dentist. I'd just sat down when there was a knock at the door and Mr Willmett entered.

'You look terrible.'

'I think I'm coming down with something,' I said. He looked startled and I said quickly, 'Toothache.'

Willmett was elderly and always looked a little unkempt. His eyes were hooded so that he gave the impression that he was very tired and somehow doubted everything you were telling him.

It was Willmett though who, as head of the Townsville Joint Epidemic Board, had appointed me the board's physician. It placed me in a difficult position. What the board decided often was at odds with what the council wanted, and I was first and foremost a council employee.

Willmett, with a foot in both camps, was my best ally. As an alderman he could speak his mind; as a council employee I had to be diplomatic. Fortunately, he backed everything I proposed.

'The Mayor called an emergency council meeting this morning,' he said. 'He had someone chasing you all over town.'

My heart sank. I told him where I'd been.

'Dr Turner put the wind up him last night,' he said.

'He told the Mayor he was going to have the town declared.'

'I wish Turner would talk to me before he makes those statements. The Mayor's saying that it's Brisbane's meddling. We need him *for* us, not against us.'

'I tried to get Turner to wait.'

'Well. The Mayor would like a word, anyway. When you're ready.'

McCreedy's door was open. I knocked anyway and heard the Mayor's voice say, 'Come in, Dr Row. Good of you to come so quickly.'

The curtains were drawn, the room dark, the way I, McCreedy, ghost moths and vampire bats seemed to like it. There was a little light behind me, and a small lamp on the mayoral desk. I found a seat and sat. A shape hovered in the corner, its single eye red in the dark.

'You know Mr Dawson, I take it.'

The red eye glowed brighter as I heard Dawson draw on his cigar, the sound of a small creature having the life sucked from it.

'Whisky?' said McCreedy.

'All right,' I said. My tongue probed the aching tooth. The whisky might do it some good.

McCreedy stood and poured it himself, Northern style: no ice, no water. There was a glass only because good manners demanded one before noon and indoors.

The Mayor brought it over and watched as I sipped the warm fluid, sloshing it around. It was the good stuff. From Melbourne. I nodded gratefully. The pain actually subsided.

'This plague issue, I think there's been a misunderstanding.'

McCreedy lit a cigarette then and puffed before continuing, 'We should get things sorted out. Nobody's worried more about the welfare of this town than me. Except perhaps Mr Dawson here.' The red eye glowed bright again. 'You follow me?'

'Yes.'

'Mr Dawson by the way is staying in Townsville for the duration of this … this issue. With Mr Philp not able to be here, well, he's left it to Mr Dawson to keep an eye on things and report back to Parliament and such.'

That seemed unlikely. Even I knew Philp the businessman and Dawson the Labourite despised each other over just about everything, and especially the question of kanakas. I couldn't see the Premier asking Dawson to keep his seat warm.

'Who's looking after The World?' I said, using the nickname for the city of Charters Towers. I never knew if The World was supposed to be a boast or an ironic slur, but everyone used it.

'Mr Dunsford's there,' said McCreedy with a wave of the hand. 'He'll take care of it. Now look, I've just this morning had council appoint a special inspector to carry out the rest of your recommendations. I've arranged for five thousand handbills to be distributed, free rat poison's being handed out to anyone who asks for it, and there's that bounty you wanted. What do you think of that?'

I said I thought it was timely. Dawson grunted from the darkness.

McCreedy leaned forward. 'It seems Dr Turner has something against me and Mr Dawson. I don't for the life of me know why. If the leaders of the North getting together for a project to benefit the North is a conspiracy, then so be it. It's Turner who's behaving unreasonably. I can't even speak to the man now without being attacked. You follow me?'

McCreedy wanted me to say something. I said I thought Dr Turner was a stickler for regulations.

'Yes? Yes? Is blackmail in the regulations?' McCreedy was getting agitated and took another sip of whisky.

I was wondering about Dawson's dark presence. Humphry told me later that it was still all about the railway. McCreedy the boodler and Dawson the unionist had formed an alliance. Each desperately wanted railway contracts, McCreedy for his sawmill and Dawson for his workers. Both also wanted North Queensland to become a separate state to further their political ambitions. Joseph Chamberlain, the British Secretary of State for the Colonies, had apparently told them they'd have a better chance of getting what they wanted under a Federal flag.

But I knew also that Humphry blamed Dawson, and Dawson alone, for the 'Commonwealth catastrophe', as Humphry called it − the coming Federation. Humphry's convoluted reasoning.

McCreedy was saying, 'Doesn't need people like Turner spreading malicious rumours.'

I said I didn't think Turner had any intention of doing that. 'Dr Turner is interested only in stopping the plague.'

'Is he? Well, fair enough. But you keep an eye on him. The man's a damned nuisance. That's an order, by the way, from the Mayor to an employee.'

Dawson came out of the shadows through a haze of blue smoke and leaned close. 'Just warn the pommy runt not to slander anyone.'

I said I'd pass the message on. I swallowed the rest of my drink and left.

At my desk I sat with a report on the plague hospital. It already had McCreedy's blessing, and the surveyor's peg at the site confirmed that. Approval should be a formality. The hospital could be up within days. Whatever Turner's faults, he had things at a gallop.

Bacot, to his credit, had already arranged for tents from the local garrison to be at the site the next day. Turner had also shown me a note from Bacot confirming the staff roster for the plague hospital.

Dr Routh's name headed the list, and he would be the medical officer in charge.

'My word,' said Humphry. 'Bacot has a sense of humour after all.'

chapter ten

> *Lay not up for yourselves treasures upon earth,*
> *where moth and rust doth corrupt, and where*
> *thieves break through and steal. But lay up for*
> *yourselves treasures in heaven, where neither*
> *moth nor rust doth corrupt, and where thieves*
> *do not break through nor steal. For where your*
> *treasure is, there will your heart be also.*
>
> Matthew 6:19–21

MCCREEDY, HOUNDED BY Turner, had employed a team of rat catchers, and the Foreman of Works started sending scores of rats daily to the incinerator. Rat catching became both a pastime and an industry, and at sixpence a rat was costing the council a small fortune.

'Is that how much a rat is worth?' said the Mayor. 'Maybe we should start farming them.'

There were rumours of a gang prowling the streets at night pinching rats from official traps. No one apparently considered it a dangerous thing to do, even though only official rat catchers were inoculated. It might have been amusing, but for the boys queuing for sixpences with rats hanging from their belts.

'Can I go rat catching?' said Allan.

'*Mon dieu!*' said Maria, glaring at me.

I promised him sixpence for any Hercules moth he could find, but the deal was off if I saw him with a rat.

The Women's Christian Temperance Union organised its own gangs. Germ parties went about knocking on doors, telling housewives to throw open their windows, burn rubbish, boil down bones, seal poultry scraps in containers and lay poison.

And it appeared that all these things might work and there'd be no use for the plague hospital.

I slept badly.

I visited the boarding house, but Mrs Gard hadn't returned.

I sat through another Townsville Municipal Council meeting and gave my report, the plague now item ten on a list of twenty-five. Council obviously believed it had done its bit and it was time to move on.

Dawson came out only at night to address union meetings. The Bowen to Charters Towers spur line had run into obstacles again – of the Brisbane kind, said Humphry, whatever that meant. Humphry thought Dawson was plotting a strike.

I was in my own office, with the door closed. In the dark I ran my palms over the cool silky top of my table and then laid my head down. I would just close my eyes for a moment. I swam across the smooth surface and floated over its depths, hoping this time they'd take me down.

Someone was knocking on the door. When the clerk entered the room he seemed to think it was empty and turned to go out.

'What is it?' I said from the darkness.

'Dr Row?'

'Yes.'

Dr Bacot at the hospital wanted to see me, said the clerk, who obviously couldn't.

I sat up slowly. 'Are you sure it's me he wants and not Dr Turner?'

He took the message back out into the hallway and held it under a light, and came back in. 'It doesn't mention Dr Turner.'

I called him over and took the message from him. On his way out he started to close the door.

'Leave it,' I said.

Turner wasn't in his office when I passed, so I went into Flinders-street and found a cab.

When Bacot saw me at his door he stood and strode towards me, and then marched straight past.

'This way,' he said, and I managed to keep up without breaking into a run, but the rapid squeak of footsteps down the corridor accompanied my anxiety.

Bacot didn't break his stride as he entered one long ward where two dozen beds, all containing patients, were lined up militarily against the walls. Someone was moaning and a few stopped chatting as we passed. Their eyes followed our march with hope born from fear and boredom.

We stopped at the end, before the doors that led to the verandah.

In the bed was a girl with a wet cloth on her head. A nurse was sitting beside her. Bacot went to the girl, who was not much more than a baby, took the towel away and replaced it with his hand.

'How are you?'

The girl opened her eyes, but they didn't seem to focus. Bacot turned to me.

'She has a fever of a hundred and four. Chills. Vomiting. You wanted to see any patient with a fever?' He waved a hand over the girl, hey presto, and stepped aside.

I took his place. The little girl must have been about three and reminded me achingly of Lillian. She was curled into a foetal position but was conscious. Her skin was pasty, the hair matted. I gently tried to force her mouth open and she moaned at the touch.

I pulled down the sheet and she flinched. Her thigh was bandaged and I started to undo the dressing and she produced a long wail. I persisted, unable to block out the sound or stop my own fear from rising.

The glands were enlarged, the swelling firm and fixed, and beginning to break the surface of the skin.

'Hush. There, there,' I said, replacing the bandage, but her sobbing continued even after I stood back. Perhaps she'd done with screaming. She must have been in terrible pain.

'When was she admitted?' I asked.

'This morning.'

I looked around at the full ward. 'You'll have to move her.'

'I know what I have to do.'

I wondered if it would always be a battle with Bacot.

'You sent for *me*,' I pointed out.

'Well, what do *you* think then, Dr Row.'

I leaned forward and whispered hoarsely, 'It looks like bubonic plague.'

'Damn right it does. But *I'm* not allowed to make that diagnosis. *Now* we can get her isolated.'

The nurse may not have heard our words, but the exchange clearly frightened her.

'Perhaps we can discuss this somewhere else,' I said.

I followed Bacot into the corridor where he turned, folding his arms across his chest, glaring at me.

'Well?' As if he knew all along I was going to cause trouble.

'We have to test her blood for the bacteria first.'

'We can do that now.' He cocked a thumb over his shoulder. 'I have a microscope.'

'It has to be done by Dr Turner.'

He sighed. 'Well, bloody hurry up.'

'Who brought her in?'

'Her mother, of course. She's waiting.'

I looked back into the ward and everyone who could was watching the door. The nurse was standing at the end of the child's bed and turned away.

'We'll have to isolate her for now,' I said. 'I need to take some serum from a gland, and I can't do it in there.'

Bacot raised his eyes to the ceiling. 'All right. All right.' He flapped off down the corridor and began poking his head through doors. He disappeared through one and yelled at someone.

In the end, bewildered patients were wheeled or limped past and the girl's bed wheeled to the vacated ward where she looked even smaller.

I filled a syringe with her fluid and the girl's screams bounced around the empty room. Even Bacot looked uncomfortable.

Feeling already like a man who was collecting too many ghosts, I went off to find her mother.

Mrs Gard wasn't as surprised to see me as I was to see her. In fact, it knocked the breath out of me.

I looked around the waiting room, but there was no other candidate for the girl's mother. I took a moment to absorb the implications.

Then I sat down next to her with what must have been a look of confusion on my own face, because she read that as something else.

'Oh Holy Mother of God,' and she started to wail, 'Oh my God.' She looked at me with horror and covered her mouth.

I told her as firmly as I could that her daughter was alive.

'She has a high fever. We've had to move her to another ward where she's not bothered by anyone else, that's all.'

She coughed and seemed to have trouble catching her breath again. Finally she managed to say, 'I want to see her.'

'I'm afraid she has a contagious disease. We can't let you see her until we're sure what it is and that she's better.'

'What do you mean? I want to see her,' but she made no move to stand.

'You can't.'

She shook her head and her words were punctuated by sobs. 'What?'

I almost formed the words, but stopped myself. It sounded bizarre, even silly.

I said, '*Pestis*.'

It didn't save me of course. She just looked confused.

'Plague.'

Quand on parle du loup, on en voit la queue, as Maria might say. Speak of the wolf, and there's his tail.

I don't think the word meant that much to her, though. What could it mean? She may not have ever heard of it, except in some childish stories. I managed to get her to tell me that, yes, she'd been away, visiting a sister in Charters Towers. The girl developed a fever on the train.

Had she been back to the boarding house?

She nodded.

Then Mrs Glendinning must surely have wasted no time telling her that her husband was dead. I looked into her eyes and they stared back in fear only for her child. It was a look I knew well.

'My baby,' she sobbed. 'Will she be all right?'

'Of course,' I said, but I could tell that she didn't believe me. Perhaps foolishly, but with good intentions, I decided to leave this bad news until the morning.

I left her with a nurse and went to Bacot's office.

'This isn't a dispensary,' but he gave me something he said he kept for hysterical women. I took it back to the waiting room and Mrs Gard, already in a swoon, drank it without a murmur.

I examined her; her body felt as light and fragile as one of Turner's desiccated moths. No fever, no swellings. Her pulse was strong, and her breathing strained and steady.

Bacot reluctantly found Mrs Gard a bed and I left the hospital carrying her daughter's serum and more bad news for Turner.

Mrs Glendinning was unhappy to see me, but the sight of the constable appearing out of the night struck her dumb. I left them at the door as he explained in a low, firm voice that no one was to enter or leave the boarding house before the doctors returned in the morning.

Turner and I went back to the hospital to tell Bacot, who immediately demanded the girl be moved to Three

Mile Creek. We persuaded him to wait. The plague hospital wasn't quite ready and the girl was far too ill to travel.

In fact, it seemed unlikely she'd live through the night. I sat by her side for a while and then saw it was growing lighter outside. I felt her fluttering pulse and reluctantly left her.

'"The Rat is the concisest tenant. He pays no rent".'

'That so?'

'"Repudiates the obligation on schemes intent".' Turner held the dead rat by the tail. 'Emily Dickinson.'

'Bloody show-off,' Humphry muttered.

Humphry was looking behind a cupboard, rattling the crockery. Turner dropped his rat into a bag for examination and incineration.

It wasn't our job to catch rats, of course, but Turner decided we should take a quick look while we were there. He had found the dead rat behind the ice box.

I'd been there since dawn. Mrs Glendinning was in the kitchen.

'I've got eighteen bloomin' mouths to feed now for three bloomin' weeks.'

I asked her when she knew that Mrs Gard was back from Charters Towers, and she said she didn't.

'And now you tell me I'm quarantined.'

I'd waited outside with the constables until Humphry and Turner arrived with the prophylactic.

We'd examined the surprised guests in the dining room and none showed any fever. The mood then, if anything, was jovial. One of the male boarders walked out on to the verandah and was cheered by a small number of people who'd heard the news and had come to have a look at this place where plague had broken out.

'There's not enough entertainment in this town,' said Humphry, and he plunged the needle into another guest.

'Cripes,' said the man, rubbing his arm. 'And what good's this going to do for us?'

'A precaution. So you don't get sick. Don't worry.'

'Don't worry? And how long before this stuff works?'

Humphry hesitated. 'Eight days.'

'Eight days? It'd all be a bit late by then, wouldn't it? I mean, if we were going to catch it, we'd have got it by then.'

'Next!' yelled Humphry.

'Cripes.' The man stormed off.

He was right. The vaccine was probably pointless in their case, but there was no questioning the regulations in front of Turner.

Unfortunately, scepticism was already spreading like a disease itself. Dawson for instance had produced the steward, Storm, when the *Cintra*, which was again plying the coast, returned from Cairns.

'Here's your plague,' he told a meeting of waterside workers. 'Plague be damned.' Cheers.

Circulating around Townsville was a pamphlet entitled 'Twenty-five Reasons Why The Australian Epidemic Is *Not* Plague!', by a Brisbane doctor, T. P. Lucas. Turner had been furious when shown a copy and sent a telegraph off to the man rebutting each claim. Perhaps it made him feel better, but I doubted it did any good.

'Lin?' Humphry waved a hand in front of my face. 'Are you all right? Turner's going back to his office.'

The crowd that had grown outside the boarding house booed Turner as he left. I didn't tell him a guest appeared to be missing.

'I want to take another look around,' I told Humphry.

The boarders were meeting in the dining room, now loudly complaining and drawing up a list of demands, by the sound of it. Humphry poked his head around the door jamb and quickly withdrew it. 'They seem to be enjoying themselves.'

He loitered in the hallway looking at a curling calendar while I went to fetch the keys from the kitchen wall.

'What're you after then?' said Humphry, nodding at the keys.

'None of your business.'

'Is it any of yours?'

There was no one on the stairs so up we went as if inspecting the place, which I suppose I had every right to. I was relieved, though, to have Humphry following along.

I looked up and down the hall. Everyone seemed to be downstairs. I tried the door knob first, and it opened. I walked through. Humphry hesitated before stepping in. I closed the door behind us and locked it this time.

The room was more chaotic than I remembered. There was an open suitcase and clothes were scattered over it, and around the floor and the bed. There was a child's cloth doll on the dresser.

I opened the thin curtains and more light fell on the open suitcase, the wardrobe, the dresser still crowded. There was the smell of scent as before.

'What are we looking for?' said Humphry.

'A letter.'

I opened a drawer of the dresser. Humphry started picking at the clothing on the floor. He plucked up a thin dress, the one she wore in church.

'Who lived here?' said Humphry. 'If we're becoming so intimately involved. Or should I guess?'

I went back to a drawer I'd just rifled and found a framed wedding photograph lying flat.

The couple didn't look happy, but who did in wedding photographs. She had sad eyes. His crooked face looked rugged, almost handsome.

I handed it to Humphry, and he stared at it for a while.

'That fellow looks familiar.'

'The steward on the *Cintra*.'

'The one who died or the one Dawson's buying drinks for?'

'The dead one.'

He put the picture face down on the bed and we fumbled through clothing, as ineptly as men do. The room rustled with our awkward, furtive violations.

'I'm assuming,' said Humphry, 'that this is also the room the child was staying in.' He picked up the doll.

'Yes.'

'That's interesting.'

'Yes, it is.'

'Where's the mother?'

'Up at the hospital.'

He sat on the bed and took out his flask. 'This isn't one of your Acts of God, I hope.'

Humphry started tapping his foot. I searched. The voices downstairs rose and fell.

'Did I tell you I nearly became a priest?' Humphry said.

It was such an unexpected confession I stopped what I was doing and looked at him.

'I wanted to know why my parents died,' he said.

He used the toe of his shoe to push the suitcase backwards and forwards.

'Died in a fire when I was very young. But I was old enough to ask why.'

'I'm very sorry.'

He took a sip from the flask and offered it to me. I shook my head.

'My sister pulled me out through a window and we watched the house go up together, a big roaring fire, in the middle of the night. It was exciting, you know. I didn't understand.

'Anyway, later a priest came along and told me it was God's will. And I believed him. You tell a child something like that and it makes an impression. I became quite religious. We'd moved in with my father's sister and they wondered if I had a calling. I started studying for the priesthood.'

I resumed looking through the last drawer.

'And then,' said Humphry, 'I had a kind of epiphany, although it probably occurred to me a little slower than that. Over months or years. But I realised that everyone I knew had had some awful tragedy in their life. Parents, brothers, sisters, children died or were terribly maimed by this or that disease and this or that accident. What I'd experienced wasn't that special. I concluded that the whole thing, the human condition if you like, must have all been a terrible accident. Don't you think it's a miracle any of us live to old age at all? Anyway, lost my vocation, became a doctor.'

I looked around the room we'd sacked.

'And that's the end of the story,' said Humphry.

She must have thrown it away.

And then I saw the scrap of cardboard. I picked it up and brushed the lint off, turned it over and over. It was the front of a box of poison.

'I don't understand,' I said aloud.

'Sometimes there is nothing left to understand,' said Humphry. 'Things are as they seem. A house burns down, people die. Happens every damned day. If anything, God's only acting when he spares us, not when he kills us. Horrible deaths and sudden accidents are natural. Nature is chaotic. It's working against us. That's my theory.'

I looked at the label. *Rough on Rats.* The company's motto was engraved beneath a picture of a supine rat: *They'll die outside.* I slipped it into my pocket.

The whisky flask sighed, and then Humphry was saying, 'You shouldn't take these things so personally. It's not healthy for a doctor. *You* should have been the priest.'

On an impulse, when we left, I took the doll.

We returned to the Town Hall and met McCreedy in the hallway.

I moved aside to let him pass, but when he saw me, he flew at me. He thrust his fist with a crushed piece of paper in my face and I flinched.

'Who on *earth* does he think he is?' he said. 'Have I shown him anything but courtesy since he arrived? Have I? By God! I'll not be lectured like a child.'

Even Humphry was too surprised to retort. McCreedy looked at his fist and then tried to straighten the bit of paper, which I took to be a telegram. His hands were shaking, he couldn't manage it, and he held it out to me again.

'Declared. *Might as well close the damned port for God's sake!*' He was choking. 'This is *exactly* what I asked *you* to deal with. The man's out of control. And he has the audacity to go running to the Home Secretary telling him *I'm* the troublemaker. *Me?*' He flung the words around the hallway and I felt the building itself grow tense, listening. 'What did I ask you to do, Dr Row? Well? *What did I ask you?*' he screamed.

'I –'

'*Keep the damned man under control. Didn't I tell you that?*' The Mayor took a few moments to get himself together. 'Your fault, you follow me? By God, wait until Dawson hears this,' and he stormed off.

My face was burning, my throat tight.

'What was that about?' said Humphry.

I croaked, 'Turner's done something.'

'Again? I might just stick around here today. Could be interesting.'

Still shaken, with Humphry following me, I went straight to Turner's office. He was at his table, writing.

'You had a chat with the Mayor. I could hear him from here,' he said without looking up.

'He's a little upset,' I said, and took a seat.

'Yes.'

'Did you close the port?'

He looked at me. 'They're not fumigating the ships. They're not following regulations. I've just quarantined a few ships, that's all.'

'How many?'

'All the ones that haven't been fumigated.'

'How many is that?'

'All of them.'

Humphry clapped his hands together.

'Did you send a telegram to the Home Secretary?' I said.

'The Mayor's been very uncooperative about it all, as you know. And now we have a human case of plague in town. There's no time for dilly-dallying. One of those ships was carrying lumber from McCreedy's mill. It could also be carrying rats. But I think that's what really upset him, having his dashed wood delayed. That, and the telegram he's received back from the Home Secretary I suppose.'

He walked over to a boiling beaker and prepared three cups with a splash of essence.

'Coffee?'

'What did the telegram say?' I said.

'Oh, I don't know. The Mayor wouldn't show me. Just kept ranting. Perhaps there was a threat in there that if he didn't pull up his socks the council would be stood down. But I'd just be guessing. Sugar?'

I tried to fathom the depth of trouble I might be in. Perhaps my loyalties should have been with my employer. Perhaps I'd aligned myself too closely with Turner. Well, too late now. I heard Turner place the cup on the table in front of me. I heard Humphry unscrew the lid of his flask and pour some whisky into his coffee. I felt as if I'd stepped into a vortex – so many Blue Tigers that they were dragging me down.

'I could have dealt with it,' I said.

'The man still doesn't appear to appreciate the gravity of the crisis. The plague's here now. People will die. How many people die rests directly on our shoulders and the Mayor's. If certain things aren't done immediately, we'll all be culpable to some extent for these deaths.'

Amen.

chapter eleven

Shall we never more behold thee;
Never hear thy winning voice again —
When the Springtime comes, gentle Annie,
When the wild flowers are scattered o'er the
plain?

'Gentle Annie', by Stephen C. Foster

THERE WAS A LOT TO DO now that the city had its first human case of plague, but I decided to go for a walk. I needed composure.

I had expected Mrs Gard to still be at the hospital.

She was gone.

'You let her go?' I asked Bacot, who sneered and brushed past me. The nurse said no one had seen Mrs Gard leave. She hadn't been officially admitted anyway. Her little girl was still alive, fighting her own demons, alone in her empty ward. The door had been locked during the night.

I went to the boarding house, but there'd been no sign of the woman.

When I returned to the Town Hall I was told Turner

had gone to Three Mile Creek, so I went to my room and laid my head on my desk for a moment.

I woke much later and went to find Turner. He was standing in the middle of his office, looking at something on the floor. I followed his gaze and there between us was a black bat.

'I'll have someone throw it out,' I said.

'No,' said Turner. 'Leave it.' He knelt and teased the dead creature on to the palm of his hand. He brought it suddenly up to my face and I flinched – but saw it was just another blasted moth! An enormous thing, its muddy wings wider than the spread of his hand.

'Another *Coscinocera*,' said Turner. 'See the sheen on its wings? That's from the tiny scales, the *lepido*, which give the name to the order Lepidoptera.' He looked at me. 'Moths and butterflies.'

'I know.'

'Are you all right?'

I nodded. Books and papers covered Turner's desk, but he found a clear corner for the thing.

'I've been thinking about the *Cintra* steward, the one who died, and his daughter,' said Turner. 'About the coincidence of their relationship, how they can both become infected from apparently different sources.'

I nodded wearily and sat, my head bowed. That indeed was the question. I should have told Turner earlier.

'You struck up some sort of friendship with the steward, didn't you?'

I nodded again. He knew. 'I wouldn't say friendship.'

'You spoke with him, though. Several times.'

'Yes, yes.' I stared at the floor.

'You knew him well enough to pay a visit to his wife. To break the news.'

Moylan had no doubt been asking questions of Turner, about me.

'Someone had to,' I said. 'I was concerned. He mentioned his wife.'

'It's important we tell each other what we're doing during this business.'

'I thought it was a personal matter.'

'Personal missions can complicate our job. We must remain objective and detached because our actions, however seemingly innocuous, have consequences.'

I nodded, knowing what he was about to say next.

'She's dead.'

My head snapped up. 'Dead?' It wasn't what I'd expected. 'She can't be?' I sat there, unable for a moment to understand what he meant. 'You are talking about the girl?'

'Her mother.'

'What?'

'Sergeant Moylan telephoned. They've just found her body at the wharves.' He was watching me closely.

'My God. It was only last night …' That I'd examined Mrs Gard. 'It was …' After she'd learnt her daughter had plague.

Turner stood. He went to make coffee. The smell of it charged the room and made me feel sick.

'What was her reaction,' said Turner, 'when you told her her husband was dead?'

'I didn't get a chance to tell her.'

'The sergeant said you did.'

I shook my head. 'I didn't see her until last night. She was in shock. Her daughter.'

I was a living curse to that family.

There was a tinkle of metal on china. Images came to me: the canvas bag, the empty room, the face of Mrs Gard at the door, Gard in his grave. A little girl screaming. I needed to put them into an order that made sense, because at the moment none of it did.

Turner brought over the coffee, bitter and black.

'How did she die?' I said.

'The sergeant didn't say. He wants to see you.'

'When?'

'Now.'

'Now?'

'Now-ish. At the sugar wharf. In my experience police like to inconvenience doctors whenever they can. We can keep him waiting, I think.'

I pushed my coffee aside and stood, a little dazed. 'I'll go now.'

'I'll come.'

But I shook my head.

It was dark by then. I found a cab and rode across the Victoria Bridge, past the hotels leaning on each other in Palmer-street, towards the wharves where Moylan was waiting. At some point the road ran out and slivers of steel flashed by in the lamplight as I bumped across the railway shunting yards.

There were lanterns ahead, moving about. I could see a blue light and part of the police wagon, a few dark figures against it.

I told the driver to stop and wait for me, and the man took out his pipe and settled back without complaining.

One of the lanterns came bobbing over and Sergeant Moylan, his face inscrutable in the light, led me to a patch of ground lit by the police-wagon lamps.

There was clothing piled carelessly on the tracks. He pointed, unnecessarily.

'We haven't moved her.'

I looked up and down the line. A locomotive was stopped a hundred yards away. I walked over the rough ground. There was an oily smell of industry. The wind ruffled the skirts and hair.

I bent over the body and put my finger to the strands of hair and gently moved them aside. Her frightened white face stared up at the stars. I saw an arm and a leg oddly placed amongst the material.

It was only then that the odours of violent death, the distinct combination of faeces and blood, hit me. I pulled a handkerchief from my pocket and held it over my face as I reached for the clothing.

'Wagon will be here soon to take her away,' said Moylan.

I gently lifted the skirt. There seemed to be an

immense amount of material about the woman. Even in the poor light I could see the lower torso had been twisted completely around. The steel wheels had severed her head without moving it more than a few inches. Black blood was spattered delicately across the pale rise above the bodice.

I stood.

'Seen enough then?' said Moylan.

Another vehicle clattered out of the night, the horses greeting each other with snorts.

I nodded.

'Good-oh.' The sergeant held a lantern up to my face. 'It *is* Mrs Gard?'

'Yes.'

He seemed to be weighing it up.

'You see, we found a purse. Name was on an envelope. Mrs Walter Gard, it said. And you'd come to collect her old man's things.'

I nodded.

'Don't go away,' and he went off to talk with someone.

I felt tired to my bootlaces. I could have dropped to the ground there and slept. Well, not there exactly.

When Moylan came back, he asked me what was Mrs Gard's reaction to the news her husband had died?

I said I never got the chance to tell her.

He rubbed his head hard at this.

'Are you telling me you never told her her husband was dead?'

'She was out.'

'But you knew who she was. You just identified her.'

'I saw her at the hospital last night,' I said, explaining that her little girl was brought in sick.

'Sick.'

I nodded. I said that I understood she'd been out of town.

'But she must have known by today. It wasn't exactly a secret. Someone must have told her. You can't live in this town and have your husband die and no one tell you about it for days.'

I wasn't going to argue that point. There was Mrs Glendinning and her lodgers, after all. He didn't ask me about Gard's belongings. I didn't tell him I'd entered her room.

'Right,' he said, closing his notebook. 'Suicide. Poor thing.' We looked over to the locomotive.

Two men walked into the lights carrying a stretcher.

'We'll need a post-mortem examination,' I said.

'Post-mortem?' He pointed at the body. 'She lay down there and along comes that loco.'

'Her sick daughter,' I said. 'She has the plague. Need to check.'

Moylan rubbed a hand over his face and nodded, as if I'd confirmed his fears that this case was never going to be as simple as it seemed.

'I'll have this one taken to Bacot then,' he said.

'And just one more thing. The envelope. Can I see that as well.'

I followed him to the police wagon. He thrust Mrs Gard's purse at me. 'It's in there. You keep it safe, mind, and return it to me tomorrow.'

I escaped to the cab. Moylan called after me. 'And even if you *don't* find anything more, I'd appreciate you telling me.'

The driver tapped out his pipe and opened the door. God knows what he made of the scene. I eased into the cab's seat made soft by thousands of weary bodies.

On the way back, I opened the purse in the dark and sensed her presence again. I felt around and found the stiff envelope, took it out and held it up so the light from the cab lamp fell across it. It was the same one – the name on the front – torn open now, and empty.

I put it back and snapped the purse shut.

I closed my eyes and it wasn't Mrs Gard's face that haunted me. It was my own daughter's.

Lillian was lying before me on the operating table, her chest fluttering, a rasping noise coming from the tube that protruded grotesquely from her throat.

It had taken all night to reach Herston. My little girl was by that stage delirious, her neck swollen so much she was wheezing. I was frantic throughout the nightmarish journey up the Brisbane River, first by boat and then by carriage. I had to keep telling myself that the new anti-toxin would save her. We just had to get to the children's hospital.

I was so relieved I was crying as I carried Lillian's feverish little body into the diphtheria ward. The doctor on duty gave her the serum and we waited. He was kind and reassuring, but as the hours crept by I became more frightened. Her breathing laboured. When her lips turned lavender we could wait no more. The membrane had spread down her throat and was strangling her.

I held her hand on the operating table and spoke gently, sang the songs she liked, *Hey diddle diddle the cat and the fiddle*, although I knew she was in another place by then, away from the pain. *The cow jumped over the moon.* Her little hand occasionally flexed and I had the impression she was squeezing my fingers, reassuring me. *The little dog laughed.*

The operation ended. Lillian breathed in liquid rasps.

Dr Turner put his hand to her forehead.

The look on his face told me.

And the dish ran away with the spoon.

Her heart failed that day. Sunlight and the drone of insects filtered through the boards. I was holding her hand when she died.

I went home to Dunwich sitting with her small coffin, thinking of her mother.

Maria woke me by shaking me by the shoulder. The sun was already up.

'Blast.'

There was some hot water in a kettle in the wash

room and I made a puddle in the sink, washing and then shaving.

I heard voices. Humphry was on the front verandah.

'A fine view,' called Humphry. 'I could sit here all morning. In fact, I think we should.'

'We'd better get going,' I shouted.

'I'm not going anywhere until we've had tea. Maria's making it now.'

He had sunk into a wicker chair when I came out and sat on the day bed. The harbour twinkled and from this distance seemed quite benign.

Maria brought tea.

'Yes, indeed,' said Humphry, 'let's stay here and drink Maria's splendid tea all morning.'

'You'd be very welcome, Ernie,' she said.

Ernie? When had Humphry become Ernie?

'What sort of wild evening did you have, Lin?' said Humphry. 'You look a little peaked and pale.'

'I went to see a body at the wharves.'

Humphry sat up a little. 'Anyone I know?'

Maria had gone back inside. I whispered, 'Mrs Gard. The room we searched.'

'Plague?'

'No. Suicide. Apparently.' I remembered the purse. It was in my coat. My coat was where? Hanging on the hallway peg. I wondered what Maria would think if she'd seen it.

Humphry sipped his tea and pulled a face.

'Sounds like you have a story to tell me.'

'Not just now.'

'Well, I have a story for you.' He reached into his pocket and brought out a piece torn from *The Northern Miner*.

A sensation was caused in town yesterday when it was reported that a plague-stricken rat had been captured in the vicinity of the Queen's Park Hotel, North Ward. The excitement was further intensified when the news was circulated that Mr Monteith, a well-known local British Association football player, had been bitten on the hand by the rat. It appears that a number of lads were chasing the rat, all eager to obtain the coveted sixpence, and several men also became engaged in the lark. Monteith seized the rat, when it turned and bit him on the knuckle of the forefinger of the right hand. He became alarmed, and went to Dr Bacot, at the Hospital, who cauterised the wound and allowed Monteith to leave. The rat was also sent to the Hospital to be analysed, and Dr Bacot made an examination of it and discovered as the result a quantity of plague bacillus. No steps have been taken for the isolation of Monteith.

'Oh, for Heaven's sake,' I said.

'I thought you'd be amused.'

'I'm flabbergasted.'

'Me, too.'

'A plague rat. Why isn't the man quarantined?'

'Oh that? I'm just worried Monteith didn't get his sixpence. He certainly earned it.'

Another case of plague would suit Humphry, I thought.

'Blast Bacot,' I said. 'What's he think he's doing?'

'I should think he's going out of his way to annoy Turner. Don't worry about him. That microscope of his is a hundred years old and I doubt he knows what plague looks like.' The wicker creaked. Humphry coughed. 'Turner seemed worried about you.'

'Yes, it's this damned tooth. I'll have to get it pulled today.'

'Good-oh.' He leaned back. 'And it's not all bad news. A new shipment of vaccine's come in. One hundred doses. Enough to inoculate all the medicos and nurses in town plus Monteith, if we can find him. And the city fathers.'

'The Mayor?'

'And any passing Members of Parliament.'

'You're not going near Dawson with a needle.'

'Turner's already told me he'd be *vewy gwateful* for my help.'

I never knew whether to believe Humphry or not. Maria came back out.

'Why don't you take the day off?' said Humphry. 'You've earned a day off.'

I knew then that the pair had been talking while I washed.

But things had just become much more complicated, and even if I wanted to, I couldn't afford to take that day off.

I grabbed my coat, felt for the purse and found it with a sense of regret, and Humphry gave me a lift to the Town Hall. My tooth behaved. I actually felt a little better for having slept.

I asked Turner if he'd heard from Dr Bacot yet.

'Bacot sent me the rat this morning. By messenger.'

Well, there was a turn up. Perhaps it was an act of contrition.

'Have you taken a look?'

'Not yet.' He would say nothing more on the subject until he'd seen for himself whether the rat had plague or not.

Turner had sent the boxes of serum to the ice works. He'd kept a dozen doses aside and placed them in his own ice chest, where he'd also placed Bacot's rat.

'So,' he said, 'tell me about last night.'

I told him, and showed him the contents of Mrs Gard's purse. A brush, coins, the envelope. An almost empty small blue bottle of Evening in Paris. The envelope … Where was the letter that had been inside?

'No suicide note?' he said.

'No.'

Turner was watching me carefully. 'Suicides usually leave a note, or at least some clue as to why they did what they did.'

'The envelope?'

'Possibly.'

'Not much of a clue without the letter.'

'Perhaps.'

Turner opened the blue bottle of Evening in Paris. The scent struck me. I recognised it from church, her room, and her body.

'Ever been to Paris?' he said.

I shook my head. Turner sealed the bottle and put the items back. He passed the purse to me and I took it to my office.

I thought about placing it in the cupboard with Gard's canvas bag, but couldn't face that reunion of Mr and Mrs Gard. Instead, I put it in my drawer.

'Come to my office,' said Bacot. He shut the door behind me. 'Drink?'

'No.'

'Sent the damned rat to Turner, didn't he tell you? Nothing I could do with Mr Monteith, if you want to know. It's not up to me to diagnose the damned disease is it? No.'

He poured me a drink anyway and I cradled it.

'Plague hospital's ready. Routh's nitpicking. Can't stand the man. Weak. And Turner, I'd rather not have anything to do with him. He's unreasonable. Sneaky.'

He stared out the window.

'What about Mrs Gard?' I said.

He turned around and looked at me as if I was mad. 'She can't damned well stay here.'

'What? I meant the dead woman from the wharves last night. The post-mortem?'

'Oh, that.' He searched his desk. 'Did that first thing. Before all this.' He found a sheet of paper and held it up to read.

'Yes,' he said. 'Death is most definitely consistent with the poor woman being run over by a train. I'd say that finished her off.'

'Finished her off?'

He put the paper down.

'Well, I thought this was why you had asked for the post-mortem. Do you want to hear it or not?'

'Sorry. Keep going,' I said.

My tooth had started to complain and I took a sip of what might have been undiluted gin and swirled it around my mouth.

Bacot was rustling the paper. 'The walls of the stomach were corroded and the mucous membrane had been entirely eaten away.'

I swallowed. The drink had made my eyes water. 'What caused that then?' I said, trying to catch my breath.

'Could have been acid. Or caustic soda. Not unheard of.' He held up a finger. 'But it wasn't. Indeed not. I found grey powder on the walls of the stomach. Maybe a teaspoon.'

I waited, but he wanted me to ask so I ventured, 'Poison?'

He made a small, scoffing laugh. 'Of course *poison*. *Rat* poison. No doubt about it. I told you there was a craze. The Mayor's been giving the stuff away.'

'Rough on Rats.' And I felt in my pocket and

brought out the label of the poison packet I'd found in Mrs Gard's room.

'Yes, and never mind the blasted rats. Rough way to kill yourself. Which I suppose explains the injuries. Didn't take enough of the poison, you'd look for something quicker too. Very uncomfortable.'

Dear God. I put the label back in my pocket.

'A very persistent suicide.'

I had one more question. 'Did you test for plague?'

'Why?'

'The woman had a room at the boarding house.'

'Boarding house? What the devil are you talking about?'

'The mother of the girl with plague. This is her. Mrs Gard. The suicide. She lived in the boarding house in Sturt-street.'

Bacot digested this for a moment. 'Ridiculous. Only other things of note were unrelated,' and he picked up the post-mortem report again. 'Small kidneys. Some inflammation of the lungs. Syphilis.'

'Syphilis? You must be mistaken. She was a married woman.'

He looked genuinely offended. 'There's no mistake.' He passed me the sheet. 'I see it quite often. Her husband, what's he do?'

'He was a ship's steward.'

'Well, then. He's been playing up.'

I read the report through. It was thorough. 'Well, there's a chance ... ' I began.

'Yes, yes, all bloody right. It'll have to be the kidney. The spleen's pulp,' and he stamped off. He returned with a specimen in a jar.

'You test it. You're the expert now. Nothing to do with me.'

I picked up the jar. 'And the Gard girl?' I'd been afraid to ask.

'Gone. Last night.'

I felt a crushing weight on my soul. 'Oh.'

'Dr Routh's problem now.'

The jar slipped and I just managed to catch it. 'She's alive?' I put it back on the table with shaking hands.

He nodded curtly. 'I wouldn't be too hopeful, though. Anyway,' he said, 'your plague hospital appears to be open for business.'

I asked Humphry to step into my room. The lamps were lit. I closed the door.

I placed the Rough on Rats label between us on the table.

'What's that?' he said.

'It's from Mrs Gard's room. I'm wondering if it was in the envelope.'

'What envelope?'

I pulled the purse from my drawer and put the envelope beside the label.

'This is Mrs Gard's purse.'

Humphry looked at me, frowning.

'It's all right. The police gave it to me. And this,'

I said, pointing at the envelope, 'is the letter her husband asked me to give to her.'

He looked at the items and then looked at me as if I really had gone mad.

'It's simple.' I picked up the label and plopped it in the envelope, and took it out again. 'Her husband had sent her this label. That was his last letter to her. A poison label.'

'Oh, I see,' said Humphry, clearly not seeing.

'It's a threat. Or a suggestion. He wanted her dead.'

'The steward wanted to kill his wife,' said Humphry, 'so he sent her a letter with a label in it?'

'Yes.'

'Yes. That would certainly do me in.' Humphry looked very closely at me.

'Well, what would you do if you were quarantined on an island and wanted to kill your wife?'

Humphry reached forward and picked up the label and envelope. He seemed to be considering the question seriously. He held the items up to the light. 'You say you delivered this letter to Mrs Gard.'

I nodded.

'Presumably before the man was dead.'

'Well, he gave it to me before he died, yes.'

'And he didn't know he was dying.'

'Right.'

'But he wanted his wife dead.'

'Yes.'

'And now she is.'

'Yes.'

'And their daughter has plague.'

'That may have been a coincidence.'

'I thought it may have been an Act of God.' Humphry held the envelope up to the light again.

'Not if Gard killed his wife. You see?'

'It lets God off the hook? Is that what this is about?' Humphry took the label and turned it blank side up. He then upended the envelope and tapped it.

'What is it?' I asked. He had his nose to the paper. He crooked a finger and pointed. I rubbed my eyes, but could see nothing.

'Fleas,' he said. He poked them with a finger. 'Dead.'

I took a magnifying glass from my drawer. There were half a dozen black dots. Humphry might have then realised what that meant to me.

'Ah, but it really doesn't matter now though, does it?' he said. 'It's probably just a coincidence.'

With Humphry almost anxious at my elbow, I went to Turner's empty office and fetched some tweezers, collected a flea and cut it open with a scalpel on a glass plate. I slid it under the microscope. There were cells there, but they were so desiccated it was impossible to tell if any was plague bacterium.

How did the fleas get into the envelope? Did God, nature or Gard put them there? The fact remained that I'd delivered them.

'It doesn't matter now,' said Humphry, at my

shoulder. 'What matters *now* is stopping the disease spreading.'

But I squeezed my head between my hands and felt the vortex grip me and drag me further down towards its fluttering core.

chapter twelve

Willy and two other brats,
Licked up all the Rough on Rats,
Father said, when mother cried,
Don't worry, dear, they'll die outside.

Anon

THE GARD GIRL HAD BECOME the plague hospital's first patient and starched nurses circled her bed and attended her every whimper.

'She won't last the week, you know,' said Routh, who spent most of the time complaining about the facilities.

It was true, the tent made a poor hospital. It was cool at night and stifling during the day, but at this stage it was quiet. I thought Bacot, though, had done a good job in equipping it and the child was probably the best cared for plague patient in the colonies. Still, she suffered.

I sat with her at Three Mile Creek all that next night. Fever and spasms twisted her small body.

'Mum–meee,' she cried out, and I gave her a little ether and drained the buboes again, but it seemed to do nothing to ease the pain that might well stop her little heart. It certainly put a strain on mine.

In the morning, though, she took some water.

I felt relieved enough to have breakfast. Routh brought his plate over and sat down with a wheeze beside me.

'Word of advice,' he said to his eggs. 'Don't expect them to be grateful. They'll hate you for this.'

He brought a forkful of egg to his mouth and it slid off. He sighed and tried again. 'They'll hate you for trying to help them. Mark my words.'

'Who hates me?' I said.

'Them,' and he docked with the fork successfully, and then jabbed it in the air in the direction of town. 'The public. If not yet, then they will. If we have more patients. And I dare say we will if this blasted Dr Turner has his way.'

He said this without looking at me. His face wobbled over the plate.

'Why?' I said.

'Why? You saw what happened on the island. I've seen it before. Many times. No one likes being quarantined. Especially if they think they're going to die. And the people you separate them from like it even less. Do you have a gun?'

'Of course not.'

'Word of advice,' he said. 'Get a gun.' He took some bread and mopped up the rest of the eggs with it, shovelling the lot into his mouth.

'Do *you* have a gun?' I said.

He nodded, chewing, and gave me a wink. 'And I suppose being stuck out here has its benefits,' he said. 'Dr Bacot has sent us a splendid cook.' He rose and carried his plate back to the table where the food was laid out.

I took a sip of my tea and left before he returned.

Back in the near-empty ward, the child was still asleep, thankfully, and I watched for a time the painful rise and fall of her chest. A nurse sat beside her and I said I'd just lie down over there on that bed, and if I dozed off to wake me when the little girl stirred.

During the previous night, I'd tried to make sense of the chain of events that had brought her here.

Of all people, it was Gard who'd been ordered to help me move Storm. It was Gard I'd somehow exposed to the disease. I'd then delivered his fateful letter and transferred the disease as effectively as a rat. Despite Humphry dismissing the theory, I couldn't see any other connection. The child caught the disease from the letter I'd delivered, and that same letter and the removal of her daughter – as well, perhaps, as news of Gard's death – all this had caused Mrs Gard to take poison *and* throw herself on the railway tracks. A breeze brought a hint of Evening in Paris through the tent flap and a breath touched my cheek, in small puffs.

Humphry was shaking me. It took me some time to drag myself away from the blessing of sleep, and when I managed to sit, I had to hold my head in both hands.

Humphry was saying Maria had been worried and wanted to know if I was coming home. I nodded, and stood.

I went over to the girl. She was still asleep and her breathing much easier. I touched her forehead. Her fever had actually come down.

And so I went home. As I sat beside Humphry in his buggy, the sea air revived me and I told him my new germ theory – the one in which I was either God's or Gard's agent.

'The way you describe it, it sounds more like a conspiracy than an Act of God,' said Humphry. 'But I'm sure there's a more rational way of looking at it.'

'Not this time.'

In morning light Humphry and I sat at the kitchen table as Maria filled the teapot from the steaming stove-black fountain.

'How is the little girl?' said Maria. She had one of those flat Irish voices, but I'd always found the lightness of it powerfully attractive. She didn't look at me. She wore a blue winter dress, rather formal for indoors. As she stirred the pot I stared at her forearms. I hadn't noticed before how brown they'd become. She must have been out in the vegetable garden.

'Better,' I said. I asked where Allan and the girls were.

'School.'

I tried to think what day it was. Monday?

Maria, my wife, wore her long dark hair in a tight bun, French style. As she turned I noticed also that her face was brown and she looked healthier than I'd seen her for some time, although there were bags under her eyes. So she hadn't slept much either. I scratched the stubble on my chin.

As she put the pot down between Humphry and me, she gave me a smile. When had I stopped noticing these things? Well, of course, I knew when. I turned to Humphry and said there must be many things waiting for us to do.

'Should we be going?'

Maria paused at the cupboard.

'Well, no,' said Humphry. 'Wouldn't you know, there's actually nothing to do at the moment.'

Maria brought over the good cups and saucers.

Humphry said, 'Funny isn't it how things run on and on at such a pace and then,' he clapped a hand on the table rattling the cups, 'it stops. Anyway, I don't know about you, Lin, but I need this cup of tea.'

I saw them exchange a glance. I wondered about conspiracies. I knew they both thought I might be mad. And I knew why.

'You're right, I suppose. I need a wash anyway.'

'Take the rest of the day,' said Humphry. 'Up all night tending the sick. Can't be expected to work twenty-four hours a day. I'll tell Turner.'

Yes, I said.

But the thought of being home alone all day with

Maria made me afraid. There were some things I couldn't face.

There was another long silence as Maria spun the teapot left, then right, and poured. She leaned over me to do this and I could smell that womanly smell of soap from the laundry. Her brown jaw was firm, a small nose, an attractive wife.

She poured herself a cup and sat at the end of the table and we politely sipped our tea.

She had an aristocratic habit of crooking a little finger as she drank. I used to say that I rescued her from Inniskillen and she'd say I kidnapped her.

Our little joke.

She missed her family, of course she did, and I often wondered why she'd married me, against her father's wishes, a young doctor from the colonies, but it seemed a long time ago and so far away. Four children ago.

'I don't know what the girl's name is.' I said this out loud. It had just occurred to me no one had told me, and it wasn't on her paperwork. Just 'Child: Gard'.

'You know, I never thought to ask the mother,' said Humphry, and I caught another fleeting look from Maria to Humphry.

I found myself staring at Humphry and he gave me a hard look back.

'You look terrible, Lin,' he said. 'You never were a pretty chap, but by God you're a sight. When was the last time you slept?'

'You woke me up only hours ago.'

'Did I? Well, don't blame me for your appearance. Maria, what are you doing to care for this husband of yours?'

If that had come from anyone else Maria might have flown at him, but she simply laughed then, knowing Humphry. And I smiled to see it.

'I think he's having an *affaire de coeur*,' she said, her eyes on me.

'I suspect something like that, too. The hours he keeps.'

The laughter petered away, and Humphry said, 'I have a better theory about the Gards. Want to hear it?'

I shook my head, looking at Maria, but she leaned forward and Humphry pressed on.

'There'd be fleas on the quarantine station goats,' he said. I shook my head again, but he said, 'Listen, it's actually along the same line as yours.'

Gard discovered the truth about his treacherous wife, he said.

'Treacherous?'

Humphry looked at Maria. 'Fallen,' he said. Perhaps the men talked. There was little else to do. And when those sorts of men talked, it always turned to women.

Gard listened coolly, said Humphry, but he had a burning rage as he recognised the woman they bragged about. The next day he shot a goat for the camp and put some fleas into a bottle.

Humphry rubbed his hands together, pleased with his theory.

'This is the best bit,' he said.

That night, with Storm in a fever, he pressed the bottle to Storm's thigh. Next day he recaptured some of them! It explained how Gard might have himself caught plague, said Humphry, if a flea escaped and bit him. Anyway, he put the fleas in the envelope with the poison label and had the honourable and reliable Dr Row deliver the message. It was cunning: a suggestion, a threat and an attempt at murder all in one. It worked. Mrs Gard, filled with remorse and guilt, took what Gard knew was at hand – Rough on Rats.

'Why would she take what she feared?' asked Maria.

'The power of suggestion,' said Humphry.

Listening to him, I wondered if Humphry wasn't inviting me to question the absurdity of the theory. Maria, though, had a hand over her mouth, shocked and fascinated by Humphry's story.

Humphry continued. The agony was too great and she took herself off to the rail yards and waited for a locomotive. Gard himself had by then succumbed to plague from the very fleas he'd enlisted as assassins.

Humphry slapped the table and sat back, pleased with himself and certain I would be comforted.

'What about the child?' I said. 'The man wouldn't put his daughter at risk, surely.'

'He wasn't thinking about his daughter,' said Humphry, lighting a cigarette. 'Only revenge. And if that's the case, it shows you what a scoundrel the man was and that even death from plague was too good for him.'

I supposed it took the act out of God's hands and put it in a man's, which should have been some comfort to me. I told Humphry it was a good theory.

'Good? It's better than good. It's damned perfect. If the man was still alive I'd shake his hand and put him on the end of a rope. I should have been a barrister.' But he winked at me.

Maria poured more tea.

I said there were a lot of 'ifs' in his theory.

'*Avec des "si" on mettrait Paris en bouteille*,' said Maria.

'What was that?' said Humphry, looking from me to Maria.

'With "ifs" one could put Paris in a bottle,' she told him.

He picked up his tea and finished it. 'Is that right?' he said, looking at me. 'Sounds a bit like "If wishes were horses, beggars would ride", and I can take a hint.'

'No, it's just an expression. Please don't leave,' said Maria.

'I do have to go,' said Humphry. I rose. 'You're staying,' he told me.

'I'll see you out.' I was too tired to argue.

When Humphry was gone I went out to the bathroom. The house was silent. There were things to be said. I watched her iron a fresh shirt.

I couldn't find the words, somehow.

I stood at the door in my undershirt and trousers, braces hanging loose, and she turned and brought me the shirt, pressing it into my chest. I felt those cool forearms against me and she was looking directly into my eyes.

'Why don't you go into the bedroom,' she said. 'And lie down.'

But I heard myself say, as if from a great distance, that I really had to get to work.

When I got to my office I laid my head on my desk and slept until well after noon.

My throbbing tooth woke me.

That afternoon I learnt from Turner that no one had claimed Mrs Gard's body. Everyone had forgotten about her husband's possessions, the bag in my cupboard, and I realised I still had her purse, despite my promise to return it to Moylan.

The newspapers that day had devoted just as many column inches to plague as to war. The first case of plague in the town was referred to as an 'Unfortunate Occurrence', but one not entirely unexpected. There was no mention of the girl's parents, and her name wasn't even published. The plague news from Sydney and Brisbane was more of a sensation, apparently.

The council had begun pouring more resources into sweeping the streets, fumigating sheds around the wharves, knocking on doors and inspecting sewers and back yards. The leaflets I'd composed and council had approved long ago were finally rolling off Willmett's presses, more rats were being found and incinerated, ships fumigated and so much carbolic poured into drains that the dead fish were again piling up along the Strand and not even the Chinamen could bury them all this time.

'The town might be clean,' said Humphry, 'but it smells like death.'

Like a heavily laden steamer, McCreedy walked with an easy rolling grace.

I was startled, though, that he had managed to appear in the centre of my office without my noticing.

'Sit, sit,' he said, looking about the room as if for the first time.

'I was about to come to your office.' I rummaged around my desk.

'Couldn't wait all day. Let's get the damned thing over with now.'

He came over to the desk and picked up a framed photograph.

'Your girl?' he said.

'My wife.'

'I didn't know you were married.'

He sat in the chair across from me and leaned back, resting hands like twin spiders on his belly.

'Well, I suppose that's that then. I suppose she must have plague if she's in the plague hospital,' but the Mayor didn't seem to enjoy his own joke. 'This serum for the plague. It works?'

'Yes.'

'You've had it?'

'Of course.'

'And it's being given to mayors. Well, well, this must be serious.'

I prepared the syringe.

'The captains,' he rambled, 'leaders of society and civilisation, people needed to keep the ship off the rocks. You follow me? Some don't want it. I could name names. They don't believe it's plague at all.'

'Mr Dawson?'

'He's just one.'

I took a teaspoon of yellow serum up into the syringe. Where was Dawson? He seemed to appear just before a disaster. I should be thankful I hadn't seen him.

'No point protecting yourself against something that doesn't exist, I suppose,' McCreedy was saying, and his hands did a little spidery dance on his stomach. 'People aren't always aware of what's good for them.'

'Please undo your trousers, Mr McCreedy.'

I didn't give him the choice. The Mayor took his jab in the flab of skin above the hip, talking throughout.

Must hardly be a blasted rat left alive in the town, he was saying, the money being dished out to grubby boys for ... *ow* ... the bounty. And what were Turner's intentions now? Was he still on about the blasted railway? He was here to scuttle it on Mr Philp's orders, that's what Dawson thought.

I said I didn't know. I supposed I wasn't a good spy.

McCreedy did up his trousers and collected his coat.

'Dr Row, your future is very much tied up in this business, you follow me? You're a servant of the town's ratepayers, just as I am. They pay your salary, and it's your job to protect them from blasted quacks.'

And the plague, I would have thought.

'Turner's anything but a quack. Zealous, perhaps,' I said.

'Well, just keep an eye on him. I'm relying on you to let me know if he has anything in mind that might jeopardise this town.'

He sailed off.

I sat. For some time. On a whim I fetched Gard's bag from the cupboard. I stood it behind my desk in case someone came in, but all I could do was stare at it. And what if I did open it? What if I found something that somehow explained Mrs Gard's death, the plague that seemed to have visited the entire Gard family? Wouldn't I be even more culpable, by not having opened the thing in the first place when there was a chance to prevent it? There was a world of opportunities in the bag, but the time for them had passed and I couldn't face knowing. I put the bag back and locked the cupboard and sat, waiting for something else to happen. My tooth was giving me a holiday. I hoped it was a good omen. I put my head on the table, but couldn't sleep.

There'd been no sign of plague in Mrs Gard's kidney and she was buried in the Presbyterian section of the West End cemetery. I didn't attend. As it turned out, the Reverend Kerr and the undertaker were the only ones who did.

Turner had examined the woman's child and said she had signs of anaemia, probably caused by leech worms in the bowels, which would complicate her recovery. He took a faecal sample for microscopic examination. I went back to Three Mile Creek and stayed there late in the evenings, risking my neck with a bicycle ride home in the dark.

It seemed for a few days that the child might be the first and last patient for the plague hospital, but the next Saturday the *Bobby Towns* returned from Picnic Bay with an English Church minister so delirious with fever that the people with him thought he was possessed.

He let go a stream of obscenities when Humphry examined him at the hospital, and as soon as plague was confirmed Bacot packed him off in the middle of the night to Three Mile Creek.

Humphry and Bacot had a falling out over this. The Reverend was a friend of Humphry's and Bacot was probably just being his acid self.

I was more worried for the girl. The Reverend Ward in the condition Humphry described would be bad company for her.

This second case worried Turner more than the first.

The Gard child fitted neatly with Turner's theories about overcrowding and filth. Her disease was more logical if we discounted the link to West Point, said Turner. There were rats in town with plague in their blood. The child was three and inhabited an unsanitary boarding house. Beneath the house flowed an open drain and there was barely room between the earth and the floorboards for a cat.

The Reverend Ward, though, had no business catching plague.

He lived in a clean house on Melton Hill. If he had any connection with infection it was an arm's-length one with his parishioners, and they should be the ones to succumb first.

When Turner had Humphry and me inspect the *Bobby Towns*, the rectory and the church, we found no rats, at least none we could catch. We laid baits, had the launch and church fumigated, and the parishioners who'd been at the picnic with him were told to report the first signs of fever. We didn't quarantine or inoculate them because their contact was slight. It was unlikely they shared the minister's mystery flea.

It was worrying.

So was my tooth. The ache came, and I swore I'd get it pulled, and then it went, and I found any excuse to put it off again.

'Are you all right?' Humphry and Turner would ask.

I was spending the evenings at the plague hospital, as was Humphry now. The fever kept the Reverend Ward blaspheming and the nurses sometimes had to cover their ears and flee the tent. On his hands, feet and face were many light red spots about the size of peas, which Routh insisted were mosquito bites.

While the Reverend burned, the girl hovered more peacefully between life and death. She would not die of plague, but she might well starve to death or one of her organs might give out.

Humphry and I sat one whole night beside our patients at opposite ends of the tent.

By this time, Turner had developed a set against Flinders-lane and now that he had two plague patients, he decided to act.

Chinatown was a place I had been ignoring as much as possible. It wasn't somewhere I wanted to investigate, but Turner insisted it had to be disinfected, and one stuffy and overcast morning we gathered a small company of council workers and armed them with kerosene, matches, shovels, brooms and buckets of lime wash, rat poison, and sulphur.

We stood at the Denham-street end, literally a stone's throw from the rear of the Town Hall and Post Office. I could see the closed and covered window of my office.

Turner gave a small speech.

Behind him was a jumble of rusty lean-tos. A greasy kind of smoke wafted down from corrugated-iron chimneys, drifting through the lane. A small muddy trench dug by a hand or a heel oozed grey water. There was little sign of life, except for a dog with three legs that limped carefully around the potholes away from us.

Turner said the lane was a possible source for infection. Did each man have his instructions and did he understand them?

There were a dozen workers dressed head to toe – in boots, white overalls, and hats – and they nodded as one. Each carried a white gauze mask and looked as though they might have come from the moon or the deep sea.

'If you come across any person, please explain what you are doing and ask them politely to leave,' said Turner. 'If they protest, explain that under the Health Act the police have the power to force them to leave. If they put up any resistance, call for the police.'

The two jaunty constables, Clark and O'Donnell, stood behind him with their batons on display.

We didn't expect to find many people. No one was supposed to live here, and most of the business went on at night, when Flinders-lane apparently seethed with slinky Chinamen who ran opium and gambling dens, sly grog shops and prostitutes.

It looked nowhere near as exotic by day.

It had been relatively easy to get support for that morning's raid on Chinatown, simply because it confirmed what many people believed about the plague – that is, if they believed in the plague at all. The consensus seemed to be that it was incubated by Chinamen. And 'Chinamen' meant anyone with Asian features. In Townsville, many Chinamen were actually Japanese.

Opinion was more divided over how the plague should be contained. A few people had fled. Some were burning drums of oil in their yards to ward off miasmas. Quarantining, inoculation and rubbish disposal were viewed with suspicion bordering on hostility.

But no one opposed ransacking Chinatown.

Turner and I led the team into the street, and the now masked workers fanned out behind us.

On our left was Ross Creek. I couldn't see it, but the air felt heavier on that side. The lane was supposed to run in a straight line in front of us, but I couldn't see the end because of the jumble of shacks and gin stalls shoehorned into such a small space. The effect was a labyrinth of walls made of crates, iron and flattened kerosene tins. There were obviously many others in the council who'd turned a blind eye to the place.

'It reminds me of Shanghai, Row,' said Turner, sniffing the air. I had my mask on as we stood in the middle of the lane. There was a lot of crashing behind us. Turner's white coat was stippled with little black flies.

'Happy memories?' I asked.

He nodded. I supposed smells could have that effect, but the only memory I associated with something that smelled like a corpse was of a corpse. The creek was undoubtedly choked with dead fish, faeces and rotting fruit, perhaps punctuated by a bloated horse.

'That smell, like burnt sugar,' said Turner. 'Opium. Don't you smell it?'

Thankfully, no.

Turner walked over to one shack and peeled back the corrugated-iron door.

Inside was another smell even more overpowering: the sharp smell of urine. When my eyes adjusted I could make out rows of empty bunks. The only light came from the doorway behind us and old nail holes in the tin roof and walls. When I walked, the floor gave with a sickly sponginess. I couldn't see my feet in the gloom. Something scuttled from one corner to another.

I found Turner leaning over a bunk and realised there was someone lying on it.

'Is he dead?'

Turner poked and the figure sighed. He turned away and picked up something from a beer crate. A pipe. On the crate were other things I didn't recognise.

I followed Turner back out into the lane and gulped the sweetish air. He called over O'Donnell.

'There's a man in there. Get him out.'

I heard the constable swear after he entered the shack. He emerged with the man under one arm and that look of distaste on his face that I remembered from when we opened Gard's coffin.

'What do I do with him?' O'Donnell said.

The man was white, I saw. And reasonably well dressed. God knew what he was doing in that place.

'Just get him out of the lane,' said Turner. 'Put him in

the shade. Try not to let anyone near him. And see if you can find out where he lives.'

O'Donnell dragged the man around the rubbish now piling up in the middle of the lane. Turner wanted it all done before a crowd could gather, but that seemed unlikely. Already a few boys had gathered at the end of the lane to watch these strange white creatures build bonfires in the street.

Even the walls of the shacks were stripped of newspaper. Horse-hair mattresses, crates and bunks, chairs and tables, clothing, anything combustible, was thrown on to the pile. When the first few shacks were emptied and lime wash had been slopped over the walls, sulphur was burned inside and the piles of rubbish were doused with kerosene and lit, to the cheers of the boys. A yellow and black smoke blew about us. I wondered what the Reverend Kerr would make of this apocalyptic vision.

An old Chinaman had come down the lane clicking his tongue furiously and waving his arms. He stood there and then suddenly took a swipe at a passing worker. Clark saw this and charged the man with his baton, chasing him in circles until Turner told him to stop. I could have laughed, but saw the old man was weeping.

With Clark at his shoulder ready to thump him, the old man came up to Turner and began yabbering away. Turner patiently pretended to listen, I thought, and then, to my astonishment, began yabbering back.

The man staggered as if hit. He probably had never met a white man who could speak his language. They spoke for a short time and the old man ended up bowing and retreating.

'What was that about?' I asked.

'He wanted to know why we were destroying his business.' Turner looked a little shaken.

'What's his business?'

'He says he sells women.'

'What did you tell him?'

'I told him to find a more honourable business.'

A few disorientated drunks lurched towards us, but seeing the flames and the creatures in white decided to exit the other way. O'Donnell returned to tell us that a fair-sized crowd had gathered at the end of the lane and what should he do with them?

'Are they causing trouble?' said Turner.

'I don't suppose so. Not yet.'

The work went on and we gradually moved up the lane. It might have been more convenient to torch the lot, but the shacks clung like ticks to the backs of Townsville's grandest buildings.

Within four hours we were looking back on our handiwork. Our white coveralls were grimy. The lime-washed shacks looked ghostly through the swirling smoke, and the feeling I had from the crowd around us, the white and yellow faces, was a disturbing mixture of excitement, fear, and resentment.

For a short time, there was cause for optimism, if one wanted it. We still had our two plague patients, but the council seemed to have had a change of heart. The effort of cleansing Chinatown would have to be rewarded.

But the conflagration in Flinders-lane might well have had the opposite effect.

People began to fall ill.

Within days, and in quick succession, the plague hospital started to fill. First came John O'Connell from North Ward, James Waldie who sold firewood, Fanny Healy from German Gardens, a married woman Henrietta Walker, John Burke from Cluden, and eight-year-old Francis Hipworth from South Townsville. They took the miserable ambulance ride to Three Mile Creek, their homes were fumigated with sulphur, and their families locked in with the smell for twenty-one days.

The removal of young Hipworth was the first to turn violent.

His mother pleaded, the family cried. They wanted to know if they'd ever see the boy again, but weren't satisfied with my assurances. The police had to draw their batons as Francis was loaded screaming into the ambulance. His father took a blow to the head. As the ambulance left, the mother turned to me and, with her eyes, wished me dead. It shook me all the more because I'd felt I was beyond shaking.

A butcher from Alderman Castling's shop near the Victoria Bridge came down with plague and that put the wind up council.

By that stage, no Chinaman nor black had been infected. At least, none had been reported, which I supposed was a completely different thing, but it was proof to some that the disease going around wasn't plague at all.

The smell of sulphur, burning rubbish and burning rats hung about town in the mornings and it must have been hard for those who didn't believe in plague to shake the physical evidence of apocalypse. Even Dawson kept a low profile.

As the new patients arrived at Three Mile Creek, Mrs Gard's daughter appeared to improve.

The Reverend Ward began to fail.

chapter thirteen

You may think I'm exaggerating. It's true, modern medicine allows me to dispassionately describe a disease by its cause, effect and treatment, as if I could pin it to a cork board to study and say 'Yes, that's it' and move on. But medicine, if it is a science, can't describe the horror of a bewildered child dying in agony of, say, diphtheria or whooping cough or one of any number of diseases. The truth is that these ancient diseases are monsters, more real and terrible than any dragon or devil or creation of Mary Shelley. So I want you to understand why I say this; that I also believe that I am a man of science, and that the hairs stood on the back of my neck when I entered the plague tent.

Dr Linford Row,
from his unpublished memoirs

HUMPHRY HAD FOR SEVERAL days insisted on tending the Reverend Ward himself. Now the minister's condition was deteriorating and Turner let Humphry stay by the bed, even though it left us with more of the work.

One afternoon, with dark clouds blowing in from the sea and smelling of rain, Routh sent for help. The note was addressed to me, Routh by then refusing to deal directly with Turner.

I gathered from the note that Bacot wouldn't free another doctor and Humphry wouldn't leave the Reverend's side, and he needed a second opinion on two patients. Medicines were late, so could I collect them and lend a hand?

No cab could take me to Three Mile Creek. Humphry had his buggy with him. There were no patients waiting for the ambulance, so I had to take the Carbine. I stopped at the public hospital to collect a box of laudanum.

The plague hospital might have been a military camp now. The tents were square and tight, centred precisely inside a barbed-wire fence creating an illusion of order. The glare from the canvas infected the scrub around it and lit the face of Routh so he seemed to be in a fever himself as he accompanied me first to his office with the supplies, and then to the lone tent to which the Reverend had been moved.

He complained about the lack of staff and what Bacot, Turner and the Epidemic Board weren't doing about it.

'Is it adequate, though?' I said.

'Adequate?' He pointed his two chins at the tents we passed. 'Primitive, I'd call it.'

'Better than West Point, surely.'

'Hmm.'

'How are you treating him?'

'The Reverend? Laudanum for the pain. What would we do without it, eh?'

Routh wanted me to go to the main tent to see his patients, particularly the Gard child whom he thought was fully recovered. He seemed keen to discharge her. He might need the bed soon, he said, the rate Turner was incarcerating people.

'I'll see Humphry first,' I said, so we cut across the grass towards a lone policeman, who got up from his chair and began fiddling with a rope that tied a gate to an inner fence, a loose affair hardly likely to stop anyone who wanted to, say, step over it. He added some sense that things were under control, but there was little chance of this patient escaping.

We stopped outside the canvas flap of the smaller tent. The Reverend Ward had had to be isolated to spare everyone further distress. He'd stopped swearing, said Routh, but his screams were torturous. We pulled up our surgical masks. And then hesitated a moment at the entrance.

'Poor bugger,' was Routh's final, muffled opinion, and we stepped from the modern world to meet this monster from the past.

The air was hot and drowsy with ether. There was nothing to stir it. The light that soaked through the canvas made every person in that tent appear drained of blood. A nurse sat on a hard hospital chair by a bed with a wet towel in her hand and a basin at her feet. Humphry was hunched over a table with some papers and bottles and might well have been asleep. On the bed lay a form covered in a white sheet.

Humphry stood suddenly and met us by the bed. All of us were perspiring now. I had to take my glasses off and wipe them.

'Where's Turner?' said Humphry. His eyes were red and had dark puffy sacks beneath them.

'Widding the town of wats,' I said. A poor joke at Turner's expense, and I felt ashamed as soon as I said it, but Routh tittered so no harm done.

Humphry summarised the medical history of the Reverend William Ward, minister of the Church of England. The Reverend Ward was taken ill five days before with abdominal discomfort, fever, chills, and such. Bacot found swollen glands in the groin and Humphry had serum taken, confirming *pasteurella pestis*.

Blasted Bacot had sent him to Three Mile Creek in the middle of the night.

'You can imagine the to-do all this caused,' added Routh. Bacot had now sent a number of patients off into the night, to Turner's disgust.

Humphry finished by saying the patient had been given vaccine, the buboes had been drained, his condition had deteriorated and it appeared the germ had entered his blood system and there were signs of septicaemia in the past few hours.

'It's not easy, you know, providing this sort of care,' said Routh. 'I need more doctors if people are going to end up like this.'

Humphry ignored Routh and nodded past me at the bed.

The Reverend Ward's eyes were open and watching us, which gave me a start. I leaned forward to see his face better. The conjunctiva was no longer white; it was livid, and I could see the tracks of bloody tears which had run down his face and puddled in an ear. His hair was wet where the nurse had been dabbing his forehead. His eyes flicked from me to Humphry. I pulled my mask away and gave him what I hoped was a reassuring smile, introduced myself.

I was astounded when the poor chap smiled back. His gums were bleeding and the blood had stained his teeth. Routh gave a small cough and excused himself from the tent.

The Reverend mouthed a word several times.

'Do you have pain? You do?' Humphry said. 'I'll find some laudanum.'

I pulled my mask up and leaned closer. The man's face looked like a pudding sprinkled with raisins, the small black patches of dead tissue, smaller than liver spots, signs of the disease in its advanced stage. I reached out my hand to touch his face, to feel if the flesh had any spring left in it.

I was staring at his open mouth when he coughed, and as I jumped back his body arched and I swear I heard his sinews crack.

The nurse was trying to force him flat on the bed, but the cough produced a seizure that created more pain, prolonging the spasm; bloody tears ran down his face and dark veins boiled at his temples.

Humphry hurried over with a syringe and quickly jabbed it into the Reverend's thigh, and after an eternal minute his body relaxed and settled back on the bed, the only sound a wet rasp from the man's chest. And my own heartbeat.

'That nearly finished him,' said Humphry, his voice slurred from fatigue. He leaned over to put a stethoscope to the man's chest and nodded at my gown.

I looked down and there was a fine spray of blood over it and I suspected it was over my mask as well. I took off my glasses and wiped the mist of blood from the lenses. I had no reason to fear for myself. I'd had several courses of Haffkine's vaccine now. Nevertheless, I tried to slow my breathing and wait for the palpitations to subside.

The sheet had fallen from the upper part of Ward's body and he was naked underneath, unable no doubt to tolerate the clinging touch of a gown. His thin mottled chest rose and fell painfully.

'How much laudanum do you have over there?'

'Enough.'

I pulled the sheet from his groin and saw the buboes were leaking from where they'd been earlier drained. The two bruises joined at the pubis. I gently replaced the sheet and the Reverend shuddered at the touch.

I turned to Humphry to say something. He was looking down at the Reverend and suddenly reached past me.

I turned and saw the man had raised his head and chest again well off the bed, and his eyes and mouth were open. Humphry grabbed him by the shoulder, but couldn't push him back. It looked as if the man was choking. His arms were straight and rigid, as if desperate to hold on to the soul that was trying to flee the wretched body. He trembled. He made no sound. The nurse looked terrified.

'I can't stand this,' said Humphry, and turned away as the nurse held the man despite her own horror.

I said nothing, but stood transfixed by the scene; a bloody drool ran from Ward's mouth as he struggled with the thing that was eating him.

Humphry appeared with the syringe and in one smooth motion plunged it into the man's thigh.

He stood back.

'How much was that?' I said.

Humphry wiped a sleeve across his forehead. 'Enough.'

The nurse had given up and the three of us stood back and simply watched.

I can tell you, I don't know at what point the man died. I thought I heard a sigh, but the eyes and mouth remained open, the back arched, arms outstretched.

After what must have been a minute, but could have been longer, Humphry stepped forward and tried to gently push the man back, but his contortions appeared to have become locked with death. Humphry put a stethoscope to the Reverend's chest, shook his head and turned away.

The nurse straightened the cadaver as best she could, and she eventually turned her head and let out one small sob herself.

I pulled the stained sheet over him, and knew that would be the image that would stay with me, the one my mind would tuck away in the gallery it saved for special horrors.

I stayed for the funeral. The Reverend Ward was buried at the cemetery by the Reverend Walsh, a Methodist minister who acted in an interdenominational capacity as the plague hospital chaplain. Humphry made a fine speech and I think he was relieved it was over.

The burial was done at an almost undignified pace. The Reverend's arched body was wrapped in a sheet soaked with sublimate and somehow fitted into a coffin with quicklime packed around the body, the coffin nailed shut and buried in a deep grave in the sandy soil. Lime was thrown over the coffin and, within an hour of death, there was a cross on the plague cemetery's first grave.

Humphry found a cot in the staff tent, and we sat and shared his flask. And then he lay down and went to sleep.

I went to see the Gard child. She was better, but not well enough to leave. Routh grumbled, but I wasn't going to release her until I had somewhere to send her, in any case. I was relieved that she would survive, but that good news couldn't erase the bad and I rode back to town to break it to Turner.

Turner was tormenting the Mayor.

'For God's sake, I'm doing everything I can,' said McCreedy, who then attacked Turner about the heavy-handed treatment of ratepayers, the reports of police using batons to enforce quarantine.

I told them my news. It quietened them both for a while.

Dawson's dark presence had apparently flitted off to Charters Towers for some urgent railway meetings. The plague crisis in Townsville had resurrected interest in the direct route to Bowen. The stagnation of trade through Townsville's declared port must have helped, turning plague into Dawson's ally. His alliance with McCreedy might well have been shaky now, but this was wishful thinking on my part, too. I never felt comfortable with Dawson hanging about. I still believed he would somehow get me, in revenge for West Point.

Word of the plague death spread. I noticed that in the street, in dealing with each other, people seemed to be trying hard to prove things were normal. Personal greetings were exaggerated, men were thicker in the hotel bars and laughed louder, and there appeared to be more women out shopping on Friday morning. There was a jagged edge to the town, as if everyone might become hysterical all at once.

That night I went home with four small bottles of serum and a large bag of boiled lollies. Maria rolled up her sleeve and smiled for the girls, but they weren't convinced and she had to hold each of them tight for my needle. Allan was a stoic, but fled to the front verandah as soon as the inoculation was done.

Maria avoided my eyes and saw to the girls. I gave Allan some time, and found him on the front steps beside a carbide lamp. He had an enormous moth in his hands.

'*Coscinocera*,' I said, remembering the moth in Turner's office. 'Is it dead?'

He nodded.

I sat beside him and started talking ridiculously about moths. I was surprised at how much I remembered from Turner's monologues. I made up a story about a silver butterfly that flew at night towards the moon. I felt him leaning against me and when I looked down I saw he was asleep. I picked him up and carried him into his room. Everyone was asleep. I put him to bed, closed his hand over a sixpence, and lay down gently beside him, hearing his gentle steady breathing.

I left before he woke, before anyone woke.

Later that morning I was still in my office when I heard the ambulance coming fast and stopping with a clang. I went downstairs and found it in the middle of the street, the horses already sweating, a few people gathering around, as they do for ambulances.

Turner had followed me down. It seemed at first that the plague might have come to the Town Hall itself, but the driver who met me on the steps told me a guest from the Commercial Hotel had ridden horseback to see Bacot at the hospital, to tell him the landlord had a fever. Bacot had said that it was nothing to do with him, and sent the ambulance to collect one of the Government doctors, who could tell whether the man needed to come to him or go to the plague hospital.

'I'll go,' I said, but Turner said he'd join me, so we fetched our bags and climbed in.

The driver swung the horses around and took us at a gallop through the main street and over the bridge.

'Are you all right, Row?' Turner said.

I had a white-knuckled grip on the side. 'I was thinking that every time I get into a carriage with you, I take my life in my hands.'

Mrs McLean sat beside her husband. 'Constitution of a steam engine.' She dabbed her eyes.

But he appeared to be out of steam. His breath was a rattle and he hadn't the strength to cough, choking instead, his wife wiping away the bloody sputum as soon as it bloomed in the corner of his mouth. The sheets were crisp and tight across his body, the room smelled fragrant, windows open and the light streaming in.

I believed she'd taken good care of him, save for the lack of proper medical attention. There was a bottle of Owbridge's Lung Tonic on the dresser.

'How long has he been ill?' said Turner, gently probing the man's body.

'Three days. Don't want any sawbones near me, he says. I says it's more than a blooming cold, perhaps you should let someone take a look, and he says over my dead body, Kathleen. Over my dead body he says,' and she gazed down at him and patted his hand.

I looked at Turner who shook his head, and I shook my head at her, and she just sat there crying silently and holding his hand.

The stretcher bearers arrived, but Turner ushered them out and asked me if I could wait. I sat in a chair on the other side of the bed and waited.

I thought how peaceful the room was, the unsteady shallow breath of a dying man, a dresser clock ticking his life away. The sprawling wooden hotel stretched in the heat of the day and a buggy passed in the street below. Someone somewhere far away coughed, and there were footfalls downstairs. How different was this death to the Reverend Ward's, I thought.

McLean died in that timeless room between a tick of the clock and a creak as a cloud cooled the iron roof. I was staring out the window and when I looked back at the bed nothing had changed except the man had stopped breathing and Mrs McLean had her mouth open in a silent wail.

* * *

When Turner returned he had the two constables with him, the dray with the yellow flags and the rope, the containers of phenyl.

He examined the dead McLean and sent for the mortuary wagon. Then he drew me aside.

'I want to have a look at his lungs.'

Mrs McLean had recovered some composure and was using the telephone to make funeral arrangements. One constable stood at the front door and the other began locking the remaining doors and pasting up the quarantine order.

'What?' She looked at the constables, and Turner led her by the elbow away from the telephone and sat her down at the bar.

He explained there could be no funeral arrangements as such, that unfortunately Mr McLean may have died of plague and that, once it was confirmed, he must by law be buried at the plague cemetery at Three Mile Creek.

'But his family's all in West End.'

'Unavoidable. Do you understand?'

'What will his mother say? She's too old to go all the way out there.'

Turner tried to explain what would happen next and she nodded at something in the distance. He asked me to fetch her a brandy, the only time I'd ever heard him prescribe alcohol. The other guests were rounded up and addressed in the bar, and the constables said they'd turn a blind eye and there was sherry all around. Some women wept, and a couple of men looked as if they might cheer at the prospect of being quarantined for three weeks in a hotel.

We left them all in the bar consoling Mrs McLean. But the shock wore off when we had McLean's body on a stretcher and were taking it to the wagon. His wife must have realised then that she wouldn't see her husband again.

'But there has to be a funeral,' said one of the men from the bar, fortified by sherry and suddenly protective of the newly widowed landlady. The constables tried to explain that there'd be a funeral but no one could attend apart from the hospital chaplain.

Turner and the wagon were fifty yards down the road when Mrs McLean broke through the line and ran after it. It was left to me to grab her and bring her back as the constables threatened the crowd with batons.

A few of the guests threw insults at me as I brought her in, and as I left one threw a glass, which smashed against the wall. The constables rushed in behind me, but I told them to leave the man alone.

Turner had had to go with the mortuary wagon and I was left alone to walk back to Flinders-street. I heard the woman's screams even as I crossed the bridge.

The police closed the bar and that was the last straw for public opinion. We were officially 'hard-hearted monsters' in the papers, although Humphry said they were simply jealous of those lucky enough to be at the hotel when the constables came.

A morgue needs no windows.

Turner and Humphry were preparing for the autopsy. The publican's skin looked yellow in the gaslight.

'Why don't you go home, Row,' said Turner, washing his hands in a basin. 'You must have other things to do. We can manage here.'

'That's what I've been telling him,' said Humphry. 'Man needs some recreation.' Humphry had returned to town that morning. 'You should get a pipe.'

We were babbling, I was sure, from exhaustion. These were the conversations we had.

'What do you suggest?' I asked Turner.

'Allan's already put together a remarkable collection of butterflies, you know,' said Turner, wiping his hands with a white towel. 'You should see it. There are some beauties there.'

'Exactly what you need, Lin,' said Humphry. 'A hobby.'

Allan *collected* butterflies? 'How do you know?' I asked Turner.

'He asked if he could borrow my net. Bright boy there, Row.'

'Never be bored with a butterfly net,' said Humphry. 'And a pipe.'

But I couldn't go home. It required more energy than I had, to fix all the things that now needed fixing.

I told them they might need me, that they were just as tired surely, and I stayed and watched, as they must have known I would.

Turner was fast. He had sheared the breast open and had the lungs out in seconds. There was a good deal of interest in the lungs, which when spread out resembled a large scarlet butterfly themselves.

'We'll take a sample anyway,' said Turner, and Humphry slit a small piece from the middle and put it in a glass tube with a cork stopper.

It wasn't long before Turner had blood up to his elbows, and Humphry tipped water from a bucket into the man's stomach to wash away some of the dark fluids so they could see the organs better. Turner lifted them out and displayed them around the cavity, telling Humphry to get a sample from the spleen and liver for examination later.

They, too, were bright red.

It was hard to tell from where I stood whether there was anything else abnormal, and Turner simply grunted here and there, and poked around. Humphry looked bored, if anything.

Last of all, Turner took a scalpel and cut the hard little buboes from the man's groin. He and Humphry repacked the organs and two inoculated orderlies cleaned the body. I watched an orderly try to shut the mouth. The tongue had turned black and now seemed to be stuck to the palate and the gums had drawn back from the teeth.

Turner said, 'The disease stopped his heart. It's become a little faster.'

A blessing for Mr McLean, but a curse for us.

Both Humphry and Turner insisted I take the afternoon off. Neither would leave off about it, so in the end I gave up arguing.

I didn't go home, though.

As John McLean began the journey to his final resting place at Three Mile Creek, I was in McKimmin and Richardson's store to look for a hat to replace the one I'd lost overboard weeks before.

I had to admit I felt a little more human for being out in public as an ordinary bloke, even though a few people stared.

I was trying on some English boaters, victims of a 'gigantic slaughter' in Drapery, Clothing, Hats, Boots and Shoes.

'Prices reduced' didn't cut it. There had to be blood on the hands of the store owner, his own blood, if customers were to be persuaded. Perhaps this was the sort of thing people expected nowadays, and a leaflet that merely said *Plague*! was probably a bit of a yawn.

I was tired and this was the direction in which my mind was drifting, when I thought I saw Dawson as a shadow in Shoes. He was accompanied by sulphurous fumes and a cloud of bats; more of an impression, I supposed.

A short time later I was standing at the counter having my boater boxed, when his dark shape flickered at the corner of my eye. I turned and might have imagined it, but for a swirl of blue smoke lingering around a tie rack.

I turned back to the counter and suddenly Dawson was at my side, displacing the air like a thunderstorm. He was swaying slightly, as if getting used to solid ground.

'Where's Humphry?' he said.

'Graveyard.'

He put his cigar to his lips and inhaled hugely. 'Dead?'

I glanced at him sideways as he produced an enormous billow of smoke that obscured his features.

'Burying the owner of the Commercial Hotel.'

'Damned shame,' and stared at the ceiling for a moment. I looked up half expecting to see something malicious hanging there.

And he walked out of the store as if he were flesh and blood.

I told Humphry later.

'Another boater? You need a boxer. More a man's hat.'

The next day things got worse.

It was the Reverend Kerr who had telephoned, and left a message for me to meet him at the home of Mrs Duffy.

Mrs Duffy who handed out the Bibles.

Mrs Duffy had no family except a rumour of a husband – a fireman on the trains. He had never shared the back pew with us and I never could quite believe he existed.

I pedalled over the Victoria Bridge through South Townsville until I found her street. There were a dozen people, mainly women, gathered in front of the house, but still standing *in* the street. Children ran about, but they all fell silent when they saw me. I might have been the next act in the Tragedy, and they seemed to be expecting some speech as I leaned the Carbine against the fence and took my medical bag from the basket.

'They're inside,' said an elderly, portly woman dressed all in black. 'Haven't come out since.'

Mrs Duffy's house was one of those spidery cottages high on stilts. It had a red iron roof and steep straight stairs front and back. The most practical thing about this sort of housing was that in the Wet, hammocks were spun like webs underneath where it was cooler during the long steamy days.

The house sent mixed messages: the door was open but the windows shut, curtains drawn. A dog was barking around the back.

'Someone should go get that bloomin' dog,' said the woman.

'Someone should shoot it,' said another, but no one moved.

I said, 'Who's with her?'

'Just the Reverend.'

'Where's her husband?'

'Between here and The World I'm told. He don't know yet.'

The gate screeched and the crowd was quiet as I climbed the steps. The house breathed hot foetid air over me as I put my head into its dark throat.

'It's Dr Row,' I called out.

Inside was quiet.

'Too damned late again,' someone yelled from the street.

I put my hand on the doorframe and felt the wood warm as fever. The dog barked incessantly.

I stepped down the hall. There were only two doorways, one each side, and in the room on the right was a figure on the floor, another on the bed. I hurried to the Reverend Kerr's side. His eyes fluttered open, but rolled upwards so I gently laid him down again. The kitchen was at the back; there was a water bucket on the sink, an enamel mug nearby and I dipped it in the bucket and took that back.

The water was warm, but I kept flicking it on his face until he shook his head and struggled to move. I slapped his cheeks. Just a little.

He moaned and blinked.

'Drink,' I said, and I held the mug to his mouth. I helped him up and out of the charnel room and into the hallway. The back door opened with a tug and cooler air passed around us. I fetched a chair and sat him in the draught and put the mug in his hands.

'My word.'

'Just sit for a moment,' I said. His eyes wandered, trying to focus. 'You fainted, that's all.'

'Cold.' Shock.

'I have to go back to Mrs Duffy,' I said.

'Dead.'

I went back into the room and stood for a moment at the door. She lay as if killed by one terrible blow, arms flung out, one leg off the bed, her head lolling sideways and her tongue out.

I opened the window with great effort and a breeze came through and rippled the curtains, dropping the temperature straight away by several degrees. The damned dog, though, was louder and wouldn't shut up.

Taking a deep breath, I turned to look at Mrs Duffy. Her forehead was still warm to my touch, the skin at her throat taut and lifeless. She hadn't been dead long. Hours perhaps.

I went to the other side and moved her leg on to the bed, brought it together with the other, straightening her dress. There was the smell of lavender and perspiration and urine, but the breeze made it bearable. Had she suffered long? She might have died from the heat, but for the blood on her tongue, her chin, and the bedspread.

I felt beneath her armpit and my fingers came away wet. I wiped them on the bedspread, and then folded her arms across her chest and tried to put her tongue back in her mouth and had to wipe them again.

Her eyes were closed. Thirst had played a part, and she may have lain unconscious and convulsed at the end. The disease had taken her violently and quickly, but perhaps it would never be fast enough.

Closing the house up was what many people did during an illness, especially an air disease. To protect her neighbours, perhaps, or to sweat out the initial fever.

The room was clean, neat, a Bible open on a table, a dark wardrobe closed, a lamp out of kerosene, a framed photograph on the wall. I took a closer look at the two faces, a man and a woman, and then back to Mrs Duffy. How different to Mrs Gard's room and yet how similar. No one should die alone, be left alone, be lonely.

I sat down at the end of the bed and felt a wave of grief sweep over me.

I felt a sudden need to see Maria and my babies and to hold them tight. Death had come into my life and wouldn't leave and I now felt a terrible fear, seeing what had happened to Mrs Duffy.

Could I protect them all from an Act of God?

'Lord have mercy.'

The Reverend Kerr was at the door and I tried to pull myself together. I nodded to him, afraid my voice would betray me.

'She looks peaceful.'

I nodded again.

'A shock, you see.'

'I understand.'

'I've seen worse.'

'The heat.' I cleared my throat.

'The poor woman,' and the Reverend started towards the bed, but I stood and put a hand out to stop him. I shook my head.

'Oh? Oh, I see.'

'You didn't touch her? Earlier?'

He shook his head, his eyes watering.

'Alive?' I asked.

'Too late. Too late.' He pulled out a handkerchief and wiped his eyes. 'A prayer.'

He closed his eyes and we both prayed for Mrs Duffy's immortal soul and her poor husband, wherever he might be. And I said a silent prayer for my own Lillian. And for Mrs Gard's daughter.

Afterwards, Kerr went into the street to talk to the neighbours and urge them to go home. We waited for the mortuary wagon.

The sight of gloved and masked orderlies was still a novelty. A fair-sized crowd watched Mrs Duffy's shrouded body being carried on to the wagon and away to the morgue. The Reverend Kerr had remained until the end, swooping like a magpie after curious boys who came too close.

Much later I heard that Mr Duffy was found in Charters Towers, caught a night train home, and shot the dog.

That evening Humphry and Turner conducted their autopsy. In Mrs Duffy's saturated lungs they found something of which we were very afraid: a fermenting contagion that, with a kiss, a cough or a sneeze, could be transmitted from one person to another, putting the rat and the flea out of business. Turner diagnosed pneumonic plague and we all slept very badly that night.

Allan was sitting on the end of the day bed. I'd fallen asleep on the verandah as the sky had begun to lighten. The sun was now in full steam.

'Where are the girls?'

'Still in bed,' he said.

I asked him to show me his butterfly collection and he brought back a box full of dead dry insects. I noticed quite a few Blue Tigers.

'What happened to that grub inside the ants' nest,' I said. I'd forgotten all about it.

He shrugged. 'Nothing. The ants are still there, though.'

Great.

'Can I come with you today?'

'No,' I said, and soon left him swiping at things in the front yard with the net Turner had given him.

chapter fourteen

Rats! Rats! Rats! Rough on Rats,
Hang your dog and drown your cats;
We give a plan for every man
To clear his house with Rough on Rats.

From the Rough on Rats poison company,

Jersey City, USA

'DO YOU KNOW WHAT today is?' said Humphry. Turner kept scribbling.

'Friday?'

'Very good, Lin. And do you know what that means?'

Turner refused now to buy into Humphry's riddles.

I gave a tired shrug. 'Fish for tea?'

Humphry looked at me as if I'd disappointed him.

'It's the day before Dawson's comeuppance.'

'The day *before*.'

'Tomorrow, as you know, is race day,' and Humphry reached into his pocket and produced a thick pile of pound notes, fanning them under my nose.

'Must be twenty quid there.'

'A very good eye you have for cash, Lin. You should be an accountant. Or a surgeon. Exactly twenty quid in pound notes.'

'What's it for?'

'It's for buying a horse.'

Turner held his pen above the paper, but did not look up. I saw his chest rise with the sigh, and then he continued writing. Humphry winked at me.

'What horse around here is worth twenty quid?' I said.

Humphry tapped the side of his nose. 'Exactly. None. Mate of mine spotted this one at a barracks in Brisbane. Goes like the clappers. Bought it from some fool going off to sort the Boer out and it's already been a big winner.'

It felt like I was rubbing grit *into* my eyes. Humphry waited patiently.

Turner put his pen down and said, 'I'm going to make coffee,' and walked over to his laboratory.

'And how's that going to be Dawson's comeuppance?' I said.

'Mare's arrived by steamer.' Humphry put the money back in his pocket and patted it. 'Cash on delivery.'

We had deeper concerns that day, of course. Mrs Duffy's death meant the disease might be gathering strength. Her self-enforced quarantine might have been the only thing that spared a far more deadly outbreak.

Turner was drafting another missive to the Mayor and the Joint Epidemic Board, urging greater care, faster work and stricter adherence to regulations. Pneumonic plague could strike again. This was the very reason that tough quarantine measures had to be enforced.

Still, we were all wrung out. Humphry was waiting for word from the harbour yards. The horse wasn't expected to have cleared quarantine until the afternoon.

'Cutting it a bit fine, aren't you?' said Turner. 'If the race is tomorrow.'

'Lucky to get her up here at all. I take it as a good sign.'

'How are you going to get her from the yards? You're not going to ride her,' I said.

'Don't be silly, Lin. I'd break my neck. I'll lead her with the buggy. Can't take any chances.'

Turner asked if he could borrow his buggy then, if he wasn't using it for a few hours.

'Just make sure you don't wear the old fellow out,' said Humphry, referring perhaps to his horse, but who really knew. 'Last time you took him he broke down for two days. He's not used to how exciting it is being around you.'

Turner collected his pith helmet and butterfly net and asked if I wanted to join him for a ride around Castle Hill.

'Just for fun.'

'What if there's a case?'

'Humphry will have to handle it. We won't be long.'

Turner was at the reins. I supposed we had no right, but we both enjoyed the truancy and despite Humphry's instructions Turner soon had the horse at an exhilarating gallop.

It was a clear and still day, the sun had a sting, but the air was relatively cool.

We followed Flinders-street west and then turned north. If we were to keep going, I thought, we'd end up at Cairns, if we didn't get lost in some swamp and eaten by crocodiles.

I wondered what Cairns was like. Would it be plague free, swaying palms, the sort of numb paradise I'd imagined and hoped Townsville would be when we set sail a year earlier? Back then, the pain of Lillian's loss was so great it seemed like a physical thing that we could outrun. She was there in every thing we could touch and all we could see. We'd both agreed, hadn't we? Maria and I had both decided in a haze of grief that the best thing to do was to leave what was familiar and take the job being offered in the North.

'What's this?' said Turner, breaking into my thoughts.

There seemed to be more traffic here, drays and wagons and men on horseback, more leaving town than riding towards it. It was when we turned back into Sturt-street that we saw the funeral procession. The cortege was small, a few men on horseback, most in buggies or sulkies, all in black suits and black hats struggling to maintain some dignity, but obviously in a hurry to catch up with the hearse.

We came up beside the stragglers. Turner leaned over the side and said, 'Whose funeral is this?'

We trotted beside the other sulky and the man looked us over, 'It's Mrs Duffy, mate. Died yesterday,' and he lowered his voice, 'Don't you know? She had the plague.'

Turner said, 'Where are they taking her?'

The man looked confused for a moment. 'The cemetery of course.'

'The *town* cemetery?' said Turner.

'Well, it's where all the Duffys are planted, mate.'

I nearly fell out of my seat as Turner flicked the reins and sent the horse off at a gallop towards the hearse.

The custom for funerals in the North was for all traffic to pull off the road and stop, and the men to remove their hats. The practice gave us a clear run. It was probably not the practice to overtake funeral corteges. I held on to my new hat this time.

As we came near, I saw the funeral director turn around and gape at us. He reached for his whip and I thought he might try to outrun us, but Turner caught him, passed him and in a spray of gravel cut in front, pulling on the brake violently and forcing the hearse to brake as well. We all stopped in a swirl of dust and snorting horses. Turner was down on the road before I had a chance to warn him.

By the time I'd tethered the reins, climbed down and reached the hearse myself, Turner was already having a go at the funeral director.

How did Mr Watt come by the body? Turner had asked.

Well, the usual way: a request and the coffin collected. The funeral director knew his way around the morgue. The coffin had been nailed shut, the sign that any autopsy or official business had been completed. He'd signed the release himself, as he had done so many times before.

'Being a Justice of the Peace,' he said, punctuating the point by spitting carefully over the footplate into the dust.

Watt was clean shaven and dressed as if business was thriving. He wore a top hat, the only one I'd seen since we left Brisbane. His teeth were yellow, probably from the small plug of tobacco he kept in the marsupial pouch of his cheek, but it didn't matter because he never smiled.

Turner had pushed his helmet back and had one hand on the footrest, as if he'd just stopped for a chat.

'You can't bury her in the town cemetery, Mr Watt,' said Turner.

Watt squirmed in his seat, feigning outrage.

'She's not your business any more, Dr Turner,' he said, 'and fat good you've done her up until now anyway. Now, I'll ask you to get out of the way. There's laws against interrupting funerals.'

'There's a law requiring plague victims to be buried in the plague cemetery.'

Watt leaned down. 'Keep your voice down, there's her husband.'

By this time a few men on horseback had come up beside the hearse and loomed over Turner. The cortege had come to a standstill.

A buggy with Mr Duffy and the Reverend Kerr pulled up on the other side. The horses were nervous. Most of the cortege were upwind, but no one wanted to get in front of the hearse in case any miasmas were leaking from the coffin.

Watt tied the reins to the bar, pulled again on the brake to make sure the horses didn't bolt, and climbed down to face us.

'We can work something out, I'm sure, doctor,' he whispered.

'There's no bargaining over this.' Turner was outwardly calm and reasonable. I noticed only that his speech impediment got worse when he was arguing and he was likely to speak his mind, a speech non-impediment, I supposed.

'It's a simple fact of plague regulations.' *Wegulations.* 'If you decide to take Mrs Duffy to the town cemetery you'll be breaking the law and I'll be back here with Sergeant Moylan.'

'Look, Dr Turner, they just want a decent funeral,' said Watt. 'What harm can it do now? You and I both know that there's no harm to be done.'

Mr Duffy was close enough now to overhear this. Turner looked around at the gathering of black suits on horseback as they pressed closer to hear what was being said.

'She will get a Christian burial. At the plague cemetery. I suggest that is where you are going. Aren't you?'

A few of the men closest to us started talking at once then, and the horses began stamping and snorting in excitement, the dust rising to our waistcoats. One man said that the funeral should proceed as planned, there was no way any damned quack could stop them anyway. There was agreement on this point.

I looked over to Mr Duffy on the other side of the hearse, but he said nothing and in fact swayed as if drunk. The Reverend Kerr had a hand on his shoulder, perhaps to comfort him, but probably to keep him from falling.

Watt knew he was in trouble if he proceeded, but out of pocket if he didn't bury his customer as instructed.

Turner said, 'I trust the church service was quick?'

'Yes, and the coffin closed.'

'You didn't prepare the body?'

'No, no. The coffin was sealed. I know the regulations.'

'No, you don't, Mr Watt. Do you know she had a very infectious strain of plague? Pneumonic. One post-mortem expiration of her lungs and you might be dead,' said Turner, reasonably.

Watt looked a little alarmed and wrung his hands, and I wondered if he'd been told this.

Turner said, 'So, you're off to the plague cemetery?'

'No,' cried someone in the gathering crowd and it was taken up and I thought there might be violence, but

Watt raised his hands and told them that there was nothing he could do now, the doctors were within their rights and he'd tried his best to reason with them.

He turned and climbed back up on to the hearse and took hold of the reins. Turner and I had to step back as the black funeral horses reared up. The other mourners grumbled and prepared to follow the hearse.

'Wait,' said Turner, and I tensed as he gave them more bad news. Only the hearse with Mrs Duffy's body and the funeral director were allowed to go to Three Mile Creek.

There was a stunned silence and then Watt spat and set off at an undignified trot. The mourners were restless and I thought for a moment they were going to ride out there anyway. But they stayed where they were, buzzing angrily. They might even have been grateful to avoid it.

The Reverend Kerr steered his buggy beside us as we climbed back into ours. Duffy had his head on his chest and the Reverend Kerr leaned over him.

'A husband can surely attend his wife's funeral?' he said.

'Not unless he's been inoculated,' said Turner. 'Sorry.'

'A Christian burial, Dr Turner? Can you guarantee that, at least?'

'You know the Reverend Walsh will do a proper job. You of all people understand the need to expose as few people as possible to this disease.'

'Yes, yes,' said Reverend Kerr, ashamed, I think.

Turner picked up the reins. 'Please be cautious, Mr Kerr. You don't want your church quarantined. That's what will happen if you bring another plague victim into it. I'm satisfied that the coffin is properly sealed, but you've run a terrible risk.'

'*The fear of the Lord tendeth to life: and he that hath it shall abide satisfied he shall not be visited by evil,*' said Kerr.

Duffy nodded and mumbled what sounded like 'Amen.'

'Won't do to tempt Him though,' said Turner, and with that we set off to catch the hearse.

'*In the sweat of thy face shalt thou eat bread, till thou return unto the ground; for out of it wast thou taken: for dust thou art, and unto dust shalt thou return.*'

She-oaks in their tattered veils moaned as Mrs Duffy's coffin was lowered into her ultimate grave, the secretary of the Women's Christian Temperance Union now being buried next to McLean the publican. There were a number of new crosses nearby. I must have known, but I couldn't think of the names.

As I walked back to the buggy, lagging behind Turner, Routh came up to me. He looked raw, as if he'd just woken up, or hadn't been to bed.

'Who was that?' he said, scratching his head.

'Mrs Duffy.'

Routh looked back towards the bare graveyard and appeared to be searching his memory, but couldn't place her.

'I'd have attended myself.' He gestured to the hospital tent. 'Busy.'

There were a dozen patients at Three Mile Creek now. Another twenty had recovered. Eight had died since Mr Gard. We'd looked for patterns of infection, but apart from poverty or close habitation, the cases appeared random.

Those, of course, were the cases we were called to. It was likely that many people fell ill, and recovered or died in their homes. A few doctors refused to believe that plague existed, and the dead were simply put down to typhoid or any of a number of fevers, and buried without any formal examination.

Many feared the hospital more than death itself; and any of those wretched races not blessed with British blood probably didn't bother seeking treatment. Turner privately said the number of cases could be doubled — even tripled. But who would know? We could only report what we saw. What we didn't see might as well not exist.

Now *there* was a theory for Humphry.

The Gard girl was actually out of her bed and playing with her rag doll between two cots. I looked for a nurse, but there was none handy, so I picked her up and sat her on the bed.

'Better?' I asked.

She nodded. I didn't believe I'd ever heard her speak, except to cry out in pain.

She let me examine her and she appeared well, if a little listless. She had neither fever nor swellings and she probably should have been discharged days ago. I'd resisted Routh's attempts to transfer her to the public hospital. She had nowhere to go but the Townsville orphanage, and I was trying to put that off for as long as possible. At Three Mile Creek, Humphry, Turner and I could look in on her. She was also better fed.

I stood and waved goodbye. She returned the wave. It lifted my heart and broke it at once.

On our way back to town I thought of Mrs Duffy in church. We'd shared the same back pew, but we spoke only about the weather. I realised that of the back-pew sitters, two were dead. Was *that* a pattern? Kerr had wondered aloud if the end of the world was coming, and I supposed it had, a chain of personal apocalypses for the Gard family, Mrs Duffy, even her dog.

I didn't know what to think. In fact, in my misery, I didn't want to think about it at all.

We rattled along the coast, and I noticed the sea breeze had dropped completely.

Turner suddenly left the road, taking a track through one of the low coastal dunes on to the beach, a childish risk, the horse straining as the wheels sank into the soft sand, until we reached the wet shoulder where the sand was firm and smooth. Humphry's horse snorted with delight at the water and drew us suddenly into the wash. Turner had some difficulty steering him back, and eventually let the horse have his way. The hooves splashed through the shallows, one wheel throwing sea water so a rainbow chased us.

After awhile Turner managed to steer the horse back on to the dry sand and we stopped.

The sea was smooth and gasped slightly as it pushed up the sand. Magnetic Island lay deep blue on the horizon, and the water was a glass green near the shore, so clear you could see the bottom. Gulls foraged through the line of rubbish and dead fish were strung along the high tide mark. Swirls farther out marked where fish fed near the surface and more gulls floated above them. There was nothing more peaceful, and all I wanted to do then was to lie down on the sand and close my eyes, listening to the sounds of nothing civilised, just the gentle rocking of nature taking a breather.

I said this to Turner, who didn't reply; probably he wished the same thing and if we both wished it, it might come true and that wouldn't do.

'Sleeping well?' Turner broke the silence.

'Yes.'

He looked like an Englishman from the Raj. The pith helmet was actually bigger than his head. There was a puffiness, a redness about the cheek, the skin sagging slightly.

'What are you looking at?' he said.

'Sleeping well?'

He flicked the reins, but the horse didn't respond.

He let them hang limply in his hands. 'You are not responsible.'

'I thought I should have been able to help,' I said.

'I don't mean the Gard child.'

I knew what he meant.

'Your daughter.'

I stiffened, nevertheless.

'Her death,' he said.

The small unbroken waves hissed in their run up the sand and recoiled as if touching a hot stove.

My mind screamed, *Stop*! but Turner of course would never be able to stop.

'Diphtheria is a cruel disease, Row. Lillian died terribly. Nothing could be done. We must face the truth as we find it.'

I was unable to speak.

'It's not your fault,' he said.

A laugh slipped from my mouth then. Didn't he know?

I swung down from the buggy and fell to my knees. I wanted to show the eminent Dr Turner my theory, but I couldn't find a stick. I wandered about, determined to show him what seemed clear to me.

If I had a stick I could trace a line in the sand, from the night I told Maria we should wait, to the day Mrs Duffy's dog died, and through all the horrors in between. The dog's fate was sealed more than a year before Mr Duffy slid the bullet into the chamber.

Turner was saying, 'Your family needs you, Row. More than this town does.'

I looked down at my boots and saw that they were under the water.

'That's funny,' I said. I didn't believe Turner was listening.

'Don't you see what you're doing to Maria?' he was saying. 'She's lost a daughter and now she believes she's lost a husband.'

'Do you think I don't know that?' I told the gulls.

'*I* could have been at the hospital sooner, too. Each of us could have done more, perhaps.'

For God's sake, stop.

'We could all blame ourselves,' I heard him say. 'But we don't, because we did what we could, and in the end we have a greater responsibility to the living.'

Do you think I don't know that? I could have screamed. If I was deluded, I could be cured. The grief of a rational man is endless.

'Many parents lose children, Row. Others aren't blessed with children in the first place. Whose loss is greater?' I heard him say.

The water lapped my knees and had soaked my trousers to the waist, but I couldn't feel it. I turned away from the buggy and looked out to sea.

My grief would not be shared.

I stood there for some time, between two worlds. Turner politely waited.

'Can you swim, Dr Turner?' I said, after awhile.

'Of course not.'

My feet took me back to the buggy and I pulled myself, dripping, back up beside Turner, who got the horse going again. We rode in silence.

I laid my head down slowly on my office table. The comforting smell of polish and the pressure against my cheek eased the tooth a little. The cupboard appeared from the gloom, leaning against the wall, as indifferent as a sarcophagus to the secrets it held inside.

I heard knocking, but I had no desire to move.

'You the doctor?'

I lay still.

'I said, are you the doctor?' It was the rasping voice of a man who worked in dust. With great effort I raised my head. The man was standing in the doorway.

'What do you want?' I said.

'I want a doctor.'

'Are you sick?'

He shook his head. 'My son.' He took a few uncertain steps forward.

I leaned across the table, lit the lamp and found my spectacles. I saw large hands holding a battered straw hat.

'Broke his leg a few days back.'

'I'm not the doctor you need.' My body gave one sudden, violent shudder. 'I can't help you with a broken leg.'

'Dr Bacot at the hospital fixed him two days ago, but he got worse and now Bacot says to see the doctor at the council and here I am.'

'Bacot sent you?' I looked down at the sand and the puddle of sea water under the chair.

'Says if my son's got a fever you was the bloke to see.'

'I thought you said he had a broken leg?'

'He does. And now he's got fever.' The man took another step towards my table.

I shook my head.

'Cockerill's the name.' He stuck out a large brown hand and, feeling numb and cold, I stood and reached across the table to have my hand wrung. He pointed over his shoulder. 'Sulky's out front.'

A crease from the middle of his forehead to the top of his nose that was so deep I could have sutured it. He fidgeted with his hat, but his gaze was steady. Fever following a broken leg was a bad sign. Why couldn't the blasted surgeon deal with this?

'What did you tell Dr Bacot?' I said. 'About the fever.'

'Just that he was red flaming hot. I'd been taking a look at the leg like he says to, but it wasn't red or oozing, no more than it was before. I told him the boy's tongue's got this white stuff over it and he had the aches and the chills. He says to come here. You are a doctor, aren't you?'

I stood, wearily found my bag and coat, and followed him down to his sulky. He glanced at my sopping gritty trousers, but didn't say a word.

I kept my eyes closed against the dust and the sun, appreciating the heat for once. He had the horse at a round gallop all the way.

chapter fifteen

Truth never needs violence to compel blessings. This Plague farce can only be kept up by tyranny and violence.

Point 24 of 'Twenty-five Reasons Why The Australian Epidemic Is *Not* Plague!' by Dr. T. P. Lucas MRCS Eng., LSA Lond., FRSQ

HIS HOUSE WAS ONE OF the small cottages along the road that led out of town to Charters Towers. The plants closest to the road, dead and live, always had a light grey dusting. Most yards, like Cockerill's, were treeless and the ground too hard for much to survive the long dry season.

Inside it smelled stale; a house of men. Cockerill junior was lying on his bed, his shirt soaked from neck to navel. He was conscious and as soon as he saw us asked for water.

'How old?' I said, as Cockerill senior lifted his son's head and helped him drink from a tin mug.

'Oh,' he stared up at the wall, 'about twenty-five.'

'What happened to his leg?'

'Slipped in the flaming yards and an old steer stood on it. Bacot set it here. Seemed all right, but this morning he was like this.'

I lifted the sheet from the lower end of the bed. Bacot had done a good job with the splint and bandage.

'Did the bone come through the flesh?' I said.

'No. I seen worse. Bacot said he'll keep his leg.' He was trying hard to keep the concern from his voice. 'He will, won't he?'

I peeled back the bandage and poked at the flesh around the broken tibia. It was chaffed and bruised where the hoof had struck it, and sticky with sweat, but it looked fine. The bone had cracked but held together. I lifted the sheet further, and stopped.

At the groin was a hard purple boil, about the size of a small chicken's egg. I raised the sheet still further and there was the same on the other thigh.

'How long has he had a fever?'

'I told you, just this morning. Said he wasn't feeling right last night but, you know, he's got a broken leg. Takes time.'

'You haven't washed him.'

'I'm not his flaming mother, God rest her. He's only been laid up a couple of days.'

'So you haven't noticed this lump before?'

He came to my shoulder.

'What's that?' he said.

'Let's go into the kitchen for a minute.'

* * *

Cockerill, to my surprise, looked relieved when I told him.

'Christ,' he said, sitting in a kitchen chair and rubbing the top of his head hard. 'You know, I was worried he'd lose his leg.'

'It's not blood poisoning.'

'Christ.' He ran his fingers through his matted hair and looked up at the ceiling. 'Don't know what I'd do if he'd lost the leg.'

'I'll have to do a test. On that boil.'

'What sort of test?'

'A test for plague.'

He nodded. 'Why didn't Bacot see that when he was splinting it?'

Good question. 'Did your son have a fever before he broke his leg?'

'No.'

'Dizziness? Headache?'

'Well, he was slacking off a bit that morning but he'd had a few the night before. Listen. You sure it's plague? I know someone who says they'd told him he had it, but he didn't. Says he wasn't any sicker than when he had dengue and some doctors, and I'm not saying who mind you, were making a few quid from it.'

I said I was paid a salary, not a commission, and didn't charge fees. I tried to explain that some people with plague were simply sicker than others. Some became very ill indeed, some recovered.

'Yeah, but my son's a strong bloke, wouldn't you say?'

'He looks strong.'

He nodded. 'Too right. Do what you like. Long as he keeps his leg.'

Junior called out, 'Dad?'

'Hold yer flamin' horses,' he yelled back. He said to me, 'How long will this take then, this test?'

'I just need to take some blood from your son and see if there are any germs in it.'

'He stays here.'

'For now.'

'He ain't going nowhere.' He nodded to himself.

'Not at the moment.'

I had Cockerill hold his son down and the pair seemed to know the drill, but junior still bellowed when I sent the needle home.

We trotted back in a sullen silence, long shadows stretching ahead of us. My trousers had almost dried, but they were stiff from the sea water. I had to stretch my legs and pluck the material away from my thigh occasionally to ease the chafing. Cockerill seemed to be getting annoyed with my fidgeting.

I saw the barber shop and on impulse told Cockerill to stop and let me out. He looked me up and down as I got off and then he simply turned his sulky around.

I sat in the barber's chair with a weary resignation. The man, who also claimed to be a dentist, bent over me. He smelled of talc and cloves. His own teeth seemed to be in good shape.

'Too many sweet things, Dr Row.'

'It's one of the molars on the left ...'

'I see it.'

He whipped a blunt chisel and a small hammer from some hiding place under his apron, and he had it in my mouth. The blow sent a shock of pain through my head and I saw stars.

'Just a tap to loosen it,' I heard him say.

The black mist started rolling across the ceiling and receded.

'Whisky working yet?'

'Ung.' Perhaps he'd hoped to knock me out.

'Keep your mouth open,' and he turned away. I allowed myself to relax a little and in a blur he had a knee on my chest and a shiny pair of pliers disappeared into my mouth. He gave a fierce sideways wrench and then a mighty tug, dragging my head up near his chest. There was a deafening crack.

We both fell back.

My mouth filled with blood. As the ceiling reappeared through the black mist I saw that he was bending over me, panting, to display the gleaming molar. It was huge. He was obviously pleased with himself, although his smile faded as he looked into my face.

'Bite on this,' he said, putting a wad of cotton into the hole in my mouth. He wound the chair up and I could see my pale, shocked reflection in the mirror. I leaned over a bucket he'd placed on the floor beside the chair and let blood dribble into it. I stayed bent over, sure I would vomit.

'Thought you might faint on me there, doctor,' I heard as the nausea came and went.

'I think you broke my jaw,' I tried to say.

I told myself, as the pain spread around my head to the back of my neck, that I'd seen worse days.

Turner was gone. Everyone was gone. I lit the gas lamp in Turner's laboratory, my jaw pumping pain. I prepared a slide, hardly able to see through the microscope lens.

The barber had sold me a bottle of whisky for rinsing and swallowing. It had had little effect, so I searched Turner's pharmacopoeia and found some laudanum.

I spat out the bloody wad of cotton and placed three drops on my tongue, and then went to the basin and wetted a cloth. I sat back in Turner's chair and draped its blessed coolness over my eyelids for a few moments, waiting for the pain to subside. For a while there was only throbbing and nausea. My tongue went to the place where the molar had been and there was a certain pleasure in finding the devil gone. The pain began to fade.

After a time, images appeared on the underside of my lids. I could see the familiar oval bacteria swimming in solution, like jellyfish under the wharves on Ross Creek, transparent and languid. They became faces underwater – of Mrs Gard, then Mrs Duffy, and then darling little Lillian, all drifting on the tide, staring up not at me but past me, and there on the surface was my own face staring blankly back.

And then another face appeared suddenly beside it, a crooked face, and I started awake, choking on blood.

I spat in a kidney dish and rinsed with whisky, before stumbling back to the microscope. The ache had gone, but there was a thick leaden fog to swim through. I couldn't get the lens to focus so I washed my face in a bowl and forced myself awake, coming back to count and sketch the bacteria from young Cockerill's groin.

No surprises in those reflected faces staring back at me through the lens.

I scrubbed my hands and went to Turner's desk with my sketch, finished a brief report and pushed it aside. I took another few drops of laudanum and leaned back in his chair, closing my eyes again, and this time the image I saw was Allan's strange flat brown grub.

When I woke it was dark, cold, and my neck so painful I could hardly turn my head. The lamp had gone out. I stood and fumbled stiffly for a blanket I knew Turner kept in a cupboard. I found it in the half-light and fell back into an uncomfortable sleep.

'Coffee?'

I opened my eyes and felt my face, pressing along the jaw line. It appeared to be intact.

I heard Turner at his laboratory and went to rise, but my neck, or the chair, creaked dangerously.

'Coffee's in front of you.'

I could see the steam rising in front of my face. I heard Turner rustling paper.

'We'll move him to the plague hospital this morning,' he said. 'Are you all right?'

'Tooth pulled.'

'About time.'

'I think the man broke my neck.'

I moved it a little and pain shot to the top of my head.

'I told you I could have done it,' said Turner. 'Saved you a few shillings.'

The whisky bottle was next to the microscope and I wanted to add some to my coffee but wasn't game to move any further. Turner hadn't mentioned it and I watched him read the report on Cockerill junior.

'The broken leg might have masked the initial symptoms,' he said. 'But broken legs in themselves don't cause fevers. Bacot must have seen that.'

Fatigue and pain still nailed me to the chair.

'Are you all right?' he said.

'Yes, yes. I wish you would stop asking,' I snapped.

Turner continued reading the report long after he should have finished.

Without looking up he said, 'I have spent some time questioning my actions and I have come to the conclusion that I could have done more.'

I longed for the pair of pliers that could rip a rotten splinter from my own heart.

* * *

We found a cab in the street and rattled off against the morning traffic.

Cockerill was sour when he opened the door. He looked us up and down as if we'd come to beg tobacco.

'What did your test say?' he said. He stared at our medical bags.

'Plague,' I said.

Cockerill grunted and glared at Turner.

'This is Dr Turner,' I told him.

The old man kept us at the door a moment and then said he supposed we'd better come in, but the boy was better anyway.

We examined the boy and I was surprised to see the sheets had been changed. The splinted leg was uncovered and raised, as I'd suggested, and the young man looked as comfortable as someone with bubonic plague could be. He was sleeping.

Turner took his temperature.

'One hundred and one,' he told me. 'What was it yesterday?'

'A hundred and four.'

'I think we can move him.'

'No. You're not moving him,' said Cockerill senior from the doorway.

I'd heard reports that in Sydney, where the plague seemed to have latched on with a particular viciousness, doctors and patients had been in fist fights. Police had used guns and batons to remove plague patients and there'd even been a riot as people queued for vaccination. I could see from Cockerill's stance that he might be trouble.

'We have to take him to hospital,' said Turner, in his quiet voice. 'Your son has bubonic plague.'

'All he's got is a broken leg. I can take care of that.'

'You told Dr Row yesterday that he had a fever.'

'Yeah, well, it's just about gone, isn't it? Look, he's better. You said so yourself. Just leave him be.' The man rubbed his nose with a dirty clenched fist. 'He's not going to flamin' hospital. That's that.'

'It's the law,' said Turner.

'The law be buggered.'

'We have to isolate him if he has plague. You don't want to get it, do you?'

Cockerill senior sneered. 'I'm not flamin' stupid, you know. I'd have got it by now if it was, wouldn't I? Dr Bacot saw him first anyway and didn't say anything about plague. Why don't you get him back here and see what he says?'

'Nonetheless, he must go to the plague hospital,' said Turner, his words hardening.

'Nonetheless, over my dead body,' said Cockerill, and he took a step forward. Turner came up to his chest.

'Let's discuss this in the kitchen.'

'Nothing to discuss. He's not going near no hospital. I already told *you*,' and he poked a finger at me, 'he's staying here, and he's gonna get better here.'

I noticed now that the tip of the finger was missing. He'd be one of those men who knew only about hard work, believed that pain had to be endured and that brute force could solve any problem.

Turner said, 'He needs medical attention. He's going to get a lot worse before he gets better. He needs help.'

'That's what they said about his mother. And his brother. Took them off to hospital and they didn't come back.'

I reached for Turner's elbow, fed up with this argument, but he wanted to keep going.

'We have to take your son to the plague hospital. You could be arrested if you prevent him from being taken away.'

Cockerill suddenly put his foot to a chair and sent it smashing against the wall. The violence of it caused his son to open his eyes and try to sit.

'Wha...?'

I grabbed Turner and pulled him past the old man and down the hall out on to the front steps. I turned around at the top of the steps, as Cockerill emerged from the kitchen with a rifle, an old Martini, solid and tarnished, looking as light as a chicken bone in those big hands.

Turner went white and I felt a moment of vindictive pleasure that he might now realise that sometimes he went too far.

I met Cockerill's eyes as he raised the rifle to my chest. I felt a curious calmness looking down that barrel, and it was Turner this time who was tugging for me to go. I turned stiffly and we retreated to the front gate.

Cockerill yelled after us, 'Any flamin' doctor comes here and tries to take my son away, I'll shoot him.'

Our cab was still waiting at the gate, and several buggies had now stopped behind it in the middle of the road to watch the commotion. It was Turner, though, who had the last word.

'Beware of that wifle,' he yelled back at Cockerill. 'It might be dangewous.'

I bundled Turner into the cab and the driver pulled away before I had the door shut. I could see through the window Cockerill at the top of the stairs, peering into the breech and then storming back inside. Turner in front of me had his colour back.

'My word, Row,' he said, 'you could have handled that better.'

Humphry's buggy was leading a sleek black mare and had just pulled up in front of us, outside the Town Hall. He jumped down and stood beside the beast with his hands on his hips, almost begging us to admire it. Turner strode straight past to telephone for the police.

'What's up?' said Humphry, watching him go inside.

'Another plague patient. Father's got a gun this time and won't let the lad go.'

'But it's race day.'

Humphry slapped the mare's glossy black shoulder-muscle and she skittered and pulled at the lead, showing the whites of her eyes. She looked as if she might bolt or kill someone herself, given a chance.

'She's a spirited thing.'

We took a few quick steps backwards as she danced sideways towards us. Humphry pointed out her best features. She was tall and long, with strong legs, a deep chest, and a sleek body. No mere saddle horse.

When Turner came back, we had a short conference in the street. The police would take over, he said, but Moylan wanted us to keep negotiating.

'Good for him,' said Humphry, and he took out his watch, swore, and started to get into his buggy.

'Where are you going?' said Turner.

'Cluden,' said Humphry. 'You boys can handle it. I'll put a few bob on Black Bird for you, if you like. On the nose.'

'Black Bird?'

'Well,' said Humphry, looking around, but no one else was in earshot, 'I couldn't very well race her as Minstrel Girl. Someone might recognise her.'

'She's a ring-in?' I said.

'Hoy, keep it down. I'm just saying,' he leaned forward and whispered, 'you should get six to one.'

Turner suggested I catch a lift with Humphry back to Cockerill's house, to keep an eye on things before the police arrived. There was a chance he'd come to his senses.

'A chance?' said Humphry, as I climbed up beside him. 'I wouldn't put my money on it.'

'Why Black Bird?' I said. We were rolling again down the main street. The dark horse trotting behind us was looking to make a break for it.

'I thought Dawson would appreciate it. I wanted to call her Quarantine, but that might spark a plunge and lower the price.'

'She's not going to be in top form, though, if she just got off the boat,' I said.

'Doesn't need to be,' said Humphry. 'She could beat Dawson's nag with one leg tied behind her back.'

Dawson's nag, he said, was called Red Nellie.

'What's wrong?' Humphry peered at my puffy face.

'My neck.'

'I thought it was your tooth.'

I told Humphry about the barber, the rifle, and Bacot's role in the Cockerill affair.

'Well, that explains the gun,' he said. 'Anything Bacot touches gets this urge to bite someone.'

The dust swirled in front of us and I spat some blood on to the road.

Low grey clouds scuttered in from the harbour and the road was busy with people in carriages and on horseback heading towards the racecourse. I hadn't been taking much notice of Townsville's social calendar and I asked Humphry if this was the usual Saturday afternoon races or a special race event.

He looked at me with pity and said it was 'Race Day'. He wouldn't have paid a small fortune to ship Black Bird up for any Saturday gallop.

* * *

Humphry dropped me near the front gate.

I stood there looking up the path to the open door. There was some laughter as a wagon-load of the younger set rumbled behind me. The dog escorting them trotted over to smell my boots. Two men galloped past and I was forced to move closer to the fence.

There was no sign of Cockerill senior or his gun. He could have fallen asleep, or gone to the races himself. Was this a chance to go inside and bundle his son away? If I'd thought I could manage it, perhaps I'd have tried, but I knew I couldn't move the lad myself, and Cockerill might well take a shot at me.

I carried four quarantine flags rolled up in my bag nowadays and I tied one to the gate and then made my way along the front fence. With the yellow bunting snapping in the breeze it seemed as if a party was in the offing – which it was for some, as it turned out. It certainly drew attention to the place. A few people appeared in their front yards to stretch their necks again. Some passers-by booed.

I stood exposed by the front fence and waited stiffly for the police, the ambulance, and some moral support.

After a while Cockerill appeared at the top of his front steps. He propped the rifle in the doorway, sat on the step and filled and lit a pipe, before lifting the stem to me, a sort of hello.

I said, raising my voice, but conversationally, 'The police will be here soon.'

He nodded and looked up and down the road, nodding too at the traffic.

'Have you changed your mind?' I said.

He reached behind him and grabbed the gun and laid it across his knees.

'How's your son?'

'He'll be right without your flamin' help.'

'Do you want me to take a look at him?'

'Only one I'll let take a look is Bacot. He comin'?'

I hoped to God he wasn't.

I waited near the gate for a while, but I was attracting too much attention from the traffic so I decided to walk fifty yards down the road to a mango tree. I set down my bag and took off my boater and leaned against the trunk wishing I'd brought some water and something for my neck, my mouth, and my back.

I heard the clanging of the ambulance from far away, coming closer, always a sound I thought the patient and the doctor could do without.

Some children who'd been playing in a ditch jumped up and down cheering as it went past. A few scampered after it when they realised it was about to stop.

It arrived in a cloud of dust and dogs outside Cockerill's gate and before I could reach them two ambulancemen had jumped from the cab in a smooth practised motion and were removing a stretcher.

'Stop!' They were almost at the gate. 'Don't go in.'

Their intent faces broke into frowns when they saw me charging them, then fortunately they recognised me and stopped.

Cockerill was standing on the top steps fingering the weapon.

I pointed at the house. 'The man has a gun.'

They saw the old man then, the gun in his hands, and took a few steps back. 'Christ!' They retreated as if it was a snake they'd nearly stepped on.

'Why didn't they tell us it was a siege?'

They put the stretcher away and we stood on the road beside the ambulance, out of the wind and line of fire. The old man had settled back on his perch. A small crowd, mostly children, had gathered on the other side of the road, watching us through the passing traffic.

'We were told it was a case of plague.' The ambulancemen looked at each other. 'They didn't say anything about gunshot wounds.'

'There's a man with plague inside,' I said. 'The police aren't going to shoot him.'

The two men leaned against the vehicle's side and began rolling cigarettes. 'Can't see how they can avoid it,' one said to the other.

They smoked patiently, the veterans of action, certain of the outcome.

'Have to shoot him. If he's mad with plague.'

'He hasn't got plague,' I said. 'It's his son.'

'That's bad.' They nodded to each other, ignoring me. 'Gonna need more stretchers.'

I left them behind the ambulance and went to see what Cockerill was doing. A few people were stopping before moving on, and the traffic was backing up. The small crowd had grown on both sides of the road. They were in loose groups and I prayed that the police would come soon. My throat was now so dry from dust I couldn't spit the vile taste from my mouth.

Two men were at Cockerill's front fence and tried to strike up a conversation. I asked them to move back.

'It's the plague,' I said.

'We can't catch it from here, can we?' The man was being belligerent.

'You could catch a bullet,' I said.

He smirked. 'He says he's quarantined.'

'Just move back. The police will be here soon.'

'Police?' The news soon spread like a ripple along the road.

A carriage belted towards us, weaving in and out of the slowing traffic. It braked and out jumped Bacot. My heart sank. The crowd, which had now grown alarmingly, became quiet as they strained to learn what might happen next.

'What's going on?' said Bacot.

'Cockerill junior has the plague.'

He sneered and looked at the house.

'Has he?'

He knew what was going on. Someone had sent a message, but he said, 'What's the old man doing with that gun?'

'He says he'll shoot anyone who tries to take his son away.'

'Well, why the devil are all these people here? Where are the police?'

I bit my tongue and looked up the road, wondering what was keeping them. People were spilling on to the road and blocking traffic, and creeping closer to the quarantine flags.

'It's under control.'

He looked around, and then at me, curling his lip. 'Really?'

'The police will be here shortly.'

'Look, Row,' he said, condescendingly, 'I'll just go in there and see the old fellow's son. He's my damned patient.'

'No. You won't.' I turned my head and the pain winded me for a moment. I took a deep breath and spoke slowly, 'He's not your patient any more. He has plague.'

I spat some blood at Bacot's feet and he backed up then, a little startled maybe. He opened his mouth a couple of times and looked me up and down. Was he actually sizing me up for a fight? A cold fury seized me.

At that moment the crowd, which may have grown to fifty people, grew louder and there was some clapping. The police wagon appeared and a wave of dust rolled around us. It parked beside the ambulance and three high white helmets floated over.

Moylan took one look at Cockerill on his steps and sent his constables to push everyone back. There was some jeering as this went on.

Bacot backed away as Sergeant Moylan walked past with his thumbs hooked in his tunic and went up to the gate.

'You should put that relic away, William. It'll not do your son any good if someone's shot.'

'A man's got a right to defend his own flamin' property. I won't shoot anyone who doesn't flamin' well deserve it.'

'Have you been drinking?' shouted Moylan.

'None of your flamin' business.'

Moylan walked back to me. 'Do you have any plans?'

Bacot jumped in and said to let him through the gate, he could examine the boy, see if it *wasn't* plague, and then persuade the old man to surrender. Or he could even disarm him when he wasn't looking. The gun probably wasn't even loaded.

Moylan shook his head as if a fly was bothering him. 'Dr Row?'

'Cockerill junior has plague,' I said. 'He has to go to the plague hospital. Anyway, the house is quarantined,' I glared at Bacot, 'and *no one's* allowed inside. We should wait.'

'Wait? Wait? What for?' said Bacot.

Turner, I said. He was the Government's expert.

'Expert!'

I wasn't sure that Turner had a plan, but if he did it wouldn't involve Bacot undermining our authority.

'He's my patient,' Bacot insisted.

I said the boy had plague, and that meant he wasn't Bacot's patient any longer, but was in the care of myself and Dr Turner.

'Speak of the devil,' said Bacot, 'and here's your boss.'

Turner was beside me, looking past us to the house. I stood aside and gave him a view of Cockerill on the steps with his rifle.

'This house is quarantined under the Health Act,' Turner told Sergeant Moylan. 'No one's to go through that gate.'

'He's asked for me,' said Bacot, reddening. 'Don't you see, you fools, I can help.'

Dr Bacot had forfeited his patient when he referred him to Dr Row, said Turner, and he went on to insist that, under the Health Act, anyone who entered a quarantined premises who wasn't a police officer or a member of the Epidemic Board would be breaking the law. Bacot wasn't on the board.

The trouble, of course, was that anybody who *was* a policeman or a board member would be shot, if Cockerill was to be taken at his word. And who would call his bluff now? Not only would he be shot, but worse, he'd look like a fool.

'It would be irresponsible to send anyone up there while the man's armed and threatening to shoot doctors, don't you think?' said Turner.

Even if Bacot had a good point, there was no budging Turner.

Bacot stamped off.

A wave of nausea suddenly hit me and I leaned against the side of the ambulance.

Turner was watching the gathering crowd.

'If we don't follow the regulations by the book now, we'll have no chance of enforcing them again.'

The nausea passed.

We stood about with nothing to do; Cockerill sat on his step and smoked as if it was a summer evening and exchanged a few comments with the crowd. Bacot paced the fence, fists thrust deep into his pockets, his body so tightly clenched he was shaking.

Cockerill taunted Bacot when he realised the doctor had been forbidden from entering the gate.

'You're not going to let that flamin' lot scare you?'

Bacot looked darkly at the two armed constables in front of the gate. He may have thought it was worth the risk. He'd be a hero because Cockerill had asked for him and wouldn't shoot him. But he'd face arrest. The longer it dragged on, the more I began to think we should have let him have a go.

Sergeant Moylan and Turner tried to persuade Cockerill to surrender his son, but the exchanges were booed and cheered and only encouraged the old man's cockiness.

I sat on the ambulance footplate watching, and within a few hours the crowd had grown to perhaps two hundred.

Some had stayed the entire time, some had gone to the races and returned, having a bet each way as it were.

Someone was selling ices.

The wind had picked up. People moved about, skittish, as if a storm was approaching.

I felt the nausea return and I climbed into the ambulance, out of sight, pressing my head against the cool wood, closing my eyes. My neck was hot and stiff, my face swollen, and I wondered if my wounded mouth had become infected. The two ambulancemen suggested causes and cures.

'Cancer.'

'I had a tooth pulled,' I told them, but they ignored me.

'I saw a man had a face ulcer. Looked like that.'

'He'll be right.' One of them climbed in and sat beside me. He slapped me on the shoulder and I nearly collapsed forward. 'He's lucky we're here. And Bacot's good with face boils.'

'What'd he say?'

'I think he said it was his tooth.'

'Cripes that can be bad. I remember once . . .'

I couldn't raise the energy to tell them both to shut up. I sat still. There was some chatter and movement, but miles away. I heard Humphry say, 'Here.'

He put something in my mouth, and then, 'Rinse and spit.'

The top of a bottle touched my lip and then my mouth was full of whisky. I bent gingerly over the side of the ambulance and spat.

'Here,' and this time it felt like a glass. 'Drink.'

It was vile, but I swallowed it with some effort.

I felt him leave and I sat. It had grown quieter. Gradually, a great knot was loosened.

When I crept to the edge of the ambulance and swung my legs down, I found Humphry smoking with the ambulancemen.

'Told him he'd be all right,' said one.

'What was it?' I said.

'Chlorodyne,' said Humphry.

'How much?'

'A dram. Sit tight.'

My jaw still felt like a kerosene tin being beaten with a hammer, but the pain was fading fast.

'Might make you a little drowsy,' said Humphry.

'Now you say.'

'Probably shouldn't have given it with whisky either.'

But I did feel better.

'Was Bacot here?' said Humphry. 'Did I miss the fun?'

I looked about. There seemed to be people everywhere. 'I can't see him now.'

'Shame.'

Women were roaming through the crowd calling men and boys home for tea. One figure amongst the faces was staring straight at me.

'Damn.'

'Still bad? Better not have another,' said Humphry.

'Dawson's there.'

'I know.' Humphry was looking the other way, as if the beauty of distant hills had caught his attention.

Dawson followed McCreedy through the crowd. A boy wilted to tears as the two men strode through a game.

I felt a little unsteady, Humphry's whisky taking effect.

The Mayor launched a thick finger as he approached.

'What in the blazes, Row? What in the *blazes*?'

I pointed my own finger back, and then crooked it as if squeezing a trigger.

'Cockerill has a gun,' I said.

The eyes of the crowd had swivelled to the Mayor. I saw Bacot then behind him and realised he must have run off to fetch McCreedy.

The crowd quietened a little.

Between Dawson and McCreedy I noticed the two constables in their white helmets and canary uniforms shooing the crowd back. I felt a surging affection for them.

McCreedy was saying, 'Why don't you let Dr Bacot handle this? He's the only blasted doctor here knows what he's doing. And where the blazes is Dr Turner, anyway?'

Dawson was standing impassively in front of Humphry. The MP took a cigar from his jacket, bit the end off, and spat it at Humphry's feet.

In front of me the Mayor was gesticulating.

In the crowd, right at the front, was a boy about Allan's age. One of the constables was pushing the crowd back and had a baton across his chest. The crowd surged around him and he looked small and frightened.

And then he was gone. I took a step forward and the Mayor caught my coat.

'Look,' McCreedy was saying, and something about another screaming bloody farce.

Dawson struck a match, a wet sizzle of red phosphorus. The murmur of the crowd rose and fell, and I saw the face again. It *was* Allan, closer to the fence.

He saw me. He waved. And then before I could raise a hand to tell him to stay where he was he'd turned to the police and I knew what he was going to do next. Moylan was marching up the line behind his constables as they pushed the crowd back.

I could see Allan form the word 'Dad'.

I looked up to the house. Cockerill was standing at the top of the steps, nervous about the sudden commotion, fidgeting with the gun.

And when I turned back, Allan had broken through the police line and was running towards me. I took a step forward, but McCreedy still had hold of me so I put my hand against his chest.

I never heard the crack of the Martini.

McCreedy opened his mouth and then his eyes went wide and he seemed to shrink away. Behind him the crowd flinched and fell to its knees as one. The constables crouched and fumbled for their pistols.

The Mayor was in the dirt in front of me, but Allan had vanished.

I passed Humphry and Dawson, who were peering like little boys around the side of the ambulance.

Allan!

There was a figure in the dust just inside the gate and I cried out. Humphry later said it was that sound that caused the crowd to finally scatter.

In a few slow dream-like strides I reached him, but it wasn't Allan's face staring up at me.

It was Bacot's.

I stepped over the surgeon's body, but I couldn't see Allan. I asked Bacot if he'd seen the boy and he shook his head. He opened his mouth and nothing came out.

It must have been comfortable in the dust inside the gate. It was a place I used to play as a boy, that soft hollow where no grass ever grew. I would have liked to have joined him.

I looked back up to the house. The old man wasn't there; he'd vanished behind the blue smoke that still lingered in the open doorway.

I told Bacot we should go now and he reached up to me with both arms, like a baby. I grabbed him, dragging him backwards through the dust, and then other hands took him away and slid him into the cool dark rear of the ambulance.

Lucky bastard.

And then the boy had his arms around my waist and I lost my balance, sitting down heavily in the road and sinking my face into Allan's hair.

chapter sixteen

A man has only one lifetime, and in it he
should combine as many lives as possible.

Dr A. J. Turner to the Entomological
Society of Queensland, 1930

HUMPHRY WORKED THE SEQUENCE out later: Bacot had decided to rush the gate while no one was looking. He picked the worst moment: the old man was on the top step, agitated by the Mayor's arrival and the police decision to push the crowd back. Cockerill couldn't have known what was going on, and still had the gun pointed loosely in that direction. He surely had no idea who it was coming up to the gate and he stood too tense, then, in a panic stumbled and the thing fired.

Bacot dropped like a bag of nails.

The recoil might have knocked the old man back into his kitchen. Whatever the reason, he didn't appear again, probably deciding to get drunk and maybe even unaware he'd hit anyone.

The surgeon had a gaping wound where the bullet had glanced off a rib and ripped his side open. It missed vital organs and his chances of survival were good, said Humphry, because he'd be spared the greater danger of being under his own knife.

After the shooting, though still not feeling sober, I'd borrowed Humphry's buggy and took Allan home to his mother. After what was some initial shock, Allan had become talkative and reconstructed the event as an adventure in which I'd stepped into the battlefield and rescued a man who'd been shot.

Maria came straight up to me and slapped my face so hard I staggered and nearly fell.

'*Tu es completement debile!*'

And then she collapsed into me, weeping. Allan seemed more horrified by this than by the shooting and began crying into her skirt and we stood that way until the girls came to see what the commotion was about and joined in.

Although I was still affected by Humphry's elixir, the blow brought back the pain. But the euphoria I felt, I believed, was genuine.

They wouldn't let go for a long time and that, more than anything that day, disturbed me. And as the sobbing subsided another knot inside me slipped loose. Just a little.

When I went to the sink and spat some blood, it caused another scene until I explained that I'd had the tooth pulled.

In an odd way, as I sat in the kitchen with Maria preparing tea and pouring French blasphemies, I felt relieved. There was something more than grief between us.

And I would have stayed. My jaw was aching again now and I'd begun to stiffen up.

But I had to return Humphry's buggy.

I squinted into the sun and could just make out the figures in a pall of yellow dust. The men stopped talking as I pulled up.

One of the constables, O'Donnell I think it was, was at the gate with a rifle loosely aimed at the house. Near his feet was a dark splash of mud, and a jagged wet trail led to the road. There was no sign of Cockerill.

'Anyway, the man's a hero,' Humphry said, pointing at me as I jumped down. 'What do you say?'

Dawson examined me as if I was a steer carcass. 'I say if he hadn't forced Cockerill into a damned corner none of this would have happened. I'll be making my own report on this fiasco.'

'Lin! Did you hear that?' said Humphry. 'Mr Dawson's going to recommend you for a medal.'

Dawson seemed to be steaming in front of the setting sun. 'You had something to do with this, too,' he hissed at Humphry.

'Just say I was right behind him, if you like. That's Dr Humphry, with no 'e', by the way.'

'All right,' said Moylan, who still looked shaky and

was cradling his silver rifle. 'Bacot broke the law and was fool enough to get himself shot. The Lord knows what the old man was aiming at – he couldn't have hit his neighbour's house if he'd been trying to. What we have to do now is avoid more bloodshed.' By that, I assumed he meant he didn't want to shoot Cockerill.

'Where's Turner now?' I said.

'Informing the Home Secretary,' said Humphry. 'Never seen him so mad.'

Most of the crowd had gone now, but some groups of men had returned, less sober. Moylan occasionally called out for Cockerill to surrender, but there was no sound from the house. The sun set, the air cooled, there was a sense that the best of the show was over.

Sergeant Moylan agonised over sending in the constables, but decided if Cockerill still had his gun they'd have to shoot him. It would soon be too dark to see and they might well shoot each other.

'What state is Cockerill junior likely to be in?' Moylan asked me.

I'd forgotten my patient. It was hard to say, I said, but he certainly needed medical attention as soon as possible.

'Could he survive the night?'

If junior's disease progressed, the pain might force the old man to seek help. He would survive the night, though.

'We'll wait until morning then. The old man might have run out of tobacco by then.'

Lanterns were brought from the rear of the police van. The ambulance returned. Moylan mounted a guard.

Dawson, at some stage, vanished into the night. I supposed he had other souls to torment.

Fatigue rooted me to the spot. I wondered aloud what had happened to Black Bird. Did she win?

Humphry struck a match and in the glow I saw him wince.

'Not exactly,' he said, lighting a cigarette and saying no more for a long time. Eventually, though, he had to tell me: Black Bird had thrown her jockey before the race, and bolted into the scrub. Humphry had got his money back, but not his horse. Dawson's comeuppance, it seemed, would have to wait.

The windows of the Cockerill house were black holes. Humphry said he'd stick around, in case something happened.

'An unmitigated disaster.' McCreedy was sitting in Turner's office. The light was second-hand, from the gas lights outside, and illuminated only the very edges of things: window, table, the Mayor's hand in mid-air, a curl of cigarette smoke, and a silver slash of jacket. 'Wouldn't you say?'

I think they'd been at it for some time. Seeing me and probably realising only then that the dark had crept up on him, Turner lit a lamp on his desk.

McCreedy continued to look out into the night, a bottle

on the table and a tumbler half full. A cigarette shook as he raised it to his mouth. 'Our hospital superintendent.'

'An unfortunate incident,' said Turner, getting up from his chair.

'Damned right.'

Turner opened the French door behind him and sat back down, McCreedy staring past him into the night and saying, 'I warned you. Didn't I damn well tell you?'

The Mayor was addressing me, I realised. He could see my reflection in the glass of the door. I didn't answer.

Turner said, 'The old man lost his temper and Dr Bacot wouldn't mind his own business.' He went over to his laboratory to light the stove.

'It *was* Bacot's business.'

'As soon as Dr Row diagnosed plague, it stopped being Dr Bacot's business.'

'Plague be damned. Plague's nothing.' McCreedy flicked his hand and cigarette ash floated to the floor. 'What's plague? A word. *Pl-ague.*' He blew out a thin stream of smoke. 'Means whatever you want and nothing. Something to scare children, if you want. The Black Death? More people have died in driving accidents around here lately.'

'The deaths are fewer only because of the measures we've taken.'

'And those measures have now resulted in someone being shot. You know, perhaps we should all be quarantined against damned doctors. You follow me?'

McCreedy drained his glass and poured another. 'You know what people fear more than death, don't you. Eh? Being separated from their loved ones.'

Turner fiddled with a pot in his laboratory, not answering.

'That's right,' the Mayor called out to him. 'You know. I've told you before. Force them off to some damned concentration camp like they're Boers and of course they're going to stick their heels in.'

Turner made his coffee. He said, 'Did you encourage Dr Bacot to enter the house?'

'Cockerill was his patient,' said McCreedy. 'I don't care what you say, he had every right. If he'd been let in in the first place it would have ended peacefully.'

'He entered the yard illegally. He broke the law.'

'No. He did not. He had the Home Secretary's permission.'

Turner froze. 'What did you say?'

'Yes. I thought that might shake you up. While you were provoking a riot, Mr Dawson sent off a telegram to Brisbane on behalf of the old man. Had a reply within the hour, so if you'd let Bacot in in the first place –'

'If he hadn't gone in at all he wouldn't have been shot,' said Turner, leaving his cup to face McCreedy. 'And why wasn't I informed of this telegram?'

'I believe Mr Dawson tried to tell you.'

'I don't believe he did.' Turner's voice had dropped ominously. 'I want to speak to Mr Dawson.'

'Well.' McCreedy stood unsteadily. 'Please yourself.

But enough damage has been done, I should think.' He grabbed his bottle and left.

I wished he'd left it behind.

During that night, Humphry took matters into his own hands. He ordered the constable on watch into the house by intimidating him with the Health Act. Cockerill was asleep under the kitchen table and it was simply a matter of taking the gun and then calling for the stretcher.

Public opinion, though, was now as firmly against us as if we'd brought the plague and shot Bacot ourselves, and given the town nothing but fear and threats and incarceration.

Which, of course, was partly true.

Turner sat at his table condensing the events of the previous day into a five-line telegram and drafting his resignation.

'Is that wise?' I said. My tongue explored the wonder of the hole in my mouth. The pain had gone and I was left with a sense of . . . detachment.

'If the Home Secretary allowed Bacot entry, then my position is untenable,' said Turner. 'I have no authority to implement plague regulations if they can be overruled. Anyway, I'm tired.'

The confession alarmed me. I relied on Turner to be strong. He'd been fighting battles on all fronts, but was now uncharacteristically bent at the table. He looked old. His shirt collar was open and he wore no tie.

'I should resign, too,' I said, but I really didn't care one way or the other this morning. I felt light-headed from actually having had some sleep.

'That would be unwise.'

Turner went to the Post Office and his telegraph flew down a wire to Brisbane.

'What now?' I said.

'Now? We wait.'

We waited.

'I was beginning to like the place,' I said, back in his office. Behind Turner I could see Castle Hill, looking small under a wider, clearer sky.

A clerk came with the reply:

> *Mayor is mistaken in reporting I authorised him defy health authorities or use force for obtaining admission for Dr Bacot or anyone else stop Both Mayor and Dr Bacot will be held responsible for any breach of regulations stop Resignation refused stop Foxton*

'What now?' I said.

'I suppose, just now, we should get back to work.'

The Mayor took the Home Secretary's telegram as a physical blow. He appeared deeply offended that Turner held so much clout; that the Home Secretary would back this small, weak-chested doctor over the Mayor of Townsville.

'He's not heard the last of it, you follow me?' he told me in the corridor.

McCreedy didn't seem to appreciate that Turner could still press charges.

I believe what happened next was the result of people mistaking the cure for the disease.

Most residents had encountered only the inconvenience of the plague: the clouds of phenyl, the stench of burning rats, news of forced evictions, quarantine flags, letters to the editor, and the sound of the ambulance in the night.

The plague itself wasn't the ultimate issue. The desecration of Mrs Duffy's funeral and the shooting of Dr Bacot confirmed the general perception that all those evils were the fault of the doctors.

And McCreedy, true to his word, would launch one more attack.

Humphry and I walked into Turner's office and sat down. Turner reached over his desk and handed me a piece of paper. I read the leaflet addressed to *All Prominent Citizens*.

Humphry sniffed at my shoulder. 'Mine must still be in the mail.'

The leaflet called for a meeting to discuss the way the health officers, *Drs Turner and Rowe*, had been administering the Health Act. It proposed forming a Vigilance Committee to protect the public.

'They've spelt my name wrong again,' I said, trying to make light of it but feeling sick to my stomach.

Vigilantes? I'd thought Routh had been exaggerating about getting a gun.

'Why isn't your name on here?' I handed it to Humphry.

'I don't go around picking fights with people who are bigger than me. Anyway,' he lit a cigarette, settling back, 'I live in this town. The pair of you just blew in. You're Southerners and you've been telling them how to save their own skins. The cheek.'

Turner, who was staring up at the hill: 'It doesn't matter. We've done our job within the law.'

'But we *did* save their damned hides, didn't we?' I said.

Humphry flicked the paper back to Turner. 'Dawson must be terrified,' he said. 'That's what this is about.'

I had assumed that Dawson had slipped back to Charters Towers, perhaps realising that the incident could turn into a political scandal that might hurt his apparent ambition to run for the Senate the next year – perhaps realising that, like McCreedy, he'd misjudged the respect with which Turner was held in Brisbane.

'It's spite,' I said. But it wasn't spite, it was raw political instinct. Humphry was right. Turner and I had threatened the authority of his Worship the Mayor and the Honourable Member of Parliament, and we still had the power to make them look like fools.

So . . . this leaflet, which now lay between us on the table.

* * *

Humphry, as a ratepayer, made a point of attending the meeting and reported back the next morning.

McCreedy had chaired the meeting and Humphry said Dawson was there, prowling the fringes, the representative MP glad-handing prospective voters, no doubt.

One hundred prominent citizens were on the platform.

'A hundred?' I couldn't believe there'd been such a set against us. Turner said nothing as Humphry described what happened.

I felt uneasy hearing things said about me that were plainly untrue. We were described as if we'd attacked the town to tear it to pieces. One man had apparently stood to say we'd forced the Reverend Ward at gunpoint to the plague hospital, in the dead of night.

Humphry said he'd made a courageous attempt to correct this, but was booed down.

The meeting had gone on in this vein for a while. The Cockerill case came up and McCreedy told the crowd Dr Bacot would not have been shot if the health officers had simply let him visit his patient. No one said that Bacot was shot *because* he was trying to do just that.

Someone moved that a collection be taken to buy Cockerill a new pair of glasses and a Snider rifle so he could hit the right doctor next time.

I must have looked horrified, but Humphry appeared to be enjoying himself. 'Don't worry, the motion was lost.'

Humphry said the whole event to that point was restrained. I looked at him with frank disbelief.

'Comparatively restrained,' he said, as he lit another cigarette. 'The best is to come.'

Everyone must have been saving their voices for the next item, said Humphry. The burial of plague victims. It seemed everyone knew someone who had died and been buried at the plague cemetery. They seemed to think that the doctors were doing this simply to throw around their misplaced power, and that we enjoyed torturing the grieving families.

'Your name came up, Lin, over some affair involving the landlady of the Commercial Hotel,' said Humphry. 'Did you really bring her down in a tackle and drag the poor woman away from her poor husband's coffin? That's something I wish I'd seen. Mind you, having seen you rush an armed man I'm not at all surprised.'

Well, then. The meeting, he said, had erupted in a chorus of *Shame!*

When that died down, Mr Ogden took the floor and told everyone he'd been in the funeral procession of poor Mrs Duffy when the health officers arrived and threatened Watt the undertaker with arrest if he didn't take the coffin out to Three Mile Creek immediately. This, despite a grave having already been dug in the family plot at West End, and the mourners left standing around with no body to bury. If he was the woman's husband, Mr Ogden told the mob, he'd have horsewhipped Dr Turner.

'You can imagine how that got them going,' said Humphry. 'I thought they might rush out, there and then, to find an appropriate whip.'

'I'm glad we weren't invited,' I said, my face in my hands.

'That's about it,' said Humphry, crushing the stub of his cigarette. 'Oh, and they resolved that Doctors Turner and Row be removed from their positions. Unanimously.'

'Unanimously?'

'I missed that vote. Call of nature.'

The Mayor unwisely sent the Home Secretary a copy of the meeting's resolutions. Foxton was furious and told Turner to bring charges against anyone who'd breached the regulations.

I was all for it. Bacot had broken quarantine, and McCreedy and probably Dawson had encouraged him. I was about to lose my job, although strangely that still wasn't worrying me.

It was Humphry who defended the Mayor. I was astonished.

'He believes he's protecting his town,' Humphry said. 'That's his job. You have to give him that.'

In the end, even Cockerill senior escaped gaol. Sergeant Moylan didn't want a trial because the police either believed the shooting was the reasonable response of a father protecting his son, or that it was an accident. Moylan charged him with resisting arrest, confiscated the Martini, and let him go.

Bacot was already pacing his corridors, no more contrite than before.

I went out to Three Mile Creek. I took the Carbine along the sandy track, which had deteriorated so much that I had to walk it the last half-mile.

There'd been no new cases since the Cockerill affair. The few rats trapped by councils' rat catchers in the previous week showed no sign of plague. It was too soon to declare the epidemic over, but that was enough for the Epidemic Board, despite my objections, to order the plague hospital closed when the last patient was discharged. It made political sense, I supposed. The siege had given everyone a fright, and even the police would baulk at packing anyone else off to Three Mile Creek.

It already had an abandoned look. The ropes had loosened and the canvas snapped in the sea-breeze.

Cockerill junior was sitting on the edge of his bed smoking, and raised a finger in greeting, thinking I was just another medico.

I asked about the girl and he shook his head. 'Not here.'

'Where?'

He shrugged.

I went to Routh's office and pushed open the flap.

'Row?' He was sitting on a box. 'Good of you to come. Packing,' he said, his sad face nodding to a box in front of him. 'Losing my last patient today.'

'Today? I didn't think he was due to leave until tomorrow.'

'Don't start that again.'

'No, no. I came to see the girl.'

'Sarah?'

'Her name's Sarah?'

'Sarah Gard. Gone, I'm afraid.'

'She can't be gone. She has nowhere to go.'

'Oh, some woman showed up from The World and said she was an aunt. She sent papers out from town. I released the child,' said Routh. 'Is that a problem?'

'No.' I shook my head, my heart in my throat. 'On the contrary. I suppose I just wanted to check that everything was all right with her.'

'Good as gold when she left. I suspect the aunt waited. You know, until . . .'

I nodded.

So I knew, suddenly, that this would be my last trip out here. And that I'd never see the child again. I wheeled my bicycle to the cemetery; not to pay my respects, more to get some sense of what had happened. The graves were marked by wooden crosses that were already leaning in the sandy soil.

But I felt no connection with the mounds of blowing sand in front of me, and I even found it hard to conjure up the once familiar face of Mrs Duffy.

I knew it would have been easier to believe it was an Act of God if I'd been lying there myself.

Turner was right. It's all a matter of perspective, and the victim's often the last person to see what really hit him.

chapter seventeen

Fifty years hence our atrocious treatment of plague patients will cause our successors to wonder what sort of thick-headed, hard-hearted monsters their ancestors were.

North Queensland Herald,
10 September, 1900

A GREAT CRANE LIFTED TURNER'S trunks over our heads. Allan watched the bulging net, fascinated.

'That would kill someone if it fell on them, wouldn't it?'

Humphry said, 'I'm sure they're insured.'

Turner looked on, a little worried, too. He carried his brown leather medical bag. Allan held Turner's best butterfly net.

We stood at the bottom of the gangway. Turner appeared to be the only passenger from Townsville heading north.

'I'm told the Mayor of Cairns is holding a ball for you,' said Humphry. 'Heard of your marvellous work in saving Townsville from itself.'

'Weally?' said Turner.

'No. I should think if anything he'll have an armed garrison waiting to repel you.'

Turner seemed cheerful enough to be going. There'd been no sign of plague for weeks and any rats we could find were the healthy kind.

He shook our hands. Allan handed him his net, but Turner said, 'You keep it. Send me some specimens.'

The ship groaned against the ropes and the planks beneath our feet trembled.

He had said he was pleased to leave Townsville, but I think that secretly he had relished the fight, although McCreedy's accusations and the hostility had hurt him.

'Public health is the future, Row,' he'd told me. 'Perhaps we need to be more flexible, though.'

We watched him walk up the gangway, a small translucent figure, and I was sad to see him go. He turned at the top, took off his pith helmet and waved it in the air.

It was the last I'd see of him for two decades.

Months later, it was I who was packing.

McCreedy stopped by the door. He was dressed for the holidays and had his hands in his pockets, puffing on a cigarette. The Town Hall was largely deserted. He stood there almost politely, waiting for me to acknowledge him.

'So you're off then?' he said.

'Yes.'

When the plague was officially over, the Townsville Joint Epidemic Board had let me go and I'd gone back to being merely the local medical officer for health. So I had handed in my resignation as soon as the Board of Health in Brisbane confirmed I had a position to return to at Moreton Bay.

'Aren't you going to ask me in?' said McCreedy.

'You're the Mayor. It's your building.'

'I suppose it is,' and he stepped into the office and closed the door behind him.

'Just wanted to say goodbye. You did your job, I'll give you that. Probably too well.' He started to laugh and stopped. 'You follow me?'

'Yes.'

He stared at me for a while and took another deep drag of a rapidly diminishing cigarette. 'Well, damn it, I told you to keep that blasted Turner under control. Look what he did.'

'I resigned.'

'Yes, yes.' He walked over to the window and opened the curtains. He looked down on to Flinders-lane, 'Dear God!' and closed the curtains again.

I had a tea chest beside it half full of medical books and items from my desk. 'You'll need someone to lift that for you?'

'They're coming to take it to the wharves this evening.'

'Your ship sails . . . when?'

'Tomorrow.'

'I suppose it's appropriate. New start and all that. I never said this and I probably should have, but

I think it was a damned thing going in to fetch Bacot like that. Took courage. Could have been shot yourself.' He puffed and stood there waiting for me to thank him. 'Look, you can stay on if you like. Why don't you, eh?'

He didn't mean it, but I supposed it was a compliment.

'It's a bit late now.'

He nodded, finishing his cigarette and looking for somewhere to put it. I fished out an ashtray and he ground the stub into it.

'I won't be seeing you tomorrow before you go?'

I shook my head.

'Well, good luck, Row.' And he leaned across the table and offered me his hand.

I took it. For auld lang syne.

The list of deaths I'd started charting more than a year ago was the last thing on my desk. The bound ledger seemed a folly now, the list unfinished. I couldn't bear to open it, so I left it there and turned to the storage cupboard.

I had to face the blue duffel bag, but felt unable to drag myself one last time back into that misery. I thought of little Sarah Gard, gone to Charters Towers with her aunt. I had asked the Reverend Kerr if there was any way to check on her, and he'd asked the Reverend Galloway at The World to look in on the family.

'A positive report, Row,' said Kerr.

The family were regular churchgoers, the uncle was at the cyanide works, and there were five other children. Sarah seemed to fit in and he was sure she was being well cared for.

I couldn't have asked for more, I supposed.

Now I opened the cupboard door and sat down again. The bag was still there, slumped over, with its chin on its chest, amongst the reams of carbon copy paper and requisition forms.

I sat for a while, and then got up and pulled the bag into the middle of the room, undid the drawstring and upended it. Gard's life poured on to the floor, sending out a cloying wave of phenyl and camphor.

It was as I'd expected, but also disappointing.

I raked aside the linen uniform, trousers, boots, shirts, belt and collar, and was left with a pile of personal things the man had accumulated. I had an image of Walter Gard's crooked face in my mind as I picked at them.

There were playing cards with furry corners, their torn packet, loose cigarette cards. A cheap watch with a scratched glass face had stopped. I set the time, wound it, and put it aside.

There was a stiff leather strop, and a razor in its case. I opened it and tested the edge.

In a leather pouch was a pipe and tobacco.

I was left with a biscuit tin and an envelope with handwriting, and I took them to my desk.

I opened the tin under the light. Inside was an eclectic jumble of little things a boy might find valuable, but which really had no use. One pearl cufflink, a glass marble, some used stamps, keys, a tiny blue glass bird with a broken leg, a whistle, and something in a cloth. I unwrapped a small, shiny tin tiger. It hardly had a scratch. Finally, there was a miniature Bible and a crucifix.

I set them aside and picked up the envelope. It was unsealed and held nothing.

I had trouble reading the writing on the front and so I held it under the light. It was a hand I recognised. It said simply, *For darling Sarah.*

I could imagine him propped up on his sick bed at West Point, struggling with the paper and pencil. He'd had to press hard and had gone over the words a few times.

I slumped wearily back into the chair. My first emotion was, as always, a purely selfish one: that I wished I'd never opened the damned bag.

For darling Sarah.

I leaned forward and picked up the tin tiger again, turning it over. The more I looked at it, the more certain I became that this was what the man intended to give his daughter. He'd bought her something he thought she might like. He may have told her stories about tigers he'd seen in far-off places.

It wasn't something I'd wanted to consider. But having done so, I couldn't now believe that the man had meant to harm his only child.

The thought stung me. I looked around my bare office and was touched again by a deep sadness, the inconsolable grief of losing a child, because Gard had lost his daughter as surely as I had lost mine.

I stood at the mouth of the council furnace watching the flames. I should, of course, have thrown the bag unopened into the furnace in the first place, to join the ashes of the rats.

'There you are.' From the back door strode Bacot. 'I wasn't sure I would catch you before you left.'

We stood side by side looking into the swirling flames which, thankfully, obscured the things they were destroying. I was still wary of the surgeon. His wound had obviously healed, but I assumed he still blamed me for his brush with death.

'I suppose I should have thanked you,' he said. 'Earlier. Been meaning to. God knows how long the police would have let me lie there. Probably bled to death by then.'

We watched the flames.

'Clearing the decks?'

'Last of the plague contacts,' I said. 'Just a precaution.'

He wanted to shake my hand goodbye, too, and then he left.

I went back up to my office, took a last look and left the door ajar behind me, the smell of Gard's tin and tobacco still on my hands.

'By the Grace of God this new Nation,' said the Reverend Kerr, 'will take its place amongst the Great Nations of the World. Australia will stand Proudly beside Canada, South Africa and India, in the Service of the Great British Empire.'

We all attended church that evening. The Reverend Kerr had organised a New Year's Eve service starting at eleven o'clock. I imagined most churches in the other colonies were doing the same, nearly four million people up past bedtime.

The Twentieth Century and a new Australia were about to be born and Queensland would be suddenly elevated, or, as Humphry said, demoted, from a colony to a state.

Reverend Kerr read from Ephesians: '*And you hath He quickened, who were dead in trespasses and sins, wherein in time past ye walked according to the course of this world . . .*'

I didn't think many people appreciated the implications of Federation, but in the lamplit Presbyterian Church at that moment everyone believed the next day would be tangibly different.

Allan's head rested heavily against my arm. I felt Maria against the other.

'*. . . that in the ages to come He might show the exceeding riches of His grace, in His kindness toward us, through Christ Jesus. For by grace are ye saved through faith; and that not of* *yourselves: it is the gift of God: not of works, lest any man should boast.'*

Amen.

The church bells sounded all around Castle Hill and we sang 'God Save the Queen'; twice, for good measure. The English Church down the road were giving us some competition.

Once outside, the congregation gathered amongst the flicker of moths around buggy lamps to wish each other Happy New Year. Men produced hip flasks and in furtive groups toasted the many things there were suddenly to toast. Allan had a new lease on life and was trying to catch insects to bait his sisters.

I'd been looking about for the Reverend Kerr to say goodbye, and then he was suddenly at Maria's side.

'My word,' he said, 'the pair of you at the same service again. I hope this becomes your habit.' And did I like the reading?

Indeed I did.

'Your ship leaves tomorrow?'

'Today.'

'Oh yes, it's today already. How silly of me. You know, Row, I'll miss our chats. I'm sure God has His plans for you, though, and knows what He's doing.'

Allan's voice in the dark started complaining about a knee, and Maria went off to see to it.

I handed Kerr a pound note and a package, sealed, Sarah's name on it.

'My word.' He looked at the writing. 'Oh yes. How thoughtful. What's in here?'

'Something from her father.'

'From her *father*?' He looked unsure, but decided not to ask. 'I'll make sure she gets it. I'll give it to Galloway when he's next here.' He shook it. 'Might get damaged in the post otherwise.'

I thanked him and we shook hands. I could see the reflection of the harbour lights in his eyes and he grabbed my arm and squeezed it with genuine warmth before turning away.

I turned and took in the view. Below us the gas lamps were blazing along Flinders-street and boats in the creek had every lantern lit. We could hear singing and cheering as Maria gathered the children. We all walked home together.

Humphry collected us late the next morning.

The girls had been moping around the empty house, moaning about leaving their friends, and then running tearfully to their bedrooms. Allan was already at the gate and eager to get going, looking forward to the ship.

They all still seemed like strangers to me and I realised only then how much I'd squandered my brief time in the North.

'You know, Lin,' said Humphry, as we stood for a moment beside his buggy, 'you should stay. There's plenty of opportunity up here for a young doctor with your experience. A modern private practice is the go.'

From the town below came the banging of many hammers and some cheering and whistles that seemed to be left over from the night before.

'Do you think people would come to my surgery?'

'There is that. But look, you could stay on in this house. It's a pleasant enough life. I might even join you in practice.'

I could see in his eyes that he was serious. He wanted me to stay. I was touched. I might even have taken up the offer under different circumstances, or given more time.

'Our ship leaves in a few hours.'

'Does it? Best get moving then.'

Most of our boxes and trunks had already been sent to the wharf. We had just a few bags with us. The girls and Allan climbed on to the back of the buggy while I squeezed next to Humphry and Maria sat beside me, and then we rattled down through the town for the last time.

This first day of the century was hot and steamy. Maria wore her broad hat and she held the rim daintily between her index finger and thumb, swearing as the buggy plunged down Denham-street through the dust of the other traffic.

'*Maudit!*'

'Sorry,' said Humphry, but we hit another bump.

'Oh, *merde!*'

'Hang on back there,' I yelled, but we slowed as we came to Flinders-street.

Celebrations were already under way, it seemed. A stage bristling with Union Jacks and Federation flags took up most of the intersection.

'I'm told there'll be many speeches,' said Humphry, as we crept around it. 'You've really cut it fine again, but I think we can make our escape before they start.'

He trotted the horse slowly down the main street. Crowds packed the sidewalks and the balconies, and a few people cheered, perhaps thinking we were part of the show.

'How's this for a send-off?' said Humphry, who might well have planned it this way.

His little surprise.

A policeman under his tall white helmet came marching sternly across the road to us with a white-gloved hand held up, but then seemed to change his mind and waved us through. I recognised Clark. Or was it O'Donnell. I turned and saw Allan salute him, and he saluted back.

A band started up 'Soldiers of the Queen', and we rode through assembling armies of pipers, Druids in white beards, Masons, butchers, Oddfellows, friendly societies and Caledonians.

'What a menagerie,' said Humphry in feigned disgust.

'*Je n'y crois pas!*' said Maria.

'Can we stop?' said Allan from the back, but Humphry said if we did we'd never get started again and, besides, this was the best view we'd ever have of the circus. He produced a bag of boiled lollies and handed them over his shoulder, a small compensation.

We crossed the bridge to the sound of cheering. I assumed McCreedy was taking the stage.

'Now there's an irony,' said Humphry.

He had pulled the buggy up on the wharf and we were staring again at the SS *Cintra*.

The ship was dressed in bunting for the celebrations and all passengers were out on the deck trying to catch a last festive glimpse.

Humphry produced his silver flask and hit me in the chest with it. I took a sip and handed it back.

'You keep it.'

'Don't be silly.'

He pushed it back. We shook hands and he just nodded, and I turned and followed my family up the gangplank before one of us embarrassed the other by saying something sentimental.

And then I was standing at the railing, watching Humphry's figure on the wharf, watching the spot where he stood even after I could see him no more, as the ship slid away.

As if on cue, as we rounded the breakwater, the Garrison Artillery let go a twenty-one-gun salute along the banks of Ross Creek. The crowd cheered. And Allan believed it was all for us.

Out in the bay, I had a last look at Townsville with its rugged backdrop, finally in context, complete and even beautiful.

The passengers eventually drifted to the bar or their cabins and I found myself alone, still staring at the spot, now part of an endless green-grey coastline.

The wind had sprung from the north-east and blue-black thunderheads rose above the distant hills, as the *Cintra* chugged down the coast.

brisbane

1921

If the alarm be warranted, Brisbane must be added to the three or four pestis pestilentiae holes of direst disease. And it then becomes our duty to Humanity to vacate the city and cleanse the corrupt centre, by making it a lake of fire and brimstone.

Point 25 of 'Twenty-five Reasons Why The Australian Epidemic Is *Not* Plague!' by Dr. T. P. Lucas, MRCS Eng., LSA Lond., FRSQ

IT WAS LATE AFTERNOON when I trudged from the Highgate Hill tram stop to Turner's house.

It was a modern suburb of a modern city. Children played in the street under spreading jacaranda trees. The place had life. I felt as if I'd stepped into the world from some other place.

Hilda answered the door and led me inside.

Turner looked up from his tray of insects. I supposed it was the strength of those spectacles that gave him the startled appearance.

'It's Dr Row, Dr Turner.' His wife stood behind me.

'I know who it is, Hilda dear. Thank you.' Fank you.

Turner and I blinked at each other like two frogs until Hilda forced me to sit.

'You will have coffee, Dr Row?' she said.

'That would be appropriate.'

Turner put a pencil down and sat back. On the table were rows of tiny moths stuck to a flat board with small silver pins.

'I'm reclassifying some of my old collections,' he said, sweeping a hand over the table. 'I'd made a mess. *Epicoma* with *Axiocleta*.'

'I can imagine.'

He scratched his beard. 'You took the position on the Epidemic Board. Congratulations.'

I nodded. 'Thank you. We're closer to the girls. Found a place to rent in Toowong.'

'Maria's happy?' he asked.

I said I supposed she was.

'She's here?'

'She's visiting the girls. Eileen,' I told him, 'is having a baby.'

'Well, splendid. Is everything all right? Perhaps I could call.'

'She lives out at Toowong, too.'

'No bother,' said Turner.

I looked at him looking at me and I nodded.

'Everything is all right, though?'

'Yes. This will be number four.'

'I meant you.'

'Dr Turner, is this a consultation?'

'If you like.'

Hilda brought coffee and we made ourselves busy with spoons and sugar.

I held the steaming cup under my nose for some time. The room was full of slowly atomising books and insects and I felt I might sneeze.

'Allan's still in Britain,' I said.

Turner nodded.

Maria and I had been visiting Allan at Oxford when war broke out, and we were stuck there. Allan enlisted. So did I.

I hadn't realised until well on in things that Turner was stationed at a war hospital near Epsom.

'And you were in France, too, Row?'

'For a year. Quite long enough,' I said. Afterwards, I told him now, I took the opportunity to study bacteriology in London. We returned. I said that Allan had stayed on to complete his medical training and was now in Edinburgh.

'Yes, I know,' said Turner.

'You know?' I put my cup down.

'He writes.'

I was flabbergasted. 'Does he?'

'Don't be so surprised. He sends me the occasional moff. For old time's sake, I suspect, but he has quite a knowledge of lepidoptera.'

'Dear God.' I felt a pang of paternal jealousy. Allan had never told me he kept in touch with Turner, and I wondered what else they discussed apart from moths. What could they have in common after all these years? Certainly not me.

'He's not a very good correspondent,' said Turner.

'Like his father.'

We finished our coffee. He stood. 'I'll show you your moff.'

He ushered me to a wide cabinet. Its drawers were long and thin and he pulled one out. On it were trays of moths, all small things, carefully arranged crumbs. He slid the drawer back and pulled out another.

'Ah. There.' He pointed a finger amongst a crowd of similar-looking insects. I bent forward and Turner handed me a magnifying glass.

Eupterote rowii looked as light as a wafer. Its wings had tiny grey-blue veins. I couldn't see what distinguished it from its neighbour.

'I'm honoured,' I said.

'So you dashed well should be.'

I stood for a moment and admired the rest of the trays. Hilda brought more coffee and we both sat again, this time in more comfortable armchairs by the window. The hibiscus bushes trembled in an afternoon breeze.

'And how are you, Row?' he said.

'You've already asked.'

'You didn't answer.'

'I'm well enough.' I sipped my coffee. 'I'm happy. Maria's happy. Is that what you want to know?'

'No need to snap,' he said. Putting his cup down. 'You know that Maria thinks you may be shell-shocked.'

'You've spoken to Maria?'

'Well, don't look so surprised. She's concerned about you.'

'And Allan?'

Turner nodded.

I put my cup down and stood up.

'Row,' he said, gently. Woe.

For God's sake. 'How deep does this conspiracy go?'

'Sit down.'

'Is that the reason for all of this? They think I'm mad.'

'Of course not.'

I remained standing, looking down at him.

'Well, we're all a bit mad, I've always thought,' he said. 'It's just a matter of degrees.'

'And this appointment with the Epidemic Board is part of this, isn't it? A job in town might do me some good.'

'No, no. That's nothing to do with it. It just so happens you are the best person for the job.' He suddenly looked tired and old. 'I was afraid you'd take this the wrong way.'

I sat back down again.

'The wrong way? Talking about me behind my back?'

'Concerned that you've been distant, perhaps unwell.'

We sat for a while, unwinding a little.

'It's not the War, you know,' I said. 'It's not even Townsville, or whatever might have been different there.'

'No.'

'You know I don't blame you,' I said. 'Or myself, any more, really. It's that I've never managed to get over Lillian.'

He nodded. He looked deeply sad then. We both stared into his front yard, into the gathering dark.

'You're a lucky man, Row.'

'Am I?'

'You have three bright, healthy children. You must be proud of them. And grandchildren. That must be a wonderful thing.'

Turner had never been able to have children. He'd thrown himself into paediatrics, especially in recent years. It was with a sense of shame that I began to realise how selfish I'd become. Distant and selfish.

And I couldn't snap out of it.

We gathered our composures, and Turner managed to say, 'I've had an opportunity to contact Humphry lately.'

'Really?' Another stab to the heart. My own sense of guilt that I'd not written in twenty years. 'Has he written back?'

Turner said, 'He asked about you.'

I sipped my coffee.

'Do you remember that grub we found in the tree ants' nest?' he said.

I shook my head.

'Small round thing, size of a half penny.'

I did remember then. Allan kept one in the back yard.

Turner stood, went to the wall. He took down a framed picture and brought it over and propped it against the windowpane in front of me.

It was a moth, of course.

'*Liphyra brassolis.* The moth butterfly,' he said. 'That's what that little half penny turned into. A beautiful thing, don't you think?'

It seemed a bit drab to me, each caramel wing a teardrop.

'Is this another analogy?' I said.

He glanced at me over the top of his glasses. 'Moths are full of analogies, aren't they. No. Not this time. Only if you want to look for one.'

I looked. The light in Turner's study probably didn't do it justice, but I supposed moths weren't meant to be seen in the light.

'Is it a moth or a butterfly?' I said.

'It's a butterfly that doesn't like the sun that much.'

It grew dark and eventually we ran out of things to say.

We finally shook hands at the door. He clasped my hand with both of his and I did the same and we stood there nodding and smiling at things said and unsaid, the usual bond between men who'd shared wars, great or small.

And I turned and walked away.

'I could give you a lift,' he called after me.

'I'll walk to the tram stop. It's not far.'

I could hear the sound of motorcars and tram bells rising up the hill.

'Come and see me again,' he said. And I turned to wave, but he'd closed the door.

postscript

Dr Linford Row died of pneumonia in Cooma in New South Wales in 1926. He fell ill while making a house call. His patient recovered.

Dr Alfred Jefferis Turner went to London in 1901 to study public health. He held honorary and consulting positions at the Brisbane Children's Hospital for many years, and was credited, along with Dr John Lockhart Gibson, with solving the riddle of the lead-poisoning epidemic amongst Queensland children. He amassed a collection of fifty thousand moths and butterflies in his lifetime. He retired in 1937, ending a remarkable medical career, but kept collecting moths until he died on 29 December 1947, aged eighty-six.

Dr Ernest Humphry remained a much-loved Townsville physician for many years. He is remembered as a sober man with few, if any, vices. Mothers named their babies after him.

Anderson Dawson was elected to the Australian Senate in 1901 and became Minister of Defence in 1904. Despite Dr Row's opinion of him, he was an eloquent politician, a champion of women's suffrage and lived a hard life. He died alone and an alcoholic at the age of forty-seven.

Allan Row became a Rhodes scholar and served in both World Wars, rising to Lieutenant Colonel. He returned to Australia and practised medicine in Toowoomba. Dr Turner stored his moth collection at Allan's home, for safe-keeping, during the Second World War. Allan married late in life, just after that war, and Dr and Mrs Turner attended the wedding.

The Reverend Richard Kerr travelled Queensland and eventually settled in Warwick. He became the Home Mission Superintendent for the Presbyterian Church in Queensland in 1911. He died in 1932. The Reverend Kerr left the church with a valuable legacy in real estate. He had collected parcels of land in each parish he visited.

author's note

This novel is based on a true story, but it is fiction. There's no way to accurately construct a personal life from old newspaper articles, photographs, telegrams, government reports, or even personal papers and oral histories. I've rebuilt the skeletons of these characters from what evidence there is and fleshed them out with fiction.

I've tried to keep to the events as they happened in Townsville in 1900, but for my own purposes I've changed the timing and the outcome of a few incidents. For instance, Dr Bacot escaped serious injury in the Cockerill siege, although the Reverend Richard Kerr's sermon is based on the actual sermon he gave just before the plague arrived in 1900.

The plague spread, from China, around the world at the end of the nineteenth century. Steamships brought it to Sydney in 1900. From Sydney it spread by steamship around the colonies. Hundreds died, and the disease re-occurred during the next two decades. The plague last broke out in Brisbane in 1921, but Dr Row played no role in it, as far as I know.

Dr Row had his personal opinions, but his colleagues in this book were all good men doing their jobs to the best of their abilities.

P.S.

Ideas,
interviews
& features
included
in a new
section…

COURTESY OF JOHN BEAN

Ian Townsend

Life at a glance

BORN

Cessnock, New South Wales, 1960.

EDUCATED

Mitchell College of Advanced Education, Bathurst.

CAREER

Newspapers: the *Western Advocate* in Bathurst, the *Daily Telegraph* in Sydney, *The Land* newspaper in New South Wales, the *Daily Mercury* in Mackay in Queensland. Radio: ABC Radio reporter and broadcaster in Mackay and Brisbane; current affairs reporter for the ABC's *AM*, *PM* and *The World Today*; currently with ABC Radio National's *Background Briefing*.

FAMILY

Married in Townsville to broadcaster Kirsten MacGregor, with three children: Charlotte, Josephine and Gabrielle.

LIVES

Brisbane

AWARDS AND HONOURS

Ian Townsend has won two Australian Museum Eureka Prizes for science and medical research journalism.

In 2005, he was awarded the State Library of Queensland's John Oxley Library Fellowship to research his next novel, based on the 1899 Bathurst Bay cyclone.

Affection has been nominated for the following literary awards:

Shortlisted:
The 2005 Victorian Premier's Awards
www.slv.vic.gov.au/programs/literary/pla/index.html

The 2006 Commonwealth Writers' Prize for Best First Book
www.commonwealthwriters.com

The 2006 Colin Roderick Award
www.faess.jcu.edu.au/soh/fals/awards.html

Longlisted:
The 2007 IMPAC Dublin Literary Award
www.impacdublinaward.ie

An interview with
Ian Townsend

This interview is based on questions composed by the Crieff Reading Group (Crieff, Scotland). Reproduced by kind permission of Mandy Moore, Penny Montgomery, Catherine Howett, Lesley Ford, Lesley Taylor, Nicola Watson, Jane White, Elaine Millar, Sian Campbell, Annette Forsyth, Sally Leger and Katy Galbraith.

Why did you call the book *Affection*?
Affection means 'love and tender feelings', but it is also a medical term, rarely used these days, meaning 'disease, or a morbid or abnormal state of the body or mind'.

Was there really a plague in Queensland in 1900?
Yes, in fact plague spread around the world at the end of the 19th century, sparking what's called the third great plague pandemic. The first was in the ninth century; the second famously included the Black Death of London. The third pandemic started in China in the late 19th century and spread to most continents, including Europe and Africa. It established a foothold in the US — in fact, plague still kills hundreds of people every year in Asia, Africa and the US. The plague reached Sydney in January 1900 and touched most Australian states during a series of outbreaks that kept occurring into the 1920s. Townsville had several outbreaks. Officially, nine people died in Townsville in that original 1900 outbreak, but the plague cemetery at Three Mile Creek, in which many of them were buried, was not gazetted and its exact location remains a mystery, as does the location of many other small plague cemeteries around Australia.

What were your reasons for the moth themes?
Dr Alfred Jefferis Turner, apart from being a paediatrician and early bacteriologist, was a lepidopterist and collected for the

Queensland Museum. During his life he collected 50,000 moths and butterflies, and his collection is now in Brisbane and Canberra. He was Australia's most prolific moth collector. Turner in fact sent his moth collection by truck to Allan Row's surgery in Toowoomba for safe keeping during the Second World War. As Turner told Row, 'Moths are full of analogies … if you want to look for one.'

The novel seems to be more a gradual revelation of characters and events than a plot-driven narrative. Was this your intention?
I wanted the book to be character-driven. The books and movies I like are driven by character and dialogue. I suppose I was lucky to find such wonderful characters. I like them all.

Dr Row doesn't express his inner pain, especially about the death of his daughter, outwardly at all. It leaks out more as the book progresses and is clearly apparent to others around him, such as his wife and the other doctors. How do you see him?
This was the end of the Victorian era and Linford Row lived in a society that believed that hardship was the grit that made the man. He had no support and was offered none, except by the enlightened Turner. Dr Row was a man of his time and was expected to cope, but he clearly wasn't coping with his loss. It is frustrating when people don't solve a problem, but I don't see

5

An interview with
Ian Townsend *(continued)*

Dr Row as cold; just lost. He tried very hard to cope, but as he said himself, 'The grief of a rational man is endless.'

How much is fiction, and how much is fact? Novelists seem to be treading on the toes of historians lately, and there's a debate about whether history is being served well by historical novelists.

The book is fiction. I've woven what evidence I've found of the characters and events into a story. Little evidence remains of Dr Linford Row, for instance, and so I've imaginatively recreated him from telegrams and reports, and birth and death certificates. Dr Turner is better recorded. There are clues to Humphry's contradictory character in the anecdotal stories told about him, and in his reports and telegrams. I've relied heavily on historians and non-fiction accounts for the fabric of this book. I wanted to tell a story and to put the remarkable characters I discovered into a context in which I could understand them. I'm interested in history, but this is an imaginative interpretation of the past. I've tried to stick to the facts, but the facts in the end aren't the point of a novel. It's a novel. History is the setting in which other truths about ourselves can be revealed. ■

> ‘ History is the setting in which other truths about ourselves can be revealed. ’

A writing life:

When do you write? Whenever I find the time, but often in slabs of time between work and family commitments. I prefer to start at 4.30am.

Where do you write? I have a small office on the end of my verandah, and I have to leave my front door to get there.

Why do you write? I'm a journalist and have no other marketable skills.

Pen or computer? Computer.

Silence or music? Silence, and the thumping of small feet.

How do you start a book? I do an enormous amount of research and the characters and events are formed before I write the first draft.

And finish? I never quite feel as if I've finished. The characters live on. They are often kind enough to show me the point at which their lives change and another story begins.

Do you have any writing rituals or superstitions? I keep telling myself something which I suspect at the time is not true: that I really can write this book.

Which writers do you most admire? Ernest Hemingway, David Lodge and William McInnes.

What or who inspires you? Queensland.

If you weren't a writer, what job would you do? I'd like to grow sugarcane. ■

The critical eye

Affection has been extraordinarily well-received, with critics describing it as 'a lyrical first novel' (*Daily Telegraph*), 'a fascinating portrait' (*Herald Sun*) and 'a literary tour de force' (*The Australian*). Many praised Townsend's deft use of historical sources: '*Affection* takes the raw material of historical fact and hews from it a finely crafted novel', said *The Age*, adding that the result was 'more skilful than most debuts'. *The Australian* declared *Affection* 'a must-read book', explaining: 'Townsend has done something quite remarkable … he has fleshed out into fiction a hitherto unknown and fascinating story of colonial Queensland on the cusp of a new century and of Australian nationhood … Townsend makes superb use of contemporary advertisements and editorials, which he effectively weaves into the plot.'

Vogue Australia agreed, adding: '*Affection* is an astonishing novel … it authentically portrays a period of Australian history that has been barely acknowledged.'

The book's depiction of Queensland also impressed many reviewers. 'Townsend evokes the pungent smells and heavy air of Townsville', wrote *The Bulletin*; '*Affection* is an engrossing and skilful debut.' Peter Pierce, reviewing for *Australian Book Review*, concurred: '*Affection* is a fine debut,' he wrote, 'which, at the risk of jinxing it, one might hail as The Great Townsville Novel.'

The *Sydney Morning Herald* admired Townsend's prose, detecting the influence of his background in journalism: 'There is a concise quality to his writing that suggests a debt to the profession,' wrote David Messer.

> ❛ A literary tour de force ❜

The result, he concluded, was 'a bona fide page-turner … Townsend has brought a very big subject back to Earth … *Affection* is, above all, a novel about the unpleasant uncertainties of life and the leap of faith – usually difficult but always necessary – needed to cope with them.' Brisbane's *Courier Mail* also enjoyed Townsend's 'journalistic economy: fast out of the gate, light on the description and with a good ear for dialogue.'

Several reviewers noted the subtle sense of humour at work in *Affection*. 'For a historical novel about such a grim topic,' observed the *Courier Mail*, '*Affection* has a surprisingly light touch. It manages to educate and elicit emotional responses without brow-beating … and it's downright hilarious at times.' *Australian Bookseller and Publisher* declared it 'a charming social comedy', explaining: 'There is a tragic core to this novel, but the quirky characters, well-chosen chapter epigraphs … and … snappy, period-yet-contemporary dialogue all combine to make this an unusually successful historical novel.' Added *The Age*: 'There is both humour and pathos here in the broad historical sweep and the intimate detail.'

Perhaps the last word should go to Australian actor and author William McInnes, who summed up *Affection*'s appeal and placed it in illustrious company: 'I love Robert Louis Stevenson, Joseph Conrad, American realists like John Steinbeck, Faulkner, not that he was a realist really. I like Hemingway. And I tell you what, I read Ian Townsend's book. Now that was fantastic. I really liked that book. Really graceful writing. Really interesting, too. A cracker.' ■

❝ A bona fide page-turner ❞

Reading group questions

1. Early in the novel, Dr Row explains his interest in collecting 'acts of God'. How does the plague epidemic challenge or confirm his theories?

2. Humans aren't the only ones afflicted by illness and injury in the novel: wheels 'maim' a road, smokestacks 'cough', a dirty wall displays 'a suppurating brown sore'. What other examples of this medical imagery can you find – and what do you make of it? Does it say something about disease, nature, the city setting? Does it reflect something in Dr Row's view of the world?

3. 'Unfortunately, scepticism was already spreading like a disease' (page 239). Nature can be deadly, but are humans even worse? How does Townsend use the plague epidemic – a natural disaster of sorts – to expose human folly?

4. 'We were heading into a new world and this capering disease was coming with us. We could even see it, but it acted with indifference, as if nothing had changed since the Middle Ages' (page 202). Partial understanding of a disease may allow us to diagnose it but not to save its victims. Is Dr Row's frustration with the limits of scientific knowledge connected somehow to his grief for his daughter?

❛ scepticism was already spreading like a disease … ❜

5. 'How fortunate to be a pastor in a time of pestilence,' remarks Dr Row (page 55). What role does his wry, melancholy humour play in the novel?

6. 'If I was deluded, I could be cured. The grief of a rational man is endless.' (329) Has Dr Row found any relief by the end of the novel? Does his rational grief require a rational cure, or does he find other sorts of comfort?

7. The postscript reveals some striking differences between the characters as they appear in the novel and the historical figures on whom they are based. Did this revelation alter your reading of the book? Do you think a novelist has any obligation to disclose how much of a story is fact and how much is fiction?

8. Are there lessons in the novel for contemporary society? If an epidemic (SARS, AIDS, avian flu) were to strike your hometown, how do you think individuals, communities and governments would behave? ∎

❝ How fortunate to be a pastor in a time of pestilence … ❞

Have you read?
The plague in literature

The Year of Wonders by Geraldine Brooks (2001)
Inspired by real events, Pulitzer prize winner Geraldine Brooks describes a young woman's struggle to save her family and her soul. When plague visits a small Derbyshire village in 1666 the villagers, inspired by a charismatic preacher, agree to quarantine themselves to stop the disease from spreading any further.

The Plague by Albert Camus (1947)
The townspeople of Oran, Algeria, are in the grip of a deadly plague that condemns its victims to a swift and horrifying death. When the town is forced into quarantine, fear and suspicion grip the inhabitants. Some try to escape, some resign themselves to fate, and others seek to lay blame. Some work to stop the plague – but others find ways to profit from it …

A Journal of the Plague Year by Daniel Defoe (1722)
In 1665 plague devastated London. In this fictional diary, a Londoner describes the city's descent into panic as the disease spreads from one neighbourhood to the next. The rich flee, while the poor take what comfort they can from faith healers and soothsayers.

The Decameron by Giovanni Boccaccio (1350)
When the Bubonic Plague comes to Florence, seven young women and three young men flee to a country villa. To pass the time and to

forget the tragedy back home, they take turns telling colourful stories of love, lust, trickery and adventure.

Australia's north

Oyster by Janette Turner Hospital (1996)
You won't find the town of Outer Maroo on any map, and the locals like it that way. United by their suspicion of outsiders, the town's two opposing cultures – the rowdy, hard-drinking opal miners and the teetotaler Christian fundamentalists – have so far co-existed peacefully. But when a strange man stumbles in from the desert spouting apocalyptic prophecies, the town will never be the same again …

Maestro by Peter Goldsworthy (1989)
Paul Crabbe and his musical parents have just moved north to steamy, exotic Darwin. Despite his protestations, Paul is signed up for weekly piano lessons with Eduard Keller, 'the maestro', a Viennese refugee with exacting standards and a mysterious – and tragic – past.

Sugar Heaven by Jean Devanny (1936)
When Dulcie moves from Sydney to Innisfail to be with her cane-cutter husband, she finds she has a lot to learn about the politics of sex and class in tropical Queensland. Meanwhile, the deadly Weil's disease, spread by rats, is sweeping the cane fields. When the cane-cutters strike to demand action, tensions in the town come to a head.

Have you read? *(continued)*

It's Raining in Mango by Thea Astley (1989)
In the 1860s Cornelius Laffey, an Irish-born
journalist living in Sydney, moves his young
family to the muddy goldfields of northern
Queensland. When he reports a massacre of
Aborigines by white settlers, he loses his job
on the local paper and the family is left
destitute. With humour and imagination,
Thea Astley charts the fortunes of the Laffey
clan over four generations, from this shaky
start in the 19th century through to the 1980s.

Capricornia by Xavier Herbert (1938)
Norman, son of a white father and an
Aboriginal mother, returns to the remote
northern settlement of Capricornia after
spending most of his childhood in
Melbourne. While trying to find his place in
the world, he encounters a colourful cast of
characters and confronts the racial tensions
underpinning the community's history.
Xavier Herbert's sprawling, epic,
controversial novel explores race relations in
Australia's north during the first half of the
20th century. ■

Visit

Magnetic Island and Cape Pallarenda

The headstone of Walter Gard and a few concrete posts are all that remain of the old quarantine station at West Point on Magnetic Island. The station's buildings were moved to Cape Pallarenda in 1915, where they continued to be used for quarantine until 1973. During the Second World War, the station was also used as a hospital and base camp by American and Australian troops. Both sites are now administered by the Queensland Parks and Wildlife Service. For more information, visit www.epa.qld.gov.au/parks_and_forests

Dunwich and Peel Island

Many of the buildings of Dr Linford Row's benevolent asylum still stand at Dunwich, on Stradbroke Island. Between 1874 and 1959, nearby Peel Island also served as a general quarantine station and a leper colony. Like Cape Pallarenda, it is now administered by the Queensland Parks and Wildlife service. Peter Ludlow's informative history of the site is available at www.users.bigpond.net.au/pludlow/peelhist.htm

North Head Quarantine Station, Sydney

Between 1828 and 1972, the Manly quarantine station was the first port of call for many new arrivals. When the plague hit Sydney in 1900, nearly 2000 people were quarantined at North Head. Later, the station was used to house survivors of Cyclone Tracey and refugees from the Vietnam War. The site is now part of Sydney Harbour National Park and is open to visitors. For more information, visit: www.nationalparks.nsw.gov.au or www.manlyquarantine.com

Explore online

Townsville's history and heritage
www.townsville.qld.gov.au/heritage

Townsville tourist information
www.townsvilleonline.com.au

Plague at the World Health Organization
www.who.int/topics/plague

Bird flu: a modern pandemic?
How prepared are we for another pandemic? Read or listen to Ian Townsend's report for ABC Radio.
origin.abc.net.au/rn/backgroundbriefing/stories/2007/1814815.htm